PENGUIN  CLASSICS

LETTERS TO SIR WILLIAM TEMPLE

Dorothy Osborne (1627–95) was one of the younger daughters of Sir Peter Osborne, royalist Governor of Guernsey garrisoned at Castle Cornet during the Civil Wars. She married William Temple (1628–99) after several years of resistance to the marriage by both families, and these letters are part of the record of their love-affair at a significant moment in English history, in which her husband was a key participant: as diplomat and statesman who helped to negotiate not only the Triple Alliance but also the marriage between William and Mary; as patron to Jonathan Swift; and as essayist of distinction, whose works include *An Essay Upon the Ancient and Modern Learning*, *Of Heroick Virtue*, *Of Health and Long Life* and *Of Popular Discontents*.

Kenneth Parker was born in South Africa, where his edition of critical essays, *The South African Novel in English: Essays in Criticism and Society* (1978), is banned. He has been a visiting professor in universities in the United States and on the Continent, and is at present Director of the Cultural Studies Graduate Centre in the North East London Polytechnic.

D0869327

Dorothy Osborne

Letters to Sir William Temple

Edited with an Introduction and Notes by
Kenneth Parker

PENGUIN BOOKS

Penguin Books Ltd, 27 Wrights Lane, London W8 5TZ (Publishing and Editorial)
and Harmondsworth, Middlesex, England (Distribution and Warehouse)
Viking Penguin Inc., 40 West 23rd Street, New York, New York 10010, USA
Penguin Books Australia Ltd, Ringwood, Victoria, Australia
Penguin Books Canada Ltd, 2801 John Street, Markham, Ontario, Canada L3R 1B4
Penguin Books (NZ) Ltd, 182–190 Wairau Road, Auckland 10, New Zealand

This edition first published 1987

Made and printed in Great Britain by
Richard Clay Ltd, Bungay, Suffolk
Filmset in 10½/12½ Monophoto Bembo

For Lady Constance Violette Osborn

Contents

Acknowledgements

This edition could not have been completed without the assistance of many individuals and institutions. The Notes will reveal my indebtedness to the two previous editors, Sir Edward Parry and Professor G. C. Moore Smith, for their pioneering excavations, and I would like to thank their respective publishers, Messrs J. M. Dent & Son Ltd and Oxford University Press, for permission to use material from their editions. To that must be added my gratitude for the support of the staff of, among others, the British Library; the National Register of Archives; the Bodleian Library; County Hall, Ipswich; Ipswich Museums and Galleries; the Norfolk Record Office; the Bedfordshire County Record Office; the National Portrait Gallery; and the North East London Polytechnic Livingstone House Library.

I am grateful to the Governors and Rector of the North East London Polytechnic for awarding me a one-term sabbatical; to the President and Fellows of St John's College, Oxford, for electing me as one of their Summer Vacation Visiting Fellows; to my wife, Gabrielle, for her translations from the French and for her assistance with French history and culture; to her, and to my colleagues at the N.E.L.P., Sally Alexander and Catherine Hall, for their guidance about feminism and gender; to Miss Dorothy Longe of Yelverton, Norwich, and to Mr G. N. B. Longe, of Woking, Surrey, for assistance with recent Longe family history.

I am particularly indebted to Sir Richard Osborn, Bart, for permission to use the portrait of Dorothy Osborne on the front cover, and to the British Library for the illustration showing her handwriting, taken from Add. Mss. 33975, f. 19v–20.

Above all, I am aware of the constant support for, and interest in, the project on the part of Lady Constance Osborn, and I am delighted to dedicate this edition to her.

Bibliography

BIOGRAPHICAL

BOYER, ABEL. *Memoirs of the Life and Negotiations of Sir William Temple* (London: for W. Taylor, 1714)

GIFFARD, MARTHA. *The Life and Character of Sir William Temple, Bart. Written by a Particular Friend. Never Before Published* (London: printed for B. Molle. At the Middle Temple Gate in Fleet Street, 1728)

COURTENAY, T. P. *Memoirs of the Life, Works and Correspondence of Sir William Temple, Bart,* by the Right Honourable Thomas Peregrine Courtenay. In Two Volumes. (London: printed for Longman, Rees, Orme, Brown, Green & Longman, Paternoster-Row, 1836)

MACAULAY, T. B. *Literary Essays. Contributed to The Edinburgh Review* (Oxford: Oxford University Press, 1913)

LONGE, JULIA G. *Martha, Lady Giffard: Her Life and Correspondence (1664–1722), a Sequel to the Letters of Dorothy Osborne* (London: George Allen & Sons, 1911)

TEMPLE, JOHN ALEXANDER. *The Temple Memoirs. An Account of this Historic Family and its Demesnes, with Biographical Sketches, Anecdotes & Legends from Saxon Times to the Present Day . . .* (London: H. F. & G. Witherby, 326 High Holborn, 1925)

WOODBRIDGE, HOMER E. *Sir William Temple, The Man and His Work* (London: Oxford University Press, 1940)

CECIL, DAVID. *Two Quiet Lives* (London: Constable & Co., and Indianapolis, The Bobbs Merrill Co., 1947, reprinted 1967)

FABER, RICHARD. *The Brave Courtier. Sir William Temple* (London: Faber and Faber, 1983)

HALEY, K. H. D. *An English Diplomat in the Low Countries: Sir William Temple and John de Witt* (Oxford: Clarendon Press, 1986)

EDITIONS OF THE LETTERS

PARRY (1888). *Letters from Dorothy Osborne to Sir William Temple 1652–54*, edited by Edward Abbott Parry (Barrister-at-Law). (Printed for Griffith, Farren, Okeden & Welsh, successors to Newbery & Harris, at the Sign of the Bible & Sun, West Corner of St Paul's Churchyard, London, and Sydney, New South Wales)

PARRY (1903). *Letters from Dorothy Osborne to Sir William Temple 1652–54*, edited by Edward Abbott Parry (London and Manchester: Sherratt & Hughes. Revised and enlarged edition)

GOLLANCZ (1903). *The Love Letters of Dorothy Osborne to Sir William Temple*, newly edited from the Original MSS. by Israel Gollancz/Alexander Morning (London: The De La More Press)

PARRY (1906). *The Letters of Dorothy Osborne to Sir William Temple*, with a new historical introduction (London: Everyman's Library, published by J. M. Dent & Son; New York: E. P. Dutton & Co.)

PARRY (1914). *The Letters from Dorothy Osborne to Sir William Temple (1652–54)*, edited by E. A. Parry (London: The Wayfarers Library, published by J. M. Dent & Son)

MOORE SMITH (1928). *The Letters of Dorothy Osborne to William Temple*, edited, by permission of Sir Edward Parry and of his Publishers ... by G. C. Moore Smith (Oxford: Clarendon Press. Reprinted lithographically 1947, 1959)

HART (1968). *Letters of Dorothy Osborne to Sir William Temple 1652–54*, edited by Kingsley Hart (London: The Folio Society, 1968)

CRITICAL COMMENTARIES

HEWLETT, MAURICE. *Last Essays* (London: William Heinemann, 1924)

IRVINE, LYN LL. *The Letter-Writers* (London: The Hogarth Press, 1932)

LUCAS, F. L. *Studies French and English* (London: Cassell & Co., 1934. Reprinted 1950, Pocket Library edition)

PARRY, E. A. *My Own Way: An Autobiography* (London: Cassell & Co., 1932)

WOOLF, VIRGINIA. *The Common Reader*, Second Series (London: The Hogarth Press, 1932).

Introduction

i Dorothy Osborne and William Temple

> ... *can there bee a more Romance story then*
> *ours would make if the conclusion should prove*
> *happy* ...

Few stories outside the realms of imaginative literature can match
that of the love-affair between Dorothy Osborne and William
Temple – in genesis, in obstacles confronted and overcome, in
social and cultural context, and in its conclusion, which proved
happy.

Martha, Lady Giffard, who wrote the first biography of her
brother,[1] tells a rather plain tale about the first meeting. She
records that:

... at Nineteen he began his travels in *France*, in 1648, a Time so
dismal in *England*, that none but they, who were the occasion for
those Troubles and Confusions in their Country, could be sorry to
leave it: He chose to pass through the Isle of *Wight*, where his
Majesty was then Prisoner in *Carisbrook* Castle, and met there with
Mrs *Dorothy Osborn*, Daughter of Sir *Peter Osborn*, then Governor
of *Guernsey* for the King, who was going with her Brother to their
Father at *St Maloes*; he made that journey with them, and there
began an Amour with that young Lady, which lasted seven years,
and then ended in a happy marriage.

Lady Giffard's initial published account omits the central
episode of that first meeting, and we have to turn to a later
reconstruction of the manuscript material, which records that:

At twenty he began his travels in France in the year 48 a time so dismal to England, that none but those who were the occasion of those disorders in their country, could have been sorry to leave it; He chose to pass by the Isle of Wight, where his uncle Sir John Dingley then Master of a good estate, & one of the auncients Fameleyes of that country liv'd, & where His Majesty was then prisoner in Carisbrooke Castle – and twas here he first met Sir Peter Osbornes Daughter goeing with her Brother to their Father at Snt Maloes, who was Governor of Garnesey, & held it out for the king; He made that journey with them, in which her brother had like to be stop'd by an Accident, that I don't know whether it will be thought worth relateing. The spite he had to se the king imprison'd, and treated by the Governour Coll. Hammond soe unlike what was due to him, provoked him to step back again after all his company were gon before him out of the line and write these words with a Diamond in the window, (And Haman was hang'd upon the Gallows he had prepar'd for Mordechai.) Twas easy to imagin what hast be made after company when he had done, but had no sooner overtaken them then he was seis'd himselfe, & brought back to ye Governour, & only escap'd by his Sister takeing it upon her selfe. In this Journey begun a amour between Sir William Temple and Mrs Osborne, of which the accidents for seven years might make a History, & the letters that pass'd between them a Volum; & though I cannot venter it myselfe, I have often wish'd the[y] might be printed, for to say nothing of his writeing, which the world has since bin made judge off, I never saw any thing more extraordinary than hers.[2]

While we might speculate about the reasons for the differences between the manuscript and the early published versions, the publication history of the letters will reveal that Lady Giffard's assessment of their importance was remarkably prescient, and since this marriage united two very important gentry families, whose intervention in the arts and in diplomacy continues to be considerable into our own time, it is therefore prudent to have a brief look at the family histories of the respective parties in order to emphasize the link between the making of family fortunes and the consolidation of political power at a key moment in English history.

Dorothy Osborne's father was Sir Peter Osborne (*c.* 1585–1654; knighted 1611), who is best remembered as the last royalist to hold out fighting for Charles I – he surrendered only because his troops were dying from starvation in Castle Cornet, Guernsey, where he had been Lieutenant-Governor of the island (with Alderney and Sark) for twenty-eight years.[3] His father was Sir John Osborne (1552–1628; knighted 1619), who studied at Eton and at King's College, Cambridge, and who was a member of five parliaments between 1576 and 1601, as well as Commissioner of the Navy under James I. Sir John married Dorothy Barlee of Elsenham Hall, Essex; she was the grand-daughter of the Chancellor of England, Lord Chancellor Rich. D.O.'s great-grandfather, Sir Peter Osborne (1521–92), studied at Cambridge and in Lincoln's Inn; he was a member of six par-liaments, became Keeper of the Privy Purse, and was made Treasurer's Remembrancer to the Exchequer (a post which was later inherited by his son as well as by his grandson). He was a close associate of the distinguished scholar Sir John Cheke (who died at his house in 1557), whose niece Ann Blyth, the daughter of the Regius Professor of Physick at Cambridge, became his wife, and by whom he had twenty-two children; one of whom, Catherine, married Cheke's grandson, Sir Thomas Cheke (see letter 27, note 1).

After studying at Emmanuel College, Cambridge, Sir Peter married Dorothy Danvers, youngest daughter of Sir John Danvers of Dauntsey, Wiltshire. Three of her brothers were to become distinguished participants in the events of their times, though on different sides: Sir John Danvers (see letter 3, note 3) became a prominent regicide; Henry Danvers, Earl of Danby, K.G., became one of the most influential statesmen after the Restoration; Sir Charles Danvers was executed for his part in the Essex Plot.

Sir Peter Osborne was a prosperous man, but he was severely penalized by the parliamentary government for his support for Charles I. D.O. mentions (letter 75) that she had seen her father's finances reduced from £4,000 to £400 per annum. Official as well as family papers record the process of relative pauperization, and include Sir Peter's answer to the Committee of Examinations, before which he was charged with high treason (10 April 1647), and a document of 1648, specifying the particulars of the estate of Chicksands Priory, for which he desired to compound. (The Osborne family estate, Chicksands Priory, was one of the few monasteries in England of the Gilbertine order, with two cloisters, admitting both monks and nuns. It was bought by Sir Peter Osborne around 1576, though he continued to live in London, and his son, Sir John, was apparently the first member of the family to live there; it continued to be the Osborne family residence until just before the Second World War, when the estate became RAF Chicksands. The building is now a shell and the estate an American air force base. A separate document of 1648 itemizes debts of £7,445 for which Sir Peter wanted an allowance to be made, but although he received his discharge from the Commissioners (2 August 1649), and a certificate from the Goldsmiths' Hall confirms that he had compounded and paid (4 October 1649), he was later assessed for an additional penalty; this additional charge is often mentioned in the Diary of his son, Henry (see letter 10, note 3). Sir Peter was discharged from his sequestration on 30 May 1650, but there exists also a receipt for payment of an additional amount of £1,437.11s. on 23 December 1650, with the certificate of final discharge dated 10 November 1651. Here, as elsewhere (and in particular in relation to marriage settlements), one is struck by the sheer size of the cash settlements involved, particularly when compared with what an ordinary worker earned – for instance, the coachman mentioned in Appendix A, letter D. The penalties also explain, in part, why the Osborne family were not enthusiastic about a match between D.O. and W.T.: they were actively looking for a marriage that would help to solve their liquidity problems. It must be emphasized that their objections were personal and financial, and not ideological: at the time of their first meeting, her father was a royalist official, while his was a member of the Long Parliament; furthermore, as we shall see from her letters, her family did not appear to object to the prospect of their daughter marrying one of Cromwell's sons. Quite without foundation, some members of the Osborne family saw in W.T. an unprincipled adventurer, without either honour or glory, someone who would be willing to render service to any party for the sake of personal advancement, whereas any dispassionate assessment might have attributed his comparative 'failure' as a statesman to his probity, a quality that was seldom evident in the Restoration court.

The charge of being prepared to serve an administration irrespective of whether it was royalist or parliamentary might well have been laid against his father, Sir John Temple (1600–1677), Master of the Rolls in Ireland. Sir John had served on the personal staff of Charles I (for which he was knighted in 1628), was appointed Master of the Rolls in 1640, and was elected a member of the Irish parliament in 1642. Because he was suspected of having republican sympathies during the Civil War, he was (with several others) confined to prison, but was released after about a year and compensated with a seat in the English House of Commons. He returned to Ireland in 1653 as one of Cromwell's commissioners, to advise the parliamentary government on the carving-up of titles and properties, after which he was once again, with excellent references from Cromwell, made Master of the Rolls (1655) – in which position he was confirmed after the Restoration. Sir John is perhaps best remembered for his history of the 'Irish Rebellion' of his times. It is clear now that what he claimed to have been an unbiased, eye-witness account of events was a partisan and propagandist document, which contributed in no small way to English clamour and hysteria, which in turn was used by Cromwell as justification for his interventions in Ireland. Temple's assertions so incensed the Irish parliament that one of its first actions when it re-assembled in 1689 was to order that the book be burnt in public by the common hangman!

This Irish connection (and it is one that recurs in the letters, with references to campaigns of subjugation by Cromwell, by Monck and by Ludlow) was not only continued by the son, as we shall see later, but had been preceded by the grandfather, Sir William Temple (*c.* 1553–1627), a distinguished Provost of Trinity College, Dublin, and at one time secretary to Sir Philip Sidney, who died in his arms at Flushing. (Jonathan Swift was, at a later date, to be secretary to his grandson.) He later joined the household of the 2nd Earl of Essex, but claimed that he was left in ignorance of that peer's attempted insurrection.

It was into this family of administrators, diplomats and patrons of the arts that D.O. married on Christmas Day, 1654; the event is recorded as follows in the marriage register in St Giles in the Fields, Holborn: 'William Temple, Esq., and Mrs Dorothie Osborne had given intenson [intention?] of marriage Saterday the ninth of this month and were thrice published, and had a certifed [certificate?] D.D. seq. 24th of the same month.'[4] Henry Osborne's Diary corroborates: 'Dec. 25, Munday. – Being Christmasse day my sister was married, and went as shee said to Mr Franklins.' The marriage was before a Justice of the Peace, and according to the Cromwellian version of the marriage vows (see letter 35, note 5).

The man she married, William Temple, was born in Black-friars, London, in 1628. His first education was under the guidance of his uncle, Dr Henry Hammond, who was then Rector of Penshurst (see letter 44, note 7), but after Hammond was sequestered from his living in 1643, W.T. was sent to Bishop Stortford School; from there he proceeded to Emmanuel College, Cambridge (1644), where he was a pupil of the celebrated Ralph Cudworth, but after two years he left without taking his degree, to travel abroad in order to improve his linguistic skills, notably in Spanish and French. The letters date from this period of travel and of residence in England and Ireland (1652–4), years in which their love was placed under considerable strain, not least by D.O. becoming a victim of smallpox. She recovered, but sustained cruel and permanent facial scars; as a result of her illness, the marriage was delayed for a year.

After their marriage the Temples settled in Ireland, where they lived either in his father's house in Dublin, or on the small family estate in Carlow; there W.T. studied philosophy and history and was chosen (on the Restoration) as a member of the Irish Convention for Carlow, later (1661) being elected for his county to the Irish parliament. After the prorogation of that parliament the family returned to England (1663), leaving behind the bodies of six children who had died at birth or in infancy. They settled at Sheen (Richmond), where his widowed sister and first biographer, Lady Giffard, joined them. (She had married, in April 1662, Sir Thomas Giffard, of Castle Jordan, Co. Meath, but was widowed about two weeks after the marriage; she never re-married, and lived permanently as part of her brother's household, surviving both him and her sister-in-law. She is buried with them in Westminster Abbey.) [5]

W.T. obtained his first diplomatic posting in 1665, when he was sent on a special mission – one of considerable delicacy and complexity – to the prince-bishop of Münster, who had agreed to invade Dutch territory from the east in order to create a diversion in favour of the English in the Anglo-Dutch War. W.T. had the twofold task of seeing that the prince-bishop kept his bargain, and paying him his 'subsidy', in instalments, for doing so. This complex exercise, in which the French became embroiled, culminated in a separate peace between the Dutch and the prince-bishop (1666). Despite this failure, W.T. was sent as resident to the vice-regal court at Brussels (1665), with a baronetcy included, and with sufficient funds to enable his household to accompany him there. It was in these years that his diplomatic skills were displayed to their greatest effect, culminating in the momentous Triple Alliance (1668) with the Dutch and Swedish governments against the French, which later led to the Peace of Aix-la-Chapelle between France and Spain.

Because of the high regard in which he was held by the Prince of Orange and the Dutch statesman De Witt, W.T. was appointed Ambassador to the Netherlands in 1668, but he was soon afterwards recalled by the Cabal – the King and his advisers were once again changing their foreign policy: this time in favour of the erstwhile enemy, France, against their former allies, the

Dutch. The King spoke to his ambassador about the latter's health, but refused to discuss affairs of state with him. Furthermore, despite appeals by the Dutch that W.T. should return to The Hague, the King let it be understood that W.T. had returned to England for personal and private reasons, knowing full well that he had been recalled at the express wish of the French king as an earnest of English good faith in the attempt at an Anglo-French alliance.[6]

W.T. returned to Sheen, where his wife joined him in 1671, and a few months later England was again at war with the Dutch. However, when in 1674 the need for a peace settlement was once again uppermost, W.T. was plucked from his retirement to become ambassador in The Hague once again in order to expedite the peace negotiations. Not only did he bring these to a successful conclusion, but he was instrumental in contriving the marriage between William of Orange and the King's niece, Mary – negotiations in which Lady Temple played no small part because of her friendship with the Dutch prince as well as with the English princess and her governess. This international diplomatic coup had several consequences: it re-established the former close friendship between W.T. and Thomas Osborne, Earl of Danby (later 1st Duke of Leeds: see letter 2, note 3), but it exacerbated the tension between W.T. and Arlington (who was, in any event, deeply at odds with Danby). It led to the King offering W.T. the position of Secretary of State, an offer which was declined: W.T. did not trust the King, and was later to have his doubts confirmed.

Sir John Temple had died in 1677 while his son was engaged in diplomacy and, when the position of Master of the Rolls in Ireland fell to him by reversion, W.T. sought, and obtained, permission to postpone taking up this task in 1680, and again in 1685, finally resigning his entitlement to the office in 1695. In the meantime he had sought to persuade the King to restructure radically his Privy Council by reducing its numbers and by means of a judicious weighing of competing interests, with the landed gentry holding the balance between an oligarchic executive and an obstructive parliament. Although a Privy Council was constituted along these lines in 1679, it soon foundered on the twin reefs of the English king's chicanery and his French counterpart's mendacity. W.T., finding himself more and more frequently excluded from the decision-making process (to the extent that, when the parliament was dissolved in 1681, he discovered that his name had been struck off the list of members of the Privy Council), retired to his estate of Moor Park near Farnham, which he had bought in 1680.

Moor Park was named in memory of the estate of the Countess of Bedford, near Rickmansworth (although A. C. Elias – see note 7, below – points out that a surviving drawing of Moor Park in the 1690s shows the garden as looking something like a scaled-down version of the gardens of the Prince of Orange at Het Loo, begun in the same year that W.T. moved to Moor Park), about which he wrote with such admiration in his essay *Upon the Gardens of Epicurus; or, of Gardening, in the year 1685*. The latter is now recollected only in the name of a golf-course, while Moor Park in Surrey has become a finishing school, having previously been a teacher training college and a station for Canadian military personnel during the Second World War. Here W.T. began to devote his time to his two major interests, fruit-growing (especially vines, apricots and cherries) and essay-writing, and it was to this place that a kinsman of his, Jonathan Swift, came in 1689 at the age of twenty-two, after being sent down from Trinity College, Dublin, to be secretary to W.T., at a salary of £20 per annum and meals at the second table.[7] It was here that W.T. completed the writings upon which his literary reputation rests, and around which much of the disputes about him have been orchestrated, not only in his own time but particularly in the nineteenth century, from which he has not yet been rescued. Apart from the essay on gardening noted earlier, he wrote, among other essays, *Of Heroick Virtue*; *Of Poetry*; *Of Popular Discontents*; *Of Health and Long Life*, and *An Essay Upon the Ancient and Modern Learning* (with a sequel) from which arose the so-called 'Battle of the Books'.

When William succeeded James as king in the protestant coup that became known as 'The Glorious Revolution', W.T. was again offered the position of Secretary of State, but he again declined to serve although he agreed that his only son, John, should become Secretary for War. A contemporary witness, Narcissus Luttrell, records the appointment in his diary for 18 April 1689, and then proceeds to record the aftermath on 24 April:

A gentleman taking water the 18th, when he came near London bridge, pull'd a written paper out of his pocket, laid it in the boat with a shilling, and suddenly leapt over the boat into the water, and was drowned. The paper contained these words: My folly in undertaking what I could not execute has done the king great prejudice, which cannot be stop't no easier way for me then this. May his undertaking prosper, may he have a blessing. This has occasioned great discourse; but the body being since found, it proves to be Mr John Temple, only son of sir William Temple: the reason thought to be this; he had engaged the king not to send over any forces to Ireland, assuring him that he had that interest with the lord Tyronells secretary, who informed him that Tyrconnel would surrender that kingdom if the king sent over no forces thither; but finding he had been deceived, and that they only pretended that till they had fortifyed that kingdom, and that his majesties reducing that kingdom would be very difficult thereby, he committed this fact upon himself.[8]

It would appear that John Temple had persuaded William to free Richard Hamilton, a brigadier-general in the Irish army, who was at that time a prisoner in the Tower, in order that he should go back to Ireland to persuade Tyrconnell to surrender. This was done, but Hamilton, once freed and back in Ireland, joined the Tyrconnell faction, and John Temple committed suicide. According to Moore Smith, a note endorsed 'child's paper he writ/ before he killed himself', in Lady Temple's handwriting, was in the possession of the Longe family; he records it as follows:

'Tis not out of any Dissatisfaction from my ffriends, from whom I have rec[eive]d Infinitely more ffriendship and kindness then I deserve, I say it is not from such reason that I do myself this violence, but having been long tired with the Burthen of this life, 'tis now become Insupportable . . . From my ffather and mother I have had especially of late all the marks of tenderness in the world, and no less from my Dear Brother and Sisters, to whom I wish all my ffriends Health and Happiness and forgetfullness of me. I am not conscious to my self of any Ill Action, I despair not of ease in a futurity, the only regret I leave the world with is, that I shall leave my ffriends for sometime (I hope but for a little time) in Affliction.

Lady Temple died on 7 February 1695, W.T. on 27 January 1699; their remains, together with those of their daughter Diana, who died of smallpox in 1679, aged fourteen, and of Lady Giffard, who died in 1722, are interred in Westminster Abbey – though W.T.'s heart was, according to instructions in his will, buried in a silver box under the sundial in the garden at Moor Park. At the behest of Lady Constance Osborn, a tablet in the floor, inscribed 'Sir William Temple Baronet 1628–1699', marks the approximate spot, while a plaque in the south aisle of the Abbey records, below the family crest:

Sibi Suisque Charissimis,
DIANAE TEMPLE
Delectissimae Filiae
DOROTHEAE OSBORN
Conjunctissimae Conjugi,
et MARTHAE GIFFARD
Optimae Sorori.
Hoc Qualecunque Monumentum
  poni curavit
GULIELMUS TEMPLE de MOORPARK
In Agro Surriensi Baronettus.[9]

DI. T		1679		14
DO. O	Obijt	1694	Aetat	66
GUL. T		1698		70
MAR.G		1722		84

ii *The Publication History of the Letters*

The publication history of these letters is a fascinating amalgam
of several elements, notably: the tenacity as well as the excavatory
skills of the first editor, Sir Edward Parry; the initial and mistaken
assumptions on the part of publishers of the literary and cultural
(therefore commercial) value of the letters; the continuing presence in British society of the 'gifted amateur' (in the sense of
someone who develops an expertise without pursuing it profes-
sionally), whose interventions in specialist journals and societies
make small but significant contributions to our study of the past;
the shift, during the period since the first edition of the letters, in
the nature and scope of criticism as well as in the nature and
interests of the reading public. It therefore becomes an exercise
in late-twentieth-century assessment of the mid-nineteenth-
century evaluation of the late seventeenth century: the transitional
contemplating the notionally stable in its estimation of the revolutionary.

We should remind ourselves at all times that these letters
were not intended for publication; that when heavily edited
extracts were first printed, they formed part of a supplement to
the biography of the man to whom they were written; and that
the aim of the biographer, the Rt Hon. Thomas Peregrine
Courtenay,[10] was to annex W.T. to conservative ideology of
his times – a most doubtful proposition both in theory and in
terms of our knowledge of beliefs expressed in the essays: being a
royalist during the English Revolution does not qualify automatic-
ally for incorporation into Victorian toryism.

Courtenay's biography of W.T. became the occasion for a
considered review essay by Lord Macaulay[11] in the *Edinburgh
Review* (1838), in which that distinguished Protestant Whig
historian sought not only to demolish the Tory biographer, but
also attempted to do the same to the subject of the biography. It

is probably true to say that, although Macaulay's strictures no longer apply, the effect of the review was that since that time the former high reputation of W.T. has not been re-established. While it is important to emphasize that Macaulay expressed unalloyed enthusiasm for the extracts from the letters, the main thrust of his review was to demonstrate how political difference could be pursued to advantage under the guise of disinterested literary criticism.

Macaulay's review did, however, have one major positive effect: it led to the letters finding their first and most dedicated editor in E.A. (later Sir Edward) Parry.[12] In his autobiography[13] (and it is instructive to follow the story in some detail in order to get the sense of events in their context a century ago), Parry tells us that after his father had had printed his nine-year-old son's manuscript on 'The Life of Queen Elizabeth', the boy was 'absolutely convinced that one day I would be an author, with my name in the British Museum catalogue, which has this advantage over being buried in Westminster Abbey, that some one is sure to come across your niche in the sepulchre – and take you down for a short airing, if only out of pity or curiosity. That cannot happen in Westminster Abbey.'

Reflecting on the chain of events which led to eventual publication, Parry comments: '. . . both these eminent writers [Courtenay and Macaulay] entirely underrated the literary and historical value of Dorothy's letters. To me she seemed one of the great English letter-writers. Curiously enough, Courtenay, a dull fellow compared to Macaulay, had the finer instinct . . . I had to admit that Macaulay, as a literary critic, had blundered badly, but I was so grateful to him for pointing out to me this treasure-trove, that I magnanimously determined to let him down gently when I came to write about it.'

Courtenay had located the original letters, and had obtained permission to publish extracts, from their owner, the Rev. Robert Longe of Spixworth Park, Norfolk, and vicar of Coddenham Church, Suffolk, who had acquired them by marriage and inheritance. When W.T. died in 1699, the letters (as well as the cabinet in which they were kept) were left to his grand-daughter, Elizabeth Temple, who had married her cousin, John Temple; on his death in 1722 they passed to John Bacon, who was the youngest son of Elizabeth Temple's youngest sister, Dorothy.

Members of the family of Bacon of Shrubland Hall, Suffolk, were also associated with the living at Coddenham, and it was here that the letters were kept. In 1875 the Rev. Nicholas Bacon left all his personal effects to his sister-in-law, Charlotte; when she later married the Rev. John Longe (the curate, who succeeded to the living), title passed to him and then to his son, from whom Courtenay obtained permission to publish.

When the Rev. Robert Longe died in 1890, the letters came to Robert Bacon Longe, and it was from him that Parry obtained permission to edit them. But, the first editor informs us, the owner would neither allow visitors to see the originals (though, in fairness, he was at that time over eighty years of age!), nor would he allow them to be sent to the editor, who therefore had to rely, for his first edition, on transcriptions made by a member of the Longe family.

That member of the Longe family was Mrs Sarah Rose Longe, wife of Francis Davy Longe, and a daughter-in-law of the Rev. Robert Longe. While Parry scrupulously records Mrs Longe's central importance to the whole enterprise, it is nevertheless important to emphasize how the operation of patriarchy in particular, and of late-nineteenth-century 'gentility' in general, deprived her of the opportunity to become the first editor of the letters. For instance, having written to Parry on 6 April 1886 that 'there are about 90 letters which, by studying every book of the time I could hear of, I have to a certain degree arranged and dated, and found out who everyone named in the letters was', a letter of two days later makes an offer that she will 'gladly give up *all* my notes etc. etc. and enter into everything – only my name not appearing. It must be "by permission of the Rev. R. Longe" – then there will be no jealousy as you know this exists in families, specially with daughters-in-law.' Later still, Sarah

Rose Longe explains to Parry why she had not herself proceeded to the preparation of an edition: the elderly Rev. Longe had consented that she should copy the letters, but when she wanted to publish them, or get someone else to do so, he would not agree, 'though his father had allowed Mr Courtenay to do so, who was a stranger'.

If Parry's biography makes this point about family and gender relations only by inference, his justification for preparing a 'modernized' edition is not only explicit, but also a fascinating insight into the contemporary national cultural assumptions about readership; he writes: '... from the first, I had made up my mind that the book would be of no use to the average reader if the letters were printed in the old spelling ... if an old English writer has any story to tell, or wisdom to impart, I think his spelling should be "modernized" – and for American readers Americanized – that is to say translated into the vulgar tongue'.

Finding a publisher was not easy. Despite Defoe's character-ization of writing as 'a very considerable Branch of the English Commerce', and despite the growth in publishing houses, as well as in circulating libraries, after 1830, Parry tells us: 'I soon dis-covered that to write a masterpiece was one thing, and to find a publisher was quite another affair. Naturally, it appeared to me that Macmillans should be honoured by the offer of the precious MS. as they had published the magazine article. On May 28 it was returned to me ... in their letters Macmillans say, "with every desire to take a favourable view of the project we cannot think that the book would be likely to pay its expenses". They thought it would only interest a limited circle of readers, and ought, if at all, to be produced by a book club or an antiquarian society.'

Following the rejection by Macmillan, Parry offered it to Smith, Elder, but the reader of that distinguished house, one James Payn, thought the letters to be of antiquarian interest only. It is perhaps instructive to note that it was around this time that Matthew Arnold observed that the book market was being infested by 'a cheap literature, hideous and ignoble in aspect, like the tawdry novels which flare in the bookshelves of our railway stations, and which seem designed, as so much else is that is produced for the use of our middle class seems designed, for people with a low standard of life'. While Raymond Williams[14] is correct to remind us that 'the whole argument about "cheap literature" has been compromised by its use as a form of class-distinction, whereas the real problem is always the relation between inexperience and the way this is met', it is nevertheless salutary to note that the publishers had miscalculated the market for this volume of letters.

Sarah Rose Longe, who had, apparently with Parry's agreement, been looking for a publisher, wrote to him on 5 July to say that 'Griffith, Farren and Okeden are publishers, and Mr Okeden is interested in Dorothy. He has written and asked me to ask you to send the MS. to his private residence and he will read it himself.' Agreement to publish was reached towards the end of August, with Parry consenting to participate in the financing of the edition, adding the proviso that 'if there were any profits they were to be shared between us. This he [Okeden] acknowledged and it was all the contract we had – but I had the letters put carefully away, for I did not think the arrangement very businesslike.'

The success of the first edition[15] was instantaneous – to such an extent that a new, and cheaper, edition (with some profits to the editor) was printed in the same year. Parry does not exaggerate when he writes that 'the reviewers strove with each other to find epithets superlative enough to express their appreciation of the literary and historical interest of Dorothy's wonderful letters'.

While the first edition was being typeset, Okeden pressed that seven of the letters (in this edition, letters 8, 12, 16, 28, 31, 37, 47) be omitted as 'of no great interest'. Parry concurred, because 'as he was paying the piper he had a right to call the tune and I accepted his advice'. One curious effect of that decision was that, when the letters were sold to the British Museum in 1891 (they are now held in the British Library as ADD. MSS. 33975), these seven letters were excluded from the purchase – not because Mr Longe did not want to sell, but because the British Museum apparently ticked off those they wanted against the printed work; it was only in 1903 that Parry, having 'acquired the sole right of publishing them from Mr Longe', was able to incorporate these seven letters in a new edition. Two further editions[16] appeared under Parry's editorship, so that the letters can legitimately be said to have become a minor classic in the lifetime of the individual who laboured with such diligence to effect their publication. But there was also a curious consequence: at least two pirated versions appeared, one in Toronto, the other in London. (I have not seen a copy of the Toronto edition, but its existence is recorded in some Canadian bibliographies.) The London version, which was brought out under the imprint of the distinguished house of Gollancz,[17] was the subject of a court case about which Parry writes with some verve and satisfaction in his autobiography, since he brought an action for breach of copyright in which he sought to show that the Gollancz edition was not based on the original manuscript sources, but on his edition, demonstrating that even typesetting errors had been carried over into the disputed edition. He further argued that the precedent was to be found in the 'Kelly's Directories' case in the Court of Appeal, 22 February 1902, before Mr Justice Farwell,[18] in which 'the astute Mr Kelly when he completed his famous directories [*Kelly's Directories of Merchants, Manufacturers, and Shippers*] used to insert decoy and fabulous addresses, so that when some enterprising printer came out with a cheap rival volume for part of a district, stolen from Kelly, it was easy to show that it was a theft and not an original publication'.

In 1928 a new edition appeared, by Professor G. C. Moore Smith.[19] Because that edition contained the seven letters not sold to the British Museum, it was, Moore Smith noted on the title page, 'Edited by permission of Sir Edward Parry and of his publishers Messrs Sherratt & Hughes, Ltd, and Messrs J. M. Dent

& Son, Ltd.' The Moore Smith edition is of considerable scholarly skill: it restored the original text (although the editor at times tends to impose twentieth-century fashion in punctuation upon a mid-seventeenth-century style which reads admirably without the need for such intervention); it clarified and extended, by notes and appendices, information either not available (or sometimes incorrect) in the Parry editions; it made use of the manuscript Diary of Henry Osborne[20] to corroborate details in the letters and as an aid to dating. This remarkable Diary, from which Moore Smith published extracts (parts were in cypher, which he decoded with specialist help),* contains fascinating comments not only about Henry Osborne's attitudes to the courtship, but also about political and financial matters affecting the family. I have made extensive use of the manuscript in the appendices and notes.

Finally, in 1968 the Folio Society published an edition of the letters,[21] based largely on the Moore Smith edition, but dispensing with much of the critical apparatus and notes.

For this Penguin edition, a new transcription has been made of the seventy letters in the manuscript held in the British Library. Unfortunately it has not been possible to trace the present whereabouts of the seven letters which were retained by the Longe family, and I have therefore had to rely on Moore Smith's edition for the text of those. We know from Parry's autobiography that the seven letters were excluded from his 1888 edition at the request of his first publishers, but that he incorporated them in later editions, having obtained the rights to publication from their owner. We know from Moore Smith's edition that the latter had been given sight of these letters, as well as other documents, by their owner, the Rev. John Charles Longe of Yelverton, Norfolk. Correspondence with Mr Longe's daughter, Miss Dorothy Longe, who still lives in Yelverton, reveals that after the sale of Spixworth Park (1936) and the death of her

---

* The parts of Henry Osborne's Diary which were written in cypher are indicated in the Notes to this book by the use of *italic type*.

father (1939), most of the family belongings were stored in a warehouse in Norwich. When that building was bombed in March 1942, the family lost 'many treasures and all family portraits'. With the assistance of Mr G. N. B. Longe of Woking, Surrey, I was able to locate a large holding of Longe documents in the archives of the County Hall, Ipswich (HA 24/50/19 acc. 136 dd 25 March 1948), but neither the letters nor the manuscript notes of Sarah Rose Longe, to which Moore Smith had access, form part of that collection. It is hoped that publication of this edition may help to locate those documents.

The majority of the letters are written on paper approximately 12″ × 8″ in size, though there are exceptions (for instance, letters 58, 59 and 60 are on paper approximately 11″ × 15″). In some cases the letters are not folded, thus giving two pages of writing; more generally there is one fold, giving four pages. The earlier letters have a wide margin on the left. In these letters D.O. would, when she came to the end of the page, turn the sheet through ninety degrees, fill up the space in the margin, and then proceed to the verso, on which she would repeat the same process. On some occasions, when she had no space left to sign her name or to initial the letter, she would return to the first page and reverse it, with the effect that her signature or initials would appear upside-down on that first page, above the opening lines.

The paper is, generally speaking, in an excellent state. There are some tears in the manuscript, but these are very few, and have been noted; the handwriting is clear and relatively easy to read – partly as a consequence of the ink, which shows scant signs of deterioration. In this transcription I have followed closely the original punctuation, making only the exceptions noted below. D.O. does not use question marks; new paragraphs are inferred from a wider than usual space between adjacent words; ends of sentences are indicated sometimes by full stops, at other times by a dash; full stops and semi-colons are used interchangeably. I have therefore retained formulations which we might now describe as archaic, such as 'wee', 'bee', 'my thinks', etc. The main concessions made to present-day usage have been: (a) to indicate a new sentence by the use of a capital letter (D.O. uses this convention randomly); (b) to substitute the £ sign for her use of 'li' (livre); (c) to amend abbreviations, for example replacing 'w^ch' with 'which', 'y^e' with 'the', etc.; (d) to make selective use of punctuation (shown in square brackets) to clarify the sense; and (e) to modernize all 'old style' dates (the custom at that time was to date the new year from 25 March, the Feast of the Annunciation – Lady Day).

It is a noteworthy feature of the letters that D.O. was always seeking for the most apposite word: the manuscript shows countless examples where a word, or words, have been meticulously inked out and replaced. For writings which were not meant for publication this is remarkable. It seems to me that she intended the letters to be discourses concerning philosophies – arguments not only with W.T. but also with herself. It is important to see the role of these letters in the formation of belief, in the testing of her resolve, and therefore not to confuse cause and effect, as a recent critic[22] does when she writes: 'Errors and lapses show that she neither proofread nor revised, and prove that, as a lady, she had no pretensions to publication, but regarded these as an inadequate substitute for conversation.'

One of the key problems is that most of the letters are undated. Both Parry and Moore Smith have suggested dates, but theirs, like mine, are conjectural. They are deduced from two sources: their relation to those letters which are dated; and internal evidence from the letters themselves regarding either public events or corroboration from Henry Osborne's Diary. Attempts at dating and ordering are not helped by the possibility that several letters have gone astray.[23] We know from the letters that there were two carriers, Harrold (letter 36) and Collins (letter 31), but we also know that D.O. made use of opportunities when these occurred, for instance via the coachman (letter 9); when her brother sent his man to London (letter 15); or via Jane Wright (letter 34). We find that the carriers came to Chicksands on a

Thursday, and left on their return journey to London on the following Monday (see letters 9, 17, 31). We learn, additionally, that she tended to start to write her letters, and then complete them in instalments when the opportunity presented itself (see, for example, letter 17, where she advises W.T. to follow her methods); that there were problems with the family – for instance, her brother's interrogation of W.T.'s boy (letter 31); that she burnt some (all?) of W.T.'s letters (see letter 22); and that even the places used as letter-drops had to be changed (letters 31, 39). The journey from Chicksands to London was approximately forty miles, and was made via Shefford, Hitchin, Welwyn, Hatfield, Barnet, Highgate, Holloway and Islington. Parry (1914) notes that, in a 1637 pamphlet, *The Carriers Cosmography or a Brief Relation of the Inns, Ordinaries, Hostelries & other lodgings in or near London where the Carriers Waggons, Footposts and Higgles do usually come up* by one John Taylor, it is recorded that 'the carriers of Bedford do lodge at the "Three Horseshoes" in Aldersgate Street'.

iii *The Political Context of the Letters*

> . . . *I doe not think these are times for any body to expect prefferment, that deserv's it, and in the best 'twas ever too uncertaine for a wise body to truste to.*

Previous editors, as well as critics, have highlighted references in the letters to the life of the country gentry at the time: how D.O. spent her days (letter 24); visits to Epsom and Hyde Park (letter 25); the round of family visits (letters 20, 40). One or two critics have sought to construct, from these comments on maypoles and shepherdesses, masques and races, shopping for orange-flower water, sharing a bottle of ale with a servant, and guests sleeping three in a bed, a picture of rural tranquillity and of social

stability co-existing with radical upheaval. Yet the evidence of
the letters would seek to point to a contrary conclusion. The
letters make copious reference to political, religious and cultural
events and disputes. They mention the ejection of Algernon
Sidney from the Commons by Cromwell (letter 18); the sharp
observation and commentary on the preaching of Erbury (letter
22) and Stephen Marshall (letter 39); the introduction of a new
form for the solemnization of marriage (letter 35); and the plot
against Cromwell (letter 64), of which one consequence was that
Lady Vavasour was sent to the Tower (letter 67). Perhaps the
most poignant of all is the description by D.O. of her personal
state, in a moment of deepest depression: '. . . like a Country
wasted by a Civill war, where two opposing Party's have
disputed theire right soe long till they have made it worth neither
of theire conquest's, tis Ruin'd and desolated by the long striffe
within it to that degree as twill bee usefull to none, nobody that
know's the condition tis in will think it worth the gaineing'
(letter 50).

This is not the place to discuss the debate on the 'English
Revolution',[24] but references in the letters force us to ask, at
least, two questions: what might we deduce, from these letters,
about the response of the participants to the events around the
revolution and its immediate aftermath? and what might we
deduce about the views of the writer? The first question is bound
up with a wider issue: why did members of the mid-seventeenth-
century ruling class catapult themselves into positions which they
would almost certainly have rejected as unthinkable before the
event – regicide, as in the case of her uncle, Sir John Danvers;
support for a republican administration, as in the case of her
father-in-law, Sir John Temple, and her cousin, Robert
Hammond; abolition of the House of Lords and of episcopacy;
toleration for Catholics; and (perhaps most intriguing of all)
operating the mechanisms for the expropriation of land and the
confiscation of property, especially of royalists? Historians tend
to agree that it was the men of property who restored the
monarchy under Charles II; they appear less willing to agree that

it was the men of property who deposed his father and elevated Cromwell. The actions of the aristocracy and gentry fascinate (particularly when we bear in mind that they, like the radicals, were a minority), especially those of the country community, with its leavening of affluent yeomanry. It would appear that we must ascribe the success of the country gentry to one dominant element which the radicals and parliament never managed to break: a monopoly of political power, an autonomy of action – what has been vividly and aptly described as a 'union of partially independent states' [25] which gave immense confidence. These letters underscore the argument that social and kinship ties were focussed upon locality: going from country house to country house; wining and dining with the Briers family, with Lady Grey de Ruthin, is as much about politics, economics and marriage as it is about entertainment, so that we have the conditions for the creation and retention of a cohesive sense of community which could withstand new pressures and new ideas. The letters therefore dramatically illustrate Professor Everitt's further contention that: 'The allegiance of the provincial gentry to the community of their native shire is one of the basic facts of English history in the seventeenth and eighteenth centuries.' Chicksands Priory may not have been one of the 'great houses', but its function was, in effect, no different from those. Mark Girouard [26] has defined their role: 'They were not, whatever they may be now, just large houses in the country in which rich people lived. Esssentially they were power houses – the houses of a ruling class.' They were certainly celebrated as such in their own time by, for example, the birth of the country-house poem as a literary genre, as expressed in, *inter alia*, Andrew Marvell's 'Upon Appleton House' and Ben Jonson's 'To Penshurst'. [27]

To see the country-house ethos in this way is not to be interpreted as support for the theory that, from the Reformation to the late nineteenth century, the English gentry survived and renewed itself by means of regular accretion to its ranks, by marriage and/or purchase of estates, of men from the cities: lawyers, merchants, factory-owners, etc. A recent study, [28] the first I know which looks at the matter quantitatively, casts doubt on this myth of relatively easy upward mobility on the part of the so-called 'self-made man' – a myth upon which were super-imposed other myths: those of national stability at home; patriotism in times of international crisis; the shaping of a unique form of government. My argument here is that even if these superstructural myths are valid, their genesis in the myth of 'upward mobility' would still be questionable. This is not the place to argue the matter, or to speculate on the reasons why the myth of an 'open elite' has been sustained with such tenacity. What is more interesting is why the landed elite itself has continued to endure. The Stone and Stone argument may be summarized as follows: the elite, which had consolidated itself by 1660, endured because it had developed effective strategies for survival – by means of careful codes of family practices, and social and economic relations. In these they were aided and abetted by the attitudes of the middle and lower classes, who were enveloped by the cultural embrace of the landed, whose culture became, for a long time, *the* national culture.

It is noteworthy that Lord David Cecil, whose particular skill in literary criticism was biographical, with considerable antipathy to historical or theoretical approaches, should offer some support for this view. Writing about D.O.,[29] he observes that: 'The cavalier gentry accepted the plain facts of existence without questioning. Money, for instance, and all the solid security that money implied, mattered to them a great deal. They never married without it; they generally married for it. And, though they felt the family bond very strongly, the closest relations would squabble for years about the terms of a dowry or an inheritance. Yet they were not materialists. Their outlook was made spiritual by the sublime background of religion.'

The questions of family, marriage and gender will be considered in the next section, but it is important not to dismiss the conclusion cited above as a romanticization of the past or of a particular class. And it is very important to recognize the religious dimension, not simply with regard to single items to which D.O.

draws our attention (that she is a 'devote' of Jeremy Taylor (letter 60, note 2), or where she questions the ideas attributed to Lord Lisle), but in the general spirit and tenor of the letters and in the evidence of how her faith sustained her during her worst moments of misery. The contrast with the beliefs of her future husband could not be more marked. His are philosophical, theoretical, those of the urbane traveller and man of letters and of affairs; hers are based on a simple, yet not uncritical, faith allied to a keen intelligence and a sharp awareness of what is going forth in current debates: with cousin Molle and his Cambridge connections; with brother Henry's orthodoxies; with observations on sermons heard; and, above all, with W.T. himself. Surely one of the most noteworthy features of the letters is not so much the content of her arguments, but the fact that from the outset this young woman, who was not substantially different from most others of her age and class, never doubts that she is right in writing to W.T. on a basis of equality. It is to this matter that we now turn.

iv *Family, Gender, and Feminism*

> *... though I can easily beleeve that to marry one for whome we have already some affection, will infinitely Encrease that kindenesse yet I shall never bee perswaded that Marriage has a Charme to raise love out of nothing, much lesse out of dislike.*

Given our present-day interest in the history of the family, in gender relations, and in feminist theories, it is appropriate that we consider the letters in these contexts.[30]

It was the Duchess of Newcastle (see letter 17) who, in 1655, outlined the territories of the male and the female as follows: 'Men and women may be compared to the sun and the moon, according to the description in the Holy Writ, which says: "God made two great lights, one to rule the day, the other night." So man is made to govern commonwealths and women their private families . . .' It is for that reason, she concludes, that women are not scientists, or skilled in the arts, in military affairs, or in state-craft. There is, of course, nothing new in such an assertion of patriarchy as both God-given and 'natural'; this gender-specific contrast is the foundation for a complex superstructure of oppositions: public vs. private; active vs. passive; authority vs. obedience; societal vs. domestic. Yet it should be pointed out that this same Lady Newcastle, in her passionate desire for literary recognition (which she deserved, but never fully achieved, either in her own time or in ours), rejected the model to which she subscribed in theory, and which she exhorted others to follow. The irony was that, try as she might, she could not rid herself of the classification into which she was born: a specifically female sphere presupposed, as well as operated, an appropriate female knowledge (domestic); an appropriate female sexuality (chastity); and an appropriate female economic status (dependency).

I am aware that at least two serious criticisms may be made to seek to invalidate what follows: (a) that it is inappropriate for a man to intervene in a debate about feminisms;[31] and (b) that letters to the person you love have only a dubious validity as documents for the measurement of feminist beliefs. But the issue has to be confronted. In letter 15, D.O. writes that she can never think of disposing (note the word!) of herself without her father's consent, and then proceeds to add, '. . . Nor could you like it in mee if I should doe otherwise, 'twould make mee unworthy of your Esteem.' To this acceptance of paternal authority and pros-pective wifely obedience should be added her acquiescence in fraternal obedience – while she is constantly at odds with her brother about his attemps to marry her off, she does not actually rebel, indeed she counsels against it. In letter 44, she says that she has observed '. . . that Generaly in great famely's the Men sildom disagree, but that the women are alway's scolding, and tis most certain that lett the husband bee what hee will if the wife have but Patience (which sure becomes her best) the disorder cannot bee great enough to make a noise'. So, by these remarks and others in the same vein, D.O. falls short. But to dismiss her in that way would be to dismiss the remarkable qualities of an exceptional woman, and would also deny us the insights the letters afford on the changing conceptions of love, family and marriage which were being forged at that time. To do her justice, D.O. should be considered in the context of the strictures she advances, the frustrations she encountered, and her awareness of the changing world of her times: it is out of female responses to those kinds of interactions and impositions that feminism was born.

Thus the observation at the beginning of this section (from letter 4) is not an isolated one. Time and time again D.O. offers a general criticism, not only of the institution of marriage itself, but also of its association with love – more precisely, with what most couples lightly assume to be that state. Thus: 'To marry for Love were noe reproachfull thing if wee did not see that of ten thousand couples that doe it, hardly one can be brought for an Example that it may bee done & not repented afterwards.' She is quite clear about the reason for such a state of affairs: 'What an Age doe wee live in where 'tis a Miracle if in ten Couple that are married two of them live soe as not to publish it to the world that they cannot agree' (letter 44). Of such situations she offers several examples: Lady Sunderland is not to be followed in her marrying of Mr Smith (letter 7), particularly since it transpires that she married him out of pity; of Lady Udall, who is resolved to marry a blind man, she notes pertinently that 'if she did not love him what could perswade her to marry him, and if she did, in my opinion she made him but an ill requitall for seventeen years' service, to marry him when she had spent all her youth & beauty with another' (letter 37). It is out of an awareness of these high standards of conduct that she writes that she had made her brother confess he agreed with her that Lady Isabella Rich 'had better have marryed a begger, then that beast with all his estate'. D.O. also extends the same critical insights to the literature (especially the romances) she reads, and which is read by other women of her time. In letter 59 she confesses that she has 'noe patience for our faiseurs de Romance, when they make women court. It will never enter into my head that tis posible any woman can Love where she is not first Loved, & much lesse that if they should doe that, they could have the face to owne it.'

Her solution is, in the context of her time and her own orthodoxies, quite radical: 'For my part I think it were very convenient that all such as intend to marrye should be together in the same house some year's of probation and if in all that time they never disagreed they should then bee permitted to marry if they pleased, but how few would doe it then' (letter 44). This is a most apposite observation, not only because of the difficulties she had to overcome, but because of the legal and financial practices which made women into dependants. Of all these, two predominate. The first is primogeniture, by which the landed gentry in particular, but property-owners generally, preserved and protected entail. (Note that D.O. has to leave Chicksands very speedily after the death of her father in order that her elder brother and his household can move in, which circumstance illustrates the double disadvantage of that system for women – discrimination by gender as well as age.) Secondly, dowries, whereby brides who were unable to offer landed property (an effect of primogeniture) were expected to offer instead an amount in cash, called a 'portion'; this was usually intended for the bridegroom's father, who would use it, in his turn, to off-load a daughter, or settle an outstanding debt (one of the strategies by which Sir Peter Osborne had hoped to liquidate his debt to the Briers family?). In return for this 'portion', the father of the bridegroom guaranteed the bride an annuity, or 'jointure', if she was left a widow. D.O. offers an excellent example of this in letter 23, when she writes: 'Just now I have news brought mee of the death of an old rich Knight [Sir William Briers; see letter 2, note 5], that had promised mee this seven year's to marry mee whensoever his wife dyed, and now hee's dead before her, and has left her such a widdow it makes mee mad to think on it,

£1200 a yeare Joynter and £20000 in mony & personall Estate, and all this I might have had, if Mr Death had bin pleased to have taken her instead of him.' She is, of course, not serious, because she immediately goes on to say, 'but since I cannot have him, would you have her. What say you, shall I speak a good word for you . . .' But the point has been made!

The general consequence, as Lawrence Stone observes, was that marriage therefore 'always involved a transfer of a significant amount of real or personal property from the family of the bride to that of the groom, with a reverse commitment in the future of a significant proportion of annual income'.[32] The letters frequently illustrate this property–power nexus – with regard to her brother's intentions, as well as those of other people. In the case of the former, she writes: '. . . my B will never bee at quiet till hee see mee disposed of, but hee do's not mean to loose mee by it . . . when this house break's up [on the death of her father], he is resolved to follow mee if hee can, which hee thinks hee might better doe to a house where I had some power, then where I am but upon Courtesy my self, besydes that hee thinks it would bee to my advantage to bee well bestow'd, and by that hee understands Richly' (letter 22). With regard to other people and their intentions, she offers a great variety of comments. These include her remarks on the gentleman who 'prottested hee liked mee soe well, that hee was very angry my Father would not bee perswaded to give up £1000 more with mee, and I him soe ill, that I vowed, if I had £1000 lesse I should have thought it too much for him' (letter 3); her admiration for Sir John Temple's patience 'that let's you reste with soe much indifference when there is such a fortune offer'd' (letter 9). Finally, what seems to me to be the key to an understanding of her position might be deduced from her predilection for an offhandedness which not only hides a scalpel-sharp discernment, but also insulates against the pain of not being free to make her own choices in the ways that a man could, and what that lack of freedom does to women. Thus she observes about her cousin Thomas Osborne, later Earl of Danby, that nothing tempted him 'to marry his Lady (soe

much) as that shee was an Earl's daughter, which mee thought
was the prittiest fancy and had the least of sence out of any I had
heard on, Considering that it was noe addition to her person . . .'
(letter 43). Similarly, about their close friend Mrs Franklin, she
can write that she 'may say fine things now she is warme in
Moore Park, but she is very much Alterd in her opinions since
her marriage, if these bee her owne. She left a Gentleman that I
could name whome she had much more of kindenesse for, then
ever she had for Mr Fr: because his Estate was lesse, and upon the
discovery of some letters that her Mother intercepted, sufferd
her self to bee perswaded that 23 hundred pound a year, was
better then twelve with a person she loved' (letter 50).

Finally, the question arises: how might D.O. justify her marriage to W.T. rather than to any of her other suitors? In this
connection it is important to give her credit for the extremely
skilful manner and techniques with which she sees off all of them,
as well as the interventions of her family – an excellent example
of the nominally dutiful daughter, but one who eventually gets
her way. This is not to accuse D.O. of being untruthful, or
making use of 'female wiles'. Indeed, the opposite is true: in letter
48 she informs W.T. that she will not dissimulate; in letter 55 she
re-states her love, and in letter 58 she outlines the reasons for her
decision to marry him. (Recall that, in letter 12, it is she who
proposes to him.) Letter 59 contains a remarkable statement,
which shows her awareness of contemporary debates: 'Tis certain
(what you say) that where devine or human Laws are not possitive wee may bee our owne Judges, nobody can hinder us, nor
is it in it selfe to be blamed', although this statement is immediately qualified with the observation that 'it is not safe to take all
the liberty is allowed us, there are not many that are sober enough
to bee trusted with the government of themselv's . . .'. This last
sentiment is followed (in letter 60) by a reference to Jeremy
Taylor's view that 'there is a great advantage to bee gained in
resigning up on's will to the comande of another, because the
same Action which in it selfe is wholy indifferent if done upon
our owne Choice, becom's an Act of Duty and Religion if don

in Obedience to the comande of any Person whome Nature the Law's or our selv's have given a power over us'. It is this tension between apparently contradictory positions which gives the clue to her singularity: her ability to do justice to the demands of those around her, yet to retain her sense of her own integrity as a woman – a feminist before feminism.

v *The Literary and Critical Contexts*

> *All letters mee thinks should bee free and Easy*
> *as ones discourse, not studdyed, as an Oration,*
> *nor made up of hard words like a Charme.*
> *Tis an abominable thing to see how some*
> *People will labour to find out term's that may*
> *Obscure a plaine sense . . .*

The letters are fascinating because of the insights they provide into attitudes to style, reading habits and critical outlook in the late seventeenth century, while their publication history affords an insight into the changing approaches to these practices.

The reviewers of the earlier editions of the letters not only tended to emphasize the myth of the enduring stability of English life despite the hiccup of the war years, to which reference has already been made, but they also sought to underpin the notion of the woman as helpmeet, to which reference was also made earlier, of which the following review is perhaps a representative sample: 'No one . . . who looks at her portrait, with its clear, pure brows, and sweet, earnest, resolute mouth, and who reads her letters . . . will doubt that the capacity for heroism was hers. In womanliness, tenderness, virtue, grace, meanwhile, she redeems an epoch which has not much of such qualities to spare.'[33]

It is Virginia Woolf who provides the sharpest insight into D.O. in the context of her times, and of ours. After pointing out that 'at that time though writing books was ridiculous for a

woman there was nothing unseemly in writing a letter', she continues: 'The art of letter-writing is often the art of essay-writing
in disguise. But such as it was, it was an art that a woman could
practise without unsexing herself. It was an art that could be
carried out at odd moments, by a father's sick-bed, among a
thousand interruptions, without exciting comment, anonymously
as it were, and often with the pretence that it served some useful
purpose. Yet into these immaculate letters, lost now for the most
part, went powers of observation and of wit that were later to
take rather a different shape in *Evelina* and in *Pride and Prejudice.*'[34]

To the issue of the development of prose I shall return, but
first it might be interesting to digress in order to consider the
material conditions under which Virginia Woolf was writing
what started off as a book review:[35] her Diary entry for Saturday,
22 September 1928, reads:

This is written on the verge of my alarming holiday in Burgundy.
I am alarmed of 7 days alone with Vita: interested, excited, but
afraid – she may find me out, I her out. I may (& theres Mabel the
Bride in her white dress at the pump. The bridegroom, a carter out
of work, wears white socks. Are they pure? I doubt it. They are
going to spend their honeymoon near Pevensey. He was 15 minutes
late & we saw her come in wearing a wreath. And I felt this is the
heart of England – this wedding in the country: history I felt;
Cromwell; The Osbornes; Dorothy's sheperdesses singing: of all of
whom Mr & Mrs Jarrad seem more the descendants than I am: as if
they represented the unconscious breathing of England & L. and I,
leaning over the wall, were detached, unconnected.'[36]

The attitude to women writers of books, to which Virgina Woolf
draws attention, occurs on several occasions in the letters: for
instance, in letter 17, D.O. asks W.T. to send her a copy of Lady
Newcastle's poems because 'they say tis ten times more Extravagant then her dresse', but she then immediately goes on to
state that 'sure the poore woman is a little distracted, she could
never bee soe rediculous else as to venture at writeing book's and
in verse too'. By letter 20, she can tell W.T. that he need not

send her the volume after all, 'for I have seen it, and am sattisfyed that there are many soberer People in Bedlam'.

If D.O.'s comments are to be taken either as proof that she shared the dominant opinion that women should not write for publication, or that she was signalling a preference for prose over poetry, then an observation in letter 40 might contribute towards providing an answer to the first comment. Unaware (like all other readers) of the fact that the author of a popular French romance of the time was female (see letter 40, note 3), D.O. writes to W.T. the common gossip masquerading as truth: 'They say the Gentelman that writes this Romance has a Sister that lives with him as Mayde and she furnishes him with all the little Story's that come between soe that hee only Contrives the main designe and when hee wants somthing to Entertaine his company withall hee call's to her for it.' It is salutary not only to compare the fate of Madame de Scudéry, the true author of these romances, with that of D.O., but to compare D.O. with the Marquise de Sévigné, whose dates (1626–96) match hers almost exactly. Like D.O., Madame de Sévigné numbered many of the famous among her friends; like D.O., her letters are a mine of information about contemporary events and attitudes, written with immense verve and style. But unlike the case of D.O., the first edition of the letters of Madame de Sévigné appeared within a year of her death.

With regard to the second element of the Virginia Woolf criticism, it is interesting to note that while the playwrights of the period (for example Massinger, Shirley, Brome, Davenant) were all close to court circles, that was not the case with the prose writers. Indeed, the most distinguished of them all, John Bunyan, spent a considerable time in prison for his beliefs. D.O.'s letters corroborate the opinion, developed in our time, that the chief fictive prose form was that of the French romance, of, for example, Madame de Scudéry, La Calprenède, Gomberville – although a domestic version also existed. These romances[37] existed side by side with the essay (of which form W.T. was to become a distinguished exponent) and the political pamphlet, but to which should be added letters, maxims, the beginnings of periodicals and of journalism and translations.[38] About the last-named, D.O. has a great deal to say; for instance, in letter 41 she tells W.T.: 'I have noe Patience neither for these Translatours of Romances. I mett with Polexandre and L'Illustre Bassa, both soe disguised that I who am theire old acquaintance hardly knew them, besydes that they were still soe much french in words and Phrases that twas imposible for one that understood not french to make any thing of them.' Again, in letter 59 she comments that, though the author 'makes his People say fine handsome things to one another yet they are not Easy and Naïve like the french, and there is a little harshnesse in most of the discourses that one would take to bee the fault of a Translatour rather than of an author'.

But it is also a question of style. D.O. clearly holds the 'common-sense' view, advanced by Francis Bacon, that language should be unambiguous, precise, specific. In letter 61 she criticizes a letter she has seen, for having 'many pritty things shuffled together which would doe better spoken then in a letter, not-withstanding the received opinion that People ought to write as they speak (which in some sence I think is true)'. It is, however, important to recognize that the argument about style was also an argument about education and about political freedom: educa-tion, to the extent that it was a rejection of the convoluted Ciceronian Latin form in favour of the more precise and un-adorned style of Seneca and Tacitus, which, it might be argued, eventually triumphs with Dryden at the end of the period. But D.O. reminds us that it is a battle still to be won, since 'these great Schollers are not the best writer's, (of Letters I mean, of books perhaps they are)' (letter 41).

It was an argument about political freedom in terms of the extent to which style became associated with ideology in the pamphlet literature, of which John Milton's attack on the bishops and their style in his *Apology . . . Against Smectymnuus* (1642), and the case he makes for liberty of speech, writing and printing in *Areopagitica* (1644), are perhaps the best known, but it also points to the radical winds that swept through England at that time.

What stands out from the letters is her gift for highlighting character and personality. She judges the fictive inhabitants of her romances using the same uncompromising yardstick with which she measures the real ones (though she makes it clear that she distinguishes between the real and imaginary), whether personal (her aunt Gargrave; cousin Molle; Sir Justinian; her 'fighting servant') or public (Lady Newcastle; Lilly; Lord Lisle; Stephen Marshall; Henry Cromwell). Thus in letter 38 she writes: 'there are fower Pritty story's in it . . . Tell mee which you have most compass[ion] for. When you have read what Every one say's for himself, perhaps you will not thinke it soe Easy to decide which is the most unhappy as you may think by the Titles theire Storry's bear, only let mee desyre you not to Pitty the Jelous one, for I remember I could doe nothing but Laugh at him, as one that sought his owne vexation.' In the letter, she records her gladness that he had concurred with her criticism, and adds, about another character in the romances, 'i'le swear I cryed for her when I read it first though she were an imaginary person . . .'

It is perhaps wholly appropriate that, in our time, D.O. has herself become the inspiration for a work of the imagination which, in its turn, sparked off a sequel. I refer to the song cycle *The Voice of Love* by Nicholas Maw,[39] with words by Peter Porter, which led to the 'Concertante Variations' by John McCabe.[40] The Maw–Porter cycle contains eight songs, including Prologue and Epilogue, and skilfully orchestrates the question D.O. asks of W.T. in letter 31: 'Shall we ever be so happy?' What makes the cycle successful, apart from the sheer elegance of the music, is that D.O. is seen from the perspective of a woman who has been happily married for over forty years, and now recalls (to use Peter Porter's apposite choice of words) 'the basilisk, the iron man' (Oliver Cromwell), and her suitors, like 'Sir Entail and Sir Gravitas . . ./The one owns all a lake and half a shire,/The other is tone deaf and keeps a choir'. D.O. surely would have recognized a kindred spirit, and approved. But the song cycle also captures her sense of unease at the strength of feeling in W.T.'s letters to her: 'Your love for me is my ruin/Hope pushed on to sin/Like a proud river –/Always in spate, or a vain mirror/Showing one face', and her relief that the engagement has at last been made public: 'Music is heard when divisions cease', leading to the last lines of the Epilogue, 'Love, come now to me –/Can we ever be so happy'.[41]

The Letters

The Letters

Letter 1

[Friday] 24 December [1652]

Sir

You may please to lett my Old Servant [1] (as you call him) know, that I confesse I owe much to his merritts, and the many Obligations his kindenesse and Civility's has layde upon mee. But for the ten poundes hee claimes,[2] it is not yett due, and I think you may do well (as a freind) to perswade him to putt it in the Number of his desperate debts, for 'tis a very uncertaine one. In all things else pray as I am his Servant.

And now Sir let mee tell you that I am Extreamly glad (whoesoever gave you the Occasion) to heare from you, since (without complement) there are very few Person's in the world I am more concern'd in. To finde that you have overcome your longe Journy,[3] that you are well, and in a place where it is posible for mee to see you, is a sattisfaction, as I whoe have not bin used to many, may bee allowed to doubt of. Yet I will hope my Ey's doe not deceive mee, and that I have not forgott to reade. But if you please to Confirme it to mee by another, you know how to dirrect it, for I am where I was, still the same, and alwayes

December the 24th [4]   Your humble Servant

For Mrs Painter [5]
In Covent Garden

Keep this letter till it bee calld for

Letter 2

[Sunday] 2 January [1653]

Sir

If there were any thing in my letter that pleased you I am Extreamly glad on't, 'twas all due to you, and made it but an
Equall retourne for the sattisfaction yours gave mee; And whatever you may beleeve, I shall never repent the Good opinion I
have with soe much reason taken up. But I forgett my self, I
meant to chide and I think this is nothing towards it. Is it posible
that you came soe neer mee at Bedford and would not see mee,[1]
seriously I should never have beleeved it from another. Would
your horse had lost all his legg's instead of a hoofe, that hee
might not have bin able to carry you further, and you, somthing
that you vallewd extreamly and could not hope to finde any
where but at Chicksands. I could wish you a thousand litle
mischances I am soe angry with you. For my Life I could not
imagine how I had Lost you, or why you should call that a
sillence of sixe or 8 week's which you intended soe much longer,
and when I had weary'd my self with thinking of all the u[n]-
pleasing Accident's that might cause it, I at length satt down
with a resolution to Choose the best to beleeve which was, that
at the End of one Journy, you had begun another (which I had
heard you say you intended) and that your hast, or some thing
else had hindred you from letting mee know it. In this ignorance your letter from Breda[2] found mee, which (by the way)
Sir Thomas[3] never saw. 'Tis true I told him I had a letter from
you, one day that hee Extreamly lamented hee knew not what
was become of you, and fell into soe Earnest comendations of
you that I cannot expect lesse from him, whoe have the
honour to be his kinswoman, (but to leave him to his Mistresse
whoe perhaps has spoyled his Memory). Let mee assure you
that I was never soe in Love with an Old Man in my life as
I was with Mr Metcalf[4] for sending me that Letter, (though

there is one not farr off that sayes hee will have mee when his
wife dy's)[.] [5] I writt so kindly to him the next Post, and hee
that would not bee in my debt, sends mee worde againe that
you were comeing over, but your's kept mee from beleeveing
that, and made mee think you in Italy when you were in
England, though I was not displeased to finde my self deceived.
But for God sake lett mee aske you what you have done all
this while you have bin away what you mett with in holland
that could keep you there soe long why you went noe further,
and, why I was not to know you went so farr[.] you may doe
well to sattisfye mee in all these, I shall soe persecute you with
questions else when I see you, that you will bee glad to go
thither againe to avoyde mee; though when that will bee I
cannot certainly say, for my Father has soe small a proportion
of health left him since my Mother's Death,[6] that I am in
continuall feare of him, and dare not often make use of the
Leave he gives mee to bee from home, least hee should at some
time want such little services as I am able to render him. Yet I
think to bee at London in the Next Terme,[7] and am sure I
shall desyre it because you are there.

                                        Sir   your humble Servant
Jan: the 2d 1652

Letter 3

                                [Saturday 8 or Sunday 9 January 1653]

There is nothing moves my Charity like Gratitude, and when a
Begger's thankfull for a small releife, I alway's repent it was not
more. But seriously this place will not afforde much towards the
inlarging of a letter, and I am growne soe dull with liveing in't
(for I am not willing to confess that I was alwayes soe) as to need
all helps. Yet you shall see I will indeavour to sattisfye you, upon
condition you will tell mee, why you quarreld soe, at your last

letter. I cannot guesse at it, unless it were that you repented you told mee soe much of your Storry, which I am not apt to beleeve neither because it would not become our freindship, a great parte of it consisting (as I have bin taught) in a mutuael confidence, and to let you see that I beleive it soe, I will give you an accounte of my self, and begin my story as you did yours, from our Parteing at Goreing House.[1]

I cam downe hither not halfe soe well pleased as I went up, with an ingagement upon mee,[2] that I had little hope of ever shakeing of, for I had made use of all the liberty my freinds would allow me, to preserve my owne, and 'twould not do, hee was soe weary of his, that hee would parte with 't upon any term's. As my last refuge, I gott my Brother to goe downe with him to see his house, whoe when he cam back made the relation I wisht. He sayed the seate was as ill, as so good a country would permitt, and the house soe ruined for want of liveing int, as it would ask a good proportion of time, and mony, to make it fitt for a woman to confine her self to, this (though it were not much) I was willing to take hold of, and made it considerable enough to break the agreement. I had noe quarrell to his Person, or his fortune but was in love with neither, and much out of love with a thing calld marriage, and have since thanked God I was soe, for tis not longe since one of my Brothers writ mee word of him, that hee was kill'd in a Duell, though since, I heare 'twas the other that was kill'd and hee is fled upont, which doe's not mend the matter much, Both made mee glad I had scaped him, and sorry for his misfortune, which in Earnest was the least retourne, his many Civility's to mee could deserve.

Presently after this was at an End, my Mother dyed, and I was left at liberty to mourne her losse a while. At length, my Aunte[3] (with whome I was when you last saw mee) comanded mee to wayte on her at London, and when I cam she told mee how much I was in her care, how well she loved mee for my Mothers sake, and somthing for my owne, and drew out a longe, sett, speech, which Ended in a good motion (as she called it) and truly I saw noe harme int, for by what I had heard of the Gentleman[4]

I guessed hee expected a better fortune then myne, and it proved soe, yet hee prottested hee liked mee soe well, that hee was very angry my Father would not bee perswaded to give up £1000 more with mee, and I him soe ill, that I vowed, if I had had £1000 lesse I should have thought it too much for him, and soe we parted. Since, hee has made a story with a new Mistresse, that is worth you knowing, but too longe for a letter, i'le keep it for you.

After this, some freinds that had observed a Gravity in my face, which might become an Elderly man's wife (as they term'd it) and a Mother in Law[5] proposed a Widdower[6] to mee, that had fower daughters, all old enough to bee my Sister's. But hee had a great Estate, was as fine a Gentleman as ever England bred, and the very Patterne of Wisdom. I that knew how much I wanted it, thought this the saffest place for me to ingage in, and was mightily pleased to think, I had met with one at last that had witt enough for himself and mee too. But shall I tell you what I thought when I knew him, (you will say nothing on't) 'twas the vainest, Impertinent, self conceated, Learned, Coxcombe, that ever yet I saw, to say more were to spoyle his marriage, which I hear hee is towards with a daughter of my Lord of Coleraines,[7] but for his sake I shall take heed of a fine Gentleman as long as I live. Before I had quite ended with him, comeing to towne aboute that, and some other occasions of my owne, I fell in Sir Thomas's way,[8] & what humor took him, I cannot imagine, but hee made very formall adresses to mee, and ingaged his mother, and my Brother to apeare in't. This bred a Story Pleasanter then any I have told you yet, but soe long a one that I must reserve it till wee meet, or make it a letter of it self; onely by this you may see 'twas not for nothing he comended mee, though to speak seriously it was, because it was to you, Otherwise I might have missed of his prayses for wee have hardly bin Cousen's since the breaking up of that buisnesse.[9]

The next thing I desyr'd to bee rid on, was a Scurvy Spleen that I have ever bin subject to, and to that purpose was advised to drink the Waters,[10] there I spent the latter end of the Sommer and at my comeing here, found that a Gentleman (whoe had some Estate in this Country), had bin treating with my Brother, and it yet goes on faire and softly, I doe not know him soe well as to give you much of his Character, 'tis a Modest, Melancholy, reserved, man, whose head is so taken up with little Philosophicall Studdy's, that I admire how I founde a roome there, 'twas sure by Chance, and unlesse hee is pleased with that parte of my humor which other People think the worst, 'tis very posible, the next new Experiment may crowde mee out againe.[11] Thus you have all my late adventur's, and almost as much as this paper will hold. The rest shall bee imployed in telling you how sorry I am that you have gott such a cold, I am the more sencible of your trouble, by my owne, for I have newly gott one my self, but I will send you that which uses to cure mee, 'tis like the rest of my medicens, if it doe noe good, 'twill bee sure to doe noe harme, and 'twill bee noe great trouble to you to eate a litle on't now and then, for the taste as it is not Excelent, soe 'tis not very ill. One thing more I must tell you, which is that you are not to take it ill that I mistook your age, by my computation of your Journy thorough this Country, for I was perswaded tother day that I could not bee lesse then 30 yeare old, by one that beleeved it himself, because hee was sure 'twas a great while since hee had heard of such a one in the world

as,   your humble Servant

Letter 4

Sir

Since you are soe easy to please, sure I shall not miss it, and if my idle thoughts, and dream's will satisfy you I am to blame if you want Long Letters. To begin this, lett me tell you I had not forgott you in your absence, I alwayes meant you one of my daughters,[1] you should have had your Choice, and trust mee, they say some of them are handsome. But since things did not succeed I thought to have sayed nothing on't, least you should imagine I expected thanks for my good intention, or rather, least you should bee too much affected with the thought of what you have lost by my impudence. It would have bin a good strengthening to my Party (as you say) but in Earnest that was not it I aymed at, I onely desyred to have it in my power to Oblige you, and 'tis certaine I had proved a most Exelent Mother in Law. O my Conscience we should all have Joyned against him as the Common Enemy, for these Poore Young Wenches are as weary of his Government as I could have bin, he gives them such precepts as they say My Lord of Dorchester[2] gives his wife, and keep's them soe much Prisoners to a Vile house he has in Northampton shyre, that if once I had but let them loose they and his Learning would have bin sufficient to have made him mad,[3] without my helpe, but his good fortune would have it otherwise, to which i'le leave him, and proceed to give you some Reasons why the other kinde motion was not accepted on. The truth is, I had not that longing to aske a Mother in Law blessing which you say you should have had, for I knew mine too well to think shee could have made a good one, besydes, I was not soe certaine of his Nature, as not to doubt whither she might not Corrupt it, nor so confident of his Kindenesse, as to assure my self it would last longer then Other Peoples of his Age, and humor. I am sorry to hear he look's ill though I think there is no great danger of him 'tis but a fitt of an Ague hee has gott that the next Charme cures, yet hee will bee apt to fall into it againe upon a new occasion, and one knows not how it may worke upon his thin body if it com's too often. It spoyled his beauty[4] sure before I knew him, for I could never see it, or else (which is as likely) I do not know it when I see it, besydes that I never look for it in Men.

It was nothing that I expected made me refuse these, but something that I feared, and seriously I finde I want Courage to marry where I doe not like. If we should once come to disputes, I know who would have the worst on't, and I have not faith enough to beleeve a doctrine that is often preached, which is, that though at first one has noe kindenesse for them yet it will grow strangly after marriage. Let them truste to it that think good, for my Parte I am cleerly of opinion (and shall dye int) that as the more one sees, and know's, a person that one likes, one has still the more kindenesse for them, soe on the other side one is but the more weary of and the more averse to an unpleasant humor for haveing it perpetualy by one, and though I easily beleeve that to marry one for whome wee have already some affection, will infinitely Encrease that kindenesse yet I shall never bee perswaded that Marriage has a Charme to raise love out of nothing, much lesse out of dislike.

This is next to telling you what I dreame and when I rise, but you have promised to bee content with it. I would now if I could tell you when I shall bee in Towne, but I am ingaged to my Lady Diana Rich,[5] my Lord of Hollands[6] daughter, whoe lyes at a Gentlewomans hard by mee, for Sore Eyes that I will not leave the country till she does, she is soe much a stranger heer, and findes soe little Company, that she is glad of mine, till her Eyes will give her leave to looke out better, they are mending, and she hopes to bee at London before the end of this next Terme,[7] and soe doe I, though I shall make but a short stay, for all my buisnesse there is at an end when I have seen you and told you my story's. And indeed my Brother is soe perpetualy from home[8] that I can bee very litle, unlesse I would leave my father altogether alone which would not bee well. Wee heare of Great disorders at your Maskes,[9] but no particulers, only, they say the Spanish Gravity was much discomposed. I shall expect the relation from you, at your leisure, and pray give mee an account of how my Medicen agrees with your Cold.

This (if you can read it, for tis strangly scribled) will bee Enough to answer yours, which is not very long this weeke, and I am growne so provident that I will not lay out more then I receive, but I am very Just withall, and therefore you know how to make mine longer when you please, though to speake truth if

I should make this soe, you would hardly have it this week, for 'tis a good while since 'twas called for   Your humble Servant

Letter 5

[Saturday] 22 January [1653]

Sir

Not to confirme you in your beleife of dream's, but to avoyde your reproches, I will tell you a pleasant one, of mine. The night before I received your first letter, I dream't one brought mee a pacquett, and told mee 'twas from you. I that remembred you were by your owne apointment to bee in Italy at that time Asked the Messenger where hee had it, who told mee, my Lady your Mother sent him with it to mee. There my memory failed mee a litle, for I forgott you had told mee she was dead,[1] and meant to give her many humble thanks if Ever I were soe happy as to see her. When I had open'd the letter, I founde in it two Rings one was as I remember an Emerald doublett but broken, in the Carriage I suppose, as it might well bee comeing soe farr, t'other was plaine Gold, with the longest & the strangest Posy[2] that Ever was. Halfe on't was Italian which for my life I could not guesse at though I spent much time about it[.] the rest was, (there was a mariage in Cana of Galilee) which though it was Scripture I had not that reverence for it in my sleep, that I should have had I think if I had been awake, for in Earnest the odnesse on't put mee into that violent Laughing, that I waked my self with it and as a Just punishment upon mee, from that hower to this, I could never learne, whome those Rings were for, nor what was in the letter besydes. This is but as extravagant as yours, for tis as likly your Mother should send mee letters as that I should make a Journy to see poore People hanged, or that your teeth should drop out at this Age. And now I am out of your dreaming debt, let mee bee bold to tell you, I beleeve you have bin with Lilly[3] your Self. Nothing but hee could tell you my Knights[4] strange Name, i'le swere I could never remember it, when I was first concern'd int, and when People asked it mee and were not sattisfyed with truth, (for they took my ignorance for a desyre to conceale him) I was faine to make names for him and soe instead of one od Servant I had gotten twenty. But in Earnest now where have you fished him out, for I think hee is as litle knowne in the world, as I could have wished hee should have bin if I had married him.

I am sory you are not sattisfyed with my Exeptions to your freind,[5] I spake in generall term's of him, and was willing to spare him as much as I could, but Every body is allowed to defend themselves. You may remember a quality that you discoverd in him when hee told you the Story of his being at St Malo, and in Earnest hee gave mee soe many Testimony's that it was Naturall to him, as I could not hope hee would Ever leave it, and consequently could not beleeve any think hee Ever had or should say. If this bee not enough I can tell you more, hereafter. And to remove the Opinion you have of my Nicenesse or being hard to please, let mee assure you, I am soe farr from desyreing my husband should bee fond of mee at threescore, that I would not have him soe at all, 'tis true I should bee glad to have him alway's kinde, and know noe reason why hee should bee wearier of being my Master then hee was of being my Servant. But it is very possible I may talke ignorantly of Marriage. When I come to make sad Experiments on't in my owne Person, I shall know more, and say lesse, for feare of disheartening other's (since tis noe advantage to forknow a misfortune that cannot bee avoyded) and for feare of being Pittyed, which of all things I hate. Least you should be of the same humor, I will not Pitty you as Lame as you are, and to speake truth if you did like it you shall not have it for you do not deserve it, would any body in this world but you, make such hast for a new cold before the old one has left him, in a yeer too when meer colds kill as many as a Plague uses to doe. Well seriously either resolve to have more care of your self, or I renounce my freindship, and as a Certain King (that my learned knight is well acquainted with) who seeing one of his Confederats in soe happy a condition, as it was not likely to last, sent his Ambassador presently to breake of the League betwixt them least hee should bee obliged to mourne the Change of his fortune if hee continued his freind,[6] Soe I, with a great deal more reason do I declare that I will noe longer be a freind to one that's none to himself nor aprehend the losse of what you hazard every day at Tennis.[7] They had served you well enough if they had cram'd a dousen ounces of that precious medicin downe your throate, to have made you remember a quinzy, but I have done, and am now at Leasure to tell you that it is that daughter of my Lord of Hollands[8] (who makes as you say soe many sore Eyes with looking at her,) that is heer, and if I know her at all, or have any Judgment, her beauty is the least of her Exelency's. And now I speake of her, she has given mee the occasion to make a request to you; it will come very seasonably after my Chideing and I have great reason to expect you should bee in the humor of doing anything for mee. She sayes that seal's are much in fashion, and by showeing mee some that she has, has sett mee a longing for some too, Such as are oldest, and oddest, are most prized, and if you know any body that is lately come out of Italy, tis ten to one but they have store for they are very common there. I do remember you once sealed a letter to mee, with as fine a one as I have seen, it was a Neptune I think rideing upon a dolphin, but I'm afrayde it was not yours, for I saw it noe more, any old roman head, is a present for a Prince if such things come your way, pray remember mee.

I am sorry the new Carrier[9] makes you rise soe early, 'tis not good for your Cold. How might wee doe that you might lye a bed, and yet I have your letter. You must use to write before hee com's I think, that it may bee sure to bee redy against hee goes, in Earnest consider on't, and take some course that your health and my letters may bee both secured, for the losse of Either would bee very sencible to your humble

Jan. the 22nth.

Letter 6

Sir

I am soe great a lover of my bed my self, that I can easily aprehende the trouble of ryseing at fower a clock, these cold mornings. In Earnest I am troubled that you should bee putt to it, and have chid the Carrier for comeing out soe soone. He sweares to mee hee never comes out of Towne before eleven a clock, and that My Lady Painters footman, (as he calls him) brings her letters two howers sooner then hee needs to doe. I told him hee was gon one day before the letter cam, hee vowes hee was not, and that your old freind Collins never brought letters of my Lady Painters in's life; and to speak truth, Collins did not bring mee that letter, I had it from this Harrold two howers before Collins cam, yet it is possible all that hee sayes may not bee soe, for I have knowne better men then hee, lye, therfore if Collins bee more for your Ease or Conveniency, make use of him hereafter.

I know not whither my letter were kinde or not, but i'le sweare yours was not, and am sure mine was meant to bee soe. It is not kinde of you to desyre an increase of my freindship; that is to doubt it is not as great already as it can bee, then which you cannot doe mee a greater injury, 'tis my misfortune indeed that it lyes not in my power to give you better Testimony's on't then words, otherwise I should soone convince you, that 'tis the best quality I have, and that when I owne a freindship, I meane soe perfect a one, as time can neither lessen nor increase.

If I sayed nothing of my comeing to Towne, 'twas because I had nothing to say, that I thought you would like to heare, the truth is, twenty little crosse accidents have made it so uncertaine, as I was more out of humor with them then you could bee with the bell's,[1] though I have noe reason to expect otherwise, for I doe not know that ever I desyred any thing (Earnestly) in my life but 'twas denyed mee, and I am many times afrayed to wish a thing meerly least my fortunes should take occasion to use me ill. She cannot see and therfore I may venture to write that I intend to bee in London[2] if it bee posible on fryday, or Satterday, come sennight, bee sure you doe not reade it aloude least she heare it and prevent mee, or drive you away before I come. It is soe like my luck too, that you should bee goeing I know not whither againe, that trust mee I have looket for't ever since I heard you were come home. You will laugh sure when I shall tell you, that hearing my Lord Lisle[3] was to goe Ambassador into Sweden, I rememberd your fathers acquaintance in that Famely with an aprehension that hee might bee in the humor of sending you with him. But for god sake whither is it that you goe, I would not willingly bee at such a losse againe, as I was after your Yorkshyre Journy.[4] If it prove as longe a one, I shall not forgett you, but in Earnest I shall bee soe possest with a strong spleenatick fancy that I shall never see you more in this world, as all the water's in England[5] will not cure. Well, this is a sad story, we'll have no more on't.

I humbly thank you for your offer of your head, but if you were an Emperour I should not bee soe bold with you, as to claime your promise, you might find twenty better imployments for it, onely with your gracious leave I think I should bee a litle exalted with remembring that you had bin once my freind, twould more indanger my groweing proud then beeing Sir Justinians Mistresse, and yet hee thought mee pretty well inclined to it then. Lord what would I give that I had a Lattin letter of his for you, that hee writt to a great freind at Oxforde where hee gives him a longe and learned Character of mee, twould serve you to laugh at this seven yeare. If I remember what was told mee on't the worste of my faults was a height (hee would not call it pride) that was as hee had heard the humor of my Famely, and the best of my commendations was, that I was capable of being company and conversation for him. But you doe not tell mee yet how you found him out, if I had gone aboute to have concealed him I had bin sweetly served[.] I shall take heed of you hereafter, because there is noe very great likelyhood of your being an Emperour, or that if you were I shall have your head. I have sent into Italy for Seales 'tis to be hoped by that time mine come over they may bee out of fashion againe, for 'tis an humor that your old acquaintance Mr Smith and his Lady[6] has brought up, they say, shee wear's twenty strung upon a riban like the nutts boy's play withall, and I doe not heare of any thing else. Mr Howard[7] presented his Mistresse but a dousen such seales as are not to bee vallewd as times now goe. But a propos de Monsieur Smith, what a scape has he made of my Lady Ban-bury,[8] and whoe would ere have dreamt hee should have had my Lady Sunderland, though hee bee a very fine Gentleman, and do's more then deserve her I think. I shall never forgive her one thing she sayed of him, which was that she marryed him out of Pitty. It was the pittyfull'st sayeing that ever I heard, and made him soe contemptible that I should not have marryed him for that very reason. This is a strange letter sure I have not time to read it over but I have sayed any thing that came in my head to putt you out of dumps, for god sake bee in better humor,[9] and assure your self I am as much as you can wish

Your faithfull freind & Servant

Letter 7

[Saturday 5 or Sunday 6 February 1653]

Sir

You have made mee soe Rich, as I am able to helpe my Neighbours.[1] There is a litle head cutt in an Onixe, that I take to bee a very good one, and the Dolphin is (as you say) the better for being cutt lesse, the odnesse of the figure makes the beauty of these things. If you saw one that my Brother sent my Lady Diana last week, you would beleeve it were meant to fright

People withall; 'twas brought out of India's and cutt there for an Idoll's head, they took the Divell himself sure for theire pattern that did it, for in my life I never saw soe ugly a thing, and yet she is as fonde on't as if it were as lovely as she her self is; her eyes have not the flames they have had, nor is she like (I am affrayde) to recover them heer, but were they irrecoverably lost, the beauty of her minde were Enough to make her outshine Every body Else and she would still bee courted by all that knew how to vallew her, like La belle aveugle, that was Phillip the 2d of France his Mistresse.[2]

I am wholy ignorant of the story you mention, and I am confident you are not well informed, for 'tis imposible she should ever have done any thing that were unhandsome. If I knew whoe the personne were that is concern'd in't, she allowes mee soe much freedom with her, that I could easily putt her upon the discourse, and I do not think she would use much of disguise in it towards mee. I should have guessed it Alger: Sidney,[3] but that I cannot see in him that likelyhood of a fortune which you seem to imply by sayeing tis not pressent, but if you should mean by that, that tis possible his witt and good Parts, may raise him to one, You must pardon if I am not of your opinion, for I doe not think these are times for any body to expect prefferment in, that deserv's it, and in the best 'twas ever too uncertaine for a wise body to truste to. But I am altogether of your minde that my Lady Sunderland is not to bee followed in her marryeng fashion and that Mr Smith never appeared lesse her Servant then in desyreing it. To speak truth 'twas convenient for neither of them, and in meaner People 't had bin plaine undoeing one another, which I cannot understand to bee kindenesse of either side; she has lost by it much of the repute she has gained, by keeping her self a widdow. It was then beleeved that Witt and discretion were to bee Reconciled in her personne that have soe seldome bin perswaded to meet in any Body else; but wee are all Mortall.

I do not mean that Howard. 'Twas Arundel Howard,[4] and the seal's were some Remainders that showed his father's love to

Antiquity's and therfore cost him deer enough if that would make them good.

I am sorry I cannot follow your councell in keeping faire with fortune, I am not apt to suspect without just cause, but in Earnest if I once finde any body faulty towards mee, they loose mee for ever. I have forsworne being twice deceived by the same person, for god sake doe not say she has the spleen, I shall hate it worse then I ever did, nor that 'tis the disease of the Witt's[.] I shall think you abuse mee, for then I am sure it would not bee mine, but were it certaine that they went together alwayes, I dare sweare there is noebody soe proude of their witt as to keep it upon such termes, but would bee glad after they had indured it a while, to lett them both goe as they came.

I know nothing yet that is likely to Alter my resolution of being in Towne on Satterday nexte;[5] but I am uncertaine where I shall bee, and therfore twill bee best that I send you word when I am there. I should be glad to see you sooner but I doe not know my self what company I may have with mee. I meant this letter longer when I began it, but an extreame cold that I have taken lyes soe in my head, and makes it Ake so violently, that I hardly see what I doe, i'le e'en to bed as soon as I have told you that I am very much

> Your faithfull freind
> & Servant
> D. Osborn

Sir[6]

This is to tell you, that you will bee Expected to morrow morning about nine a clock at a Lodging over against the place where Chareing Crosse stood and two doores above the Goate Taverne. If with these dirrections you can finde it out you will finde one there that is very much

> Your servant

For Mr Temple

You are mistaken if you think I am in your debt for both these day's. Satterday I confesse was devoted to my Lady, but yesterday though I rise[7] with good intentions of goeing to Church, my Cold would not suffer mee but kept mee Prisoner all the day; I sent to your lodging to tell you that Visetting the Sicke was part of the worke of the day, but you were gon, and soe I went to bed againe where your letter found mee this morning, but now I will rise and dispatch some Visetts that I owe that to morrow may bee intirely   Yours

Letter 8

[Tuesday 22 February 1653]

Sir

Though I am very weary after my Journy, and not well, haveing added much to a sufficient Colde I had at London, yet guessing at your inclinations by my owne, I thought you would be pleased to heare how wee gott home and therfore resolved to say something though it were nonsense rather than omitt the giveing you satisfaction that is in my Power. I am soe perfectly dosed with my Cold and m[y] Journey together that all I can say is, that I am heer and that I have only soe much sence left as to wish you were soe too. When that Leaves mee you may conclude mee past all. Till then I'me sure I shall bee

Your faithfull freind
& Servant

Chicksands[1]
For Mr Temple[2]

Letter 9

[Saturday 26 or Sunday 27 February 1653]

Sir

I was soe kinde as to write to you by the Coachman, and let mee
tell you, I think 'twas the greatest testimony of my freindship
that I could give you, for truste mee I was soe tyr'd with my
Journy, soe dosed with my Colde, and soe out of humor with
our parteing, that I should have done it with great unwillingnesse
to any body else. I lay a bed all next day to recover my self, and
risse[1] a thursday to receive your letter with the more Ceremony. I founde noe fault with the ill writeing, 'twas but too
Easy to reade, my thought, for I am sure I had done much sooner
then I could have wished. But in Earnest I was heartily troubled
to finde you in soe much disorder.[2] I would not have you soe
kinde to mee, as to bee cruell to your self, in whome I am more
Concern'd; noe, for godsake let us not make afflictions of such
things as these, I am affrayde we shall meet with too many Reall
on's.

I am glad your Journy holds,[3] because I think twill bee a good
diversion for you this summer, but I admyre your fathers Patience, that let's you reste with soe much indifference when there
is such a fortune offer'd.[4] I'le sweare I have great scruples of
Conscience my self in the pointe, and am much affrayde I am
not your freind if I am any part of the Occasion that hinders
you from accepting it; yet I am sure my intentions towards you
are very innocent and good, for you are one of those whose
interest's I shall ever preffer much above my owne and you are
not to thank mee for it, since to speake truth I secure my owne
by it for I defy my ill fortune to make mee miserable unlesse she
do's it in the Person of my freinds. I wonder how your father
came to know I was in towne, unlesse my old freind your Cousen
Hamond[5] should tell him. Pray for my sake bee a very Obedient
Sonne, all your fault's will bee layde to my Charge else, and alas

I have too many of my owne. You say nothing how your Sister[6] do's, which makes mee hope there is noe more danger in her Sicknesse. Pray when it may bee noe trouble to her, tell her how much I am her Servant, and have a care of your self this colde weather. I have read your Reyne Margerite[7] and will retourne it you when you please. If you will have my opinion of her, I think she has a good deale of witt, and a greater deal of Patience for a woman of soe high a Spiritt, she speakes with too much indifference of her husbands severall Amour's, and comends Busy as if she were a litle concern'd in him. I think her a better Sister then a wife, and beleeve she might have made a better wife to a better husbande. But the storry of Mademoisell de Tournon,[8] is soe sad that when I had read it I was able to goe noe further, and was faine to take up somthing else to divert my self withall. Have you read Cleopatra,[9] I have six Tomes on't heer that I can lend you, if you have not, there are some Storry's in't you will like I beleeve. But what an asse I am to think you can bee idle enough at London to reade Romances. Noe i'le keep them till you come hither,[10] heer they may bee welcome to you for want of better Company. Yet that you may not imagine wee are quite out of the world heer, and soe bee frighted from comeing, I can assure you wee are seldome without news, such as it is, and at this present wee doe abounde with Story's of my Lady Sunderlande and Mr Smith, with what Reverance hee approaches her, and how like a Gracious Princes she receives him that they say 'tis worth on's goeing twenty miles to see it. All our Lady's are mightily pleased with the Example but I doe not finde that the men intende to follow it, and i'le undertake Sir Soloman Justinian[11] wishes her in the Indias for feare she should Perverte his new wife.

Your fellow Servant[12] kisses your hands and say's if you mean to make love to her Olde woman this is the best time you can take for shee is dyeing, this cold weather kills her I thinke, it has undone mee I'me sure in killing an Old Knight[13] that I have bin wayteing for this seven yeare, and now hee dy's and will leave mee nothing I beleeve, but leaves a Rich Widdow for somebody.

I think you had best come a wooing to her, I have a good interest in her and it shall bee all imployed in your Service if you think fitt to make any addresses there. But to bee sober now againe for godsake send mee worde how your Journy goes forward[,] when you think you shall begin it, and how longe it may last, when I may expect you comeing this way, and of all things remember to provide a safe addresse for your letters when you are abroad, this is a strange confused one I beleeve, for I have bin call'd away twenty times since I sate downe to write it to my father whoe is not very well[.] but you will pardon it, wee are past Ceremony and Excuse mee if I say noe more now but that I am tousjours la mesme, that is Ever

                                        Your affectionate
                                        freind & servant

Letter 10

                              [Saturday 5 or Sunday 6 March 1653]

Sir

Your last letter came like a pardon to one upon the block. I had given over hopes on't, haveing received my letters by the other Carrier,[1] whoe uses alway's to bee last. The losse put mee hugely out of order, and you would both have pittyed and laught at mee, if you could have seen how woddenly I entertain'd the widdow[2] whoe came hither the day before, and surprised mee very much. Not being able to say any thing, I gott her to Card's, and there with a great deal of Patience lost my Mony to her, or rather I gave it as my Ransome. In the middest of our Play in comes my blessed Boy with your letter, and in Earnest I was not able to disguise the Joy it gave mee, though one was by that is not much your freind,[3] and took notice of a blush that for my life I could not keep back. I putt up the letter in my Pockett, and made what hast I could to loose the mony I had left, that I might take occasion to goe fetch some more, but I did not make such hast back againe I can assure you, I took time enough to have Coyned my self some mony if I had had the Art on't, and left my Brother enough to make all his addresses to her, if hee were soe disposed. I know [not] whither he was pleased or not, but I am sure I was.

You make soe reasonable demandes, that 'tis not fitt you should bee deny'd, you aske my thought's but at one hower. You will think me bountifull I hope, when I shall tell you, that I know noe hower when you have them not. Noe, in Earnest my very dream's are yours, and I have gott such a habitt of thinking of You, that any other thought intrudes and grow's uneasy to mee. I drink your health every morning in a drench that would Poyson a horse I beleeve, and 'tis the only way I have to perswade my self to take it, 'tis the infusion of steell,[4] and makes mee soe horridly sick that every day at ten a clock I am makeing my will, and takeing leave of all my freind's, you will beleeve you are not forgot then. They tell mee I must take this ugly drink a fortnight, and then begin another as Bad, but unlesse you say soe too I do not thinke I shall, 'tis worse then dyeing, by the halfe.

I am glad your father is soe kinde to you, I shall not dispute it with him because 'tis much more in his power then in myne, but I shall never yeeld that tis more in his desyr's. Sure hee was much pleased with that which was a truth when you told it him but would have bin none if hee had asked the question sooner, hee thought there was noe danger of you since you were more ignorant and lesse concern'd in my being in Towne then hee; if I were Mrs Cl:[5] hee would bee more my freind but howsoever I am much his Servant as hee is your father.

I have sent you your booke, and since you are at Leasure to consider the moone you may bee enough to reade Cleopatra, therefore I have sent you three Tomes. When you have done with those you shall have the rest, and I beleeve they will please, there is a story of Artemise that I will recomende to you, her disposition I like extreamly, it has a great deal of Gratitude int, and if you meet with one Brittomart pray send mee word how you like him.

I am not displeased that my Lord makes noe more hast for though I am very willing you should goe the Journy for many reason's, yet two or three months hence sure will bee soone enough to visett soe cold a Country and I would not have you indure two winters in one year, besydes I looke for my Eldest brother[6] and my Cousen Molle[7] heer shortly and I should bee glad to have noe body to entertaine but you, whilest you are heer, Lord that you had the invisible Ring,[8] or [I?] Fortunatas[9] his Wisheing hatt, now, at this instante you should bee heer. My Brother is gon to wayte upon the widdow homeward's, She that was borne to persecute you and I, I think. She has soe tyred mee with being heer (but two days) that I doe not think I shall accept of the offer she has made mee of liveing with her in case my Father dy's before I have disposed of my self, yet wee are very great, and for my comfort she say's she will come againe about the latter ende of June, and stay longer with mee.

My Aunt is still in Towne, kept by her buisnesse which I am affrayde will not goe well, they doe soe delay it, and my pretious Uncle do's soe visett her, and is soe kinde that without doubt some Mischeife will follow. Doe you know his sonne my Cousen Harry,[10] tis a handsome youth, and well natured but such a goose, and hee has bred him soe strangly, that hee needs all his ten thousand pound a yeer. I would faine have him marry my Lady Diana, she was his Mistresse when hee was a boy. Hee had more witt then, then hee has now I think, and I have lesse witt then hee sure for spending my paper upon him when I have soe litle. Heer is hardly Roome for Your affectionate freind and Servant

Letter 11

Sir

I am soe farre from thinking you ill natured for wisheing I might not outlive you, that I should not have thought you at all kinde, if you had done otherwise. Noe, in Earnest, I was never soe in love with my life, but that I could have parted with it upon a much lesse occasion then your Death, and 'twill bee noe complement to you, to say it would bee very uneasy to meet then, since 'tis not very pleasant to mee now. Yet you will say I take great paines to preserve it, as ill as I like it, but noe I'le sweare 'tis not that I intende in what I doe, all that I ayme at, is but to keep my self from groweing a Beast, they doe soe fright mee with strange story's of what the Spleen will bring mee to in time, that I am kept in awe with them like a Childe. They tell mee 'twill not leave mee common sence, that I shall hardly bee fitt company for my own dog's, and that it will ende, either in a stupidnesse that will have mee uncapable of any thing, or fill my head with such whim's as will make mee, rediculous. To prevent this, whoe would not take steel or any thing, though I am partly of your opinion, that 'tis an ill kinde of Phisick.[1] Yet I am confident that I had take it the safest way, for I doe not take the powder, as many doe, but onely lay a peece of steel in white wine over night, and drink the infusion next morning, which one would think were nothing, and yet 'tis not to bee imagin'd how sick it makes mee for an hower or two, and, which is the missery all that time one must be useing some kinde of Exercise. Your fellow servant[2] has a blessed time on't, I make her play at Shuttlecock[3] with mee, and she is the veryest bungler at it that ever you saw, then am I ready to beate her with the batledore and grow soe peevish as I grow sick, that i'le undertake she wishes there were noe steele in England, but then to recompence the morning I am in good humor all the day after, for Joy that I am well againe. I am tolde 'twill doe mee noe good, and am content to beleeve; if it do's not, I am but where I was.

I doe not use to forget my old acquaintances, Almanzor[4] is as fresh in my memory, as if I had visitted his Tombe but Yesterday, though it bee at least seven yeare agon since. You will beleeve I had not bin used to great afflictions, when I made his Story such a one to mee, as I cryed an hower together for him, and was so angry with Alcidiana that for my life I could never love her after it. You doe not tell mee whither you received the Book's I sent you, but I will hope you did, because you say nothing to the contrary. They are my deare Lady Diana's and therfore I am much concern'd that they should bee safe. And now I speake of her, shee is acquainted with your Aunte my Lady R.[5] and say's all that you say of her. If her Neece has soe much witt will you not bee perswaded to like her, or say she has not quite soe much, may not her fortune make it up, in Earnest I know not what to say, but if your father do's not use all his kindenesse, and all his power, to make you consider your owne advantage, hee is not like other fathers. Can you imagin that hee, that demands £5000 besydes the reversion of an Estate, will like bare £4000, such mirracles are seldome seen, and you must prepare to suffer a strange persecution, unlesse you grow conformable, therfore consider what you doe, 'tis the parte of a freind to advise you. I could say a great deal to the purpose, and tell you that 'tis not discreet, to refuse a good offer, nor safe to trust wholy to your owne Judgment in your disposall. I was never better provided in my life, for a grave admonishing discourse, Would you had heard how I have bin Chatechised for you, and seen how soberly I sitt and answer to interogatory's.[6] Would you think, that upon Examination it is founde that you are not an indifferent person to mee, but the mischeif is, that what my intentions or resolutions are, is not to bee discoverd, though much pain's has bin taken to collect all scattering Circumstances, and all the probable conjectur's that can bee raised from thence has bin urged, to see if any thing would bee confessed. And all this done with soe much Ceremony and complement, soe many pardon's asked for undertakeing to councell, or inquire, and soe great kindenesse and Passion for all my

Interest's professed, that I cannot but take it well, though I am very weary on't. You are spoken of with the Reverence due to a person what I seem to like, and for as much as they know of you, you doe deserve a very good Esteem, but your fortune and mine, can never agree, and in plaine term's wee forfait our discretions and run willfully upon our owne ruin's, if there bee such a thought. To all this I make noe reply, but that if they will need's have it, that I am not without kindenesse for you, they must conclude withall that 'tis noe parte of my intention to Ruine you, and soe the conference breaks up for that time.

All this is my freind, that is not your's, and the Gentleman that cam up stayers In a baskett.[7] I could tell him that hee spends his breath to very little purpose, and has but his labour for his paines. Without his precept's my owne Judgment would preserve mee from doeing any [thing ?][8] that might bee pre-judiciall to you, or unjustifiable to the worlde, but if these may bee secured, nothing can alter the resolution I have taken of settling my whole stock of happinesse upon the affection of a person that is deare to mee whose kindenesse I shall infinitly preffer before any other consideration whatsoever, and I shall not blush to tell you, that you have made the whole world besydes soe indifferent to mee, that if I cannot bee yours They may dispose mee how they please, H.C.[9] will bee as acceptable to mee as any body else. If I may undertake to councell, I think you shall doe well to comply with your father as farr as is possible and not to discover[10] any aversion to what hee desyrs farther then you can give reason for. What his disposition may bee I know not, but 'tis that of many Parents to Judge there Childrens dislikes, to bee an humor of aproveing nothing that is Chosen for them, which many times makes them take up another of denyeing theire Children all they Chuse for themselv's.

I finde I am in the humor of talkeing wisely if my paper would give mee leave, tis great Pitty heer is roome for noe more but, your faithfull freind and Servant

Letter 12

[Thursday 17 or Friday 18 March 1653]

Sir

Your fellow servant upon the news you sent her is goeing to Looke out her Captain. In Earnest now she is goeing to sea, but 'tis to Guarnesey to her freinds there.[1] Her going is soe sudden that I have not time to say much to you, but that I Longe to heare what you have done, & that I shall hate my selfe as Longe as I live if I cause any disorder between your father and you, but if my name can doe you any service, I shall not scruple to trust you with that,[2] since I make none to trust you with my heart. She will dirrect you how you may sende to mee, and for god sake though this bee a short letter let not yours bee soe, 'tis very late & I am able to hold open my Eyes noe longer, good night. If I were not sure to meet you againe by and by, I would not Leave you soe soone.   Your

Letter 13

[Saturday 19 or Sunday 20 March 1653]

Sir

I am glad you scaped a beating but in Earnest would it had lighted upon my Brothers Groome, I think I should have beaten him my self if I had bin able. I have Expected your letter all this day with the Greatest impatience that was posible, and at Last resolved to goe out and meet the fellow, and when I came downe to the stables, I found him come, had sett up his horse, and was sweeping the Stable in great Order. I could not imagin him soe very a beast as to think his horses were to bee served before mee, and therfor was presently struck with an aprehension hee had noe letter for mee, it went Colde to my heart as Ice, and hardly left mee courage enough to aske him the question, but when hee had drawled out that hee thought there was a letter for mee in his bag I quickly made him leave his broome. 'Twas well 'tis a dull fellow hee could not but[1] have discern'd else that I was strangly overjoyed with it, and Earnest to have it, for though the poor fellow made what hast hee could to unty his bag, I did nothing but chide him for being soe slow. At last I had it, and in Earnest I know not whither an intire diamond of the bignesse on't would have pleased mee half soe well, if it would, it must bee only out of this consideration that such a Juell would make mee Rich Enough to dispute you with Mrs Cl: and perhaps make your father like mee as well. I like him i'le sweare, and extreamly too, for being soe calme in a buisnesse where his desyr's were soe much Crossed, Either he has a great power over himself or you have a great interest in him, or both. If you are pleased it should end thus, I cannot dislike it,[2] but if it would have bin happy for you, I should think my self strangly unfortunate in being the cause that it went noe further. I cannot say that I preffer your interest before my owne, because all yours are soe much mine, that 'tis imposible for mee to bee happy if you are not soe. But if they could bee devided I am certain I should, – and though you reproached mee with unkindenesse for adviseing not to refuse a good offer yet I shall not bee discouraged from doeing it againe when there is occasion, for I am resolved to bee your freind whether you will or noe, and for example though I know you doe not need my Councell, yet I cannot but tell you that I think 'twere very well that you took some care to make my Lady R. your freind, and oblige her by your Civilitys to beleeve that you were sencible of the favour was offer'd you, though you had not the grace to make good use on't, in very good Earnest now, she is a woman (by all that I have heard of her) that one would not loose. Besydes that 'twill become you to make some sattisfaction for downright refuseing a Young Lady, twas unmercifully done. Would to god you would leave that trick of makeing Excuses, can you think it necessary to mee, or

Extract from letter 13, showing Dorothy Osborne's handwriting

beleeve that your Letters can bee so long as to make them un-
pleasing to mee, are mine soe to you, if they are not, yours,
never will bee soe to mee. You see I say any thing to you, out of
a beleife, that though my letter's were more impertinent then
they are, you would not bee without them nor wish them
shorter, why should you bee lesse kinde.

If your fellow servant had bin with you, she has tolde you that
I part with her but for her advantage. That I shall alway's bee
willing to doe, but whensoever she shall think fit to serve againe
and is not provided of a better Mistresse, she know's where to
finde mee.

I have sent you the rest of Cleopatra[3] pray keep them all in
your hands, and the next week I will send you a letter and dirrections where you shall deliver that & the books for my Lady.
Is it possible that she can bee indifferent to anybody, take heed of
telling mee such Story's. If all those Exelency's she is rich in
cannot keep warme a passion without the sunshine of her Eyes,
what are poor People to expect, and were it not a strange vanity
in mee to beleeve yours can bee long lived. It would be very
pardonable in you to Change, but sure in him 'tis a marke of
soe great inconstancy as shews him of a humor that nothing
can fixe.

When you goe into the Exchange,[4] pray call at the great Shop
above, (The Flower Pott).[5] I spoke to Heam's the man of the
Shop, when I was in Towne for a quart of Oringe flower water,
hee had none that was good then, but promised to gett mee
some, pray putt him in mind of it, and let him show it you
before hee sends it mee, for I will not altogether trust to his
honesty. You see I make no scruple of giveing you litle idle
comissions, tis a freedom you allow mee, and that I should bee
glad you would take. The French man that sett my seal's lives
between Salisbury House[6] & the Exchange at a house that was
not finished when I was there, and the Master of the Shop his
name is Walker, hee made mee pay 50s for three but twas too
deare.

You will meet with a story in these parts of Cleopatra that

pleased mee more then any that ever I read in my life, 'tis one of Delie pray give mee your opinion of her and her Prince. This letter is writt in great hast as you may see, tis my brothers sick day and I am not willing to leave him longe alone. I forgott to tell you in my last that he was come hither to try if he can loose an ague heer that hee got in Glocestershyre. Hee asked mee for you very kindly and if hee knew I writt to you, I should have some thing to say from him besydes what I should say for my self if I had roome.

Yr

Letter 14

[Friday] 25 March [1653]

Sir

I know not how to Oblige soe Civill a person as you are, more, then by giveing you the occasion of serving a faire lady. In sober Earnest, I know you will not think it a trouble, to let your Boy deliver those books and this inclosed letter, where it is dirrected, for my Lady,[1] whome I would the fainest in the world have you acquainted with that you might Judge whither I had not reason to say, somebody was too blame. But had you reason to bee displeased, that I sayed a Change in you, would bee much more pardonable then in him; certainly you had not, I spake it very innocently and out of a great Sence how much she deserv's more then any body else. I shall take heed though, hereafter, what I write, since you are so good at raiseing doubts to persecute your self withall, and shall condemne my owne easy faith no more, for sure tis a better natured, and a lesse fault to beleeve too much, then to distruste where there is noe cause. If you were not soe apt to quarrell I would tell you that I am glad to heare your Journy goes forward, but you would presently imagin that 'tis because I would bee glad if you were gon. Need I say that 'tis because I preffer your interest's much before my owne, because I would not have you loose soe good a diversion and soe pleasing an Entertainment as (in all likelyhood) this voyage will bee to you, & because (which is a powerfull argument with mee) the sooner you goe, the sooner I may hope for your retourne. If it bee necessary I will confesse all this, and somthing more, which is, that notwithstanding all my Gallantry and resolution, 'tis much for my creditt, that my courage is putt to noe greater a tryall then parteing with you at this distance. But you are not goeing yet neither, and therfor we'll leave the discourse on't till then if you please, for I finde noe great Entertainment in't. And let mee aske you whither it bee possible that Mr Grey makes Love,[2] they say hee do's, to my Lady Jane Seymor.[3] If it were Expected that one should give a reason for theire Passions, what could hee say for himself, hee would not offer sure to make us beleeve my Lady Jane a Lovelyer person then my Lady Anne Percy.[4] I did not think I should have lived to have seen his frozen heart melted[,] 'tis the greatest conquest she will ever make, make it bee happy to her, but in my opinion hee has not a good natur'd look. The Younger Brother was a Servant a great while to my faire Neighbour,[5] but could not bee received, and in Earnest I could not blame her. I was his confidente and heard him make his addresses[,] not that I brag of the favour hee did mee, for any body might have bin soe that had bin as often there and hee was lesse scrupulous in that point, then one would have bin that had lesse reason. But in my life I never heard a man say more, nor lesse to the purpose, and if his Brother have not a better Guift in Courtship hee will owe my Lady's favour to his fortune rather then to his addresse.

My Lady Anne Wentworth[6] I heare is marryeng but I cannot learne to whome nor is it Easy to guesse whoe is worthy of her, in my Judgment she is without dispute the finest Lady I know, (one alway's Excepted)[7] not that she is at all handsome but infinitly Vertuous and discreet, of a sober and very different humor from most of the Young People of these times, but has as much witt and is as good company as any body that Ever I saw.

What would you give that I had but the Witt to know when to make an End of my letter. Never any body was persecuted with such long Epistles but you will pardon my unwillingnesse to leave you. And notwithstanding all your litle doubts, beleeve, that I am very much

Your faithfull freind
& humble servant
March the 25th   D. Osborn

Letter 15

[Tuesday 29 March 1653]

Sir

There shall bee two Post's this week, for my Brother sends his groome up and I am resolved to make some advantage of it. Pray what the paper denyde mee in youre last let mee receive by him. Your fellow servant is a sweet Juell to tell tales of mee. The truth is I cannot deny but that I have bin very carelesse of my self but alas whoe would have bin other, I never thought my life a thing worth my care whilest nobody was concern'd in't but my self, now I shall looke upon't as something that you would not loose, and therfore shall indeavour to keep it for you. But then you must retourne my kindenesse with the same care of a life that's much dearer to mee. I shall not bee soe unreasonable as to desyre that for my sattisfaction you should deny your self a recreation that is pleasing to you, and very innocent sure when tis not used in excesse, but I cannot consent you should disorder your self with it, and Jane was certainly in the right when she told you I would have chid if I had seen you soe in danger a health that I am soe much concern'd in. But for what she tels you of my melancholy you must not beleeve, she thinks noebody in good humor unlesse they Laugh perpetualy as Nan[1] and she do's, which I was never given to much, and now I have bin soe long accustom'd to my owne naturall dull humor nothing can alter it, tis not that I am sad, (for as longe as you and the rest of my freinds are well), I thanke God I have noe occasion to bee soe, but I never apeare to bee very merry, and if I had all that I could wish for in the World I doe not thinke it would make any visible change in my humor. And yet with all my Gravity I could not but Laugh at your Encounter in the Parke though I was not pleased that you should leave a faire Lady, and goe lye upon the Colde Grownde[.] that is full as bad as Over heating your self at Tennis,[2] & therfore remember 'tis one of the things you are forbiden.

You have reason to think your father kinde and I have reason to think him very Civill, all his Scruples are very just on's, but such as time and a litle good Fortune, (if wee were either of us Lucky to it) might sattisfy; hee may bee confident I can never think of disposeing my self without my fathers consente, and though hee has left it more in my Power then almost any body leav's a daughter, yet certainly I were the worst natured person in the world if his kindenesse were not a greater lye upon mee then any advantage hee could have reserved, besyd's that tis my duty from which nothing can ever tempt mee. Nor could you like it in mee if I should doe otherwise, 'twould make mee unworthy of your Esteem. But if ever that may bee obtayned or I left free, and you in the same condition, all the advantages of fortune, or person imaginable mett together in one man should not be preffered before you. I think I cannot leave you better then with this assurance, 'tis very Late and haveing bin abroade all this day I knew not till e'en now of this messenger, good night to you. There needed noe Excuse for the conclusion of this Letter nothing can please mee better. Once more good night I am half in a dreame already.   Your

For Mr Temple[3]

Letter 16

Sir

I did receive both your letters, and yet was not sattisfyed but resolved to have a third, you had defeated mee strangly if it had bin a blank. Not that I should have taken it ill, for 'tis as imposible for mee to doe soe, as for you to give mee the occasion, but though by sending a blank with your name to it, you had given mee a power to please my self, yet I should ne'er have don't half soe well as your letter did, for nothing pleases mee like being assured that you are pleased. Will you forgive mee if I make this a short letter. In earnest I have soe many to write and soe litle time to doe it, that for this once I think I could imploy a Secretary if I had one. Yet heer's another letter for you though I know not whither tis such a one as you desyr'd,[1] but if it bee not you may thank your self. If you had given larger instructions you had bin better obayed, and notwithstanding all my hast I cannot but tell you, 'twas a little unkinde to aske mee if I could doe it for your sattisfaction, soe poor a thing as that. If I had time I would chide you for't extreamly, and make you know that there is nothing I cannot doe for the sattisfaction of a Person I esteem and to whome I shall alway's bee a

faithfull freind &
servant

Letter 17

Sir

I received your letter to day when I thought it almost impossible that I should bee sencible of any thing but my father's sicknesse,[1] and my owne affliction in it. Indeed hee was then soe dangerously ill that wee could not reasonably hope hee should outlive this day, yet hee is now I think thank God much better, and I am come soe much to my self with it as to undertake a longe letter to you whilest I watch by him. Towards the latter end it will bee Exelent stuffe I beleeve, but alas you may allow mee to dream somtimes, I have had soe litle sleep since my father was sick that I am never thoroughly awake. Lord how have I wisht for you, heer doe I sit all night by a Poore moaped fellow that serv's my father, and have much adoe to keep him awake and my self too, if you heard the wise discourse that is between us, you would sweare wee wanted sleep, but I shall leave him to night to entertain himself and try if I can write as wisely as I talk.

I am glad all is well againe[.] in Earnest it would have laine upon my conscience if I had bin the occasion of makeing your poore boy loose a service that if hee has the witt to know how to valew it, hee would never have forgiven it mee while hee had lived,[2] but while I remember it let mee aske you if you did not send my letter & Cleopatra where I dirrected you for my Lady, I received one from her to day full of the kindest reproaches that shee has not heard from mee this three week's. I have writt constantly to her, but I doe not soe much wonder that the rest are lost as that she seem's not to have received that which I sent to you nor the book's, I do not understand it but I know there is noe fault of yours int. But harke you, if you think to scape with sending mee such bitts of letters you are mistaken. You say you are often interupted and I believe you, but you must use then to begin to write before you receive mine, and whensoever you have any spare time allow mee some of it. Can you doubt that any thing can make your letters Cheap. In Earnest twas unkindly sayed, and if I could bee angry with you, it should bee for that. Noe Certainly they are, and ever will bee, deare to mee, as that which I receive a huge contentment by. How shall I long when you are gon your Journy[3] to heare from you, how shall I aprehende a thousands accidents that are not likly nor will never happen I hope. O if you doe not send mee long letters then you are the Cruellest person that can bee. If you love mee you will and if you doe not I shall never love my self. You need not feare such a commande as you mention, alas I am too much concern'd that you should love mee ever to forbid it you, 'tis all that I propose of happinesse to my self in the world.

The turning of my paper[4] has waked mee, all this while I was in a dream, but tis noe matter I am content you should know they are of you, and that when my thoughts are left most at liberty they are the kindest. ile swear my Eys are soe heavy that I hardly see what or how I write, nor doe I think you will bee able to read it when I have done. The best on't is twill bee noe great losse to you, if you doe not, for sure the greatest part on't is not sence and yet on my conscience I shall goe on with it, tis like people that talke in theire sleep, nothing interupts them but talking to them againe and that you are not like to doe at this distance[,] besyd's that at this instant you are I beleeve more asleep then I, and doe not soe much as dream that I am writeing to you. My fellow watchers have bin a sleep too till just now, they begin to stretch and yawne, they are goeing to try if eating and drinking can keep them awake and I am kindly invited to bee of theire company. My fathers man has gott one of the mayd's to talk nonsense to to night and they have gott between them a botle of Ale, I shall loose my share if I doe not take them at theire first offer, your patience till I have drunk and then I am for you againe.

And now in the strength of this Ale I beleeve I shall bee able to fill up this Paper that's left with something or other.[5] And first let mee aske you if you have seen a book of Poems newly come out, made by my Lady New Castle[6] for God sake if you meet with it send it mee, they say tis ten times more Extravagant then her dresse. Sure the poore woman is a litle distracted, she could never bee soe rediculous else as to venture at writeing book's and in verse too. If I should not sleep this fortnight I should not come to that. My Ey's grow a litle dim though for all the Ale and I beleeve if I could see it this is most strangly scribled[.] sure I shall not finde fault with you writeing in hast for any thing but the shortnesse of your letter, and twould bee very unjust in mee to tye you to a Ceremony that I doe not observe my selfe, noe, for god sake, let there bee noe such thing between us, a reall kindenesse is soe farr beyond all Complement that it will never apear's more then when there is least of t'other mingled with it. If then you would have mee beleeve yours to bee perfect confirme it to mee by a kinde freedom, tell mee if there bee any thing that I can serve you in[,] imploy mee as you would doe that sister that you say you love soe well, chide mee when I doe any thing that is not well, but then make hast to tell mee that you have forgiven mee, and that you are what I shall Ever bee a   faithfull freind

Letter 18

[Saturday 23 or Sunday 24 April 1653]

Sir

That you may bee sure it was a dreame that I writ that part of my letter in, I doe not now remember what it was I writt, but it seem's it was very kinde, and possibly you owe the discovery on't to my being asleep, but I doe not repent it, for I should not Love you if I did not think you discreet enough to bee trusted with the knowledge of all my kindenesse. Therfor 'tis not that I desyre to hyde it from you, but that I doe not love to tell it, and perhaps if you could read my heart, I should make less scruple of your seeing on't there, then in my letters.

I can easily guesse whoe the Pritty young Lady is, for there are but two in England of that fortune, and they are Sisters, but I am to seek who the Gallant should bee. If it bee noe secrett you may tell mee, however I shall wish him all good successe if hee bee your friend as I suppose hee is, by his confidence in you. If it bee neither of the Spencers[1] I wish it were, I have not seen two young Men that looked as if they deserv'd good fortunes soe much as those Brothers. But blesse mee what will become of us all now, is not this a strange turne.[2] What do's my Lord L.[3] Sure this will at least deffer your Journy. Tell mee what I must think on't, whither it bee better or worse or whither you are at all concern'd in it, for if you are not I am not, onely if I had bin soe wise as to have taken hold of the offer was made mee of H.C.,[4] I might have bin in a faire way of prefferment for sure they will bee greater now than Ever. Is it true that Al: S. was soe unwilling to leave the house, that the G.[5] was faine to take the Pain's to turne him out himself. Well tis a pleasant world this, if Mr Pim[6] were alive again I wonder what hee would think of these proceedings and whither this would apeare as great a breach of the Privilidge of Parliament as the demanding of the 5 members. But I shall talk treason by and by if I doe not look to my self, tis saffer talking of the Oringe flower water you sent mee.

The Carrier has given mee a great charge to tell you that it came safe and I must doe him right, as you say 'tis not the best I have seen, nor the worst. I shall expect your Diary next week though this will bee but a short letter, you may allow mee to make Excuses too somtimes. But Seriously my Father is now so Continualy ill that I have hardly time for any thing, tis but an Ague that hee has, but yet I am much affrayde that is more then his Age & weaknesse will bee able to beare, hee keeps his bed and never rises but to have it made, and most times faints with that. You ought in Charity to write as much as you can for in Earnest my life heer since my Fathers sicknesse, is soe sad, that to another humor then mine it would bee unsuportable, but I have bin soe used to misfortun's that I cannot bee much surprised with them, though perhaps I am as sencible of them as another. I'le leave you for I finde that thoughts begin to putt mee in ill humor. Farwell, pray you bee Ever happy, if I am soe at all tis in being   Your

Letter 19

[Saturday 30 April or Sunday 1 May 1653]

Sir

I am sory my last letter frighted you soe,[1] 'twas noe part of my intention it should, but I am more sory to see by your first Chapter[2] that your humor is not always's soe good as I could wish it, 'twas the only thing I ever desyr'd wee might differ in and (therfore) I think it is denyde mee. Whilest I read the description on't I could not believe but that I had writt it my self it was soe much my owne. I pitty you in Earnest much more then I dare doe my self, and yet I may deserve yours when I shall have told you, that besyd's all that you speake of I have gotten an Ague that with two fitts has made mee soe very weak that I doubted Extreamly yesterday whether I should bee able to sitt up to day to write to you. But you must not bee troubled at this, that's the way to kill mee indeed, besydes it is impossible I should keep it long for heer is my Eldest Brother and my Cousen Molle[3] & two or three more of them that have great Understanding in Agues as People that have bin long acquainted with them and they doe soe tutor & governe mee that I am neither to eate drink nor sleep without their leave, and sure my Obedience deserv's they should cure mee or else they are great Tyrants to very litle purpose. You cannot imagin how Cruell they are to mee and yet will perswade mee tis for my good, I know they mean it soe and therfore say nothing but submitt, and sigh to think those are not heer that would bee kinder to mee. But you were Cruell your self when you seem'd to aprehende I might oblige you to make good your last offer.[4] Alasse if I could purchase the Empire of the world at that rate I should think it much too deare, and though perhaps I am too unhappy my self ever to make any body else happy, yet sure I shall take heed that my misfortun's may not prove infectious to my freinds.

You ask Councell of a person that is very litle able to give it. I cannot imagin whither you should goe since this Journy is broake,[5] you must een bee content to stay at home I think and see what will become of us though I expect nothing of good, and sure you never made a truer remarke in your life then that all changes are for the worse. Will it not stay your fathers Journy too,[6] my thinks it should. For god sake write mee all that you heare or can think of that I may have something to Entertaine my self withall, I have a scurvy head that will not let mee write longer. I am   Your

For Mrs Painter at her house
in Bedford Street next the Goate
In Coven Garden [7]

Letter 20

[Saturday 7 or Sunday 8 May 1653]

Sir

I doe not know that any body has frighted mee or beaten mee, or putt mee into more Passion then what I usually carry aboute mee, but yesterday I missed my fitt,[1] & am not without hope I shall heare noe more on't. My Father has lost his too & my Eldest Brother[2] but wee all look like People risen from the dead. Onely my Cousen Molle keeps his still and in Earnest I am not certain whither hee would loose it or not, for it gives him a lawfull occasion of being nice and cautious about himself, to which hee in his owne humor is soe much inclined that 'twere not easy for him to forbear it.

You need not send mee lady Newcastles book at all for I have seen it, and am sattisfyed that there are many soberer People in Bedlam,[3] i'le swear her friends are much to blame to let her goe abroade. But I am hugly pleased that you have seen my Lady.[4] I know you could not chuse but like her, but yet let mee tell you you have seen but the worst of her, her Conversation has more charmes then can bee in meer beauty, and her humor & disposition would make a difform'd person apeare lovely.

You had strange luck to meet my brother soe soone hee went up but last Tuesday.[5] I heard from him on Thursday but hee did not tell mee hee had seen you[,] perhaps hee did not think it convenient to put mee in minde of you besyd's hee thought hee told mee enough in telling mee my Cousen O.[6] was marryed. Why did you not send mee that news and a Garland.[7] Well the best on't is I have a squire now that is as good as a knight,[8] hee was comeing as fast as a Coach & horses 6 hours could bring him, but I desyr'd him to stay till my Ague was gon and give mee a little time to recover my good look's, for I protest if hee saw mee now, hee would never desyr to see mee againe. O mee I can but think how I shall sitt like the Lady of the Lobster[9] and give audience at Babram. You have bin there I am sure, nobody that is at Cambridge scapes it, but you were never soe wellcome thither as you shall bee when I am Mistresse on't. In the mean time I have sent you the first Tome of Cyrus[10] to read, when you have don with it leave it at Mr Hollingsworths and i'le send you another.

I have my Ladys with mee all this Afternoon that are for London to morrow, and now have I as many letters to write as my Lord Generall's Secretary, forgive mee that this paper is no longer, for I am   Yours

For Mrs Painter at her
house in Bedford Street next the Goate
In Coven Garden[11]

Letter 21

[Saturday 14 or Sunday 15 May 1653]

Sir

I'le tell you noe more of my Servants. I can noe sooner give you some litle hint's whereabout's they live, but you know them presently;[1] and I meant you should bee beholding to mee for your acquaintance. But it seem's this gentleman is not of soe easy accesse but that you may acknoledge somthing due to mee if I incline him to looke Graciously upon you; and therfore there is not much harme done. What has kept him from marryeng all this while, or how the humor com's soe furiously upon him now, I know not, but if hee may be believ'd, hee is resolved to bee a most Romance[2] Squire and goe in quest of some inchanted Damzell, whome if hee likes, as to her person, (for fortune is a thing below him & wee doe not reade in History that any knight, or squire, was ever soe discourtious as to inquire what portions theire Lady's had) then hee comes with the Power of the County[3] to demande her, (which for the present hee may dispose of, being Sheriff) soe that I doe not see whoe is able to resist him, all that is to bee hoped for, is, that since he may reduce whomsoever hee pleases to his Obedience, hee will bee very Curious in his choise, and then I am secure.

It may bee I dreampt it that you had mett my Brother, or else it was one of the Resvery's[4] of the Ague; if soe, I hope I shall fall into noe more of them, I have misst 4 fitts, and had but 5, and have recoverd soe much strength as made mee venture to meet your letter on Wednesday,[5] a mile from home. Yet my Recovery will bee nothing towards my leaveing this place, where many reasons will oblige mee to stay at least all this Summer, unlesse some great Alteration should happen in this family;[6] that which I most owne, is my fathers ill health, which though it bee not in that Extreamity it has bin, yet keeps him still a Prisoner to his Chamber and for the most part to his bed, which is reason

enough, but besydes I can give you others. I am heer much more
out of Peoples way then in Towne, where my Aunte[7] and such
as prettend an interest in mee and a power over mee, doe soe
persecute mee with theire good motions, and take it soe ill that
they are not accepted, as I would live in a hollow tree to avoyde
them. Heer I have noe body but my Brother[8] to Torment mee,
whome I can take the liberty to dispute with, and whome I have
prevailed with hitherto, to bring none of his prettenders to this
place, because of the noyse all such People make in a Country &
the tittle tattle it breed's amongst neighbours that have nothing
to doe but to inquire whoe marry's and who makes love. If I can
but keep him still in that humor, Mr B., and I, are likely to
preserve our State, and Treat at distance like Princes, but wee
have not sent one another our Pictures yet, though my Cousin
M. whoe was his Agent heer begg'd mine very Earnestly. But I
thank God an imagination took him one morning that hee was
falleing into a Dropsey, and made him in such hast to goe back to
Cambridge to his Doctour, that hee never rememberd any thing
hee had to ask of mee, but the Coach to carry him away. I lent it
most Willingly, and gone hee is; my Eldest Brother goes up to
Towne on Monday too, perhaps you may see him but I cannot
dirrect you where to finde him for hee is not yet resolved himself
where to lye, only tis likely Nan may tell you when hee is there,
hee will make noe stay I believe. You will think him Alterd and
(if it bee posible) more Melancholy then hee was. If marriage
agrees noe better with other People than it do's with him, I shall
pray that all my freinds may scape it.

Yet if I were my Cousen H: Danvers,[9] my Lady Diana should
not if I could help it, as well as I love her. I would try if ten
thousand pound a yeer with a husband that doated on her, as I
should doe, could not keep her from being unhappy. Well in
Earnest if I were a Prince that lady should bee my Mistresse but I
can give noe rule to any body Else, and perhaps those that are in
noe danger of looseing theire hearts to her, may bee infinitely
taken with one I should not vallew at all, for soe (say the Justinians)[10] wise providence has ordained it, that by theire different

humors Every body might finde somthing to please themselv's withall without Envying theire neighbours, and now I have begun to talk gravely and wisely i'le try if I can goe a litle further without being out. Noe, I cannot, for I have forgott already what 'twas I would have sayed, but 'tis noe matter for as I remember it was not much to the Purpose, and besydes, I have paper litle enough left, to chide you for askeing soe unkinde a question as whither you were still the same in my thoughts. Have you deserved to bee otherwise, that is, am I noe more in yours, for till that bee tis imposible the other should. But that will never bee, and I shall bee alway's the same I am, my heart tels mee soe and I may believe it, for if twere otherwise fortune would not persecute us thus. Oh mee shee's Cruell and how farr her power may reach I know not, only I am sure, she cannot call back time that is past and it is long since wee resolved to bee for Ever   most faithfull freinds

Letter 22

[Saturday 21 or Sunday 22 May 1653]

Sir

You must pardon mee I could not burn your other letter for my life;[1] I was soe pleased to see I had soe much to reade, & soe sorry I had don soe soone, that I resolved to begin them again and had like to have lost my dinner by it. I know not what humor you were in when you writt it, but Mr Arbry's[2] Prophesy and the falling downe of the forme, did a litle discompose my Gravity, but I quickly recovered my self with thinking that you deserved to bee Chid for goeing where you knew you must of necessity loose your time. In Earnest I had a litle Scruple when I went with you thither,[3] and but that I was assured it was too late to goe any whither else, and believ'd it better to heare an ill Sermon then none, I think I should have missed his Belles remarques. You had repented you I hope of that, and all other faults before you thought of dyeing. What a sattisfaction you had found out to make mee for the injury's you say you have don mee; and yet I cannot tell neither (though 'tis not the remedy I should choose) whither that were not a Certaine one for all my misfortunes, for sure I should have nothing then to perswade mee to stay longer where they Grow, and I should quickly take a resolution of leaveing them and the world at once.

I agree with you too, that I doe not see any great likelihood of the Change of our fortunes, and that we have much more to wish then to hope for, but 'tis soe common a Calamity that I dare not murmur at it, better People have indured it, and I can give noe reason why (Almost,) all are denyed the sattisfaction of disposeing themselves to theire owne desyr's, but that it is a happinesse too great for this world, and might indanger on's forgetting the next, whereas if wee are Crossed in that which only can make the world pleasing to us, wee are quickly tyred with the length of our Journy and the disquiet of our Inn's and long to bee at home. One would think that it were I that had heard the three Sermons, and were trying to make a fourth, these are truths that might become a Pulpitt better than Mr Arbrey's predictions; but least you should think I have as many wormes in my head as hee, i'le give over in time And tell you how farr Mr Luke [4] and I are acquainted. Hee lives within 4 or 5 mile of mee, and one day that I had bin to visett a Lady, that is nearer him then mee, as I cam back I mett a Coach with some company int that I knew, and thought my self obliged to salute. Wee all lighted and mett and I found more then I looked for, by two damzells, and theire squires. I was afterwards told they were of the Lukes and posible this man might bee there, or else I never saw him, for since these times, wee had noe commerce with that famely, but have kept at great distance, as haveing upon severall occasions bin disobliged by them. But of late I know not how Sr Sam: has growne soe kinde as to send to mee for some things hee desyr'd out of this Garden, and withall made the offer of what was in his, which I had reason to take for a high favor, for hee is a nice florist, &

since this, wee are insensibly come to as good degrees of Civility for one another, as can bee expected from People that never meet.

Whoe those Damoisells should bee that were at Heamses[5] I cannot imagin, and I know soe few that are concern'd in mee or my Name, that I admire you should meet with soe many of them that seem to bee acquainted with it. Sure if you had liked them you would not have bin soe sullen, and a lesse occasion would have served to make you Entertaine theire discourse if they had bin handsome, and yet I know noe reason I have to believe that beauty is any Argument to make you like People; unlesse I had more out of my self. But bee it what it will that displeased you, I am glad they did not fright you away before you had the Orange flower water for it is very good, and I am soe sweet with it a day's that I dispise Roses. When I have given you humble thanks for it, I meane to looke over your other letter and take the heads, to treat of them in order, as my time, and your Patience shall give mee leave.

And first for my Sheriff,[6] let mee desyre you to believe hee has more Courage then to Dye, upon a denyall. Noe (thanks bee to god) none of my Servants are given to that, I heare of many, every day that marry, but of none that doe worse. My Brother sent mee word this week that my fighting Servant[7] is marryed too, and with the news, this Ballad, which was to be sunge in the grove that you dreampt of I think, but because you tell mee I shall not want company there you may dispose of this peece of Poetry as you please, when you have suffitiently admired with mee, where hee found it out, for 'tis much older then that of my Lord Lorn.[8]

You are Altogether in the right that my B will never bee at quiet till hee see mee disposed of,[9] but he do's not mean to loose mee by it, hee knows that if I were marryed at this present, I should not bee perswaded to leave my father, as long as hee lives, and when this house break's up, hee is resolved to follow mee if hee can, which hee thinks hee might better doe to a house where I had some power, then where I am but upon Courtesy my self, besydes that hee thinks it would bee to my advantage to bee well bestow'd, and by that hee understands Richly. Hee is much of your Sisters humor, and many times wishes mee a husband that loved mee as well as he do's, (though hee seem's to doubt the possibility ont) but never desyr's that I should love that husband with any Passion, and plainly tells mee soe, hee sayes it would not bee soe well for him, nor perhaps for mee that I should, for hee is of opinion that all passions, have more of trouble then sattisfaction in them and therfore they are happiest that have least of them. You think him kinde from a letter that you mett with of his, Sure there was very litle of any thing in that, or else I should not have imployed it to wrap a Book up, but Seriously I many times receive letters from him that were they seen without an addresse to mee, or his Name, noe body would believe they were from a brother, & I cannot but tell him somtimes that sure hee mistakes and sends letters that were meant to his Mistresse, till hee swear's to mee that hee has none. Next week my persecution begins againe, hee com's downe, and my Cousen Molle is already Cured of his imaginary dropsey and means to meet him heer. I shall bee baited most sweetly, but sure they will not easily make mee consent to make my life unhappy to sattisfy theire importunity; I was borne to bee very happy or very miserable, I know not which, but I am certaine that as long as I am any thing I shall be

> your most faithfull freind
> & Servant

You will never read half this letter, tis soe scribled, but noe matter, tis much worth it.

Letter 23

Sir

If it were the Carryers fault that you stayed soe longe for your letter, you are revenged, for I have chid him most unreasonably. But I must confesse twas not for that, for I did not know it then, but goeing to meet him, (as I usualy doe), when hee gave mee your letter I found the uper seale broake open, and underneath, where it uses to bee only Closed with a litle waxe there was a seale, which though it were an Anchor & a heart, mee thoughts it did not looke like yours, but lesse, and much worse cutt. This suspition was soe stronge upon mee, that I chid till the Poore fellow was redy to Crye, and Swore to mee that it had never bin Touched since hee had it, and that hee was soe carefull of it, as hee never putt it with his other letters, but by it self, and that how it cam amongst his mony, which perhaps might break the seale, and least I should think it was his Curiousity, hee tolde mee very ingenuously hee could not reade and soe wee parted for the present, but since hee has bin with a Neighbour of mine, whome hee somtimes delivers my letters to, and begged of her that she would goe to mee, and desyre my worship to write to your worship to know how the letter was sealed, for it has soe griev'd him that I should think him soe dishonest that hee has neither eate nor slept (to doe him any good) since hee came home, and in grace of god this shall bee a warning to him as long as hee lives. Hee takes it soe heavily that I think I must bee freinds with him againe but pray hereafter seale your letters soe as the difficulty of opening them may dishearten any body from attempting it.

It was but my Guesse that the Lady's at Heamses were unhandsome but since you tell mee they were remarkably soe, sure I know them by it, they are two sisters, and might have bin

mine, if the fates had soe pleased, they have a Brother that is not
like them, and is a Barronett besydes.

'Tis strange that you tell mee of my Lord Shanday's &
Arundell,[1] but what becom's of young Compton's estate. Sure
my Lady Carey,[2] cannot neither in honnor nor Conscience keep
it, besydes that she needs it lesse now then Ever, her son (being as
I heare) dead.

Sir T.[3] I suppose avoyd's you as a freind of mine, my Brother
tells mee they meet somtim's and have the most adoe to pull of
theire hatts to one another that can bee, and never speake. If I
were in Towne i'le undertake, hee would venture the being
Choaked for want of Aire rather then stirre out of doores, for
feare of meeting mee.

But did not you say in your last that you took somthing very
ill from me; & twas my humble thanks. Well you shall have noe
more of them then, nor noe more Servant's,[4] I think indeed they
are not Necessary amongst freinds. I take it very kindely that
your father asked for mee, and that you were not pleased with
the question hee made of the continuance of my freindship. I can
pardon it him because hee do's not know mee, but I should
never forgive you if you could doubt it; were my face in noe
more danger of changing then my minde I should bee worth the
seeing, at threescore, and that which is but very ordinary now,
would then bee counted handsome for an old woman, but alasse
I am more likely to look old before my time, with Greife, never
anybody had such luck with Servants, what with marryeng, and
what with dyeing, they all leave mee. Just now I have news
brought mee of the death of an old rich Knight,[5] that had
promised mee this seven year's to marry mee whensoever his
wife dyed, and now hee's dead before her, and has left her such a
widdow it makes mee mad to think on it, £1200 a yeare Joynter[6]
and £20000 in mony & personall Estate, and all this I might
have had, if Mr Death had bin pleased to have taken her instead
of him. Well whoe can help these things, but since I cannot have
him, would you have her. What say you, shall I speak a good
word for you, shee will marry for certain, and though perhaps

my Brother may Expect I should serve him in it, yet if you give mee comission, i'le say I was ingaged before hand for a freind and leave him to shift for himself. You would bee my Neighbour if you had her and I should see you often; think on't, and let mee know what you resolve.

My Lady has writt mee word, that she intends very shortly to sitt at Lilly's[7] for her Picture for mee. I give you notice on't that you may have the pleasure of seeing it somtimes whilest tis there. I imagin twill bee soe to you, for I am sure it would bee a greate one to mee, and wee doe not use to differr in our inclinations, though I cannot agree with you that my Brothers kindenesse[8] to mee has any thing of trouble int, noe sure I may bee Just to you and him both, and to bee a kinde sister, will take nothing from my being a Perfect ffriende.

Letter 24

[Thursday 2 – Saturday 4 June 1653]

Sir

I have bin reckoning up how many faults you lay to my Charge in your last letter, and I finde I am severe, unjust, unmercifull, and unkinde; O mee how should one doe to mende all these, 'tis work for an Age and tis to bee feared I shall bee Old before I am good, that 'twill not bee considerable to any body but my self whither I am soe or not. I say nothing of the Pritty humor you fancy'd mee in, in your dream because 'twas but a dream, Sure if it had bin any thing Else, I should have rememberd that my Lord L.[1] loves to have his Chamber, and his Bed to himself. But seriously now, I wonder at your Patience, how could you heare mee talke soe sencelessly (though twere but in your sleep) and not bee redy to beate mee. What nice, mistaken points of honnor, I prettended to and yet could allow him a roome in the same bed with mee. Well dream's are pleasant things to People whose humor's are soe, but to have the spleen and to dream upont is a punnishment I would not wish my greatest Enemy. I seldome dream, or never remember them unlesse they have bin soe sad as to put mee into such disorder as I can hardly recover when I am awake, and some of those I am confident I shall never forgett.

You aske mee how I passe my time heer, I can give you a perfect accounte not only of what I doe for the present, but what I am likely to do this seven yeare if I stay heer soe long. I rise in the morning reasonably Early, and before I am redy I goe rounde the house til I am weary of that, and then into the garden till it grows to hott for mee. About ten a clock I think of makeing mee redy, and when that's don I goe into my fathers Chamber, from thence to dinner, where my Cousin Molle[2] and I sitt in great State, in a Roome & at a table that would hold a great many more. After dinner wee sitt and talk till Mr B[3] com's in question and then I am gon. The heat of the day is spent in reading or working and about sixe or seven a Clock, I walke out into a Common that lyes hard by the house where a great many young wenches keep Sheep and Cow's and sitt in the shade singing of Ballads; I goe to them and compare theire voyces and Beauty's to some Ancient Sheperdesses that I have read of and finde a vaste difference there, but trust mee I think these are as innocent as those could bee. I talke to them and finde they want nothing to make them the happiest People in the world, but the knoledge that they are soe.[4] Most Comonly when wee are in the middest of our discourse one looks aboute her and spyes her Cow's goeing into the Corne and then away they all run, as if they had wing's at theire heels. I that am not soe nimble stay behinde, & when I see them driveing home theire Cattle I think tis time for mee to retyre too. When I have supped I goe into the Garden and soe to the syde of a small River that runs by it where I sitt downe and wish you with mee, (You had best say this is not kinde neither) in Earnest tis a pleasant place and would bee much more soe to mee if I had your company. I sitt there somtimes till I am lost with thinking and were it not for some cruell thoughts of the Crossenesse of our fortun's that will not lett mee sleep there, I should forgett there were such a thing to bee don as going to bed. Since I writt this my company is increased by two, My Brother Harry, and a faire Neece, the Eldest of my Brother Peyton's Daughter's,[5] she is soe much a woman, that I am almost ashamed to say I am her Aunte, and soe Pritty that if I had any designe to gaine a Servant I should not like her company[.] but I have none, and therfore, shall indeavour to keep her heer as long as I can perswade her father to spare her, for she will easily consent to it haveing soe much of my humor (though it bee the worst thing in her) as to like a melancholy place, and litle company.

My Brother John is not come down againe nor am I certaine when hee will bee heer, hee went from London into Gloucestershyr to see my Sister who was very ill, and his youngest Girle of which hee was very fonde is since dead, but I beleeve by that time his wife had a litle recoverd her sicknesse and the losse of her Childe, hee will bee comeing this way. My father is reasonably well but keeps his Chamber still, and will hardly I am affrayde Ever bee soe perfectly recoverd as to come abroade againe.

I am sorry for Poore Walker,[6] but you need not doubt of what hee has of yours in his hands, for it seems hee do's not use to do his worke himself, (I speake seriously) hee keeps a french man that setts all his Seal's and Ring's. If what you say of my Lady Lepington[7] bee of your owne knoledge I shall beleeve you, but otherwise I can assure you I have heard from People that prettend to know her well, that her kindenesse to Compton was very moderate, and that she never liked him soe well, as when hee dyed and gave her his Estate[.] but they might bee deceived, and tis not soe strange as that you should imagin a Coldenesse and an indifference in my letter where I soe litle meant it, but I am not displeased you should desyre my kindenesse, enough to aprehende the losse of it, when it is safest, Only I would not have you aprehende it soe farr as to belie[ve][8] it posible. That were an injury to all the assurances I have given you and if you love mee you cannot think mee unworthy. I should think my self soe, if I founde you grew indifferent to

mee, that I have had soe long and soe perticuler a freindship for.
But sure this is more then I need to say, you are Enough in my
heart to know all my thoughts, and if soe, you know better then
I can tell you how much I am   Yours

Letter 25

[Saturday 11 or Sunday 12 June 1653]
Sir

If to know I wish you with mee, pleases you, tis a satisfaction
you may alway's have, for I doe it perpetualy, but were it realy
in my Power to make you happy, I could not misse being soe
my self, for I know nothing Else I want towards it. You are
admitted to all my Entertainments, and 'twould bee a pleasing
surprise to mee to see you amongst my Sheperdesses,[1] I meet
some there somtimes that look very like Gentlemen (for tis a
Roade) and when they are in good humor they give us a
Complement as they goe by, but you would bee soe Courteous
as to stay I hope if wee intreated you, tis in your way to this
place, and Just before the house. Tis our Hide Park,[2] and every
fine Evening any that wanted a Mistresse might bee sure to finde
one over there, I have wanderd often to meet my faire Lady
Ruthin there alone,[3] mee thinks it should bee dangerous for an
heire, I could finde in my heart to steale her away my self, but it
should bee rather for her person then her fortune.

My Brother say's not a worde of you, nor your Service, nor
doe I expect hee should, if I could forgett you, hee would not
help my memory. You would laugh sure if I could tell you how
many Servant's hee has offerd mee since hee came downe, but
one above all the rest I think hee is in love with himself, and
may marry him too, if hee pleases, I shall not hinder him, tis one
Talbott;[4] the finest gentleman hee has seen this seven yeer, but
the mischeif on't is hee has not above fifteen or 16 hundred

pound a year, though hee swear's hee begins to think one might bate £500 a yeer fór such a husband. I tell him I am glad to heare it, and that if I were as much taken (as hee) with Mr Ta: I should not bee lesse Gallant, but I doubted the first Extreamly.

I have spleen enough to carry mee to Epsum [5] this summer, but yet I think I shall not goe. If I make one Journy I must make more, for then I have noe Excuse, and rather then bee obliged to that, i'le make none. You have soe often reproached mee with the losse of your liberty that to make you some amends I am contented to bee your Prisoner this summer, but you shall doe one favour for mee into the bargain. When your father goe's into Ireland,[6] lay your Commands upon some of his Servant's to gett you an Irish Greyhound. I have one that was the Generalls[7] but tis a bitch and those are alway's much lesse then the dog's, I gott it in the time of my favour there and it was all they had. H.C. undertook to write to his Brother Fleetwood[8] for another for mee, but I have lost my hope there. Whomsoever it is that you imploy hee will need noe other instructions but to gett the biggest hee can meet with, 'tis all the beauty of those dogs or of any indeed I think, a Masty[9] is handsomer to mee then the most exact[10] litle dog that ever Lady playde withall. You will not offer to take it ill that I imploy you in such a comission, since I have tolde you that the generals Sonne did not refuse it, but I shall take it ill if you do not take the same freedom whensoever I am capable of serving you.

The Towne must needs bee unpleasant now, and mee thinks you might Contrive some way of haveing your letters sent to you without giveing your self the trouble of comeing to Towne[11] for them when you have noe other buisnesse, you must pardon mee if I think they cannot bee worth it.

I am told that R: Spencer[12] is a Servant to a Lady of my acquaintance, a Daughter of my Lady Lexingtons[.][13] is it true and if it bee true what is become of the £2500 Lady[?]

Would you think it, that I have an Ambassador from the Emperour Justinian,[14] that com's to renew the Treaty in Earnest 'tis true, and I want your Councell Extreamly what to doe in it.

You tolde mee once that of all my Servants you liked him the best, if I could doe soe too there were noe dispute int. Well i'le think on't, and if it succeed I will bee as good as my word, you shall take your Choice of my fower daughters. Am not I beholding to him think you, hee says that hee has made adresses (tis true) in severall places since wee parted, but could not fixe any where, and in his opinion hee see's nobody that would make soe fitt a wife for him as I. Hee has often inquired after mee to heare if I were not marryeng, and sombody told him I had an ague, & hee presently fell sick of one too, soe Naturall a Simpathy there is between us, and yet for all this on my Conscience wee shall never marry. Hee desyr's to know whither I am at liberty or not, what shall I tell him, or shall I send him to you to know, I think that will bee best. I'le say that you are much my freind and that I have resolved not to dispose of my self but with your consent and aprobation, and therfore hee must make all his court to you, and when hee can bring mee a Certificate under your hand, that you think him a fitt husband to mee, 'tis very likely I may have him, till then I am his humble Servant and your faithfull freind.

Letter 26

[Saturday 18 or Sunday 19 June 1653]

Sir

You are more in my debt then you imagin, I never deserved a long letter, soe much as now when you sent mee a short one. I could tell you such a Story, ('tis too longe to bee written) as would make you see (what I never discovered in my selfe before) that I am a Valiant Lady. In Earnest, wee have had such a Skirmish and upon soe foolish an occasion, as I cannot tell which is strangest; the Emperour and his proposall's began it. I talked merrily on't till I saw my B. put on his sober face and could hardly then beleeve hee was in Earnest. It seem's he was, for when I had spoke freely my meaning, it wrought soe much with him as to fetch up all that lay upon his stommack, all the People that I have Ever in my life refused were brought againe upon the Stage, like Richard the 3rd Ghosts[1] to reproach mee withall, and all the kindenesse his discovery's could make I had for you was Layed to my Charge, my best quality's (if I had any that are good) served but for agravations of my fault, and I was allowed to have witt and understanding, & discretion in other things, that it might apear I had none in this. Well twas a pritty Lecture, and I grew warme with it after a while, and in short wee came soe neer an absolute falling out, that twas time to give over and wee sayed soe much then that wee have hardly spoken a word together since; but tis wonderfull to see what Courtesy's and Legg's[2] passe between us, and as before wee were thought the kindest brother & sister wee are certainly now the most Complementall Couple in England. Tis a Strange change and I am very sorry for it, but i'le sweare I know not how to help it, – I look upont as one of my great misfortunes, and I must bear it, as that which is not my first, nor likely to bee my last. Tis but reasonable (as you say) that you should see mee, and yet I know not, now, how it can well bee; I am not for disguises it looks like Guilt, and I would not doe a thing I durst not owne. I cannot tell whether (if there were a necessity of your comeing) I should not Choose to have it when hee is at home, and rather Expose him to the trouble of Entertaining a Person whose company (heer,) would not bee pleasing to him; and perhaps an opinion that I did it purposely to Crosse him, then that your comeing in his absence should bee thought a concealement, 'twas one reason more then I could tell you, why I resolvd not to goe to Epsum[3] this Summer, because I knew hee would imagin it an agreement between us, and that somthing besydes my Spleen carryed mee thither. But whither you see mee or not you may bee sattisfied I am safe enough and you are in noe danger to loose your Prisoner since soe great a Violence as this has not broke her Chaines. You will have nothing to thank mee for after this, my whole life will not yeeld such another occasion to let you see at what rate I valew your freindship and I have bin much better then my Word, in doeing but what I promised you, since I have found it a much harder thing not to yeeld to the Power of a neer relation and a great kindenesse then I could then imagin it. To let you see, I did not repent mee of the Last Comission i'le give you another, heer is a seale that Walker[4] sett for mee, and tis dropt out, pray give it him to mende.

If any thing could bee wonderd at in this Age, I should very much, how come you by your information, tis more then I know him if Mr Freeman[5] bee my Servant I saw him not long since and hee told mee noe such thing. Doe you know him[?] in Earnest hee's a Pretty gentleman and has a great deale of good Nature I think, which may oblige him perhaps to speak well of his acquaintances without designe. Mr Fish[6] is the Squire of Dames, and has soe many Mistresses that any body may prettend a share in him and bee beleev'd; but though I have the honour to bee his neer neighbour, to speak freely I cannot bragge much that hee makes any Court to mee, and I know noe young woman in the Country that hee do's not Visett oftener.

I have sent you another Tome of Cyrus pray send the first to Mr Hollingsworth for my Lady. My Cousen Molle went from hence to Cambridge on Thursday and there's an End of Mr B. I have noe Company now but my Neece Peyton, My Brother will bee shortly for the Terme[7] but will make noe long stay in Towne. I think my Youngest Brother[8] com's downe with him; remmember that you owe mee a longe letter and somthing for forgiving your last. I have noe roome for more than   Your

Letter 27

[Saturday 25 or Sunday 26 June 1653]

Sir

You amaze mee with your story of Tom Cheek,[1] I am certaine hee could not have it where you imagin, and tis a miracle to mee that hee remembers there is such a one in the worlde as his Cousin D.O. I am sure hee has not seen her this sixe yeare, and I think but once in his life. If hee has spred his opinion in that Famely, I shall quickly heare on't, for my Cousen Molle is now gon to Kimolten[2] to my L. Manchester[3] and from thence hee goe's to Moore Parke[4] to my Cousen Franklins, and in one, or both, hee will bee sure to meet with it. The matter is not great for though I confesse I doe naturaly hate the noise and talk of the worlde, and should bee best pleased never to have to bee knowne int upon any occasion whatsoever, yet since it can never bee wholy avoyded one must sattisfye on's selfe by doeing nothing that one need care whoe know's. I doe not think it (a propos) to tell any body that you and I are very good friends, and it were better sure, if nobody knew it but wee our selves, but if in spight of all our Caution it bee discoverd, 'tis no Treason, nor any thing else that's ill, and if any body should tell mee that I had a greater kindenesse and Esteem for you, then for any one besydes, I doe not think I should deny it. Howsoever you doe oblige mee in not owning any such thing, for as you say, I have noe reason to take it ill that you indeavour to preserve mee a Liberty, though I am never likely to make use on't, besydes that I agree with you too, that certainly tis much better you should owe my kindenesse to nothing but your owne merritt and my inclination then that there should lye any other Necessity upon mee of makeing good my worde to you.

For god sake doe not complaine soe that you doe not see mee, I beleeve I doe not suffer lesse in't then you, but tis not to be helpt. If I had a Picture that were fitt for you, you should have it, I have but one that's any thing like and that's a great one, but I will send it some time or other to Cooper or Hoskins,[5] and have a litle one drawne by it, if I cannot bee in Towne to sitt my selfe.

You undoe mee by but dreaming how happy wee might have bin, when I consider how farr wee are from it in reality. Alasse, how can you talk of deffyeing fortune, noe body lives without it, and therfore why should you imagin you could. I know not how my B. coms to bee soe well informed as you say but I am certaine hee know's the utmost of the injury's you have received from her, tis not posible she should have used you worse then hee say's. Wee have had another debate, but much more calmly, 'twas just upon his goeing up to Towne and perhaps hee thought it not ffitt to parte in Anger. Not to wrong him hee never sayed to mee (what ere hee thought) a word in prejudice of you, in your owne person, and I never heard him accuse any thing but your fortune, and my indiscretion, and wheras I did Expect that (at least in Complement to mee) hee should have sayed wee had bin a Couple of Fooles well mett, hee says by his Troath hee do's not blame you, but bids mee not deceive my self to think you have any great passion for mee.

If you have done with the first Part of Cyrus I should bee glad Mr Hollingsworth had it, because I mentiond some such thing in my Last to my Lady, but there is noe hast of restoreing the other unlesse she should send to mee for it which I beleeve she will not. I have a third Tome heer against you have done with the second, and to Encourage you let mee assure you that the more you read of them you will like them still better.

O mee whilest I think ont let mee aske you one question seriously, and pray resolve mee truely, doe I look soe Stately as People aprehende. I vowe to you I made nothing on't when Sir Emperour sayed soe, because I had noe great opinion of his Judgment, but Mr Freeman makes mee mistruste my self Extreamly (not that I am sorry I did apeare soe to him since it kept mee from the displeasure of refuseing an offer, which I doe not perhaps deserve), but that is a scurvy quality in it self, and I am

affrayde I have it in great measure if I showed any of it to him,
for whome I have soe much of respect and Esteem. If it bee soe
you must need's know it, for though my kindnesse will not let
mee look soe upon you, you can see what I doe to other People,
and besydes there was a time when wee our selves were indifferent to one another, did I doe soe then or have I learn't it since[.]
for god sake tell mee that I may try to mend it. I could wish too,
that you would lay your commands on mee to forbeare fruite,
heer is Enough to kill a 1000 such as I am, and soe Exelently
good, that nothing but your power can secure mee, therfor forbid
it mee that I may live to bee   Your

Letter 28

[Saturday 2 or Sunday 3 July 1653]

Sir

In my opinion you do not understande the Law's of freindship
right. 'Tis generaly beleeved it owes it's birth to an agreement &
conformity of humors, and that it lives no longer then tis preserved by the Mutuall care of those that bred it, tis wholy
Governde by Equality, and can there bee such a thing in it, as a
distinction of Power. Noe sure, if wee are friends wee must both
comande & both obay alike. Indeed a Mistresse and a Servant,
soundes otherwise, but that is Ceremony, and this is truth.[1] Yet
what reason have I to furnish you with a stick to beat my selfe
withall or desyre you should comande, that doe it so severely.
I must Eate fruite noe longer then I could bee content you should
bee in a feavour; is not that an absolute forbiding in mee[?] it has
frighted mee just now from a baskett of the most tempting
Cherry's that Ere I saw; though I know that you did not mean I
should eate none, but if you had, I think I should have Obayed
you. I am glad you lay noe fault to my charge but indiscretion,
though that bee too much tis a well natured one in mee. I confesse

it is a fault to beleeve too easily but tis not out of vanity that I doe it, as thinking I deserve you should love mee and therfor beleeving it, but because I am apt to think People so honnest as to speake as they meane, and the lesse I deserve it the more I think my self obliged. I know 'tis a fault in any one to bee mastered by a passion, and of all passions love is perhaps the least pardonable in a woman; but when tis mingled with Gratitude, 'tis sure the lesse to bee blamed. I doe not think if there were more that loved mee I should love them all, but I am certaine I could not love the most Perfect Person in the worlde unlesse I did first firmly beleeve hee had a passion for mee. And yet you would perswade mee I am not Just, because I did once in my life deny you somthing.[2] I'le swere you are not, if you doe not beleeve that next the happy ende of all our wishes, I desyre to see you, but you know the inconveniences that will Certainly follow and if you can dispence with them I can, to show that my Obedience is not lesse then yours. I cannot heare how often that you are kinde & noble enough to preffer my interest above your owne, but sure if I have any measure of either my selfe, the more liberty you give mee the lesse I shall take. Tis most Certaine, that our Emperour,[3] would have bin to mee rather a Jaylor then a husband, and tis as true that (though for my own sake I think I should not make an ill wife to any body) I can not bee a good one to any, but one. I know not with what constancy you could heare the sentence of your Death, but I am certaine there is nothing I could not heare with more, and if your interest in mee bee dearer to you then your life, it must necessarily follow that tis dearer to mee then any thing in the worlde besydes, therfore you may bee sure I will preserve it with all my care. I cannot promise that I shall bee yours, because I know not how farr my misfortunes may reach, nor what punishments are reserved for my faults, but I dare almost promise you shall never receive the displeasure of seeing mee anothers. Noe, in Earnest, I have soe many reasons to keep mee from that, besydes your interest, that I kno[w] not whither it bee not the least of the Obligations you have to mee. Sure the whole worlde could never perswade mee (unlesse a Parent comanded it) to marry one that I had noe Esteem for, and where I have any, I am not lesse scrupulous then your father,[4] for I should never bee brought to doe them the injury as to give them a wife whose affections they could never hope for, besydes that I must sacrifice my self int and live a walking missery[5] till the only hope that would then bee left mee, were perfected. O mee this is soe sad, it has put mee out of all I had to say besydes. I meant to chide you for the shortnesse of your last letter and to tell you that if you doe not take the same liberty of telling mee of all my faults, I shall not think you are my freind. In Earnest tis true you must use to tell mee freely of any thing you see amisse in mee, wither I am too stately[6] or not enough, what humor pleases you and what do's not, what you would have mee doe & what avoyde, with the same freedom that you would use to a person over whome you have an absolute Power and were concerned in. These are the Laws of ffreindship as I understande them, and I beleeve I understande them right, for I am Certaine noe body can bee more perfectly a freind then I am   Yours

Letter 29

[Saturday 9 or Sunday 10 July 1653]

Sir

I can give you leave to doubt any thing but my kindenesse; though I can assure you I spake as I meant when I sayed I had not the Vanity to beleeve I deserved yours. For I am not certaine wither tis possible for any body to deserve that another should love them above themselv's, though I am certaine many may deserve it more then I. But not to dispute with you, let mee tell you that I am thus ffarr of Your opinion, that upon some Natur's nothing is soe powerfull as kindenesse, and that I should give that to yours, which all the merritt in the Worlde besydes would not draw from mee. I speake as if I had not don soe already, but you may choose whither you will beleeve mee or not, for to say truth I doe not much beleeve my selfe in that point. Now, all the kindenesse I have, or Ever had, is yours, nor shall I ever repent it soe, unlesse you shall ever repent yours. Without telling you what the inconveniency's[1] of your comeing hither are, you may beleeve they are considerable or else I should not deny you or my selfe the happinesse of seeing one another, and if you dare trust mee where I am Equaly concerned with you, I shall take hold of the first opertunity that may either admitt you heer, or bring mee neerer you.

Sure you took sombody else for my Cousin Peters,[2] I can never beleeve her beauty able to smite any body. I saw her when I was last in Towne but shee appear'd wholy the same, to mee, she was at St Malo, with all her innocent good nature too, and asked for you soe kindly that I am sure she cannot have forgott you, nor doe I think she has soe much addresse as to doe it meerly in Complement to mee. Noe, you were mistaken Certainely, what should she doe amongst all that Company (unlesse she bee towards a wedding). She has bin kept at home Poore Soule and sufferd soe much of Purgatory in this worlde that she needs not feare it in the next, and yet she is as merry as Ever she was, which perhaps might make her look young but that she Laughs a litle too much and that will bring wrinkles they say.[3]

O mee now I talk of Laughing it makes mee think of Poore Jane.[4] I had a letter from her the other day, she desyred mee to present her humble Service to her Master, she did mean you sure, for she named Every body Else that she ow's any Service to, and bid mee say that she would keep her worde with him, god knows what you have agreed together. Shee tells mee she shall stay long enough there to heare from mee once more and then she is resolved to come away.[5]

Heer is a seale which pray give Walker[6] to sett for mee, very handsomely & not any of those fashions hee made my Others, but of some thing that may differ from the rest. Tis a plaine head but not ill Cutt I think.

My Eldest Brother[7] is now heer, and wee expect my Youngest[8] shortly and then wee shall bee all together, which I doe not think wee ever were twice in our lives. My Neece[9] is still with mee, but her father threatens to fetch her away. If I can keep her till Michelmas I may perhaps bring her up to Towne my selfe and take the occasion of seeing you for I have noe other buisnesse that is worth my takeing a Journy for. I have had another summons from my Aunt[10] and I prottest I am afrayde I shall bee in rebellion there, but tis not to bee helpt. The Widdow[11] writes mee worde too that I must expect her heer about a month hence, and I finde that I shall want noe company but only that which I would have and for which I could willingly spare all the rest. Will it bee ever thus[?] I am affrayde it will. There has bin complaints made on mee already by my Eldest Brother, only in generall (or at least hee takes notice of noe more) what offers I refuse and what a strange humor has possest mee of being deafe to the advice of all my freinds. I finde I am to bee bayted by them all by turn's[.] they weary themselv's and mee too, to very litle purpose, for to my thinking they talke the most impertinently that Ever People did, and I believe they are not in my debt, but think the same of mee. Somtimes I tell them I will not marry, and then they Laugh at mee, somtimes I say not yet, and then they Laugh more, and would make mee beleeve I shall bee old within this twelve months. I tell them I shall bee wiser then, they say, twill bee then to noe purpose. Somtimes wee are in Earnest and somtimes in Jest, but alway's sayeing somthing, since my Brother Harry found his Tongue againe. If you were with mee I could make sport of all this, but Patience is my Pennance,[12] is sombody's motto, and I think it must bee mine.   I am

Your

Letter 30

[Saturday 16 or Sunday 17 July 1653]

Sir

The day I should have received your letter I was invited to dine at a rich widdow's[1] (whome I think I once told you of and offered my service in case you thought fitt to make addresses there), and she was soe kinde and in soe good humor, that if I had any comission I should have thought it a very fitt time to speak. Wee had a huge dinner, though the company was only of her owne kindred that are in the house with her, and what I brought, but she is broke loose from an Old Miserable husband that lived soe long she thinks if she do's not make hast she shall not have time to spend what hee left. She is old and was never handsom, and yet is Courted a thousand times more then the greatest beauty in the world would bee that had not a fortune, wee could not eate in quiet for the letters and the presents that cam in from People that would not have looked upon her when they had mett her, if she had bin left Poore. I could not but laugh to my self at the meanesse of theire humor, and was merry enough all day, for the company was very good and besydes I Expected to finde when I cam home a letter from you that would bee more a feast and company to mee then all that was there. But never any body was so deffeated[2] as I was to finde none. I could not imagin the reason, only I assured my self it was noe fault of yours, but perhaps a Just punishment upon mee for haveing bin too much pleased in a company where you were not. After supper my Brother and I fell into dispute about riches, and the great advantages of it, hee instanced in the widdow, that it made one respected in the world. I sayed twas true, but that was a respect I should not at all value when I owed it only to my fortune, & wee debated it soe long till wee had both talked our selv's weary enough to goe to bed. Yet I did not sleep soe well but that I chid my mayde for wakeing mee in the morning, till shee stoped my mouth with sayeing she had letters for mee. I had not patience to stay till I could rise, but made her tye up all the Curtains to let in light, and amongst some others, I quickly founde my deare letter that was first to bee read, and which made all the rest not worth the reading.

I could not but wonder to finde in it that my Cousin Fr:[3] should want a true friend, when 'tis thought she has the best husband in the world. Hee was soe passionate for her before hee had her, and soe pleased with her since, that in Earnest I doe not think it posible she could have any thing left to wish that she had not already, in such a husband with such a fortune. But she can best tell whither shee's happy or not, only if she bee not I doe not see how any body else can hope for it. I know her the least of all the sisters,[4] and perhaps tis to my advantage that shee knows mee noe more, since she speaks soe Obligingly of mee, but doe you think it was altogether without designe that she spoke it to you when I remember she is T.C. Sister,[5] I am apt to think she might have heard his news, and meant to try whither there was any thing of truth int. My Cousin Molle I think means to End the Summer there. They say indeed tis a very fine seate, but if I did not mistake Sir Thomas Ch: hee told mee there was never a good roome in the house. I was wondring how you cam by an acquaintance there because I had never heard you speak that you knew them. I never saw him, in my life, but hee is famous for a kinde husband, only twas found fault with, that hee could not forbeare kissing his wife before company, a foolish trick that young marryed men it seem's are apt to. Hee has left it long since I suppose. But seriously tis as ill a sight as one would wish to see, and appear's very rude mee thinks to the Company.

What a strange fellow this Goldsmith[6] is, hee has a head fitt for nothing but horn's. I chid him once for a seale hee sett mee just of this fashion and the same coulers (as) if hee were to make twenty they should all bee soe, his invention can stretch noe further then blew and red. It makes mee think of the fellow that could paint nothing but a flower de luce[7] whoe when hee mett

with one that was soe firmly resolved to have a Lyon for his
signe that there was noe perswading him out ont, Well say's the
painter, let it bee a Lyon then but it shall bee as like a flower de
Luce as ere you saw, soe because you would have it a dolphin
hee consented to it but it is liker an ilfavoured knot of riban.

I did not say any thing of my father's being ill of late. I think I
tolde you before hee kept his chamber ever since his last sicknesse,
and soe hee do's still, yet I cannot say that hee is at all sick but has
soe generall a weaknesse upon him that I am much affrayde
theire opinion of him, has too much of truth in't, and doe Extreamly aprehende how the winter may worke upon him. Will
you pardon this strang scribled letter, and the disorderlinesse on't.
I know you would, though I should not tell you that I am not
soe much at liesure as I use to bee. You can forgive your friends
any thing, and when I am not the faithfullest of those never
forgive mee.

You may dirrect your letter how you please heer will bee
nobody to receive it,[8] but   Your

Letter 31

[Saturday 23 or Sunday 24 July 1653]

Sir

I received your last sooner by a day then I Expected, it was not
the lesse welcom but the Carrier was who brought mee none. I
admired at my self to remember how I have bin transported
with the sight of that pittifull fellow, and how that I knew hee
has noe letter for mee, how coldly I looked upon him. Nan [1] tells
mee hee had the curiosity to aske your Boy questions, I should
never have suspected it, and yet hee had the witt to doe a thing
last week few such People would have don. My B. comeing
from London,[2] mett him goeing up & cald to him, & asked
what letters hee had of mine, the fellow sayed none, I did not use

to send by him. My B. sayed I tolde him hee had and bid him call for them, hee sayed there was some mistake int for hee had none, and soe they Parted for a while. But my B. not sattisfied with this rides after him, and in some anger threatned the Poore fellow, whoe would not bee frighted out of his letter, but looked very simply and sayed now hee rememberd himselfe hee had carried a letter for mee aboute a fortnight or three weeks agon, to my Lady D.R.[3] but hee was sure hee had none now. My B. smiled at his innocence and left him, and I was hugely pleased to heare, how hee had bin defeated. You will have time Enough to think of a new addresse, hee goes noe more till after harvest, and you will receive this by your old freind Collins.[4] But because my B. is with him every week as soone as hee com's and takes up all the letters, if you please lett yours bee made up in some other forme then usuall, and directed to Mr Gibson at Ch:[5] in some od hande, and bee at the Charge pray of buyeng a twopeny seale a propos for the letters.

Would you could make your words good, that my Ey's can dispell all mellancholy Clouded humors, I would looke in the glasse all day longe but I would cleare up my owne. Alasse, they are soe farr from that, they would teach one to bee sad, that knew nothing on't, for in other peoples opinions as well as my owne they have the most of it in them that Ey's can have. My Mother (I remember) used to say I needed noe tear's to perswade my trouble, and that I had lookes soe farr beyonde them, that were all the friends I had in the world, dead, more could not bee Expected then such a sadnesse in my Ey's, this indeed I think is naturall to them, or at least long custome has made it soe. 'Tis most true that our friendship has bin brought up hardly enough, and posibly it thrives the better for't, tis observed that surfeits kill more then fasting do's, but ours is in noe danger of that. My B. would perswade mee there is noe such thing in the worlde as a constante friendship, People (hee say's) that marry with great passion for one another as they think, come afterwards to loose it they know not how, besydes the multitude of such as are false and meane it. I cannot bee of his opinion (though I confesse there are too many Examples on't) I have alway's beleeved there might bee a friendship perfect like that you describe and mee thinks I finde somthing like it in my selfe, but sure tis not to be taught, it must come Naturaly to those that have it, and those that have it not can ne'ere bee made to understand it. You needed not have feared that I should take occasion from your not answering my last, not to write this week. You are as much pleased (you say) with writeing to mee as I can bee to receive your letters, why should you not think the same of mee, in Earnest you may, and if you love mee you will. But then how much more sattisfied should I bee if there were noe need of these, and wee might talke all that wee write and more, shall wee Ever bee soe happy. Last night, I was in the Garden till Eleven a clock, it was the Sweetest night that ere I saw, the Garden looked soe well, and the Jessomin smelt beyond all perfumes, and yet I was not pleased. The place had all the Charmes it used to have when I was most sattisfied with it and had you bin there I should have liked it much more than Ever I did, but that not being it was noe more to mee then the next feilde, and only served mee for a place to resve in without disturbance.

What a sad story you tell mee of the litle Marquise.[6] Poore Woman, yet shee's happy, shee's dead, for sure her life could not bee very pleasing to her. When wee were both Girl's I had a greater acquaintance there, they lived by us at Chelsey, and as long as his son lived Sir Theador did mee the honour to call mee daughter. But whilest I was first in France hee dyed, and with him my converse with the Famely, for though my Mother had occasion to bee often there yet I went very seldome with her, they were still soe passionate for theire son that I never failed of setting them all a Cryeng and then I was noe company for them. But this poore Lady had a greater losse of my Lord Hastings[7] who dyed Just when they should have bin marryed, and sure she could not think she had recoverd it at all, by Marryeng this Buffle headed Marquis. And yet one knows not neither what she might think, I remember I saw her with him in the Parke a litle while after they were marryed and she kist him the kindliest that could bee in the middest of all the Company. I shall never wish to see a worse sight then twas, nor to bee any thing longer then I am   Your faithfull

Letter 32

[Saturday 30 or Sunday 31 July 1653]

Sir

Your Last cam safe, and I shall follow your dirrection for the addresse of this, though as you say I cannot imagin what should tempt to soe severe a search for them, unless it bee that hee is not yet fully sattisfyed to what degrees our friendship is growne and thinks hee may best informe himself from them.[1] In Earnest 'twould not bee unpleasant to heare our discourses, hee formes his with soe much art and designe, and is soe pleased with the hopes of makeing some discovery, and I that know him as well as hee do's himselfe cannot but give my selfe the recreation (somtimes) of confounding him and distroying all that his buisy head had bin working on since the last conference. Hee gives mee some trouble with his suspitions, yet on my conscience hee is a greater to himself and I deale with soe much franchise[2] as to tell him soe, many times, and yet hee has noe more the heart to aske mee dirrectly what he would soe faine know, then a Jealous man has to aske (one that might tell him) whither hee were a cuckolde or not for feare of being resolved of that which is yet a doubt to him.

My E. B. is not soe inquisitive, hee sattisfy's himself with perswading mee Earnestly to marry, and takes noe notice of any thing that may hinder mee but a Carelessenesse of my fortune or perhaps an aversion to a kinde of life that appears to have lesse of freedom in't then that which I at present injoy. But sure hee gives himself another reason, for tis not very long since hee took occasion to inquire for you very kindly of mee, and though I could then give but a little account of you, hee smiled as if hee did not altogether beleeve mee, and afterwards maliciously sayed hee wondered you did not marry. I seem'd to doe soe too, & sayed if I knew any woman that had a great fortune and were a person Worthy of you, I should wish her you with all my heart. But Sister say's hee, would you have him love her. Doe you doubt it would I say, – hee were not happy int else.[3] Hee laughed and sayed my humor was pleasant but hee made some question whither it was naturall or not. Hee cannot bee soe unjust as to let mee loose him sure.[4] I was kinder to him though I had some reason's not to take it very well when hee made that a Secrett to mee, which was knowne to soe many people that did not know him, but wee shall never fall out I beleeve, wee are not apt to it neither of us.

If you are come back from Epsum,[5] I may aske you how you like drinking water. I have wished it might agree as well with you as it did with mee and if it were as certaine that the same things would doe us good, as tis that the same things would please us I should not need to doubt it, Otherwise my Wishes doe not signifye much. But I am forbid complaint's or to expresse my fear's,[6] and bee it soe, only you must pardon mee if I cannot agree to give you false hopes, I must bee deceived my self before I can deceive you, and I have soe accustomed my selfe to tell you all that I think, that I must Either say nothing, or that which I beleeve to bee true.

I cannot say but I have wanted Jane, but it has bin rather to have sombody to talk with of you, then that I needed any body to put mee in minde of you and with all her dilligence I should have often prevented[7] her in that discourse.

Were you at Althrop[8] when you saw my Lady Sunderland and Mr Smith, or were they in towne. I have heard indeed that they are very happy but withall that as she is a very Extreordinary person her self, soe she aymes at Extreordinary things, and when she had marry'd Mr Smith because some People were soe bold as to think she did it because she loved him, she undertook to convince the worlde that what shee had don was in meer Pitty to his sufferings, and that she could not goe a step lower to meet any body then that led her[,] though where she thought there were noe Ey's upon her, she was more gracious to him, but perhaps this might not bee true, or it may bee she is now growne weary of that constraint she putt upon herself. I should have bin sadder then you if I had bin theire Neighbour to have seen them soe kinde, as I must have bin if I had marryed the Emperour,[9] hee used to brag to mee alway's of a great acquaintance hee had there, what an Esteem my Lady[10] had for him, & had the Vanity, (not to call it impudence) to talke somtimes as if hee would have had mee beleev'd hee might have had her, and would not, i'le sweare I blushd for him when I saw hee did not. Hee told mee too that though hee had carryed his addresses to mee with all the privacy that was possible, because hee saw I liked it best, and that twas partly his owne humor too, yet shee had discoverd it, and could tell that there had bin such a thing, and it was broake of againe she knew not why, which certainly was a lye as well as the other for I doe not think she Ever heard there was such a one in the world as   Your faithfull freind

Letter 33

[Saturday 6 or Sunday 7 August 1653]

Sir

I do not lay it as a fault to your charge, that you were not good at disguise.[1] If it bee one, I am too guilty on't my self, to accuse another, and though I have bin tolde it shows an unpractisdnes in the world, and betray's one to all that understande it better, yet since it is a quality I was not borne with, nor ever like to gett, I have alway's thought good to maintaine that it was better not to need it, then to have it.

I give you many thanks for your care of my Irish dog, but I am Extreamly out of countenance your father should bee

troubled with it.[2] Sure hee will think I have a most Extravagant
fancy but doe mee the right as to let him know I am not so
possest with it, as to consent hee should bee imployed in such a
comission.

Your opinion of [my][3] E.B. is I think very Juste and when I
say'd maliciously, I meant a french malice which you know do's
not signifye the same with an English one.

I know not whither I tolde it you or not, but I concluded
(from what you sayed of your indisposition), that it was very
like the spleen. But perhaps I forsaw you would not bee willing
to owne a disease, that the severe part of the worlde holde to bee
meerly imaginary and affected, and therfore proper only to
women. However, I cannot but wish you had stay'd longer at
Epsum,[4] and drink the waters with more order, though in a lesse
proportion. But did you drink them imediately from the well[?] I
remember I was forbid it, and mee thought with a great deal of
reason, for (Especialy at this time of the yeare) the well is soe
low, and there is such a multitude to bee serv'd out on't, that
you can hardly gett any but what is thick, and troubled. And I
have marked that when it had stood all night (for that was my
dirrection) the bottom of the Vessell it stood in, would bee
coverd an inch thick, with a white clay, which sure has noe great
vertue in't, and is not very pleasant to drink.

What a Character of a young couple you give mee. Would
you would aske somebody that knew him, whither hee bee not
much more an Asse since his Marryeng then hee was before. I
have some reasons to doubt that it alters People strangly. I made
a Visett[5] t'other day to welcom a Lady into this Country whom
her husband has newly brought down, and because I knew him,
though not her, and shee was a stranger heer 'twas a civility I
owed them. But you cannot imagin how I was surprised to see, a
Man that I had knowne soe handsom, soe capable of being made
a pritty gentleman (for though hee was noe grande Philosophe as
the french men say yet hee was not that, which good company
and a litle knowledge of the world, would have made Equall to
many that think themselv's very well, and are thought soe),

Transformed into the dirrect shape of a great Boy newly come
from scoole. To see him wholy taken up with running on
Errand's for his wife, and teaching her little dog, tricks, and this
was the best of him, for when hee was at leasure to talke, hee
would suffer noebody Else to doe it, and by what hee sayd, and
the noyse hee made, if you had heard it you would have concluded him drunk with joy that hee had a wife and a pack of
houndes. I was so weary on't that I made hast home and could
not but think of the change all the way, till my Brother (whoe
was with mee) thought mee sad and to putt mee in better humor,
sayd hee beleev'd I repented mee I had not this Gentleman, now
I saw how absolutely his wife govern'd him. But I assured him
that though I thought it very fitt, such as hee should be govern'd,
yet I should not like the imployment by noe mean's, it became
noe woman, and did soe ill with this Lady, that in my opinion it
spoyld a good face, and a very fine gowne. Yet the woman you
mett upon the way govern'd her husband, and did it handsomly,
it was (as you say) a great Example of friendship and much for
the creditt of our sex.

You are too severe on Walker,[6] i'le undertake hee would sett
mee twenty seal's for nothing rather then undergoe your wish. I
am in noe hast for it and soe hee do's it well, wee will not fall
out. Perhaps hee is not in the humor of keeping his word, at
present, and noe body can blame him if hee bee often in an ill
one. But though I am mercifull to him as to one that has suffered
Enough alredy, I cannot Excuse you that proffesse to bee my
friend, and yet are content to let mee live in such ignorance,
write to mee Every week and yet never send mee any of the
new phrases of the Towne. I could tell you without abandoning
the truth, that it is part of your devoyre to correct the im-
perfections you finde under my hand, and that my trouble resem-
bles my wonder, you can lett mee bee dissattisfyed. I should
never have learnt any of these five things from you, and to say
truth I know not whither I shall from any body else, if to learne
them bee to understand them. Pray what is meant by wellness[7]
and unwellnes, and why is, to some Extream, better then to

some Extreamity[?] I beleeve I shall live heer till there is quite a new Language spoke where you are, and shall come out like one of the Seven Sleepers,[8] a Creature of another Age, but tis noe matter, soe you understande mee, though nobody else doe, when I say how much I am

your faithfull

Letter 34

[Friday 12 August 1653]

Sir

Jane[1] was soe unlucky as to come out of towne before your retourne, but she tels mee she left my letter with Nan Stacy[2] for you. I was in hope she would have brought mee one from you, and because she did not I was resolved to punish her, and kept her up till one a clock telling mee all her Storry's. Sure if there bee any truth in the olde observation your Cheeks glowed notably and tis most certaine that if I were with you I should chide notably, what doe you mean to bee soe melancholy, by her report your humor is growne insuportable. I can allow it not to bee altogether what she say's & yet it may bee very ill too, but if you loved mee you would not give your self over to that which will infallibly kill you if it continue. I know, too well, that our fortunes have given us occasion Enough to complaine and to bee weary of her Tirrany but alasse would it bee better if I had lost you, or you mee. Unlesse wee were sure to dye together, 'twould but increase our missery and adde to that which is more alredy then wee can well tell how to beare. You are more Cruell then she is in hazarding a life that's dearer to mee, then that of the whole worlds besyds, and which makes all the happiness I have or ever shall be capable of. Therfore by all our friendship I conjure you, and by the power (you have given mee) comande you to preserve your self with the same care that you would have mee live, 'tis all the Obedience I require of you, and will bee the greatest Testimony you can give mee of your faith. When you have promis'd mee this, tis not imposible but I may promise you shall see mee shortly, though my B. Peyton (whoe says hee will come downe to fetch his daughter [3]), hinders mee from makeing the Journy in Complement to her yet I shall perhaps find buisnesse enough to carry mee up to Towne, 'tis all the service I expect from two Girl's whose friends have given mee leave to provide for [them] [4] that some order I must take for the disposall of them may serve for my pretence to see you, but then I must finde you pleased and in good humor, merry, as you were wont to bee when wee first mett, if you will not have mee show that I am nothing a kin to my Cousin Osborn's [5] Lady. But what an Age tis since wee first mett and how great a Change it has wrought in both of us. If theire had bin as great a one in my face it would bee either very handsom or very ugly. For god sake when wee meet let us designe one day to remember old story's in, to aske one another by what degree's our friendship grew to this height tis at, in Earnest I am Lost somtimes with thinking on't, and though I can never repent the share you have in my heart, I know not whither I gave it you willingly or not at first, noe, to speak ingenuously I think you gott an interest there a good while before I thought you had any, and it grew soe insensibly and yet soe fast that all the Traverses it has mett with since, has served rather to discover it to mee, then at all to hinder it. By this confession you will see I am past all disguise with you, and that you have reason to bee sattisfyed with knowing as much of my heart as I doe my self.

Will the Kindenesse of this letter Excuse the shortnesse on't pray le[t] [6] it for I have twenty more I think to write and the hopes I had of receiving one from you last night kept mee from writeing this when I had more time, or if all this will not sattisfye, make your owne conditions soe you doe not returne it mee by the shortnesse of yours. Your Servant [7] kisses your hands, and I am

Your faithfull

For Mr T
Let the answer bee sent by Harrold [8]

Letter 35

[Saturday 13 or Sunday 14 August 1653]

Sir

You cannot imagin how I was surprised to finde a letter that began Deare Brother.[1] I thought sure it could not belong at all to mee, and was affrayde I had lost one by it, that you intended mee another, and in your hast had mistook this, for that. Therfor till I founde the permission you gave mee, I had layde it by mee, with a resolution not to read it, but send it again. If I had done soe I had mist of a great deal of sattisfaction, which I received from it. In Earnest I cannot tell you how kindly I take all the Obligeing things you say in it of mee, nor how pleased I should bee (for your sake) if I were able to make good the Character you give mee of your Brother, and that I did not owe a great part of it wholy to your friendship for mee. I dare call nothing ont my owne, but faithfullnesse. That, I boast of with truth, and modesty, since 'tis but a single Vertue, and though some are without it, yet tis soe absolutely necessary, that nobody wanting it, can bee worthy of my Esteem.

I see you speak well of mee, to other People, though you complain alway's to mee. I know not how to beleeve, I should misuse your heart as you prettende, I never had any quarrell to it, and since our friendship it has bin dear to mee as my owne. 'Tis rather sure that you have a minde to try another, then that any dislike of yours makes you turn it over to mee. But bee it as it will, I am contented to stand to the losse, & perhaps when you have changed you will finde soe litle difference, that you'l bee calling for your owne againe.

Doe but assure mee that I shall finde you almost as merry as my Lady A.W.[2] is always and nothing shall fright mee from my purpose of seeing you as soone as I can with any conveniency. I would not have you insencible of our misfortun's but I would not neither that you should revenge them upon your self. Noe, that show's a want of constancy (which you will hardly yeeld to bee your fault) but tis certaine that there was never any thing more mistaken then the Roman Courage when they kill'd them-selv's to avoyde misfortun's that were infinitly worse then death.

You confesse 'tis such an Age since our Story began, as is not fitt for mee to owne. Is it not likely then, that if my face had ever bin good it might bee alterd since then or is it as unfitt for mee to owne the Change as the time that makes it[?] bee it as you please. I am not enough concern'd in't to dispute it with you, for trust mee if you would not have my face better, I am sattisfyed it should bee as it is, since if I ever wish'd it otherwise, 'twas for your sake.

I know not how I stumbled upon a new's book[3] this week, and for want of something else to doe read it. It mentions my L. L.[4] Embassage againe, is there any such thing towards. I mett with somthing else too in't, that my concerne any body that has a mind to marry, 'tis a new forme[5] for it, that sure will fright the Country people Extreamly, for they aprehend nothing like going before a Justice, they say noe other Marriage shall stand good in Law. In conscience I beleeve the olde one is the better, and for my part I am resolvd to stay till that com's in fashion againe.

Can your father have soe perfectly forgiven alredy the injury I did him (since you will not allow it to bee any to you) in hindring you of Mrs Cle,[6] as to remember mee with kindenesse. Tis most certaine that I am obliged to him, and in Earnest if I could hope it might ever bee in my power to serve him I would promise somthing for my self. But is it not true too, that you have rep-resented mee to him rather as you imagin mee, then as I am, and had not you given him an Expectation that I shall never bee able to sattisfye[?] if you have, I cannot forgive you because I know you meant well in it. But I have knowne some women that have comended others meerly out of spite. And if I were malicious enough to Envy any body's beauty I would crye it up to all that had not seen them, ther's noe such way to make any body apear lesse handsom then they are.

You must not forgett that you are some letters in my debt besydes the Answer to this, if there were more conveniencys of sending I should persecute you strangly, and yet you cannot wonder at it, the constant desyre I have to hear from you and the sattisfaction your letters give mee, would Oblige one that had lesse time to write often, but yet I know what tis to bee in the Towne, I could never write a letter from thence in my life of above a dousen lines and though I see as litle company as any body that com's there, yet I always mett with somthing or other that kept mee idle. Therfor I can Excuse it though you doe not Exactly pay all that you owe, upon condition you shall tell mee (when I see you) all that you should have writt if you had had time, and all that you can imagin to say to a person that is

Your faithfull friend

Letter 36

[Saturday 20 or Sunday 21 August 1653]

Sir

That you may be at more certainty hereafter what to think let mee tell you that nothing could hinder mee from writeing to you (as well for my owne sattisfaction as yours) but an imposibillity of doing it, nothing but death or a dead Palsey in my hands, or somthing that had the Same Effects.

I did write,[1] and gave it Harrold, but by an accident his horse fell lame soe hee could not set out on munday, but a Tuesday hee did com to Towne on wednesday, carryed the Letter himself (as hee tell's mee) where twas dirrected which was to Mr Copyn in Fleetstreet,[2] 'twas the first time I made use of that dirrection

noe matter and I had not don't then since it proves noe better.
Harrold cam late home on thursday night with such an account
as your boy gave you, that comeing out of Towne the same day
hee cam in, hee had bin at Fleetstreet again but there was noe
letter for him. I was sorry, but I did not much wonder at it
because hee gave soe litle time, and resolved to make my best of
that I had by Collins. I read it over often enough to make it
Equall with the Longest letter that ever was writt and pleased
my self in Earnest (as much as it was posible for me in the humour
I was in) to think how by that time you had asked mee pardon
for the litle reproaches you had made mee and that the kindenesse
and lengh [*sic*] of my letter had made you amends for the trouble
it had given you in Expecting it. But I am not a litle amazed to
finde you had it not, I am very confident it was diliverd and
therfor you must serch where the fault lyes.

Were it not that you had suffer'd[3] too much alredy I would
complain a litle of you, why should you think mee soe carelesse
of any thing that you were concerned in, as to doubt that I had
not writt, though I had received none from you I should not
have taken the occasion to revenge my self, nay I should have
concluded you innocent, and have imagin'd a thousand way's
how it might happen rather then have suspected your want of
kindenesse, why should you not bee as Just to mee. But I will
not Chide, it may bee (as long as we have bin friends) you doe
not know mee soe well yett as to make an absolute Judgment of
mee, but if I know my self at all, if I am capable of being any
thing, tis, a perfect friend, Yet I must Chide too, why did you
gett such a Colde[?] good God how carelesse you are of a life
that (by your owne confession) I have told you makes all the
happinesse of mine, tis unkindly don, what is left for mee to say
when that will not prevaile with you, or how can you perswade
mee to a care of my self when you refuse to give mee the Example. I know nothing in the world that gives mee the least
desyr of preserving my self but the opinion I have you would
not bee willing to loose mee, and yet if you saw with what
Caution I live, (at least to what I did befor) you would reproach

it to your self somtim's, and might grant perhaps that you have not gott the advantage of mee in friendship soe much as you imagin. What (besydes your consideration) could Oblige mee to live and loose all the rest of my friends thus one after another. Sure I am not insensible nor very ill natur'd, and yet i'le swear I think I doe not afflict my self halfe soe much as another would doe that had my losses. I say nothing of sadnesse to the memory of my poore Brother,[4] but I presently disperse it with thinking what I owe in thankfullnesse, that tis not you I mourne for.

Well give mee noe more occasion's to complaine of you, you know not what may follow, heer was Mr Freeman[5] yesterday that made mee a very kinde Visett and sayed soe many fine things to mee that I was confounded with his Civility's and had nothing to say for my self. I could have wish'd then, that hee had considerd mee lesse and my Neece[6] more, but if you continue to use mee thus, in Earnest i'le not bee soe much her friend hereafter. Mee thinks I see you Laugh at all my Threatnings and not without reason Mr Freeman you beleeve is designed for sombody that deserv's him better, I think soe too, and am not sorry for it, and you have reason to beleeve I never can bee other then

Your faithfull friend

Letter 37

[Saturday 27 or Sunday 28 August 1653]

Sir

'Tis most true that I could not Excuse it to my selfe if I should not write to you, and that I owe it to my owne sattisfaction as well as to yours. Or rather, tis a pleasure to mee, because 'tis acceptable to you. But I cannot think it deserv's that you should quitt all other Entertainments and leave your self nothing to bee

happy in, but that which is an Effect of the absence you complaine of, and that which if wee were but a litle more happy,
wee should quickly dispise. At the same time that my Letters tell
you I am well and still your friend, they tell you too that I am
where you cannot see mee and where I vainly wish you, and
when they are kindest and most welcom to you, they only show
that 'tis imposible I should desyr your happinesse more, or have
lesse power to make it. You shall not perswade mee to bee your
Mistresse if you would, I am too much your friend to act that
part well. I knew a Lady that rather then she would want an
occasion to bee Cruell, made it a fault in her Servant that hee
Loved her too much, and another, that hers was not Jealous of
her. Sure they forsee their Raign's are to bee but short and that
makes them such Tyrants.

I heard a good while agon that my Lady Udall[1] was resolvd
to marry a blinde man that lived in the house with her, and mee
thought twas an od story then, but since then you tell mee hee
has bin in love with her seventeen year, it apear's stranger to mee
a great deal, for if she did not love him what could perswade her
to marry him, and if she did, in my opinion she made him but
an ill requitall for seventeen years' service, to marry him when
she had spent all her youth & beauty with another. She was
handsom Enough once, or Else som Pictur's that I have seen of
her flattere her very much, that, and her witt together, gott her
soe many servant's, that they hinderd one another and he too I
think. Sir William Udall and his sonn were Rivalls and (which
was stranger) shee pleased them both, the son thought himself
sure of her as longe as hee lived, and the Father knew hee might
have her when his son was dead. This word, dead, makes mee
remember to ask a question that I have forgott twice or thrice,
they say my Lady St John is dead in childbirth, is it true, or
not[?] if it bee, Poore Mrs Fretcheville[2] is neerer being mad that
ere she was in her life, to Loose such a daughter and Eight thousand pound is more then her head can beare. 'Twas the younger
Mrs Bishop[3] that was courted like mee, but when that was, she
was not thought a beauty, for her elder sister (whoe in my Judg-

ment has noe Excesse ont neither) was Esteem'd the handsomer
in those day's, but a year or two mend's some as much as it
impaires other's and she may have now outgrowne what shee
had, of like mee, to her advantage, but 'tis most certain that wee
have somthing of likenesse in our humors still, for I should have
made the same ingenuous confession that shee did, if I had bin
putt to it, and Mr Hemingham's[4] £4000 a year would have
tempted mee as litle. Lord I would not bee soe perplex'd for the
whole world, as that poore man is where to finde a wife that
may bee young & handsome and that hee may bee secure in, for
hee say's she must bee a very sweet natur'd Lady, or else hee is in
danger of dyeing as meritoriously as the good husband you
mention, that hang'd himself. 'Twere noe great losse I think (as
you say) if his Brain's were broke as well as his heart, but for a
man that has noe more witt hee is the fullest of Caution that I
have heard of. & Sir Justinian[5] could not bee more wary in his
choice, and to say truth they are much in a condition, and have
both the same hopes and fear's. Only the last has somthing the
better opinion of himselfe and is (therfor) the most likly to bee
deceived.

I had a letter the last week from my Lady[6] whoe tell's mee
she has bin ill of a Paine at her stomack and that she has bin
drinking Barnett[7] waters, and has founde her self better since. I
thought they had bin soe Lately found out that nobody had
knowne what they had bin good for yett, or had ventur'd to
take them. I could wish they were as Proper for the Spleen as
Epsum, or Tunbridge, they would lye much more conveniently
for mee, besyd's that I have noe more heart to goe to Epsum
since Sir Robert Cook[8] dyed. Ah that good old man, I woulde
soe faine have had him but I have noe luck to them, they all dye,
if hee would have marry'd mee first and then have dyed twoul'd
not have greev'd mee half soe much as it do's now. Yet I was
offerd a new servant tother day, and after two howr's talk, and
that they[9] had tolde mee hee has as good as two thousand pound
a year in present, and a thousand more to come, I had not the
Curiosity to ask who twas, which they took soe ill that I think I

shall hear noe more on't. Never man made a worse bargain then
you did when you played for the ten Pounde I am to pay you
when I marry.[10] In conscience now, what would you give mee
to bee quit on't. Because you shall see I am your friend I will
release you for a favour at your wedding, but you must keep
your owne councell then, for there are a great many others
whome I have at the same advantage that must not Expect to
bee soe favourably used. My paper has not dealt soe well with
mee, I thought I had a side good still, but I see I must make an
End in Earnest and say I am your faithfull

Letter 38

[Saturday 3 or Sunday 4 September 1653]

Sir

It was sure a lesse fault in mee to make a scruple of reading your
letter to your Brother,[1] which in all Likelyhood I could not bee
concern'd in, then for you to condemn the freedome you take of
giveing mee dirrections in a thing where we are Equaly concern'd, therfor if I forgive you this you may Justly forgive mee
t'other, and upon these Term's wee are friend's againe, are wee
not[?]. Noe stay I have another fault to chide you for, you
doubted whither you had not writt too much and whither I
could have the Patience to read it or not. Why do you disemble
so abominably[?] you cannot think these things. How I should
Love that plaineheartednesse you speak of if you would use it,
nothing is civill but that, amongst friends.

Your kinde Sister ought to chide you too for not writeing to
her, unlesse you have bin with her to Excuse it,[2] I hope you
have, and pray take some time to make her one Visett for mee
carry my humble Service with you, and tell her that tis not my
fault you are noe better.

I doe not think I shall see the Towne before Michaelmas,

therfore you may make what sally's you please. I am tyed hear to Expect my Brother P.[3] and then posibly wee may goe up together, for I should bee at home againe before the Terme[.][4] then I may show you my Neece, and you may confesse that I am a kinde aunte to desyr her company since the disadvantage of our being together will lye wholy upon mee, but I must make it in my bargaine that if I come, you will not bee frighted to see mee. You think i'le warrant you have courage enough to Endure a worse sight, you may bee deceived, you ne're saw mee in mourning[5] yet, noebody that has, will ere desyre to doe it againe, for theire owne sakes, as well as mine. O tis a most dismall dresse, I have not dared to looke in the glasse since I wore it, and certainly if it did soe ill with Other People as it do's with mee, it would never bee worne. You told mee of writeing to your father,[6] but you did not say whither you had heard from him, or how hee did, may not I aske it him[?]. Is it possible that hee saw mee, where were my Ey's that I did not see him [?], for I beleeve I should have guessed at least twas hee, if I had; they say you are very like him. But tis noe wonder neither that I did not see him, for I saw not you when I mett you there, 'tis a place I looke upon nobody in, and it was reproached to mee by a Kinsman, (but a litle before you cam to mee) that hee had follow'd mee halfe a dousen shops to see when I would take notice of him, and was at last goeing away with a beliefe twas not I because I did not seem to know him. Other People make it soe much their buisnesse to gape that i'le swear they put mee soe out of Countenance I dare not look up for my life.

I am sory for Gen. Monk's[7] misfortune because you say hee is your friend, but Otherwise shee will suite well enough with the rest of the great Lady's of the tim's and become Greenwich as well as some Others doe the rest of the kings houses. If I am not mistaken that Monke has a brother lives in Cornwall,[8] an honnest Gentleman I have heard, and one that was a great acquaintance of a Brother of mine whoe was kill'd there during the Warr,[9] and soe much his friend that upon his death hee putt himself and his Famely into mourning for him, which is not usuall I think where there is noe relation of kindred.

I will take Order that my letters shall bee left with Jones,[10] and yours call'd for there. As long as your last was, I read it over thrice in lesse then an hower, though to say truth I skipt some on't the last time, I could not read my owne confession soe offten. Love is a Terrible word, and I should blush to death if any thing but a letter accused mee on't, pray bee mercifull and lett it run friendship in my next charge. My Lady sends mee word she has received those parts of Cyrus[11] I lent you, heer is another for you which when you have read you know how to dispose, there are fower Pritty story's in it L'Amante Absente, L'Amant non Aymé, L'Amant Jaloux, et L'Amant dont la Maitresse est mort. Tell mee which you have most compass[ion][12] for. When you have read what Every one say's for himself, perhaps you will not thinke it soe Easy to decide which is the most unhappy as you may think by the Titles theire Storry's bear, only let mee desyre you not to Pitty the Jelous one, for I remember I could doe nothing but Laugh at him, as one that sought his owne vexation. This and the litle Journy's (you say) you are to make, will Entertain you till I come, which sure will bee as soone as possible I can, since tis Equaly desyr'd by you and

Your faithfull

Letter 39

[Saturday 10 or Sunday 11 September 1653]

Sir

If want of kindenesse were the only Crime I exempted from pardon,[1] twas not that I had the least aprehension you could bee Guilty of it, but to show you (by Excepting only an imposible thing) that I Excepted nothing. Noe in Earnest, I can fancy noe such thing of you. Or if I could, the quarrell would bee to my self I should never forgive my owne ffolly that led mee to choose a friend that could bee false. But i'le leave this (which is not much to the purpose) and tell you how with my usuall impatience I Expected your letter, and how colde it went to my heart to see it soe short a one, twas soe great a paine to mee that I am resolved you shall not feell it nor can I in Justice, punnish you for a fault unwillingly committed. If I were your Enemy I could not use you ill, when I saw fortune doe it too, and in gallantry & good nature both I should think my self rather Obliged to prottect you from her injuryes (if it lay in my power) then double them upon you. These things considerd I beleeve this letter will bee longer than ordinary, kinder I think it cannot bee, I alway's speak my heart to you, and that is soe much your friend it never furnishes mee with any thing to your disadvantage.

I am glad you are an admirer of Telesile as well as I, in my opinion tis a fine Lady, but I know you will pitty Poore Amestris[2] strangly when you have read her Storry[.] i'le swear I cryed for her when I read it first though shee were an imaginary person, and sure if any thing of that kinde can deserve it her misfortunes may.

God forgive mee I was as neer Laughing Yesterday where I should not. Would you beleeve that I had the grace to goe heare a sermon upon a week day, in Earnest tis true, and Mr Marshall[3] was the Man that preached, but never any body was soe defeated,[4] hee is soe famed that I Expected rare things from him and seriously I listned to him at first with as much reverence and attention as if hee had bin Snt Paul. And what doe you think hee told us, why that if there were noe kings no Queens, noe Lord's no Lady's noe Gentlemen nor Gentlewomen, in the world, twould bee noe losse at all to God Almighty. This we had over some forty times which made mee remember it whither I would or not, the rest was much at this rate, Enterlarded with the prittyest od phrases that I had the most adoe to look soberly enough for the place I was in that ever I had in my life. Hee do's not preach soe alway's sure. If hee do's I cannot beleeve his Sermon's will doe much toward's the bringing any body to heaven, more then by Exerciseing there Patience.[5] Yet i'le say that for him, hee stood stoutly for Tyth's[6] though in my opinion few deserved them lesse then hee, and it may bee hee would bee better without them. Yet you are not Convinced you say that to bee miserable is the way to bee good[.] to some Natures I think it is not, but there are many of soe carelesse & vaine a Temper that the least breath of good fortune swell's them with soe much Pride, that if they were not putt in minde somtimes by a sound Crosse or two, that they are Mortall, they would hardly think it posible, and though tis a signe of a servile Nature when feare produces more of reverence in us then love, yet there is more danger of forgetting on's self in a prosperous fortune then in the contrary, and affliction may bee the surest (though not the pleasantest) Guide to heaven. What think you might I not preach with Mr Marshall for a wager[?] but you could fancy a perfect happinesse[7] heer you say. That is not much, many People doe soe, but I never heard of any body that had it more then in fancy soe that twill not bee Strange if you should misse on't. One may bee happy to a good degree I think in a faithfull friend, a Moderate fortune and a retired life, farther then this I know nothing to wish, but if there bee any thing beyond it I wish it you.

You did not tell mee what carryed you out of Towne in such hast, I hope the occasion was good. You must account to mee for all that I lost by it, I shall Expect a whole Pacquett next week. O mee I have forgott this once or twice to tell you that if it bee noe inconvenience to you I could wish you would change the place of dirrection for my letters[.] certainly that Jones[8] know's my Name I bespoke a sadle of him once, and though it bee a good while a gon, yet I was soe often with him aboute it haveing much adoe to make him understand how I would have it, it being of a ffashion hee had never seen though since it bee common, that I am confident hee has not forgott mee besydes that upon it hee gott my Brothers Custom and I cannot tell whither hee do's not use the shop still.

Jane presents her humble service to you and has sent you

somthing in a boxe,[9] tis hard to imagin what shee can finde heer to present you withall, and I am in doubt whither you will not pay to dear for it if you discharge the Carriage, tis a pritty freedom she takes but you may thank your selfe, shee thinks because you call her ffellow Servant she may use you accordingly, I bred her better, but you have spoyled her.

Is it true that my Lord Whitlock[10] goes Ambassador where my Lord L. should have gon[?]. I know not how hee may apear in a Swedish Court, but hee was never meant for a Courtier at home I beleeve. Yet tis a gracious Prince, hee is often in this Country and always do's us the favour to send for his fruit hither, hee was makeing a Purchase of one of the best houses in the County, I know not whither hee go's on with it, but tis such a one as will not become any thing lesse then a lord and there is a talke as if the Chancery[11] were goeing downe, if soe his title goes with it I think. Twill bee sad news for my Lord Keebles[12] son hee will have nothing left to say when my Lord my father[13] is taken from him. Were it not better that I had nothing to say neither, then that I should entertaine you with such sencelesse things. I hope I am halfe asleep nothing Else can Excuse mee, if I were sound asleep I should say fine things to you[,] I often dream I doe but perhaps if I could remember them they are noe wiser then my wakeing discourses, good night.

Letter 40

[Saturday 17 or Sunday 18 September 1653]

Sir

All my quarrells to you are kinde on's, for sure tis alike imposible for mee to bee angry as for you to give mee the occasion. Therefor when I chide[1] (unlesse it bee that you are not carefull Enough of your selfe and hazarde too much a health that I am more concerned in, then in my owne), you need not studdy much for

Excuses, I can Easily forgive you any thing but want of kindenesse. The Judgment you have made of the fower Lovers[2] I recomended to you do's soe perfectly agree with what I think of them, that I hope it will not Alter when you have read their Story's. L'Amant Absent has (in my opinion) a Mistresse, soe much beyonde any of the rest that to bee in danger of loosing her, is more then to have lost the others. L'Amant non Aimé was an Ass under favour, (notwithstanding the Princesse Cleobulines letter), his Mistresse had Caprices that would have suited better with our Amant Jaloux then with any body else. And the Prince Artibie was much too blame that hee outlived his belle Leontine. But if you have mett with the beginning of the story of Amestris & Aglatides, You will find the rest of it in this part I send you now, and tis to mee one of the Prittiest I have read and the most Naturall. They say the Gentelman that writes this Romance has a Sister that lives with him as Mayde[3] and she furnishes him with all the litle Story's that come between soe that hee only Contrives the maine designe and when hee wants somthing to Entertaine his company withall hee call's to her for it. Shee has an Exelent fancy sure, and a great deal of witt, but I am sorry to tell it you, they say tis the most ilfavourd Creatur that ever was borne, and it is often soe, how seldome doe wee see a person Exelent in any thing but they have some great deffect with it that pulls them low enough to make them Equall with Other People, and there is Justice in't. Those that have fortunes have nothing else, and those that want it deserve to have it. That's but small comfort though you'le say, 'tis confess't. But there is noe such thing as perfect happynesse in this world, those that have come the nearest it, had many things to wish, and – O mee whither am I goeing, sure tis the Deaths head I see stand before mee putt mee into this grave discourse, (pray doe not think I meant that for a conceite neither) how idly have I spent two sides of my paper and am affrayde besides I shall not have time to write two more, therfor i'le make hast to tell you, that my friendship for you, makes mee concern'd in all your relations, that I have a great respect for Sir meerly as hee is your Father, and that tis much increased by his kindnesse to you, that hee has all my Prayers and wishes for his safety and that you will Oblige mee in letting mee know when you heare any good news from him. Hee has mett with a great deal of good company I beleeve.

My Lady Ormonde[4] I am told is wayting for a passage and divers others, but this winde (if I am not mistaken) is not good for them. In Earnest 'tis a most sad thing that a person of her quality should bee reduced to such a fortune as she has lived upon these late year's and that shee should loose that which she brought as well as that which was her husbands. Yet I heer shee has now gott some of her owne Lands in Ir: granted her, but whither she will gett it when she com's there is I think a question. Wee have a Lady new come in this Country that I pitty too Extreamly. She is one of my Lord of Valentia's[5] daughters and has marryed an old fellow that is some threescore and ten whoe has a house that is fitter for the hoggs then for her, and a fortune that will not at all recompence the least of these inconveniency's. Ah tis most Certain I should have chosen a handsome Chaine to Leade my Apes in,[6] before such a husband but marryeng and hanging goe by destiny they say.[7] It was not mine it seem's to have an Emperour the spitefull man, meerly to vexe mee has gon and Marryed my Country Woman my Lord Lee's[8] daughter. What a multitude of willow garlands[9] shall I weare before I dye, I think I had best make them into fagotts this cold weather, the flame they would make in a Chimny would bee of more use to mee then that which was in the hearts of all those that gave them me and would last as long.

I did not think I should have gott thus farr, I have bin soe persecuted with Vissetts[10] all this week I have noe time to dispatch any thing of buisnesse soe that now I have don this I have 40 letters more to write. How much rather would I have them all to you then to any body else, or rather how much better would it bee if there needed none to you and that I could tell you without writeing

how much I am   Yours

Letter 41

[Saturday 24 or Sunday 25 September 1653]

Sir

Pray let not the aprehension that other's say finer things to mee make you[r] letters all the shorter, for if it were soe, I should not think they did, and soe Long you are safe. My Brother P.[1] indeed do's somtim's send mee letters that may bee Excelent for ought I know, and the more likely because I doe not understand them, but I may say to you (as to a friend) I doe not like them, and have wonderd that my Sister whoe (I may tell you too and you will not think it Vanity in mee) had a great [deale?][2] of Witt and was thought to write as well as most Women in England, never perswaded him to Alter his Stile and make it a litle more Intelligeble. Hee [is][3] an honnest Gentleman in Earnest, has understanding Enough, and was an Excelent husband to two very different Wives, as two good on's could bee. My Sister was a melancholy retir'd woman, and besydes the Company of her husband and her book's, never sought any, but could have spent a life much longer than hers was in lookeing to her house and her Children. This Lady is of a free Jolly humor, loves cards and company and is never more pleased then when she see's a great many Others that are soe too. Now with both these hee soe perfectly complyed that tis hard to guesse, which humor hee is more inclined to in himself perhaps to neither which makes it soe much the more strange. His kindenesse to his first wife may give him an Esteem for her Sister, but hee [was?][4] too much smitten with this Lady to think of marryeng any body else, and seriously I could not blame him, for she had, and has yet, great Lovlinesse in her, she was very handsom and is very good, one may read it in her face at first sight, a Woman that is hugely Civill to all People, and takes as Generaly as any body that I know. But not more then my Cousen M:[5] letters doe, which yet you doe not like you say, nor I neither i'le swere, and if it bee

ignorance in us both we'el forgive it one another. In my
Opinion these great Schollers are not the best writer's, (of
Letters I mean, of books perhaps they are) I never had I think
but one letter from Sir Jus:[6] but twas worth twenty of any body's
else to make mee sport, it was the most sublime nonsense that
in my life I ever read and yet I beleeve hee decended as low
as hee could to come neer my weak understanding. Twill bee
noe Complement after this to say I like your letters in themselv's, not as they come from one that is not indifferent to
mee. But seriously I doe. All Letters mee thinks should bee free
and Easy as ones discourse, not studdyed, as an Oration, nor
made up of hard words like a Charme. Tis an admirable thing
to see how some People will labour to finde out term's that
may Obscure a plaine sence, like a gentleman I knew, whoe
would never say the weather grew cold, but that Winter began
to salute us. I have noe patience for such Coxcomb's and
cannot blame an old Uncle of mine that threw the Standish[7]
at[8] his mans head because he writt a letter for him where instead of sayeing (as his Master bid him) that hee would have
writ himself but that hee had the Goute in his hand; hee sayed
that the Goute in his hand would not permitt him to put pen
to paper. The ffellow thought hee had mended it Mightily and
that putting pen to paper was much better then plaine writeing. I have noe Patience neither for these Translatours of
Romances. I mett with Polexandre and L'Illustre Bassa,[9] both
soe disguised that I who am theire old acquaintance hardly
knew them, besydes that they were still soe much french in
words and Phrases that twas imposible for one that understood
not french to make any thing of them. If Poore Prazimene[10]
bee in the same dresse I would not see her for the worlde she
has sufferd enough besydes. I never saw but 4 Tomes of her
and was told the Gentleman that writt her Storry dyed when
those were finnish'd, I was very sorry for it I remember, for I
liked [it?][11] soe farr as I had seen of it Extreamly. Is it not my
Good Lord of Monmouth[12] or some such honourable person-
age that presents her to the English Lady's. I have heard many

People wonder how hee spends his Estate, I beleeve hee undo's himself with printing his Translations, nobody else will undergoe the Charge because they never hope to sell enough of them to pay themselv's withall. I was lookeing tother day in a book of his where hee Translates Pipeur, a Piper and twenty words more that are as false as this.

My Lord Broghill[13] sure will give us somthing worth the reading. My Lord Saye,[14] I am told has writ a Romance since his retirement in the Isle of Lundee, and Mr Waller[15] they say is makeing one of Our Warr's, which if hee do's not mingle with a great deal of pleasing fiction cannot bee very diverting sure the Subject is soe sad. But all this is nothing to my comeing to Towne you'le say, tis confest, and that I was willing as long as I could to avoyde sayeing any thing when I had nothing to say worth your knoweing. I am still Obliged to wayte my Brother P. and his Lady's comeing I had a letter from him this week which I will send you that you may see what hopes hee gives.[16] As litle Roome as I have left too, I must tell you what a present I had made mee to day two [of][17] the finest Young Ireish Greyhounds[18] that ere I saw, a Gentleman that serv's the Generall sent them mee they are newly come over and sent for by H.C. hee tels mee but not how hee gott them for mee. However I am glad I have them and much the more because it dispenses with a very unfitt imployment that your father out of his kindenesse to you & his Civility to mee was content to take upon him.[19]

Letter 42

[Saturday 24 or Sunday 25 September 1653]

Nothing that is paper can scape mee[1] when I have time to write and tis to you. But that I am not willing to Excite your Envy, I would tell you how many Letters I have dispatch'd since I Ended yours and if I could shew them you, twould bee a certaine Cure for it, for they are all very short on's and most of them meerly complement which I am sure you care not for.

I had forgott, in my Other to tell you what Jane requir's for the Sattisfaction of what you confesse you owe her. You must promise her to bee merry and not to take Colde when you are at the Tennis Court for there shee hear's you were founde.

Because you mention my Lord Broghill and his witt I have sent you some of his Verses.[2] My B. urged them against mee one day in a dispute where hee would needs make mee confesse that noe Passion could bee long lived and that such as were most in love forgott that ever they had bin soe within a twelve month after they were Marryed, and in Earnest the want of Examples to bring for the Contreary puzled mee a litle, soe that I was faine to bring out these Pittifull Verses of my Lord Biron[3] to his wife, which was soe poore as Agument that I was e'en ashamed on't my self, and hee quickly Laught mee out of Countenance with sayeing they were Just as a marryed mans flame would produce, and a wife inspire. I send you a Love Letter too, which simple as you see it was sent in very good Earnest, and to a person of quality as I was told. If you read it when you goe to bed twill certainly make you sleep, aproved.[4]

I am Yours

Letter 43

[Saturday 1 or Sunday 2 October 1653]

Sir

You have furnish'd mee now with Arguments to convince my B:[1] if hee should ever enter upon the dispute againe. In Earnest I beleev'd all this before, but twas somthing an ignorant kinde of faith in mee, I was sattisfyed my self but could not tell how to perswade another of the truth on't, and to speak indifferently, there are such Multitudes that Abuse the names of Love and friendship, and soe very few, that either understand or practice it in reality, that it may raise great doubt's whither there is any such thing in the world or not and such as doe not finde it in themselv's, will hardly beleeve tis any where. But it will Easily bee granted that most People make hast to bee miserable, that they put on theire ffetter's as inconsideratly as a woodcock run's into a noose, and are carryed by the weakest considerations imaginable, to doe a thing of the greatest Consequence of any thing that concern's this worlde. I was tolde by one (whoe pretend's to know him very well) that nothing Tempted my Cousin O.[2] to marry his Lady (soe much) as that shee was an Earl's daughter, which mee thought was the prittiest fancy and had the least of sence out of any I had heard on, Considering that it was noe addition to her person, that hee had honour enough before for his Fortune, and how litle tis esteem'd in this Age. If it bee any thing in a better, which for my Part I am not well sattisfyed in besyd's that in this perticuler it dos not sound handsomly. My Lady Bridgett O: makes a worse name a great deal mee thinks then plaine my Lady O: would doe. And now I speak of Cousin's let mee tell you that (allowing all that Mrs F:[3] sayd of the person she recomended to you, to bee but complement, or that she thought she could not say lesse upon such an occasion) I may confesse, I think shee meant mee and spoke it as you say Malicieusement,[4] for tis true that her husband was proposed by one that is our Neighbor and has some interest in the Famely as a Trustee for the Estate I think. I heard my Mother speak of it once but how it fell to the grownd I cannot tell, perhaps hee was a litle ingaged then where hee is now fast. I have bin studdieng how Tom C. might come by his intelligence and I verily beleeve hee has it from my Cousin Peetres,[5] she lives neer them in Essex, and in all liklihood for want of Other discourse to Entertaine him withall she has come out with all shee know's. The last time I saw her she asked mee for you before she spoke six words to mee and I whoe of all things doe not love to make Secretts of Trifles told her I had seen you that day. She sayed noe more nor I neither but perhaps it worked in her litle braine. The best on't is the matter is not great, for though I confesse I had rather nobody knew it, yet tis that I shall never bee ashamed to owne.[6]

How kindly doe I take these civility's of your fathers in Earnest you cannot imagin how his letter[7] pleased mee. I used to respect him meerly as hee was your Father, but I begin now to owe it to himselfe, all that hee say's is soe kinde and soe Obligeing, soe Naturall and soe Easy that one may see tis perfectly his disposition and has nothing of disguise int. Tis long since that I knew how well he writ's perhaps you have forgott that you showed mee a letter of his (to a french Marquis I think or some such man of his acquaintanc[e][8]) when I first knew you. I remember it very well, & that I thought it as handsome a letter as I had seen, but I have noe skill it seem's, for I like Yours too.

You shall Excuse mee for giveing you leave to beleeve that I might have bin happy If I could have resolved to have bin soe without you. 'Tis very true that I never tryed to resolve it, for if I had, I think it had bin to very litle purpose, but If I could have don that, I know not whither I should have bin e're a whit the neerer being happy. If one could bee soe for resolving it, twere not soe hard a thing to get as tis beleev'd.

Is not your Cousin Rante left a Rich Widdow,[9] I was tolde soe to day and that shee is very handsome too a fine house I am sure shee has, it was my Lord Pagetts.[10] That name makes mee remember to tell you that I had a letter t'otherday from my Lady where she sends mee the news of her sister Izabella's[11] being come over, if you saw it you would conclude with mee that where she loves, tis with passion, she is as absolutly wilde with Joy, as any thing in Bedlam[12] is mad, and all that she say's is soe strangly disjoynted that one whoe did not know her would think she were a very od body, but yet it is a thousand times more naturall then the Oxford letter you sent mee,[13] I doe not Envy that kinde of witt by noe mean's, such Extravagancy's as you say seldom mean any thing.

I can pardon all my Cousin Fr: litle plotts of discovery if shee beleeved her self when she say'd she was confident our humors would agree Extreamly well. In Earnest I think they doe, for I marke that I am always of your opinion unlesse it bee when you will not allow that you write well for there I am too much concern'd. Jane told mee t'other day very soberly that wee writt very much alike[,] I think she say'd it with an intent to please mee and did not faile int, but if you write ill twas noe great complement to mee. A propos de Janne she bids mee tell you that if you liked your Marmelade of Quince[14] she could sende you more and she thinks better, that has bin made since.

Twas a strange Caprice as you say of Mrs Harrison,[15] but there is fate as well as love in those things. The Queen tooke the greatest pain's to perswade her from it that could bee, and (as sombody say's I know not who) Majestye is noe ill Oratour.[16] But all would not doe, when she had nothing to say for her self she told her shee had rather begg with Mr Howards then live in the greatest plenty that could bee with either my Lord Br:, Charles Rich or Mr Nevill,[17] for all these were dyeng for her then. I am affray'd shee has Alterd her opinion since twas too late, for I doe not take Mr H: to bee a person that can deserve one should necglect all the world for him, and where there is noe reason to uphold a passion it will sinke of it self but where there is it may last   Eternaly   I am   Yours[18]

Letter 44

[Saturday 8 or Sunday 9 October 1653]

Sir

You would have mee say somthing of my comeing. Alasse, how faine I would have somthing to say, but I know noe more then you saw in that letter that I sent you.[1] How willingly would I tell you any thing that I thought would please you, but I confesse I doe not love to give uncertaine hopes because I doe not care to receive them, and I thought there was noe need of sayeing I would bee sure to take the first occasion and that I wayted with impatience for it, because I hoped you had beleev'd all that already. And soe you doe I am sure, say what you will you cannot but know my heart enough to bee assur'd that I wish my self with you for my owne sake as well as yours. Tis rather that you love to heare mee say it often, then that you doubt it, for I am noe dissembler, I could not Cry for a husband that were indifferent to mee (like your Cousen)[2] noe nor for a husband that I loved neither I think, twould break my heart sooner then make mee shed a tear, 'tis ordinary greifs that only make mee weep. In Earnest you cannot imagin how often I have bin told that I had too much franchise in my humor and that 'twas a point of good breeding to disguise handsomly, but I answerd still for my self that twas not to bee Expected I should bee Exactly bred that had never seen a Court since I was capable of any thing. Yet I know soe much that my Lady Carlisle[3] would take it very ill if you should not let her get the point of honnour. Tis all she Aim's at to goe beyond every body in Complement. But are you not affrayde of giveing mee a strang Vanity with telling mee that I write better then the most Extreordinary person in the Kingdom[?] if I had not the sence to understand that the reason why you like my letters better is only because they are kinder then hers, such a word might have undon mee.

But my Lady Izabella[4] that speaks & looks and sings & play's & all soe Prittily, why cannot I say that she is as free from fault's as her Sister beleev's her. Noe, I am affray'd she is not, and sorry that those she has are soe generaly known. My B. did not bring them for an Example but I did, and made him confesse she had better have marryed a begger, then that beast with all his Estate; she canot bee excused but certainly they run a strange hazard that have such husbands as makes them think they cannot bee more undon whatever course they take, O tis ten thousand pitty's. I remember she was the first woman that ever I took notice of for Extreamly handsom, and in Earnest shee was then the Lovlyest thing that could bee lookt on I think, but what should she doe with beauty now. Were I as shee I would hide my self from all the world, I should think all people that Looked on mee read it in my face and dispised mee in theire hearts, and at the same time they made mee a leg or spoke Civily to mee I should beleeve they did not think I deserved theire respect. I'le tell you whoe hee urged for an Example though, my Lord Pembrok[5] and my Lady whoe they say are upon Parteing after all his Passion for her, and his marryeng her against the consent of all his friends. But to that I answer'd that though hee prettended great Kindnesse hee had for her, I never heard of much she had for him, and knew she marryed him meerly for advantage. Nor is she a woman of that discretion as to doe all that might become her, when she must doe it rather as things fitt too bee don then as things she is inclined to, besyd's, that what with a spleenatick side and a Chimickall head, hee is but an odd body himself. But is it possible what they say that my Lord Liec:[6] and my Lady are in great disorder, and that after 40 years patience hee has now taken up the Cudgells and resolves to Venture for the Mastery. Meethinks hee wakes out of his long sleep like a froward Childe that wrangles and fights with all that com's neer it, they say hee has turned away almost every servant in the house and left her at Penshurst[7] to disgest[8] it as she can. What an Age doe wee live in where 'tis a Miracle if in ten Couple that are marryed two of them live soe as not to publish it to the world that they cannot agree. I begin to bee of the opinion of him that (when the Roman Church first propounded whither it were not convenient for Priest[s] not to marry) sayed that it might bee convenient enough but sure it was not our Saviours intention for hee comanded that all should take up theire Crosse and follow him, and for his part hee was Confident there was noe such Crosse as a wife. This is an ill doctrine for mee to preach but to my friends I cannot but confesse that I am affrayde much of the fault lyes in us, for I have observed that Generaly in great famely's[9] the Men sildom disagree, but that the women are alway's scolding, and tis most certain that lett the husband bee what hee will if the wife have but patience (which sure becoms her best) the disorder cannot bee great enough to make a noise.

His anger alone when it meet's with nothing that resists it cannot bee loude enough to disturbe the Neighbours, and such a wife may bee sayd to doe, as a kinswoman of Ours, that had a husband whoe was not alway's him self, and when hee was otherwise, his humor was to rise in the night, and with two bedstaves[10] tabour[11] upon the table an houre together, shee took care every night to lay a great Cushen upon the table for him to strike on that noebody might heer him and soe discover his madnesse. But tis a sad thing when all on's happinesse is only that the world dos not know you are miserable. For my part I think it were very convenient that all such as intend to marrye should live together in the same house some year's of probation and if in all that time they never disagreed they should then bee permitted to marry if they pleasd, but how few would doe it then. I doe not remember that I ever saw or heard of any couple that were bred up soe together, (as many you know are, they that are design'd for one another from Children) but they alwayes disliked one another Extreamly and parted if it were left in theire Choise. If People proceeded with this caution the world would End sooner then is Expected I beleeve, and because with all my Warinesse tis not imposible but I may bee caught, nor likely, that I should bee wiser then Every body Else, twere best I think that I sayed noe more in this point.

What would I give to know that Sister[12] of yours that is soe good at discovery Sure she is Excelent Company. Shee has reason to Laugh at you when you would have perswaded her the mosse was sweet. I remember Jane brought some of it to mee to ask mee if I thought it had noe ill smell and whither shee might venture to put it in the boxe[13] or not. I told her as I thought she could not putt a more innocent thing there for I did not finde that it had any Smell at all, besyd's that I was willing it should doe mee some Service in requitall of the Pain's I had taken for it. My Neece[14] and I wanderd through some 6 hundred Acres of wood in search of it, to make rocks, and strang things that her head is full of, and she admires it more then you did. If she had known I had consented it should have bin used to fill up a boxe she would have condemn'd mee Extreamly. I told Jane that you liked her present, and she I finde is resolved to spoyle your complement and make you confesse at last that they are not worth the Eateing. She Threatens to send you more, but you would forgive her if you saw how she baites mee Every day to goe to London, all that I can say will not sattisfye her. When I urge (as tis true) that there is a necessity of my stay heer, she grow's furious, cry's you will dye with melancholy and confounds mee soe with Storry's of your ill humor that i'le swere I think I should goe meerly to bee at quiett, if it were posible, though there were noe other reason for it. But I hope tis not soe ill as she would have mee beleive it though I know your humor is strangly Alterd from what it was, and I am sorry to see it. Melancholy must needs doe you more hurt then to another to whome it may bee Naturall, as I think it is to mee, therfore if you loved mee you would take heed ont. Can you beleeve that you are dearer to mee then the whole world besyd's and yet necglect yourself. If you doe not, you wrong a perfect friendship, and if you doe, you must consider my interest in you and preserve your self to make mee happy[.] promise mee this or I shall haunte you worse then she doe's mee.

Scrible how you please soe you make your Letters longe enough You see I give you good Example. Besyd's I can assure you wee doe perfectly agree if you receive noe sattisfaction but from my letters I have none but what yours give mee.

Letter 45

[Saturday 15 or Sunday 16 October 1653]

Sir

Why are you soe sullen, and why am I the cause. Can you beleeve that I doe willingly deffer my Journy, I know you doe not. Why then should my Absence now bee lesse suportable to you then heretofore. It cannot, nay it shall not bee long (if I can help it) & I shall break thorough all inconvency's [*sic*] rather then deny you any thing that ly's in my power to grant. But by your owne rules then may not I expect the same from you. Is it possible that all I have sayed cannot Oblige you to a care of your Selfe. What a pleasant distinction you make when you say tis not melancholy that makes you doe these things but a carelesse forgetfulnesse, did ever any body forget themselv's to that degree that was not melancholy in Extreamity. Good God how are you Alterd[1] and what is it that has don it. I have knowne you when of all the things in the world you would not have bin taken for a discontent, you were as I thought perfectly pleased with your condition, what has made it soe much worse since. I know nothing you have lost and am sure you have gained a friend, A friend that is capable of the highest degree of friendship you can propounde that has already given an intire heart for that which she received and tis noe more in her will then in her power ever to recall it or devide it. If this bee not Enough to sattisfye you, tell mee what I can doe more. I shall finde lesse difficulty in the doeing it then in imagining what it may bee. And will not you then doe soe much for my sake as to bee careful of a health I am soe infinitely concern'd in and which these Courses must need's distroy. If you Loved mee you would, I am sure you would, and let mee tell you, you can never bee that perfect friend you describe if you can deny mee this. But will not your wife[2] beleeve there is such a friendship. I am not of her opinion at all but I doe not wonder neither that she is of it. Alas how few there are that ever heard of such a thing, and ffewer that understand it, besyd's it is not to bee taught or Learn'd it must come Naturaly to those that have it and those must have it before they can know it. But I admire, since she has it[3] not, how she can bee sattisfyed with her condition, nothing else sure can recompence the Alteration you say is made in her fortune. What was it took her, her husbands good face, what could invite her where there was neither fortune witt nor good usage and a husband to whome she was but indifferent which is all one to mee if not worse then

an Aversion and I should sooner hope to gaine upon one that
Hated mee then upon one that did not consider mee enough
either to Love or hate mee. I'le swere she is much Easyer to
please then I should bee, there are a great many ingredients must
goe to the makeing mee happy in a husband. First as my Cousin
Fr: say's our humors must agree,[4] and to doe that hee must have
that kinde of breeding that I have had and used that kinde of
company, that is hee must not bee soe much a Country Gentleman as to understand Nothing but hawks and dog's and bee
fonder of Either then of his wife, nor of the next sort of them
whose aime reaches noe further then to bee Justice of peace and
once in his life high Sheriff, who read noe book but Statut's and
study's nothing but how to make a speech interlarded with Latin
that may amaze his disagreeing poore Neighbours and fright
them rather then perswade them into quietnesse. Hee must not
bee a thing that began the world in a free scoole was sent from
thence to the University and is at his farthest when hee reaches
the Inn's of Court has noe acquaintance but those of his forme[5]
in these places speaks the french hee has pickt out of Old Law's,
and admires nothing but the Storry's hee has heard of the Revells
that were kept there before his time. Hee must not bee a Towne
Gallant neither that lives in a Tavern and an Ordinary,[6] that
cannot imagin how an hower should bee spent without company
unless it bee in sleeping that makes court to all the Women hee
sees thinks they beleeve him and Laughs and is Laught at Equaly;
Nor a Traveld Monsieur whose head is all feather inside and
outside, that can talk of nothing but dances and Duells, and has
Courage Enough to were slashes when every body else dy's with
cold to see him.[7] Hee must not bee a foole of noe sort, nor
peevish nor ill Natur'd nor proude nor Coveteous, and to all this
must bee added that he must Love mee and I him as much as
wee are capable of Loveing. Without all this his fortune though
never soe great would not sattisfye mee and with it a very
moderat one would keep mee from ever repenting my disposall.

I have bin as large and as perticular in my discriptions as my
Cousin Molle in his of Moore Park;[8] but that you know the

place soe well I would send it you, nothing can come neer his Patience in writing it but my reading ont. But would you had sent mee your fathers letter,[9] it would not have bin lesse welcome to mee then to you, and you may safely beleeve that I am Equaly concern'd with you in any thing. I should bee pleased too to see somthing of my Lady Carlisles[10] writeing because she is soe Extreordinary a Person.

I have bin thinking of sending you my Picture till I could come my self but a Picture is but dull company and that you need not, besyd's I cannot tell whither it bee very like mee or not though tis the best I have ever had drawne for mee and Mr Lilly[11] will have it that hee never took more pain's to make a good one in his life. And that was it I think that spoiled it. Hee was condemned for makeing the first hee drew for mee a little worse then I, and in makeing this better hee has made it as unlike tother. Hee is now I think at my Lord Pagetts[12] at Marloe where I am promised hee shall draw a Picture of my Lady for mee, she giv's it mee she say's as the greatest testimony of her friendship to mee, for by her owne rule she is past the time of haveing Pictur's taken of her, After Eighteen shee say's there is noe face but decay's aparantly. I would faine have had her Excepted such as had never bin beauty's, for my comfort, but she would not.

When you see your friend Mr Heningham[13] You may tell him in his Eare there is a Willow Garland[14] coeming towards him. Hee might have sped better in his suite if hee made court to mee as well as to my La: Ru:,[15] shee has bin my wife[16] this Seven year and who soever pretends there must ask my Leave; I have now given my consent that she shall marry a Very pritty litle Gentleman Sir Chr: Yelverton's Son[17] and I think wee shall have a wedding ere it bee long. My Lady her Mother[18] in great kindenesse would have recomended Hen:[19] to mee and told mee in a Complement that I was fitter for him then her daughter whoe was younger and therfore did not understand the world soe well, that she was certain if hee knew mee hee would bee Extreamly taken, for I would make just that kinde of wife hee looked for. I humbly thankt her but sayed that without knowing him (more then by relation) I was certain hee would not make that kinde of husband I looked for, and soe it went noe further.

I expect my Eldest brother heer shortly whose fortune is well mended by my Other brothers death, soe as if hee were sattisfyed himself with what hee has don,[20] I know noe reason why hee might not bee very happy, but I am affrayd hee is not. I have not seen my Sister[21] since I knew shee was soe, but sure she can have lost noe beauty, for I never saw any shee had but good black Ey's which cannot Alter. Hee Lov's her I think at the Ordinary rate of husbands, but not enough I beleeve to marry her soe much to his disadvantage if it were to doe again, and that would kill mee were I as shee for I could bee infinitly better sattisfyed with a husband that had never Loved mee in hope hee might, then with one that began to Love mee lesse then hee had don.   I am   Yours

Letter 46

[Saturday 22 or Sunday 23 October 1653]

Sir

You say I abuse you, and Jane say's you abuse mee when you say you are not melancholy, which is to bee beleev'd. Neither I think, for I could not have sayd soe positively as (it seem's) she did, that I should not bee in Towne till my B: came back. Hee was not gon when she writt nor is not yet, and if my B: Peyton had come before his goeing, I had spoyld her prediction. But now it cannot bee for hee goes on Monday or Tuesday at farthest.[1] I hope you deal truely with mee too in sayeing that you are not melancholy (though she dos not beleeve it). I am thought soe many times when I am not at all guilty on't. How often doe I sitt in company a whole day and when they are gon am not able to give an account of six words that was sayd, and many times could bee soe much better pleased with the Entertainment my owne thoughts give mee, that tis all I can doe to bee soe civill as not to let them see they trouble mee, this may bee your disease. However remember you have promised mee to bee carefull of your self and that if I secure what you have intrusted mee with, you will answer for the rest. Bee this our bargain then, and look that you give mee as good an account of one, as I shall give you of tother. In Earnest I was strangly vexed to see my self forst to disapoint you soe, and felt your trouble and my owne too. How often have I wisht my self with you though but for a day for an hower, I would have given all the time I am to spend heer for it with all my heart. You could not but have Laught if you had seen mee last night. My Br: and Mr Gibson[2] were talking by the fyre and I satt by, but as noe part of the company. Amongst other things (which I did not at all minde) they fell into a discourse of fflyeing and both agreed that it was very posible to finde out a way that people might fly like Birds and dispatch theire Journy's soe I that had not sayd a word all night started up at that and desyr'd they would say a litle more in it, for I had not marked the begining, but instead of that they both fell into soe Violent a Laughing that I should apeare soe much concern'd in such an Art; but they litle knew of what use it might have bin to mee. Yet I saw you last night but twas in a dream, and before I could say a word to you, or you to mee, the disorder my Joy to see you had put mee into waked mee.

Just now I was interupted too and call'd away to Entertain two dumbe Gentlemen.[3] You may imagin whither I was pleased to leave my writeing to you for theire company, they have made such a tedious Visett too, and I am soe tyred with makeing of sign's and tokens for every thing I had to say, good god, how doe those that live always with them. They are Brothers and the Eldest is a Barronett, has a good Estate, a wiffe & three or 4 Children, hee was my Servant heretofore and com's to see mee still for old Lov's sake, but if hee could have made mee Mistresse of the worlde, I could not have had him, and yet i'le swere hee has nothing to bee disliked in him but his want of Tongue, which in a woman might have bin a Vertue.

I sent you a part of Cyrus[4] last week where you will meet with one Doralize in the Story of Abradate and Panthée[,] the whole story is very good but her humor makes the best part of it. I am of her opinion in most things that she say's, in her Character of L'honnest hôme that she is in search of, and her resolution of receiveing noe heart that had bin offerd to any body else. Pray tell mee how you like her, and what fault you finde in my Lady Car:[5] letter, my thinks the hand and the Stile both show her a great person, and tis writt in the way that's now affected by all that pretend to witt and to good breeding, only I am a litle scandalised I confesse that she uses that word faithfull, she that never knew how to bee soe in her life.

I have sent you my Picture[6] because you wisht for it, but pray let it not presume to disturbe my Lady Sunderlands,[7] put it in some Corner where noe Ey's may finde it out but yours to whome it is only intended, tis noe very good one but the best I shall ever have drawne of mee for as my Lady say's my time for Pictur's is past, and therfor I have alway's refused to part with this because I was sure the next would bee a worse. There is a beauty in Youth that every body has once in theire lives, and I remember my Mother used to say there was never any body (that was not deformed) but were handsom to some reasonable degree, once between fowerteen and twenty. It must hang with the light on the left hand of it, and you may keep it if you please till I bring you the Originall, but then I must borrow it, (for tis noe more mine if you like it) because my Br: is often bringing People into my Closet where it hangs to show them Other Pictur's that are there and if hee should misse this long from thence 'twould trouble his Jealous head.[8]

You are not the first that has told mee I knew better what quality I would not have in a husband, then what I would, but it was more pardonable in them, I thought you had understood better what kinde of person I liked then any body else could posibly have don, and therfor did not think it necessary to make you that discription too, those that I reckon'd up were only such as I could not bee perswaded to have, upon noe term's, though I had never seen such a person in my life as Mr T. not but that all those may make very good husbands to some women, but they

are soe different from my humor that tis not posible wee should
ever agree, for though it might bee reasonable enough expected
that I should conforme mine to their's, (to my shame bee it
spoken) I could never doe it, and I have lived soe longe in the
world and soe much at my owne liberty that whosoever has mee
must bee content to take mee as they finde mee, without hope of
ever makeing mee other then I am, I cannot soe much as disguise
my humor. When it was designed that I should have had Sir
Jus:,[9] my Br: used to tell mee hee was confident that with All his
wisdom, any woman that had witt and discretion might make
an Asse of him and Govern him as shee pleased. I could not deny
but posibly it might bee soe, but twas that, I was sure I could
never doe, and though 'twas likely I should have forced myselfe
to soe much complyance as was necessary for a reasonable wife,
yet farther then that noe designe could ever have carryed mee,
and I could not fflattered him into a beleife that I admir'd
him, to gaine more then hee and all his Generation are wor[th].[10]
Tis such an Ease (as you say) not to bee sollicitous to please
Others, in Earnest I am noe more concern'd whither people think
mee hands[om][11] or ilfavourd whither they think I have witt or
that I have none then I am whither they think my name Eliz: or
Dor:. I would doe nobody noe injury, but I should never desyre
to please above one and that one I must Love too, or else I
should think it a trouble and consequently not doe it. I have
made a generall confession to you, will you give mee absolu-
tion[?] mee thinks you should for you are not much better by
your own relation, therfor tis easyest for us to forgive one another. When you hear any thing from your father remember
that I am his humble Servant and much concern'd in his
health.   I am   Yours

MESSAGES DURING THE LONDON VISIT[12]

A

I finde my conscience a litle troubled till I have asked your pardon for my ill humor Last night, will you forgive mee in Earnest, I could not helpe it, but I mett with a Cure for it. My B. kept mee up to hear his Learned Lecture till after two a clock and I spent all my ill humor upon him and yet wee parted very quietly and look'd as if a litle good fortune might make us good friends. But your speciall friend my E.B.,[13] I have a story to tell you of him. Will my Cousen Fr:[14] come think you, send mee word it may bee twas but a complement, if I can see you this morning I will but I dare not promise it.

B

Now I have gott the trick of breaking my word I shall doe it Every day. I must goe to Roe hampton[15] to day, but tis all one you doe not care much for seeing mee, well my Master remember Last Night you swaggerd like a Young Lord, i'le make y[our][16] Stomack come downe, rise quickly you had [best?][17] and come hither that I may give you you[r][18] Lesson this morning before I goe.

C

Je n'ay guere plus dormie que vous et mes songes n'ont pas Estes moins confuse au rest un bande de Violons, qui sont venu Jouer sous ma fennestre m'ont tourmentés de tel façon que je doubt fort si je pourvi jamais, les souffrire encor je ne suis pourtant pas en fort mavaise humeur et je m'envoy ausi tost que je Seray habillie Voire ce qu'il est posible de faire pour Vostre sattisfaction apres je Viendre vocy rendre contre de nos affairs et quoy qui'l en sera vous ne sçaurois jamais doubté que Je ne vous ayme plus que toutes les Choses du monde.[19]

D

I have slept as litle as you and may bee allowed to talk as unreasonably yet I find I am not quite sencelesse[,] I have a heart still that cannot resolve to refuse you any thing within its power to grant But Lord where shall I see you People will think mee mad if I goe abroade this morning after having seen mee in the condition I was in Last night, and they will think it strang to see you heer, could you not stay till they are all gone to Roe hampton[?] they goe this morning, I doe but aske though doe what you please only beleeve you doe a great injustice if you think mee false I never resolvd to give you an Etternell ffarwell but I resolved at the same time to part with all the comfort of my life and whither I told it you or not I shall dye yours

tell mee what you will have mee doe

E

Heer comes the note again to tell you I cannot call on you to night, I cannot help it and you must take it as patiently as you can but I am ingaged to night at the three Kings to sup and play. Poore man I am sorry for you in Earnest I shall be quite spoyld I see noe remedy[,] think whither it were not best to leave mee and begin a new adventure

Letter 47

[Saturday 26 November 1653]

Had you the bitt of paper I sent you from St Albon's[1] twas a strang one I beleeve as my humor was when I writt it. Well heer I am,[2] God know's for how long or short a time, nor shall I bee able to guesse till all our Company that we expect is come,[3] then, as I finde theire humors I shall resolve. Why did you not

tell mee how ill I looked[?] all People heer will not beleeve but
I have bin desperatly sick. I doe not finde that I am ill though
but I have lost a Collop[4] that's Certaine, and now I am come
to my owne glasse I finde I have not brought downe the
same face I carryed up,[5] but tis noe matter, tis well enough
for this place. I shall hear from you a Thursday, and next week
I shall bee able to say much more then I can this, both because
I shall have more time, and besyd's I shall know more. You
will send the Picture[6] and forgett not that you must walke
noe more in the Cloisters,[7] noe, in Earnest tis not good for
you and you must bee ruled by mee in that point, besyd's if
wee doe not take care of our selv's I find nobody else will. I
would not live though, if I had not some hope left that a litle
time may breed great Alterations, and that tis posible wee may
see an End of our misfortunes. When that hope leav's us,
then tis time to dye, and if I know my self I should need
noe more to kill mee. Let your letter bee as much too long
as this is too short, I shall finde by that how I must write. I
doe not think this is sence nor have I time to look it over.

I am yours

Letter 48

[Thursday 8 – Saturday 10 December 1653]

Haveing tyr'd my selfe with thinking, I mean to weary you with
reading, and revenge my selfe that way for all the unquiet
thoughts you have given mee. But I intended this a sober letter,
and therfor (sans Raillerie) let mee tell you I have seriously considerd all our misfortunes,[1] and can see noe End of them but by
submitting to that which wee cannot avoyde and by yeelding to
it, break the force of a blowe which if resisted brings a certain
Ruine. I think I need not tell you how dear you have bin to mee
nor that in your kindenesse I placed all the sattisfaction of my

life, 'twas the onely happinesse I proposed to my selfe, and had sett my heart soe much upon it, that it was therfore made my punishment, to let mee see that how innocent soever I thought my affection, it was guilty, in being greater then is allowable for things of this world. 'Tis not a melancholy humor gives mee these aprehensions and inclinations, nor the perswasions of Others, tis the result of a longe Strife with my selfe, before my Reason could overcome my passion, or bring mee to a perfect Resignation to whatsoever is alotted for mee. Tis now don I hope, and I have nothing left, but to perswade you to that which I assure my self your owne Judgment will aprove in the end and your reason has often prevailed with you to offer. That which you would have don then out of kindenesse to mee, and point of honnor,[2] I would have you doe now out of wisdome and kindenesse to your self, not that I would disclaime my part in it, or lessen my Obligation to you, noe, I am your friend as much as ever I was in my life, (I think more), and am sure I shall never bee lesse. I have knowne you long enough to discerne that you have all the quality's that make an excelent friend, and I shall indeavour to deserve that you may bee soe to mee. But I would have you doe this upon the justest grownd's and such as may conduce most to your quiett and future sattisfaction. When wee have tryed all wayes to happinesse, there is noe such thing to bee found, but in a minde conformed to on's condition whatsoever it bee, and in not aymeing at any thing that is either imposible, or improbable. All the rest is but Vanity and Vexation of Spirritt,[3] and I durst pronounce it soe from that litle knowledge I have had of the world though I had not Scripture for my warrant. The Shepheard that bragged to the Travelour whoe asked him what weather it was like to bee, that it should bee what weather pleased him,[4] and made it good by sayeing it should bee what weather pleased God and what pleased God should please him, sayed an Excelent thing in rude Language, and knew enough to make him the happiest person in the worlde if hee made a right use on't. There can bee noe pleasure in a struggling life, and that ffolly which wee condemne in an

Ambitious man, that's ever labouring for that which is hardly gott and more uncertainly kept, is seen in all according to theire severall humors. In some tis Coveteousnesse in others Pride, in some a Stubbornesse of Nature that chooses to goe alway's against the Tide, and in others, an unfortunate ffancy to things that are in themselv's innocent, till wee make them otherwise by desyreing them too much. Of this sort I think you and I are, wee have lived hitherto upon hopes soe Aïrye that I have often wonderd how they could support the weight of our misfortunes. But passion gives a Strength above Nature, wee see it in mad People, (and not to fflatter our selves) ours is but a refined degree of madnesse. What can it bee else, to be lost to all things in the world but that single Object that takes up on's ffancy to loose all the quiet and repose of on's life in hunting after it, when there is soe litle likelyhood of ever gaineing it, and soe many, more probable, accidents, that will infallibly make us misse of it. And (which is more then all) tis being Masterd by that, which Reason & Religion teaches us to governe, and in that onely gives us a preheminence above Beasts. This soberly considerd is enough to let us see our errour, and consequently to perswade us to redeeme it. To another Person I should Justifie my selfe that tis not a lightnesse in my Nature, nor any interest that is not Common to us both, that has wrought this Change in mee. To you that knowe my heart and from whome I shall never hide it, to whome a thousande Testimony's of my Kindenesse can wittnesse the reality of it, and whose ffriendship is not built upon common grownd's, I have noe more to say, but that I impose not my opinions upon you and that I had rather you tooke them up, as your owne Choice, then upon my intreaty's. But if as wee have not differd in anything else wee could agree in this too, and resolve upon a friendship that will bee much the Perfecter for haveing nothing of passion in it, how happy might wee bee. Without soe much as a fear of the Change that any accident could bring, wee might deffye all that fortune could doe, and putting of all disguise & constraint, (with that which onely made it necessary) make our lives as Easy to us as the condition of this worlde will permitt. I may owne You as a Person that I Extreamly Value and Esteem and for whome I have a particuler friendship, and you may consider mee as one that will alway's bee

Your faithfull

This was writt when I expected a letter from you,[5] how cam I to misse it. I thought at first it might bee the Carriers fault in changeing his Inne, without giveing notice, but hee assur's mee hee did to Nan.[6] My Brothers groome cam downe to day too and saw her hee tells mee, but brings mee nothing from her. If nothing of ill bee the cause I am contented. You heare the noise my Lady Anne Blunt[7] has made with her marryeng, I am soe weary with meeting it in all places where I goe, from what is shee ffallen, they talked but the week before that shee should have my Lord of Strafford.[8] Did you not intende to write to mee when you writt to Jane[?] that bit of paper did mee great service, without it I should have had strange aprehensions, all my sad dreams and the severall frights I have waked in would have run soe in my head that I should have concluded somthing of very ill from your silence.

Poore Jane is sick but she will write she say's if she can.

Did you send the last part of Cyrus[9] to Mr Hollingsworth.[10]

Letter 49

[Saturday 10 or Sunday 11 December 1653]

Sir

Tis most true what you say that few have what they merritt; if it were Otherwise you would bee happy I think; but then I should bee soe too, and that must not bee, a falce and an inconstant person, cannot merit it I am sure.

You are kinde in your good wishes but I aime at noe friends, nor noe Princes,[1] the honour would bee lost upon mee. I should become a Crowne soe ill there would bee noe Striveing for it after mee; and sure I should not weare it longe. Your letter was a much greater losse to mee then that of H:C: and therfor tis that with all my care and dilligence I cannot inquire it out. You will not complaine I beleeve of the shortnesse of my last, whatsoever else you dislike in it. And if I spare you at any time tis because I cannot but imagin, since I am soe wearisom to my self that I must needs bee soe to Every body else[2] though at present I have other occasions that will not permitt this to bee a longe one. I am sorry it should bee only in my Power to make a friend misserable, and that where I have soe great kindenesse I should doe soe great injurie, but tis my fortune and I must bear it, twill bee none to you I hope to pray for you, nor to desire that you would (all passion laide aside) freely tell mee my faults that I may at least aske your forgivnesse where tis not in my power to make you better sattisfaction. I would faine make Even with all the worlde, and bee out of danger of dyeng in any body's debt, then, I have nothing more to doe in it but to Expect when I shall bee soe happy as to leave it, and alway's to remember that my misfortune makes all my fault towards you, and that my faults to god made all my misfortunes.   Your unhappy

Letter 50

[Saturday 17 or Sunday 18 December 1653]

Sir

I am extreamly sorry that your letter miscaryed but I am confident my B: has it not.[1] As cunning as hee is, hee could not hide it soe from mee, but that I should discover it some way or other. Noe hee was heer, and both his men, when this letter should

have come, and not one of them stird out that day, indeed the
next day they went all to London. The note you writt to Jane[2]
cam in one of Nans by Collins but nothing else. It must bee lost
by the Porter that was sent with it, and twas very unhappy that
there should bee any thing in it of more consequence then ordinary, it may bee numbred amongst the rest of our misfortun's, All
which an inconsiderat passion has occasioned. You must pardon
mee I cannot bee reconciled to it, 't has bin the ruine of us both.
Tis true that nobody must imagin to themselv's, ever to bee
absolute Masters ont, but there is great difference betwixt that
and yeelding to it, between striveing with it, and soothing it up
till it grow's too strong for one. Can I remember how ignorantly
and innocently I sufferd it to steall upon mee by degrees, how
under a maske of friendship I cousen'd my self into that, which
had it apeard to mee at first in its true shape, I had fear'd and
shunn'd. Can I discerne that it has made the trouble of your life,
and cast a cloude upon mine that will help to cover mee in my
grave. Can I know that it wrought soe upon us both as to make
neither of us friends to one another, but agree in running wildely
to our owne distructions and perhaps of some more innocent
persons whoe might live to curse our ffolly that gave them soe
misserable a being. Ah if you love your self or mee, you must
confesse that I have reason to condemne this sencelesse passion,
that wheresoere it com's distroy's all that Entertaine it, nothing
of Judgment or discretion can live with it, and putts every thing
else out of Order, before it can finde a place for its self. What
has it not brought my Poore Lady Anne Blunt[3] to, she is the
talk of all the footmen and Boy's in the street, and will bee
company for them shortly, who yet is soe blinded by her
passion as not at all to perceave the missery shee has brought
her self to, and this fond love of hers, has soe rooted all sence
of Nature out of her heart, that they say shee is noe more
moved then a Statue, with the affliction of a Father and
Mother that doated on her, and had placed the comfort of
theire lives in her preferment. With all this, is it not manifest
to the whole world that Mr Blunt could not consider any thing

in this action but his owne interest, and that hee makes her a very ill retourn for all her kindenesse. If hee had loved her truly, hee would have dyed rather then have bin the occasion of this misfortune to her.

My Cousin Fr:[4] (as you observe very well) may say fine things now she is warme in Moore Park, but she is very much Alterd in her opinions since her marriage, if these bee her owne. She left a Gentleman that I could name whome she had much more of kindenesse for, then ever she had for Mr Fr: because his Estate was lesse, and upon the discovery of some letters that her Mother intercepted, sufferd her self to bee perswaded that 23 hundred pound a year, was better then twelve though with a person she loved, and has recoverd it soe well that you see shee confesses there is nothing in her condition she desyr's to Alter, at the Charge of a wish. Shee's happyer by much then I shall ever bee, but I doe not envy her, may she long injoy it, and I, an early, and a quiet grave, free from the trouble of this buissy world, where all with passion persue theire owne interests at theire Neighbours Charges, where nobody is pleased but sombody complain's ont, and where tis imposible to bee without giveing and receiveing injury's. You would know what I would bee at, and how I intend to dispose of my self.[5] Alasse were I in my owne disposall you should come to my Grave to bee resolved, but Greif alone will not kill. All that I can say then is, that I resolve on nothing but to Arme my self with patience, to resist nothing that is layd upon mee, not struggle for what I have noe hope to gett. I have noe End's nor noe designes nor will my heart ever bee capable of any, but like a Country wasted by a Civill warr, where two opposeing Party's have disputed theire right soe long till they have made it worth neither of theire conquest's,[6] tis Ruin'd and desolated by the long striffe within it to that degree as twill bee usefull to none, nobody that know's the condition tis in will think it worth the gaineing, and I shall not cousen any body with it. Noe Realy if I may bee permitted to desyre any thing it shall bee only, that I may injure nobody but my self, I can bear any thing that reflect's only upon mee, or if I cannot, I can dye, but I would faine dye innocent that I might hope to bee happy in the next world though never in This.

I take it a litle ill that you should conjure mee by any thing, with a beleife that 'tis more powerfull with mee then your kindenesse. Noe, assure your self what that alone cannot gaine, will bee denyed to all the world. You would see mee you say, You may doe soe if you please though I know not to what end, you deceive your self if you think it would prevaile upon mee to Alter my intentions. Besides I can make noe contrivances, all must bee heer,[7] and I must indure the noise it will make and undergoe the Censors of a People that Choose ever to give the worst interpretation that any thing will bear. Yet if it can bee any Ease to you to make mee more misserable then I am, never spare mee, consider your self only and not mee at all, tis noe more then I deserve for not accepting what you offer'd mee whilest twas in your Power to make it good, as you say it then was. You were prepared it seem's, but I was surprized I conffesse it, 'twas a kinde fault though, and you may pardon it with more reason then I have to forgive it my self. And let mee tell you this too, as lost and as wretched as I am, I have still some sence of my reputation left in mee. I finde that to my last I shall attempt to preserve it as Cleer as I can, and to doe that I must if you see mee thus, make it the last of our interviews. What can Excuse mee if I should Entertaine any Person that is knowne to pretend to mee, when I can have noe hope of ever marryeng him, and what hope can I have of that when the fortune that can only make it posible to mee, depends upon a thousand accidents and contingencys, the uncertainty of the place tis in, and the Government it may fall under, Your fathers life, or his successe, his disposeall of himself and then of his fortune, besyd's the time that must necessarily bee requir'd to produce all this, and the changes, that, may proba[bly][8] bring with it which tis imposible for us to forsee. All this considerd what have I to say for my self when People shall aske what tis I Expect, can there bee any thing Vainer then such a [hope?][9] upon such grownds. You must needs see the ffolly on't your self, and therfore Examine your owne heart what tis fitt for mee to doe, and what you can doe for a Person you Love, and that deserv's your compassion if Nothing Else, A Person that will alway's have an inviolable friendship for you, a friendship that shall take up all the roome my Passion held in my heart and govern there as Master till Death come to take possession and turn it out. Why should you make an imposibility where there is none. A thousand accidents might have taken mee from you, and you must have borne it, why should not your owne resolution work as much upon you, as necessity and time do's infalibly upon all People. Your Father would take it very ill I believe if you should pretende to love mee better, then hee did my Lady, yett shee is dead, and hee liv's and perhaps may doe to love again. There is a Gentlewoman in this Country that loved soe pasionatly for sixe or seven years, that her freinds who kept her from marryeng, fearing her death consented to it, and within halfe a year her husband dyed, which afflicted her soe strangly nobody thought she would have lived, she saw noe light but candles in three year nor cam abroad in five, and now that tis some nine years past she is passionatly taken again with another and how long she has bin soe nobody knows but her self. This is to let you see tis not imposible what I aske, nor unreasonable, think ont and Attempt it at least but doe it sincerely and doe not help your passion to master you. As you have ever loved mee doe this. The Carrier shall bring you[r] letters to Suffolk house to Jones.[10] I shall long to hear from you, but if you should deny mee the only hope thats left mee, I must beg you will deffer it till Christmasse day bee past, for to deale freely with you I have some devotions to performe then which must not bee disturbed with any thing, and nothing is like to doe it soe much as soe sencible an Affliction. Adieu.

Letter 51

Sir

I can say litle more then I did, I am convinced of the Vilenesse of the worlde and all that's in't and that I deceived my self Extreamly when I Expected any thing of comfort from it. Noe I have noe more to doe in it but to grow every day more and more weary of it, if it bee posible that I have not yet reached the highest degree of hatred for it. But I thank god I hate nothing else but the bare world and the Vices that make a part of it, I am in perfect Charrity with my Enemy's and have compassion for all peoples misfortunes as well as for my owne, Espetialy for those that I may have caused, and I may truly say I bear my share of such, but as nothing Obliges mee to releive a person that is in Extream want till I change conditions with him and come to bee where hee began, and that I may bee thought compassionat enough if I doe all that I can without prejudicing my self too much, soe let mee tell you that if I could help it I would not love you, and that as long as I live I shall strive against it, as against that which has bin my Ruine, and was certainly sent mee as punishment for my Sinn's. But I shall alway's have a sence of your misfortun's Equall, if not above my owne, I shall pray that you may Obtain a quiett, I never hope for but in my grave, and I shall never Change my condition but with my life. Yet let not this give you a hope, nothing can ever perswade mee to enter the worlde againe, I shall in a short time have disingaged my self of all my litle affaires in it and settled my self in a condition to aprehend[1] nothing but too long a life, therfore I wish you would forgett mee, and to induce you to it let mee tell you freely that I deserve you should. If I remember any body tis against my will, I am possessed with that strange insencibility that my neerest relations have noe tye upon mee,[2] and I finde my selfe noe more concerned in those that I have hertofore had great tendernesse of affection for then in my kindred that dyed long before I was borne. Leave mee to this, and seek a better fortune, I beg it of you as heartily as I forgive you all those strange thoughts[3] you have had of mee, think mee soe still if that will doe any thing towards it, for god sake doe, take any course that may make you happy or if you cannot bee, lesse unfortunate at least then

> Your friend and humble Servant[4]
> D. Osborne

I can hear nothing of that letter[5] but I hear from all people that I know part of my unhappy Story[6] and that from some that I doe not know. A Lady whose face I never saw sent it mee as news she had out of Ireland.

Letter 52

[Thursday 5 January 1654]

If you have Ever Loved mee doe not refuse the Last request I shall Ever make you, tis to preserve your self from the Violences of your passion.[1] Vent it upon mee call mee and think mee what you please make mee if it bee posible more wretched then I am, i'le beare it all without the Least murmure, nay I deserve it all, for had you never seen mee you had certainly bin happy, tis my misfortunes only that have that infectious quality to strike at the same time mee, and all thats d[ear][2] to mee. I am the most unfortunate woman breathing but I was never falce,[3] noe I call heaven to witnesse that if my life could sattisfye for the least injury my fortune has don you, (I cannot say twas I that did them to you) I would Lay it downe with greater Joy then Any person Ever received a Crowne, and if I ever forgett what I owe you, or Ever Entertaine a thought of kindenesse for any person in the world besydes may I live a long and misserable life, tis the

greatest Curse I can invente if there bee a greater may I feel it.
This is all I can say. Tell mee if it bee posible I can doe any thing
for you and tell mee how I may deserve your pardon for all the
trouble I have given you, I would not dye without it.

For Mr Temple[4]

Letter 53

[Saturday 7 or Sunday 8 January 1654]

Sir

That which I writt by your Boy was in soe much hast and
distraction,[1] as I cannot bee sattisfyed with it nor beleeve it
has Expressed my thoughts as I meant them. Noe, I finde it is
not Easily don at more Leasure and I am yet to seek what to say
that is not too litle nor too much.

I would faine let you see that I am Extreamly sencible of your
affliction, that I would Lay downe my life to redeem you from
it, but that's a mean Expretion my life is of soe litle Valew that I
will not mention it. Noe let it bee rather, what, in Earnest, if I
can tell any thing I have left that is considerable enough to
Expose for it, it must bee that small reputation I have amongst
my friends[.] that's all my wealth and that I could part with to
restore you to that quiet you lived in when I first knew you. But
on the Otherside I would not give you hopes of that I cannot
doe. If I loved you lesse I would allow you to bee the same
person to mee and I would bee the same to you as hertofore but
to deal freely with you, that were to betray my self and I finde
that my passion would quickly bee my Master again if I give it
any liberty. I am not secure that it would not make mee doe the
most Extravagant things in the worlde, and I shall bee forced to
keep a continuall warr alive with it, as long as there are any
remainders of it left, I think I might as well have sayed as long as I
lived. Why should you give your self over soe unreasonably to it[?]

good God, noe woman breathing can deserve halfe the trouble you give Your Self. If I were Yours from this minute I could not recompence what you have sufferd from the Violence of your passion though I were all that you can imagin mee, when god know's I am an inconsiderable person born to a thousand misfortun's which have taken away all sence of any thing else from mee and left mee a walking missery only. I doe from my soule forgive you all the Injury's your passion has don mee, though let mee tell you I was much more at my Ease whilest I was angry, Scorne and dispite would have cured mee in some reasonable time which I dispaire of now. However I am not displeased with it and if it may bee of any advantage to you, I shall not consider my self in it. But let mee beg then that you will leave of those dismall thoughts I tremble at the desperate things you say in your letter. For the Love of God consider Seriously with your selfe what can Enter into comparison with the Safety of your soule are a thousand Women or ten thousand world's worth it. Noe you cannot have so litle reason left as you prettende; nor soe litle religion, for god sake let us not necglect what can only make us happy for a triffle. Iff God had seen it fitt to have sattisfyed our desir's wee should have had them, and Every thing would not have conspired thus to crosse them, since hee has decreed it otherwise (at least as farr as wee are able to Judge by Event's) wee must submitt and not by striveing make an innocent passion a sinne and show a Childeish Stubbornesse. I could say a thousand things more to this purpose if I were not in hast to send this away that it may come to you at least as soone as the Other.[2]

Adieu.

I cannot imagin whoe this should bee that Mr Dr:[3] meant and am inclined to beleive twas a Storry made to disturbe you perhaps not by him.

For Mr T.[4]

Letter 54

[Saturday 14 January 1654]

Tis but an howr since you went,[1] and I am writeing to you already, is not this kinde[?] how doe you after your Journy[,] are you not weary[?] doe you not repent that you tooke it, to soe little purpose[?] Well god forgive mee and you too, you made mee tell a great lye, I was faine to say you came only to take your leave before you went abroad and all this nott only to keep quiett[2] but to keep him from playeing the mad man, for when hee has the least suspition hee carry's it soe strangly that all the worlde takes notice on't, and often Guesse at the reason or else hee tel's it. Now doe but you Judge whither if by mischance hee should discoverd the truth whither hee would not raile most Sweetly at mee, (and with some reason) for abuseing him. Yet you helped to doe it, a sadnesse that hee discoverd at your goeing away inclined him to beleeve you were ill sattisfyed, and made him Creditt what I sayed. Hee is kinde now in Extremity and I would bee glad to keep him soe till a discovery is absolutely necessary. Your goeing abroad will confirme him much in his beleife, and I shall have nothing to Torment mee in this place but my owne doubts and fear's. Heer I shall finde all the repose I am capable of, and nothing will disturbe my Prayers and wishes for your happinesse which can only make mine. Your Journy cannot bee to your disadvantage neither, you must needs bee pleased to Visett a place you are soe much concern'd in,[3] and to bee a wittnesse your self of the probability of your hopes though I will beleive you need noe other inducement to this Voyage then my desyreing it. I know you Love mee, and you have noe reason to doubt my kindenesse. Let us both have patience to wayte what time and fortune will doe for us, they cannot hinder our being perfect friends.

Lord there were a thousand things I rememberd after you

were gon that I should have sayed, and now I am to write not one of them will come into my head, Sure as I live it is not setled yet. Good god the fear's and surprizes, the crosses and disorders of that day,[4] twas confused Enough to bee a dream and I am apt to think somtimes it was noe more[.] but noe I saw you, when I shall doe it againe god only know's, can there bee a more Romance Story[5] then ours would make if the conclusion should prove happy. Ah I dare not hope it, somthing that I cannot discribe draw's a cloude over all the light my fancy discovers somtimes, and leav's mee soe in the darke with all my fear's about mee that I tremble to think on't. But noe more of this sad talke, whoe was that Mr Dr:[6] tolde you I should marry[?] I cannot imagin for my life[.] tell mee or I shall think you made it to Excuse your self. Did not you say once you knew where good french tweeses[7] were to bee had[?] pray send me a payer, they shall Cutt noe Love.[8] Before you goe I must have a ring[9] from you too, a plaine Golde one, if I Ever marry it shall bee my wedding ring or when I dye, i'le give it you againe.[10]

What a dismall Story this is you sent mee, but whoe could Expect better from a Love begun upon such growndes. I cannot pitty neither of them they were both soe Guilty yes they are the more to bee pittyed for that.[11]

Heer is a note comes to mee Just now[,] will you doe this service for a fair Lady[12] that is my friend. Have not I taught her well shee writes better then her Mistresse. How merry and pleased she is with her marryeng because there is a plentifull fortune, Otherwise she would not valew the man at all, this is the worlde would you and I were out on't, for sure wee were not made to live in it. Doe you remember Arme[13] and the little house there[?] shall we goe thither[?] that's next to being out of the worlde[.] there wee might live like Baucis and Philemon,[14] grow old together in our litle Cottage and for our Charrity to some shipwrakt stranger obtaine the blessing of dyeing both at the same time. How idly I talk tis because the Storry pleases mee, none in Ovide soe much. I remember

I cryed when I read it, mee thought they were the perfectest Characters of a con[ten]ted[15] marriage where Piety and Love were all theire wealth and in theire poverty feasted the Gods where rich men shutt them out. I am called away far-well

Your faithfull

Letter 55

[Saturday 21 or Sunday 22 January 1654]

Sir

Tis never my humor to doe injury's, nor was this meant as any to you. Noe in Earnest if I could have perswaded you to have quitted a passion that injures you I had don an act of real friendship and you might have lived to thank mee for it, but since it cannot bee I will Attempt it noe more.[1] I have Layed before you the inconveniencys it brings alonge, how certain the trouble is, and how uncertain the reward, how many accidents may hinder us from Ever being happy, and how few there are, (and those soe unlikely) to make up our desyr's. All this makes noe impression in you You are still resolved to ffollow your blinde Guide and I to pitty where I cannot helpe. It will not bee amisse though to let you see that what I did was meerly in considera-tion of your interest and not at all of my owne that you Judge of mee accordingly, and to doe that I must tell you that unlesse it were affter the receite of those letters that made mee Angry, I had never had the least hope of wearing out my passion, nor to say truth much desyre, for to what purpose should I have strived against it, twas innocent enough in mee that resolved never to marry, and would have kept mee company in this solitary place[2] as long as I lived, without being a trouble to my self or any body else. Nay in Earnest if I could have hoped that you would bee soe much your owne friend as to seek out a happinesse in some other person, nothing under heaven could have sattisfyed mee like Entertaining my self with the thought of haveing don you service in diverting you from a troublesome persuite of what is soe uncertain, and by that, giveing you the occasion of a better fortune. Otherwise whither you loved mee still or whither you did not, was equally the same to mee, your interest sett aside. I will not reproach how ill an interpretation you made of this because wee'l have noe more quarrell's, on the contreary because I see tis Vaine to think of cureing you i'le studdy only to give you what Ease I can, and leave the rest to better Phisitians, to Time, and Fortune.

Heer then I declare that you have still the same power in my heart that I gave you at our last parteing;[3] that I will never marry any Other, and that iff Ever Our fortun's will allow us to marry you shall dispose mee as you please, but this to deal freely with you I doe not hope for, noe, tis too great a happinesse, and I that know my self best must acknoledge I deserve crosses and affliction but can never merritt such a blessing. You know tis not a fear of want that frights mee, I thank god I never distrusted his providence nor I hope never shall and without attributeing any thing to my self I may Acknoledge hee has given mee a minde that can bee sattisfyed within as narrow a compasse as that of any person liveing of my rank. But I confesse that I have an humor will not suffer mee to Expose my self to Peoples Scorne, the name of Love is growne soe contemptible by the ffolly of such as have falcely prettended to it, and soe many Giddy People have marryed upon that score and repented soe shamefully afterwards, that nobody can doe any thing that tends towards it without being esteem'd a rediculous person. Now as my Young Lady Holland[4] say's, I never prettended to witt in my life, but I cannot bee sattisfyed that the worlde should think mee a foole; soe that all I can doe for you, will bee to preserve a constant kindenesse for you which nothing shall Ever Alter or diminish. Ile never give you any more Alarm's by goeing about to perswade you against that you have for mee, but from this hower wee'l live quietly, noe more fear's noe more Jelousy's[,] the wealth of the whole world by the grace of God shall not Tempt mee to break my worde with you, nor the importunity of all the friends I have. Keep this as a testimony against mee if ever I doe and make mee a reproach to them by it therfore bee secure; and rest sattisfyed with what I can doe for you.

You should come hither but that I expect my Brother every day,[5] not but that hee designed a longer stay when hee went but since hee keep's his horses with him tis an infalible Token that hee is comeing. Wee cannot misse ffitter times then this twenty in a year and I shall bee as redy to give you notice of such, as you can bee to desyre it, only you would doe mee a great pleasure if you could forbear writeing unlesse it were somtimes on great occasions. This is a strange request for mee to make that have bin fonder of your letters then my Lady Protector[6] is of her new honnour and in Earnest could bee soe still but there are a thousand inconveniencys int that I could tell you, tell mee what you can doe. In the mean time think of some imployment[7] for your self this summer, whoe know's what a yeare may produce. If nothing, wee are but where we were and nothing can hinder us from being at least perfect friends.

Adieu.

Ther's nothing soe Terrible in my Other Letter but you may venture to read it; have not you forgott my Lady's Book.[8]

Letter 56

[Saturday 28 or Sunday 29 January 1654]

... of what she saw till hee was gon[1] but then I had it in full measure. Tis pitty I cannot show you what his witt could doe upon soe ill a subject but my Lady Ru:[2] keeps them to abuse[3] mee withall, & has putt a tune to them that I may hear them all manner of way's, and yet I doe prottest I remember nothing more of them but this lame peece:

> *A stately and majestick brow*
> *Of force to make Prottectours bow.*

Indeed if I have any stately looks I think hee has seen them
but yet it seem's they could not keep him from playeing the
foole. My Lady Grey tolde mee that one day talkeing of mee
to her, (as hee would finde way's to bring in that discourse by
the head & shoulders whatsoever any body else could inter-
pose), hee sayed hee wonderd I did not marry. She, (that
understood him well Enough but would not seem to doe soe)
sayed she knew not, unlesse it were that I liked my present
condition soe well that I did not care to change it, which she
was apt to beleeve because to her knoledge I had refused very
good fortunes, and named some, soe farr beyond his reach, that
she thought she had dashed all his hopes, but hee confident still,
sayed twas perhaps that I had noe fancy to theire Person's (as
if his owne were soe takeing) that I was to bee looked upon
as one that had it in my power to please my self, and that
perhaps in a person I liked I would bate somthing of fortune.
To this my Lady answerd again for mee, that twas not imposible but I might doe soe, but in this pointe she thought mee
nice and Curious[4] enough. And still to dishearten him the
more, she tooke occasion (upon his nameing some gentlemen
of the Country that had been talked of heretofore as my servant's and are since disposed of,) to say (very plainly) that twas
true they had some of them prettended, but there was an End
of my Bedfordshyre Servants, she was sure there were noe
more that could bee admitted into the Number. After all this
(which would have sattisifed an ordinary young man) did I this
last thursday receive a Letter from him by Collins, which hee
sent first to London, that it might come from thence to mee.
I threw it into the fyre, and doe you but keep my councell
noe body shall Ever know that I had it, and my Gentleman
shall bee kept at such a distance as I hope to heare noe more
of him, yett i'le sweare of late I have used him soe neer to
Rudely that there is litle left for mee to doe.

Fye, what a deal of paper have I spent ypon this idle ffellow[,] if I had thought his storry would have proved soe long you should have missed on't and the losse would not have bin great.

I have not thanked you yet for my tweeses and essences they are both very good[,] I kept one of the litle glasses my self; remember my ring and in retourne if I goe to London whilest you are in Ireland i'le have my Picture taken in litle [5] and send it you. The sooner you dispatch away will bee the better I think since I have noe hopes of seeing you before you goe, there lyes all your buisnesse your father & fortune must doe the rest, I cannot bee more yours then I am. You are mistaken if you think I stand in Awe of my B: noe I feare nobody's Anger, I am proofe against all Violence, but when People haunte [6] mee with reasonings and Entreaty's when they looke sadly [7] and prettende kindenesse, when they begg upon that score tis a strange paine to mee to deny. When hee raunt's and renounces mee I can dispise him, but when hee askes my pardon with tear's pleades to mee the long and constant friendship between us and call's heaven to wittnesse that nothing upon Earth is dear to him in comparison of mee, then, I confesse I feel a strange unquietnesse within mee, and I would doe any thing to avoyde his importunity. Nothing is soe great a Violence to mee, as that which moves my compassion[.] I can resist with Ease any sort of People but beggers. If this bee a fault in mee, tis at least a well natured one, and therfore I hope you will forgive it mee, You that can forgive mee any thing you say, and bee displeased with nothing whilest I love you, may I never bee pleased with any thing when I doe not. Yet I could beat you for writeing this last strange letter, was there Ever any thing sayed like, if I had not a Vanity that the worlde shoulde admire mee, I would not care what they talked of mee. In Earnest, I beleeve there is nobody displeased that People speak well of them and reputation is esteem'd by all of much greater Valew then life it selfe. Yet let mee tell you soberly, that with all my Vanity I could bee very well contented, upon condition noe body should blame mee or any action of mine, to quitt all my part of the praises and admiration of the worlde and if I might bee allowed to choose my happinesse, part of it should consist in concealment there should not above two persons in the worlde know that that there were such a one in it as

Your faithfull

Stay I have not done yet, heers another side good still[,] heer then i'le tell you that I am not angry for all this[,] noe I allow it to your ill humor, and that to the Crosses that have bin common to us. But now that is clear'd up I shall Expect you should say finer things to mee,[8] Yet take heed of being like my Neighbours Servant,[9] hee is soe transported to finde noe rubb's in his way that hee knows not whither hee stands upon his head or his feet[,] tis the most troublesome, buisy, talkeing litle thing that ever was borne, his Tongue goes like the Clack of a Mill but to much lesse purpos, though if twere all Oracle my head would ake to heare that perpetuall noise. I admire at her Patience, and her resolution that can laugh at all his ffooleries and love his fortune. You would wonder to see how tyred she is with his impertinences,[10] and yet how pleased she is to think she shall have a great Estate with him; but this is the world and shee makes a part of it betimes, two or three great glistering Jewells has bribed her to wink at all his faults and she hears him as unmoved and unconcern'd as if another were to marry him. What think you[?] have I not don faire for once[?] would you wish a longer letter[?] see how kinde I grow at parting, whoe would not goe into Ireland to have such another. In Earnest now, goe as soone as you can, twill bee the better, I think, whoe am   Your faithfull friend

Letter 57

[Saturday 4 or Sunday 5 February 1654]

Whoe would bee kinde to one that reproaches one soe cruelly. Doe you think in Earnest I could bee satisfyed the world should think mee a dissembler, full of Avarice, or Ambition noe you are mistaken. But i'le tell you what I could suffer, that they should say I marryed where I had noe inclination, because my friends thought it fitt rather then that I had run willfully to my owne Ruine in a persuit of a fond passion of my owne. To marry for Love were noe reproachful thing if wee did not see that of ten thousand couples that doe it, hardly one can be brought for an Example that it may bee done & not repented afterwards, is there any thing soe indiscreet, or that makes one more contemptible. Tis true that I doe firmly beleeve wee should bee as you say tousjours les mesmes[1] but if (as you confesse) tis that which hardly happens once in two Ages, wee are not to Expect the worlde should discerne wee were not like the rest.

I'le tell you story's another time you retourne them soe handsomly upon mee. Well the next servant I tell you of shall not bee called a whelp.[2] If twere not to give you a stick to beat my self with, I would confesse that I looked upon the impudence of this ffellow as a punishment upon mee for my care in avoyding the talk of the world. Yet the case is very different and noe Woman shall ever bee blamed that an inconsiderable person prettends to her when she gives noe allowance[3] to it, whereas none shall scape that own's a passion though in retourne of Persons much above her. The little Taylor[4] that loved Queen Elizabeth was sufferd to talke ont, and none of her Councell thought it nescesary to stop his mouth but the Queen of Swedens kinde letter to the King of Scott's[5] was intercepted by her owne Ambassador, because hee thought it was not for his Mistresses honnour, (at least that was his prettended reason and thought

Justifiable enough). But to come to my Beagle again,[6] I have heard noe more of him though I have seen him since, wee mett at Wrest[7] again, I doe not doubt but I shall bee better able to resist his importunity then his Tutor[8] was but what doe you think it is that giv's him his incouragement, hee was told that I had thought's of marryeng a Gentleman that had not above two hundred Pounde a yeer only out of a likeing to his person, and upon that score his vanity allows him to think hee may prettende as farr as another. Thus you see tis not altogether without reason that I aprehend[9] the noise of the worlde since tis soe much to my disadvantage.

Is it in Earnest that you say your being there keeps mee from the Towne, if soe, tis very unkinde. Noe if I had gon it had bin to have wayted on my Neighbour,[10] whoe has now alterd her resolution and goes not her self, I have noe buisnesse there, and am soe litle taken with the place that I could sitt heer seven yeer without soe much as thinking once of goeing to it. Tis not likely as you say that you should much perswade your father[11] to what you doe not desyre hee should doe, but it is harde if all the Testimony's of my kindenesse are not enough to sattisfye without my Publishing to the world that I can forgett my friends and all my interest to ffollow my Passion; though perhaps it will admitt of a good sence, tis that which nobody but you or I will give it, and wee that are concerned int can only say twas an act of great kindenesse and somthing Romance,[12] but must confesse it had nothing of prudence, discretion, nor sober councell in't. Tis not that I Expect by all your Fathers offers to bring my friends to aprove it, I don't deceive my self thus farr, but I would not give them occasion to say that I hid my self from them in the doeing it, nor of makeing my action apear more indiscreet then it is, it will concerne mee that all the worlde should know what fortune you have and upon what term's I marry you that both may not bee made to appeare ten times worse then they are. Tis the Generall Custome of All People to make those that are Rich to have more Mines of Golde then are in the Indias, and such as have small fortun's to bee beggers. If an Action take a litle in the

worlde it shall bee magnified and brought into Comparison with
what the Hero's, or Senatours of Rome perform'd, but on the
Contreary if it bee once condemned nothing can bee founde ill
enough to compare it with, and People are in Paine till they
finde out some Extravagant Expression to represent the ffolly
on't. Only there is this difference that as all are more forcibly
inclined to ill then good, they are much apter to Exceede in
detraction then in praises. Have I not reason then to desyre this
from you, and may not my ffriendship have deserved it[?] I
know not, tis as you think, but if I bee denyed it, you will teach
mee to consider my self. Tis well the side ended heer.[13]

If I had not had occasion to stop there I might have gon too
farr and showed that I have more passions then one, Yet tis fitt
you should know all my faults, least you should repent your
bargen when twill not bee in your power to release your self.
Besides I may owne my ill humor to you that cause it, tis the
discontents my Crosses in this buisnes has given mee, makes mee
thus Peevish, though I say't my self, before I knew you I was
thought as well an humord Younge Person as most in England[,]
Nothing displeased nothing troubled mee. When I cam out of
France[14] nobody knew mee againe, I was soe alterd, from a
Cheerful humor that was alway's alike, never over merry but
always pleased, I was growne heavy, and sullen, froward and
discomposed, and that Country which usualy gives People a
Jollynesse and Gayete that is naturall to the Climate, has wrought
in mee soe contreary effects that I was as new a thing to them as
my Cloth's. If you finde all this to bee sad truth hereafter, remember that I gave you faire warning. Heer is a ring it must not
bee at all wider then this, which is rather to [*sic*] bigge for mee
then Otherwise but that is a good fault and counted Lucky by
Superstitious People. I am not soe though, tis indifferent to mee
whither there bee any word int[15] or not, only tis as well without, and will make my wearing it the lesse Observed.

You must give Nan[16] leave to Cutt of a Lock of your haire
for mee too. O my heart what a sigh was there,[17] I will not tell

you how many this Journy [18] causes nor the fear's and Aprehen-si[ons] I have for you, noe I long to bee rid on you [I] am afrayde you will not goe soone enough doe not you beleeve this[?] Noe, my Dearest, I know you doe not, what Ere you say You cannot doubt but I am   Yours

Letter 58

[Saturday 11 or Sunday 12 February 1654]

Tis well you have given over your reproches;[1] I can allow you to tell mee of my faults kindly and like a friend; Posibly it is a weaknesse in mee, to ayme at the worlds Esteem as if I could not bee happy without it; but there are certaine things that custom has made Almost of Absolute necessity, and reputation I take to bee one of those; if one could bee invisible I should choose that, but since all people are seen and knowne, and shall bee talked of in spight of theire Teeth's,[2] whoe is it that do's not desyre at least that nothing of ill may bee sayed of them whither Justly, or Otherwise, I never knew any soe sattisfied with theire owne innocence as to bee content the worlde should think them Guilty; some out of pride have seem'd to contemme ill reports when they have founde they could not avoyde them; but none out of strength of reason though many have prettended to it; noe not my Lady New Castle with all her Philosophy;[3] therfore you must not Expect it from mee; I shall never bee ashamed to owne that I have a particular Valew for you above any Other, but tis not the greatest merritt of Person will Excuse a want of fortune; in some degree I think it will, at least with the most rationall part of the worlde, and as farr as that will reach I desyre it should; I would not have the worlde beleeve I married out of Interest and to please my friends, I had much rather they should know I chose the Person, and took his fortune because twas necessary and that I preffer a competency with one I esteem infinitly before a Vaste Estate in Other hands; Tis much Easier sure to get a good fortune then a good Husband but whosoever marry's without any consideration of fortune shall never bee allowed to doe it out of soe reasonable an aprehension; the whole worlde (without any reserve) shall pronounce they did it meerly to sattisfie theire Giddy humor. Besides though you imagin twere a great argument of my Kindenesse to consider nothing but you, In Earnest I beleeve twould bee an injury to you, I doe not see that it putts any Valew upon men, when Women marry them for Love (as they terme it), 'tis not theire merritt but our ffolly that is alway's presumed to cause it; and would it bee any advantage to you to have your wife thought an indiscreet person. All this I can say to you, but when my Brother[4] disputes it with mee I have Other Arguments for him, and I drove him up soe close t'other night that for want of a better gap to gett out at, hee was faine to say that hee feard as much your haveing a fortune as your haveing none, for hee saw you held my Lord Lls[5] principles, that Religion or honnour were things you did not consider att all, and that hee was confident you would take any Engagement, serve in any employment or doe any thing to advance yourself. I had noe patience for this, to say you were a begger, your Father not worth £4000 in the whole world, was nothing in comparison of haveing noe Religion nor noe honnour. I forgott all my disguise and wee talked our selves weary hee renounced mee againe and I defyed him, but both in as Civill Language as it would permitt, and parted in great Anger with the Usuall Ceremony of a Leg and a Courtesy,[6] that you would have dyed with Laughing to have seen us; the next day I not beeing at dinner saw him not till night; then hee cam into my Chamber, where I supped but hee did not; Afterwards Mr Gibson[7] and hee and I talked of indifferent things till all but wee two went to bed, there hee sate halfe an hower and sayed not one word nor I to him, at Last in a pittifull Tone, Sister say's hee, I have heard you say that when any thing troubles you, of all things you aprehend goeing to bed, because there it increases upon you and you lye at the mercy of all your sad thoughts which the silence and the darknesse of the night adds a horror to; I am at that passe now, I vow to God I would not indure another night like the last to gaine a Crowne; I whoe resolvd to take noe notice of what ayled him, sayd twas a knoledge I had raised from my Spleen[8] only; and soe fell into a discourse of Melancholy and the Causes, and from all that (I know not how) into Religion, and wee talked soe long of it and soe devoutely that it layed all our anger, wee grew to a calme and peace with all the world; two hermitts conversing in a Cell they Equaly inhabitt, never Expressed more humble Charritable Kindenesse one towards another then wee, hee asked my Pardon and I his, and hee has promised mee never to speak of it to mee whilest hee liv's but leave the Event to God Almighty and till hee sees it don,[9] hee will bee always the same to mee that hee is; then hee shall leave mee hee say's not out of want of Kindenesse to mee, but because hee cannot see the Ruine of a Person that hee lov's soe passionatly and in whose happinesse hee had layed up all his.

These are the Term's we are at, and I am confident hee will keep his word with mee; soe that you have noe reason to fear him in any respect for though hee should break his promise hee should never make mee break mine; noe let mee assure you, this Rivall nor any other shall Ever Alter mee Therfor spare your Jelousy or turne it all into Kindenesse.

I will write Every week, and noe misse of letters shall give us any doubts of one another, Time nor accidents shall not prevaile upon our hearts, and if God Almighty please to blesse us, wee will meet the same wee are, or happyer; I will doe all you bid mee, I will pray, and wish and hope, but you must doe soe too then; and bee soe carfull of your self that I may have nothing to reproche you with when you come back. That vile wench[10] let's you see all my Scribles I beleeve, how doe you know I tooke care your haire should not bee spoyled, tis more then Ere you did I think, You are soe necgligent on't and keep it soe ill tis pitty you should have it. May you have better luck in the Cutting it then I had with mine I cutt it two or 3 year agon and it never grew since; Looke to it, if I keep the Lock you give mee better then you doe all the rest, I shall not spare you Expect to bee soundly Chidden. What doe you mean to doe with all my Letters leave them behinde you. If you doe it must bee in safe hands, some of them concerne you, and mee, and Other People besydes us, very much, and they will almost loade a horse to carry.

Dos not My Cousins at MP[11] mistrust us a little[?] I have a great beleife they doe, I'me sure Robin C[12] tolde my Brother of it since I was last in Towne. Of all things I admire[13] my Cousin Molle has not gott it by the End, hee that frequents that Famely soe much and is at this instant at Kimbolton.[14] If hee has, and conceals it, hee is very discreet I could never discerne by any thing that hee knew it. I shall indeavour to accustome my self to the noyse on't and make it as Easy to mee as I can, though I had much rather it were not talked of till there were an absolute nescessity of discovering it, and you can oblige mee in nothing more then in concealing it.

I take it very kindly that you promise to use all your interest in your F.[15] to perswade him to indeavor our happinesse, and hee apears soe confident of his power that it gives mee great hopes, Deare, shall wee ever bee soe happy, think you; Ah I dare not hope it, yet tis not the want of love gives mee these fear's. Noe in Earnest, I think, (nay I am sure) I love you more then Ever, and tis that only gives mee these dispaireing thoughts, When I consider how small a proportion of happines is allowed in this worlde, and how great mine would bee in a person for whome I have a passionate Kindenesse and whoe has the same for mee; As it is infinitly above what I can deserve, and more then God Almighty usually allotts to the best People, I can finde nothing in reason but seems to bee against mee, and mee thinks tis as vaine in mee to Expect it as twould bee to hope I might bee a Queen (if that were realy as desyrable a thing as tis thought to bee). And it is Just it should bee soe; Wee complaine of this world and the Variety of Crosses and afflictions it abound's in, and yet for all this whoe is weary on't (more then in discourse), whoe thinks with pleasure of leaving it, or preparing for the next; Wee see olde folks that have ou[t]lived all the comforts of life, desyre to continue it, and nothing can wean us from the ffolly of preffering a mortall beeing subject to great infirmity's and unavoydable decays, before an immortall one and all the Glorry's that are promised with it. Is not this very like preaching[?] well tis too good for you, you shall have noe more on't, I am affrayde you are not mortified [16] Enough for such discourses to worke upon, though I am not of my Brothers opinion neither (that you have noe religion in you) [17] in Earnest I never tooke any thing hee ever sayd halfe soe ill, as nothing sure is soe great an injury, it must suppose one to bee a Divell in human Shape. O mee now I am speaking of Religion lett mee aske you is not his Name Bagshaw [18] that you say railes on Love & Women because I heard one tother day speaking of him & comending his witt but withall sayed hee was a Perfect Atheist, if soe I can allow him to hate us, and Love, which sure has somthing of devine in it, since god requir's it of us; I am comeing into my preaching vaine againe what think you were it not a good way of prefferment as the times are[?] if you advise mee to it ile venture. The woman at Somercett house [19] was Cryed up mightily, think on't;

Deare I am   Yours

Letter 59

[Saturday 18 or Sunday 19 February 1654]

The lady was in the right you are a very pritty gentleman,[1] and a modest; were there Ever such story's as these to tell; the best on't is I beleeve none of them, unlesse it bee that of my Lady Newport [2] which I must confesse is soe like her, that if it bee not true twas at least Excellently fancyed.[3] But my Lord Rich [4] is not caught though hee was neer it, my Lady Devonshyre [5] whose daughter his first wife was has ingaged my Lord War: to put a stop to the buisnesse Otherwise I think his present want of fortune and the litle sence of honour hee has, might have bin prevailed on to marry her.

Tis strange to see the folly that possesses the young People of this Age, and the libertys they take to themselv's; I have the Charrity to beleeve they apear very much worse then they are, and that the want of a Court to govern themselv's by is in great part the cause of theire Ruine. Though that was noe perfect scoole of Vertue yet Vice there wore her maske, and apeard soe unlike her self that she gave noe scandall; Such as were realy as discreet as they seem'd to bee; gave good Example, and the Eminency of theire condition made others strive to imitate them, or at least they durst not owne a contreary Course; All whoe had good principles and inclinations were incouraged in them, and such as had neither were forced to putt on a handsome disguise that they might not bee out of countenance at themselves; Tis certain (what you say) that where devine or human Laws are not possitive wee may bee our owne Judges, nobody can hinder us, nor is it in it selfe to bee blamed;[6] but sure it is not safe to take all the liberty is allowed us, there are not many that are sober enough to bee trusted with the government of themselv's, and because others Judge us with more severity then our indulgence to ourselv's will permitt, it must necessarily ffollow that tis saffer being ruled by theire opinion then by our owne. I am disputeing againe though you tolde mee my fault soe Plainly, ile give it over and tell you that Parthenissa[7] is now my company[,] my Brother[8] sent it downe and I have almost read it, tis hansome Language you would know it to bee writt by a person of good Quality though you were not tolde it, but in the whole I am not very much taken with it, all the Story's have too neer a resemblance with those of Other Romances there is nothing of new or surprenant[9] in them the Ladys are all soe kinde they make noe sport, and I meet only with one that tooke mee by doeing a handsome thing of the kinde. She was in a beseiged Towne, and perswaded all those of her Sexe to goe out with her to the Enemy (which were a barbarous People) and dye by theire swords, that the provision of the Towne might last the longer for such as were able to doe service in deffending it.[10] But how angry I was to see him spoile this againe, by bringing out a letter this woman left behinde her for the Governour of the Towne, where she discovers a passion for him and makes that the reason why she did it. I confesse I have noe patience for our faiseurs de Romance, when they make women court. It will never enter into my head that tis posible any woman can Love where she is not first Loved, & much lesse that if they should doe that, they could have the face to owne it. My thinkes hee that writes L'illustre Bassa [11] sayes well in his Epistle, That wee are not to imagin his Heroe to bee lesse takeing then those of Other Romances because the Ladys doe not fall in love with him whither hee will or not. Twould bee an injury to the Lady's to suppose they could doe soe, and a greater to his Heroe's Civility if hee should putt him upon being Cruell to them, since hee was to love but one. Another fault I finde too in the stile, tis affected. Ambition'd is a great word with him, and ignore; my concerne, or of great concern, is it seem's properer then concernment; [12] and though hee makes his People say fine handsome things to one another yet they are not Easy and Naïve like the french, and there is a little harshnesse in most of the discourses that one would take to bee the fault of a Translatour rather then of an Author. But perhaps I like it the worse for haveing a peece of Cyrus [13] by mee, that I am hugely pleased with and that I would faine have you read, i'le send it you. At least read one Story that ile marke you downe, if you have time for noe more; I am glad you stay to wayte on your sister,[14] I would have my Galant Civill to all[,] much more where it is soe due and kindenesse too. I have the Cabinett [15] and tis in Earnest a pritty one, though you will not owne it for a present i'le keep it as one and tis like to bee yours noe more but as tis mine. I'le warrant you would ne're have thought of makeing mee a present of Charcole, as my Servant James [16] would have don to warme my heart I think hee meant it. But the truth is I had bin inquireing for some, (as tis a comodity scarce enough in this Country) and hee hearing of it told the Bayly [17] hee would give him some if twere for mee; but this is not all, I cannot forbear telling you that tother day hee made mee a Visett, and I to prevent his makeing discourses to mee made Mrs Gouldsmith [18] and Jane [19] sitt by all the while. But hee cam better provided then I could have imagin'd, hee brought a letter with him, and gave it mee as one that hee had mett with dirrected to mee, hee thought it came out of Northamptonshyre. I was upon my guard and suspecting all hee say'd Examined him soe Strictly where hee had it before I would open it that hee was hugely confounded and I confirmed that twas his. I layd it by and wished then they would have left us that I might have taken notice on't to him but I had forbid it them soe strictly before that they offerd not to stirr further then to look out at window as not thinking theire was any necessity of giveing us theire Ey's as well as theire Ear's. But hee that saw himself discoverd took that time to confesse to mee (in a whispering voyce that I could hardly hear my self) that the Letter (as my Lord Broghill says) was of great concern to him, and beggd I would read it and give him my answer. I took it up presently [20] as if I had meant it, but threw it sealed into the fire and told him (as softly as hee had spoke to mee) I thought that the quickest and best way of answering it. Hee satt a while in great disorder without speaking a word and soe rise [21] and took his leave. Now what think you shall I ever hear of him more[?] You doe not thank mee for useing your Rivall soe scurvily nor are not Jealoux of him though your father thinks my intentions were not handsom towards you, [22] which my thinks is another Argument that one is not to bee on's owne Judge, for I am very confident they were, and with his favour shall never beleeve Otherwise; I am sure I had noe End's to serve my owne in what I did, it could bee noe advantage to mee that had firmly resolved never to marry, but I thought it might bee an Injury to you to keep you in Expectation of what was never likely to bee as I aprehended; why doe I enter into this wrangling discourse. Let your father think mee what hee pleases, if hee com's to know mee the rest of my Actions shall Justifie mee in this, if hee dos not, i'le begin to practise upon him (what you have soe often preachd to mee) to necglect the report of the world and sattisfye my self in my owne innocency. Twill bee pleasinger[23] to you I am sure, to tell you how fond I am of your Lock;[24] well in Earnest now and setting aside all complement, I never saw finer haire nor of a better Couler, but cutt noe more on't I would not have it spoyled for the world, if you love mee bee carefull on't, I am combing and Curling and kissing this Lock all day, and dreaming ont all night

　　The ring[25] too is very well only a little of the biggest, send mee a Torto[ise] shell one to keep it on that is a little lesse then that I sent for a patt[ern]. I would not have the rule absolutely true without Exception that hard hairs are ill natured, for then I should bee soe; but I can allow that all soft hairs are good, and soe are you or I am deceived, as much as you are if you think I doe not love you enough; Tell mee my dearest am I, you will not bee if you think I am　　Yo[urs]

Letter 60

[Saturday 4 or Sunday 5 March 1654]

They say you gave order for this Vaste paper,[1] how doe you think I should ever fill it or with what. I am not alway's in the humor to wrangle or dispute, for Example now. I had rather agree to what you say then tell you that Dr Taylor[2] (whose devote you must know I am) say's there is a great advantage to bee gained in resigning up on's will to the comande of another, because the same Action which in it selfe is wholy indifferent if done upon our owne Choice, becom's an Act of Duty and Religion if don in Obedience to the comande of any Person whome Nature the Law's or our selv's have given a power over us. Soe that though in an Action already don wee can only bee our

owne Judges because wee only know with what intentions it was
don, yet in any wee intende tis safest sure to take the advice of
Another. Let mee practise this towards you as well as preach it to
you, and i'le lay a wager you'le aprove on't. But I am cleerly of
your opinion that contentment (which the spanish proverbe say's
is the best paint) [3] gives the Lustre to all on's injoyments, putts a
beauty upon things which without it would have none, increases
it Extreamly where tis already in some degree and without it all
that wee call happinesse besides looses its property. What is
contentment must bee left to every perticuler person to Judge
for themselv's, since they only know what is soe to them, which
differs in all according to there severall humors; only you and I
agree tis to bee found by us in a True friend, a moderat fortune,
and a retired life. The last I thank god I have in perfection, my
cell is almost finishd [4] and when you come back you'le finde mee
in it and bring mee both the rest I hope; I finde it much Easier to
talke of your comeing back then your goeing, you shall never
perswade mee I send you this Journy,[5] noe, pray let it bee your
fathers comand's or a necessity your fortune putts upon you;
twas unkindly sayed to tell mee I banish you, Your heart never
told it you I dare swear, nor mine ne're thought it; noe my Dear
this is I hope our last misfortune lett's beare it nobly; nothing
show's wee deserve a punishment soe much as our murmuring at
it, and the way to lessen those wee feel and to scape those wee
fear, is to suffer patiently what is imposed, makeing a Vertue of
necessity. Tis not that I have lesse kindenesse or more Courage
then you, but that mistrusting my self more (as I have more
reason) I have armed my self all that is posible against this occasion; I have thought that there is not much difference between
your beeing at Dublin or at London as our affair's stand. You
can write and hear from the first and I should not see you sooner
if you continued still at the last; besides I hope this Journy will
bee of advantage to us; when your Father pressed your comeing
over hee tolde you you needed not doubt either his power or his
will; have I don any thing since that deserves hee should Alter
his intentions towards us, or has any accident lessend his power,

if neither, wee may hope to bee happy, and the sooner for this Journy. I dare not send my Boy to meet you at Brickill,[6] nor any other of the Servants they are all too talkative but I can gett Mr Gibson[7] if you will to bring you a letter, tis a Civill well natur'd man as can bee, of Excellent Principles, and an Exact honesty. I durst make him my Conffessor though hee is not Obliged by his orders to conceal any thing that is told him. But you must tell mee then which Brickill tis you stop at, little or great, they are neither of them farr from us. If you stay there you'le write back by him, will you not, a long letter. I shall need it besides that you owe it mee for the Last's being soe short. Would you saw what Letters my Brother writes mee, you are not halfe soe kinde, well hee is alway's in the Extream's. Since our last quarrell hee has Courted mee more then ever hee did in his life and made mee more presents, which considering his humor is as great a testimony of his kindenesse as twas of Mr Smiths to my Lady Sunderland[8] when hee presented Mrs Camilla.[9] Hee sent mee one this week which in Earnest is as pritty a thing as I have seen, a China Trunke[10] and the finest of the kinde that ere I saw.

By the way this putts mee in minde ont, have you read the Story of China written by a Portuguese, Fernando Mendez Pinto[11] I think his name is, if you have not, take it with you, tis as diverting a book of the kinde as ever I read, and is handsomly written. You must allow him the Priviledge of a Travellour[12] & hee dos not abuse it, his lyes are as pleasant harmlesse on's as lyes can bee, and in noe great number considering the scope hee has for them; there is one in Dublin now that ne're saw much further, has tolde mee twice as many (I dare swear) of Ireland. If I should ever live to see that Country and her in it, I should make Excelent Sport with them[,] tis a Sister of my Lady Grey's her name is Pooley,[13] her husband liv's there too but I am affrayde in noe very good condition. They were but Poore and shee lived heer with her Sister, when I knew her, tis not halfe a yeer since she went I think, if you hear of her send mee word how she makes a shift there. And heark you can you tell

whither the Gentleman that Lost a Cristall boxe the 15 of february in Snt Jameses Parke or Olde spring garden [14] has found
it again or not I have a strang[e] Curiosity to know, tell mee,
and i'le tell you somthing that you dont know which is that I
am your Valentine [15] and you are mine. I did not think of
drawing any but Mrs Gouldsmith and Jane [16] would needs make
mee write some for them and my self, soe I writt downe our
three names and for Men Mr Fish, [17] James B. [18] and you. I cutt
them all Equall and made them up my self before they saw
them, and because I would owe it wholy to my good fortune if I
were pleased I made both them Chuse first that had never seen
what was in them and they left mee you, then I made them
Choose again for theirs and my name was left. You cannot
imagin how I was delighted with this little accident, but by
takeing notice that I cannot forbear telling you it. I was not halfe
soe pleased with my Encounter next morning, I was up Early
but with noe desig[n]e of getting another Valentine and goeing
out to walk in my Nightcloths and Nightgowne I mett Mr Fish
goeing a hunting I think hee was, but hee stayed to tell mee I
was his Valentine, and I should not have bin rid on him quickly
if hee had not thought himself a little too Necgligeé his haire
was not pouderd and his Cloths were but ordinary, to say truth
hee looked then my thought like Other Mortall People, yet hee
was as handsom as your Valentine, i'le swear you wanted one
when you took her, and had very ill fortune that nobody mett
you before her. Oh if I had not terrified my little Gentleman
when hee brought mee his owne letter, how sure I had had him
for my Valentine, on my conscience I shall follow your councell
if ere hee com's againe; but I am perswaded hee will not. I writt
my Brother that story for want of somthing else, and hee say's I
did very well there was noe Other way to bee rid on him; makes
a remarke upon't that I can bee severe enough when I please and
wishes I would practise it somwhere else as well as there. Can
you tell where that is, I never understand any body that dos not
speak plain English and hee never uses that to mee of late, but
tells mee the finest story['s] [19] (I may apply them how I please)

of People that have married where they thought there was great kindnesse and how misserably they have foun[d] themselv's deceived, how dispiseable they have made themselv's by it and how sadly they have repented it; hee reckons more inconvenienc[y's] then you doe that ffollow good natur's, say's it makes one credulous, apt to bee abused, betrays one to the cunning of People that make advantage on't and a thousand such things which I hear half asleep and halfe awake and take little notice of unlesse it bee somtimes to say that with all thes[e] faults I would not bee without it. Noe in Earnest, nor I could not love any Person that I thought had it not to a good degree, twas the first thing I liked in you, and without it I should nere have lik[ed] any thing; I know tis counted simple but I cannot imagin why. Tis true some People have it that have not witt but there are at leas[t] as many foolish People that have noe good Nature, and those are the person's I have ever observed to bee fullest of tricks, litle ugly plotts, and design's, unnecessary disguises, and mean Cunnings; which are the basest quality's in the whole worlde, and makes one the most contempti[ble] I think, and where I once discover them they loose theire Creditt with mee for Ever; some will say they are cunning only in theire owne defence & that there is noe liveing in this world without it, but I cannot understand how any thing more is necessary to on's owne safety besides a prudent caution that I now think is, though I can remember wh[en] noe body could have perswaded mee that any body meant ill when it did not apear by their words and actions. I remember my Mother, whoe (if it may bee allow'd mee to say it) was counted as wise a woman as most in England, when she seem'd to distrust any body and saw I took notice on't, wou[ld] aske if I did not think her too Jelous & a little ill natur'd, come I know you doe say's she if you would confesse it and I cannot blame you. When I was young as you are I thought my Father in Law[20] (who was a wise man) the most unreasonably suspitious person that ever was and disliked him for it huge[ly] but I have lived to see that tis almost imposible to think People worse then they are, and soe will you. I did not beleeve her, and leste that I should have more to say t[hen] this paper would holde it shall never bee sayed I began another at this time of Night I have spe[nt] [t]his idly, that should have told you with a little more circumstance how perfectly I am

Yours

Letter 61

[Saturday 11 or Sunday 12 March 1654]

You bid mee write Every week and I am doeing it without considering how it will come to you,[1] let Nan[2] look to that with whome I suppose you have left the orders of conveiance. I have your last letter, but Jane[3] to whome you refferr mee is not yet com downe, on Tewsday I expect her and if she bee not ingaged I shall give her noe cause hereafter to be[leeve] that she is a burthen to mee, though I have noe imployment for her but that of talking to mee when I am in the humor of sayeing nothing. Your dog is come too, and I have received him with all the Kindenesse that is due to any thinge you sende have deffended him from the Envy and the Mallice of a troupe of greyhounds that used to bee in favour with mee, and hee is soe sencible of my care over him that hee is pleased with nobody else and follow's mee as if wee had bin of longe acquaintance.

Tis well you are gon past my recovery, my heart has failed mee twenty times since you went, and had you bin within my call I had brought you back as often, though I know 30 miles distance and 300 are the same thing. You will bee soe kinde I am sure as to write back by the Coach and tell mee, what the successe of your Journy soe farr has bin, after that I Expect noe more (unlesse you stay for a winde) till you arrive at Dublin. I Pitty your Sister in Earnest,[4] a Sea Voyage is welcome to noe Lady,

but you are beaten[5] to it, and twill become you now you are a
conducter to shew your Valour, and keep your company in heart.
When doe you think of comeing back again, I am askeing that
before you are at your Journy's Ende, you will not take it ill that
I desyre it should bee soone, in the mean time i'le practise all the
Rules you give mee. Whoe told you I goe to bed late, in Earnest
they doe mee wronge. I have bin faulty in that point heretofore I
confesse, but tis a good while since I gave it over with my reading
a nights; but in the day time I cannot live without it, tis all my
diversion, and infinitly more pleasing to mee then any company
but yours, and yet I am not given to it in any Excesse now, I
have bin very much more. Tis Jane I know tells all these tales of
mee, I shall bee Even with her some time or Other, but for the
present I longe for her with some impatience that she may tell
mee all you have told her. Never trust mee if I had not a Suspition
from the first that twas that ill looked fellow B[6] who made up
that story Mr D.[7] told you. That which gave mee the first inclination to that beleife was the Circumstance you told mee of
theire seeing mee at Snt Gregory's,[8] for I rememberd to have
seene B. there, and had occasion to looke up into the Gallery
where hee sate to answer a very civill Salute given mee from
thence by Mr Freeman,[9] and saw B in a great whisper with
another that satt next him and pointing to mee. if Mr D. had not
bin soe nice in discovering[10] his name you would quickly have
bin cured of your Jellousy, never beleeve I have a Servante that I
doe not tell you of as soone as I know it my self, as for Example
now My B.P.[11] has sent to mee for a Country man of his Sr
John Tufton, hee marryed one of my Lady Wottens daughters
and heir's whoe is lately dead, and to invite mee to think of it.
Besides his Person and his Fortune without Exception, hee tell's
mee what an Excelent Husband hee was to this Lady thats dead
whoe was but a Crooked ill favour'd woman, only shee brought
him £1500 a year. I tell him I beleeve Sr J.T.[12] could bee content
I were soe too, upon the same term's, but his loveing his first
wife can bee noe Argument to perswade mee, for if hee loved
her as hee ought to doe, I cannot hope hee should Love another

soe well as I expect any body should that has mee, and if hee did
not Love her, I have lesse [reason][13] to Expect hee should mee. I
doe not care for a devided heart, I must have all or none, at least
the first place in it; Poore James[14] I have broake his hee say's,
twould pitty you to hear what sad complaints hee makes, and
but that hee has not the heart to hange himself, hee could bee
very well contented to bee out of the worlde.

I have read your wives[15] letter and by it finde shee has a great
deal of witt though I doe not think the manner of her writeing
very Exact; there are many pritty things shuffled together which
would doe better spoken then in a letter, notwithstanding the
received opinion that People ought to write as they speak (which
in some sence I think is true). She say's you used to say you
loved long letters which being spoken without any limitation or
qualification was in her opinion a great Error, and says shee intends your conversion by this long one of hers, and your mor-
tification[16] too, which is propper this lent, Askes you if Mrs
Kempston[17] and all her messengers were ever halfe soe troublesome, and whither you doe not think it fitt to com to com-
position w[ith] her, but yet that you should not think she dos
this meerly to torment you, You are to know that her Sister and
your Cousin Jenny[18] have urged her Often to write to you, (as
not thinking it soe fitt for them to doe it themselv's one being a
widdow and t'otther a mayde) to reproach your necglect of them;
talkes somthing of the little creditt she gives to the report of Mrs
Brooxes and Mrs Mildemays[19] reconciliation to their husband[s],
ask's you Earnestly whither you were at Mrs Mildemay's lodging
or not and whither tis likely she should ever see the famous
beauty you told her of; this is all, now whither any thing of this
bee of concernment you can only tell. That house of your Cousin
R. is fatall to Phisitians Dr Smith[20] that took it is dead already,
but may bee this was before you went and soe is noe news to
you; I shall bee sending you all I heare which though it cannot
bee much liveing as I doe yet it may bee more then ventur's into
Ireland. I would have you diverted whilest you are there as much
as is posible but not enough to tempt you to stay one Minute

Longer then your Father and your buisnesse Obliges you. Alasse I have already repented all my Shares i[n] Your Journy and begin to finde I am not half soe Valiant as I somtimes take my self to bee; The Knoledge that our interest's are the same and that I shall bee happy or unfortunate in your Person as much or more then in my owne dos not give mee that confidence You speak of, it rather increases my doubts, and I durst trust your ffortune alone rather then now that mine is Joyned with it, yet I will hope yours may bee soe good as to overcome the ill of mine and shall indeavor to mend my owne all I can by striveing to deserve it may bee better; My dearest will you pardon mee that I am forced to leave you soe soone the next shall bee longer though I can never bee more than I am,   Yours.

For your Master [21]

All else is but a circle

when your Mistress pleases

what makes that dash

between us

Letter 62

[Saturday] March the 18th 1653 [1654] [1]

How true it is that a misfortune never com's single; [2] wee live in Expectation of some one happinesse that wee propose to our selv's, an Age almost, and perhaps misse it at the last; but sad accidents have winges to overtake us, & come in fflocks like ill boading Raven's; You were noe sooner gon, but (as if that had not bin Enough) I lost the best Father [3] in the worlde, and though as to himself it was an infinite Mercy in God Almighty to take him out of a worlde that can bee pleasing to none, and was made more uneasy to him by many infirmity's that were upon him; Yet to mee it is an affliction much greater then People Judge it; Besides all that is due to Nature, and the memory of many (more

then ordinary) Kindenesses received from him, besides what hee
was to all that knew him, and what hee was to mee in Particuler;
I am left by his death in the condition (which of all Others) is
the most insuportable to my Nature; To depende upon Kindred
that are not friends, and that though I Pay as much as I should
doe to a stranger,[4] yet think they doe mee a Curtesy.

I Expect my Eldest B:[5] to day if hee com's I shall bee able to
tell you before I seale up this where you are likely to finde mee,
if hee offers mee to stay heer, this hole will bee more agreeable
to my humor, then any place that is more in the worlde. I take it
kindly that you used Art's to conceale our story and sattisfie my
nice aprehensions,[6] but i'le not impose that constraint upon
you any longer, for I finde my kinde B. Publishes it with more
Earnestnesse then ever I strove to conceale it,[7] and with more
disadvantage then any body else would; Now hee has tryed all
way's to what hee desyr's and findes it is in vaine, hee resolves to
revenge himself upon mee by representing this Action in such
Coulers as will amaze all People that know mee, and doe not
know him enough to discerne his mallice to mee; hee is not able
to forbear shewing it now, when my condition deserv's pitty
from all the worlde, I think, and that hee himself has newly lost
a Father, as well as I, but takes this time to Torment mee, which
appear's (at least to mee) soe barbarous a Cruelty that though I
thank god I have Charrity Enough perfectly to forgive all the
injury's hee can doe mee, yet I am afrayde I shall never look
upon him as a brother more.

An now doe you Judge whither I am not very unhappy, and
whither that sadnesse in my face you used to complaine off was
not suited to my fortune; You must confesse it; and that my
kindnesse for you is beyond Example. All these troubles and
persecutions that make mee weary of the world before my time,
cannot lessen the concernment I have for you and instead of
being perswaded, as they would have mee, by theire malicio[us]
storry's, mee thinks I am Obliged to love you more, in recompence of all the injury's they have don you upon my score; I
shall need nothing but my owne heart to fortifie mee in this

resolution; and desire nothing in retourne of it; but that your care of your self may answer that which I shall alway's have for your interest's.

I received your letter of the 10th of this month, and I hope this will finde you at your Journy[s] Ende. In Earnest I have pittyed your Sister Extreamly and can Easily aprehende how troublesome this Voyage must needs bee to her, by knowing what Others have bin to mee; Yet pray assure her I would not scruple at undertakeing it my self to gaine such an acquaintance, and would goe much farther then where (I hope) she is now, to serve her. I am affrayde shee will not think mee a fitt Person to choose for a friend that cannot agree with my owne Brother; but I must trust you to tell my storry for mee, and will hope for a better Charracter from you, then hee gives mee; whoe least I should complaine resolves to prevent[8] mee, and possesse[9] my faults first, that hee is the injured party. I never magnified my Patience to you but I begin to have a good opinion on't since this triall, yet perhaps I have noe reason, and it may bee as well a want of sence in mee as of Passion; however you will not bee displeased to know that I can indure all that hee or any body else can say, & that setting aside my Fathers death and your absence I make nothing an affliction to mee, though I am sorry I confesse to see my self forced to keep such distances with one of his relation[s] because Religion and Nature and the Custom of the worlde teaches Otherwise.

I see I shall not bee able to sattisfie you in this[10] how I shall dispose of my self, for my Brother is not come,[11] the next will certainly tell you, in the mean time I Expect with great impatience to heare of your safe arrivall. Twas a dissapointment that you mist those faire windes,[12] I pleased my self Extreamly with a beleife that they had made your Voyage rather a diversion then a trouble either to you or your company, but I hope your passage was as happy if not as sudden as you Expected it. Let mee hear often from you, and long letters, I doe not count this soe, have noe aprehensions for mee but all the care of your self that you please, my melancholy has not danger int, and I beleeve the accidents of my life would worke more upon any Other then they doe upon mee whose humor is alway's more prepar'd for them then that of gayer persons. I hear nothing that is worth your knowing when I doe you shall have it; Tell mee if theire bee any thing I can doe for you, & assure your self I am perfectly

Yours

Letter 63

[Sunday] April the 2d 1654

There was never any body more surprised then I was with your Last, I read it soe coldely and was soe troubled to finde that you were noe forwarder on your Journy [1] but when I cam to the last, and saw dublin at the date I could scarce beleeve my Ey's, in Earnest it Transported mee soe that I could not forbear Expressing my Joy in such a manner, as had any body bin by to have observed mee they would have suspected mee noe very sober Person; You are safe Arived you say and pleased with the place alredy only because you meet with a letter of mine there, in your next I Expect some other comendation's on't, or Else I shall hardly make such a hast to it as People heer beleeve I will. All the servants have bin to take theire leav's on mee and say how sorry they are to heer I am goeing out of the Lande, some begger's at the dore has made soe ill a report of Irlande to them, that they Pitty mee Extreamly; but you are pleased I hope to heer I am comeing to you, the next faire winde Expect mee. Tis not to bee imagined the ridiculous storry's they have made nor how J.B. [2] cryes out on mee for refusing him and choosing his Chamber ffellow Yet hee Pitty's mee to [*sic*] and swear's I am condemned to bee the misserablest Person upon Earth, with all his quarrell to mee hee do's not wish mee soe ill as to bee marryed to the Proudest imperious insulting ilnatured man that Ever was, one that before hee has had mee a week shall use mee with contempt, and beleeve that the favour was of his Side; is not this very comfortable, but pray make it noe quarrell, I make it none I can assure you, and though hee knew you before I did I doe not think hee know's you soe well; besides that his Testimony is not of much Valew. I am to spend this next week in Takeing leave of this Country and all the company int, perhaps never to see it more, from hence I must goe into Northamptonshyre to my Lady R. and soe to London,[3] where I shall finde my Aunt,[4] and my B: P.[5] betwixt whome I think to devide this Summer.

Nothing has happend since you went worth your knoledge. My Lord Marquis Hartford[6] has lost his eldest son my Lord Beuucham, whoe has left a fine Young Widdow[.] in Earnest tis great Pitty at the rate of our Young Nobillity hee was an Extreordinary Person, and remarkable for an Excelent husband. My Lord Cambden[7] has fought too, With Mr Stafford but ther's noe harme don; You may discerne the hast I am in by my writeing[8] there will come a time for Long letters againe but there will never come any wherein I shall not be   Yours

For Mr William Temple
at Sir John Temples house
in Damask Street
Dublin[9]

Letter 64

[London, Thursday 25 May 1654]

This world is composed of nothing but contrariety's and sudden accidents, only the proportions are not at all Equall for to a great measure of trouble it allow's soe small a quantitye of Joy that one may see tis meerly intended to keep us alive withall; this is a formall preface and looks as if there were somthing of very usefull to ffollow, but I would not wish you to Expect it, I was only considering my owne ill humor Last night, I had not heard from you in a week & more; my B[1] had bin with mee and wee had talked our selv's both out of breath and patience too, I was not very well, and rise[2] this morning only because I was weary of lyeing a bed.

When I had dined I took a Coach and went to see whither there was ever a letter for mee and was this once soe lucky as to finde one;[3] I am not partiall to my self I know and am contented that the pleasure I had received with this, shall serve to sweeten many sad thoughts that has interposed since your last and more that I may reasonably Expect before I have another, and I think I may (without vanity) say that nobody is more sencible of the least good fortune nor murmur's lesse at any ill then I doe, since I owe it meerly to custome and not to any constancy[4] in my humor or somthing that is better; noe in Earnest any thing of good com's to mee like the sun to the inhabitants of Groenland[5] it raises them to life when they see it and when they misse it it is not strange they Expect a night of half a yeer long. You cannot imagin how kindly I take [it] that you forgive my B. and let mee assure you, shall never presse you to any thing unreasonable. I will not Oblige you to Court a person that has injured you, I only beg that whatsoever hee dos in that kinde may bee Excused by his relation to mee, and that whensoever you are moved to think hee dos you wrong, you will at the same time remember his sister Loves you passionatly & nobly that if hee Valew's nothing but fortune shee dispises it and could Love you as much a begger as she could doe a Prince, and shall without question Love you Etternally but whither with any sattisfaction to her self or you is a sad[6] doubt; I am not apt to hope and whither it bee the better or the worse I know not, all sorts of diffidencys are naturall to mee, and that which (if your Kindenesse would give you leave) you would terme a weaknesse in mee, is nothing but a reasonable distrust of my owne Judgment which makes mee desyre the aprobation of my friends. I never had the confidence in my life to presume any thing well don that I had nobody's

opinion in but my owne, and as you very well observe there are
soe many that think themselv's wise when nothing Equalls theire
ffolly but theire pride, that I dread nothing soe much as discovering such a thought in my self because of the consequence of
it.

Whensoever you come you need not doubt your welcome[7]
but I can promise you nothing for the manner ont; I am affrayd
my surprise and disorder will bee more then Ever[.] I have good
reason to think soe and none that you can take ill; but I would
not have you Attempt it till your F. is redy for the Journy too,
noe realy hee deserv's that all your occasions should wayte on
his, and if you have not much more then an ordinary Obedience
for him I shall never beleeve you have more then an ordinary
Kindenesse for mee since (if you will pardon mee the comparison)
I beleeve wee both merritt it from you upon the same score, hee
as a very indulgent Father and I as a very kinde Mistres. Don't
laugh at mee for comending my self, you will never doe it for
mee and soe I am forced to it.

I am still heer in Towne, but had noe hand I can assure you in
the new discoverd plott against the Protector[8] but my Lord of
Dorchester[9] they say has and soe might I have had if I were as
rich as hee, and then you might have bin sure on mee at the
Tower, now a worse lodging might serve my Turne, tis over
against Salisbury house,[10] where I have the honnor of seeing my
Lady M. Sandis[11] Every day unlesse some race or other carry
her out of Towne. The last week she went to one as far as
Winchester, with Coll: Paunton,[12] (if you know such a one);
and there her husband mett her, and because hee did soe (though
it were by accident), thought himself Obliged to invite her to his
house but seven miles off, and very modestly say'd no more for it
but that hee thought it better then an Inne or at least a Crouded
one as all in the Towne were now because of the race, but she
was soe good a Companion that she would not forsake her
company, soe hee invited them too but could prevaile with
neither[.] only my Lady grew kinde at parting and sayd indeed if
Tom Paunton and J. Morton[13] and the rest would have gon she

could have bin contented to have taken his offer; thus much for
the marryed People, now for those that are towards it there is
Mr Stanley and Mrs Withrington [14] Sir H: Littleton and Mrs
Philadelphia Cary [15] whoe in Earnest is a fine Woman such a one
as will make an Excelent wife; and some say my Lord Rich [16]
and my Lady betty Howard [17] but Others that prettend to know
more say that his court to her is but to countenance a more
serious one to Mrs Howard her Sister in Law, [18] hee not haveing
the courage to pretende soe openly (as some doe) to anothers
wife. O but your old acquaintance poore Mr Heningham [19] has
noe luck hee was soe neer (as hee thought at least) marryeng Mrs
Gerhard [20] that any body might have gott his whole Estate in
Wagers upont that would have ventured but a reasonable proportion of theire owne, and now hee looks more like an Asse
then ever hee did, she has cast him off most unhandsomly that's
the truth on't and would have tyed him to such conditions as
hee might have bin her slave with but could never bee her
husband; is not this a great deal of news for mee that never stirr
abroad, nay I had brought mee to day more, then all this, that I
am marryeng my self, and the pleasantnesse ont is that it should
bee to my Lord Snt Johns, [21] would hee look of mee think you
that has pritty Mrs Fretcheville my comfort is I have not seen
him since hee was a widdower and never spoke to him in my
life; I found my self soe innocent that I never blushed when they
told it mee[,] what would I give I could avoyde it when People
speak of you, in Earnest I doe prepare my self all that is posible
to heare it spoken of and yet for my life I cannot hear your
name without discovering [22] that I am more then ordinarily concerned int. A blush is the foolishest thing that can bee and betray's
one more then a red nose dos a drunkerd, and yet I would not
soe wholy have lost them as some women that I know has, as
much injury as they doe mee.

I can assure you Now that I shall bee heer a fortnight Longer[,]
they tell mee noe lodger upon paine of his highnesses displeasure
must remove sooner [23] but when I say I may have to leave to
goe into Suffolk for a month and then come hither again to goe

into Kent[24] where I intend to bury my self alive again as I did in Bedfordshyre unlesse you call mee out and tell mee I may bee happy; alasse how faine I would hope it but I cannot and should it ever happen twould bee long before I should beleeve twas meant to mee in Earnest or that twas other then a dream; to say truth I doe not love to think ont, I finde soe many things to fear and soe few to hope; tis better telling you that I will send my letters where you dirrect that they shall bee as long on's as posibly my time will permitt, and when at any time you misse of one I give you leave to imagine as many kinde things as you please and to beleeve I mean them all to you

farwell

may the 25th

Letter 65

[London, Tuesday] 6 June 1654

I see you know how to punish mee in Earnest I was soe frighted with your short letter as you cannot imagin and as much troubled at the cause ont[.] what is it your Father Ailes and how long has hee bin ill; if my prayers are heard hee will not bee soe long; Why doe you say I failed you indeed I did not Jane[1] is my witnesse she carryed my letter to the White-hart by Snt Jameses,[2] and twas a very long one too; I carryed one thither since my self and the woman of the house was soe very angry because I desyr'd her to have a care ont that I made the Coachman drive away with all posible speed least she should have beaten mee; to say truth I prest her too much considering how litle the letter deserved it twas writt in such disorder the company prateing about mee and some of them soe bent on doeing mee litle mischeifs that I knew not what I did and beleive it was the most sencelesse disjoynted thing that Ever was read; I remember now that I writt Robin Spencer instead of Will, tis hee that has marryed Mrs Gerhard,[3] and I admire theire courages, she will have 6 hundred pound a year tis true after her mother but how they will live till then I cannot imagin; I shall bee Even with you for your short letter i'le swear they will not allow mee time for any thing and to show how absolutely I am governed I need but tell you that I am every night in the park and at new spring garden[4] where though I come with a mask I cannot scape being knowne nor my conversion being admired; are not you in some fear what will become on mee[?] these are dangerous Courses[.] I doe not finde though that they have Alter'd mee yet, I am much the same person I was at least in being   Yours

June the 6th 1654[5]

Letter 66

[London, Tuesday] 13 June [1654]

You have sattisfied mee very much with this last long letter and made some amends for the short one I received before; I am convinced too that happinesse is much such a kinde a thing as you discribe, or rather such a nothing for there is noe one thing can properly bee called soe, but Every one is left to Create it themselv's in somthing which they either have or would have, and soe farr it's well Enough; but I doe not like that ones happinesse should depende upon a perswasion that this is happinesse because nobody know's how long they shall continue in a beleife built upon noe ground's; only to bring it to what you say and to make it absolutly of the same Nature with Faith; wee must conclude that nobody can either Creat or continue such a beleife in themselv's, but where it is, there is happinesse; and for my part at this present I verely beleeve I could finde it in the Long Walk at Du:[1] You say nothing of your fathers Sicknesse therfore I will hope hee is well againe, for though I have a quarrell to him, it dos not Extende soe farr as to wish him ill[,] but hee made noe good retourne, for the councell I gave you, to say that there might come a time when my kindenesse might faile, doe not beeleeve him I charge you unlesse you doubt your self that you may give mee occasion to change; and when hee tells you soe againe, ingage what you please upon't and put it upon my accounte.

I shall goe out of Towne² this week and soe cannot possibly get a Picture drawne for you till I come againe which will bee within these six week's but not to make any stay at all[.] I should bee glad to finde you heer then; I would have had one drawne since I cam and consulted my glasse every morning when to begin, and to speak freely to you that are my friend I could never finde my face in a condition to admitt on't, & when I was not sattisfied with it my selfe I had noe reason to hope that any body else should; but Ime affrayed as you say that time will not mend it and therfore you shall have it as it is, as soone as Mr Cooper³ will voutch safe to take the pain's to draw it for you; I have made him twenty Courtesys and promised him £15 to perswade him; I am in great trouble to think how I shall write out of Suffolk to you, or receive Yours, however doe not faile to write though they lye a while I shall have them at last, and they will not bee the lesse welcome, and though you should misse of some of mine let it not trouble you but if it bee my fault ile give you leave to demande sattisfaction for it when you come; Jane⁴ kisses your hands and say's she will bee redy in all places to doe you service; but i'le prevent her[,] now you have put mee into a Jealous humor i'le keep her in chains before she shall quit scores with mee; doe not beeleeve Sir I beseech you that the Young heirs are for you content your self with your Old Mistresse you are not soe handsome as Will Spencer⁵ nor I have not soe much courage nor wealth as his Mistresse nor she has not soe much as her Aunt say's by all the mony; I should not have call'd her his Mistresse now, they have bin marryed almost this fortnight. Ile write againe before

I leave the Towne and should have writt more now but company is come in.   Adieu my Dearest

June the 13th

Letter 67

[London, Thursday 15 June 1654]

I promised in my last to write againe before I went out of Towne, and now i'le bee as good as my word, they are all gon this morning[1] and have left mee much more at liberty then I have bin of late, therfore I beleeve this will bee a long letter, perhaps too long, at least if my letters are as little entertaining as my company is.

   I was carryed yesterday abroade[2] to a dinner that was designed for mirth, but it seem's one ill humord person in the company is Enough to put all the rest out of tune, for I never saw People performe what they intended worse and could not forbear telling them soe, but to Excuse themselv's and silence my reproaches they all agreed to say that I spoyled theire Jollity by wearing the most unseasonable look's that could bee put on for such an occasion; I tolde them I know noe rememdy[3] but leaving mee behinde next time, and could have told them that my looks were suitable to my fortune though not to a feast; fye I am gott into my complaining humor that tyres my self as well as every body else and which (as you observe) help's not at all[.] would it would leave mee and that I could beleeve I shall not alway's have occasion for it, but thats in nobody's power, and my Lady Talmach[4] that say's she can doe whatsoever she will cannot beleeve whatsoever she pleases[.] tis not unpleasant mee thinks to hear her talke how at such a Time she was sick and the Phisitians tolde her she would have the small Poxe and shewed her where they were comeing out upon her but she bethought her self that it was not at all convenient for her to have them at that time; some buisnesse she had that required her goeing abroade, and soe shee resolved shee would not bee sick; nor was not, twenty such storry's as these she tell's and then fall's into discourses of the streng[t]h of reason, and the power of Philosophy till she confound's her self and all that hear her; You have noe such Lady's in Irelande. Oh mee, but I heard to day of Your Cousin Hamond[5] is goeing thither to bee in Ludlows[6] place[,] is it true[?] you tell mee nothing what is don there but tis noe matter the lesse one knows of State affayr's I finde it is the better; my Poore Lady Vavasor[7] is carryed to the Tower & her great belly could not Excuse her because she was acquainted by somebody that there was a plott against the Prottector[8] and did not discover it, she has tolde now all that was tolde her but vow's she will never say from whence she had it; wee shall see whither her resolutions are as unalterable as those of my Lady Talmach I wonder how shee behaved her self when she was marryed. I never saw any body yet that did not look simply and out of Countenanc[e] nor ever knew a wedding well designed but one, and that was of two person's whoe had time enough to confesse to contrive it; and noebody to please int but themselves[.] hee came downe into the Country where she was upon a Visett and one morning marryed her, as soone as they cam out of the Church they took coach and cam for the Towne, dined at an inne by the way and at night cam into Lodgings that were provided for them where nobody knew them and where they passed for marryed People of seven years standing; the truth is I could not indure to bee Mrs Bride in a Publick wedding[9] to bee made the happiest person on Earth. Doe not take it ill for I would indure it if I could rather then faile but in Earnest I doe not think it were posible for mee; You cannot aprehende the Formality's of a Treaty more then I doe, nor soe much the successe on't; Yet in Earnest your f: will not finde my B: Peyton wanting in civility[10] (though hee is not a man of much complement unlesse it bee in his letters to mee) nor an unreasonable Person in any thing soe hee will allowe him out of his Kindnesse to his wife to sett a higher valew upon

his sister then she deserv's; I know not how hee may bee pre-
judiced as to the buisnesse but hee is not deaf to any reason when
tis civily deliverd and is as easily gained with compliance and
good usage as any body I know but by noe other way, when hee
is roughly dealt with hee is like men ten times the worse fort. I
make it a case of consciens to discover my faults to you as fast as
I know them that you may consider what you have to doe, my
Aunt told mee no longer agon then Yesterday that I was the
most willfull woman that ever she knew and had an obstinacy of
spirritt nothing could overcome.[11] Take heed you see I give you
faire warning. I have missed a letter this Monday what is the
reason; by the next I shall bee gon into Kent and my other
Journy is layed aside[12] which I am not displeased at because it
would have broken our intercourse very much; heer are some
Verses of Cowly's[13] tell mee how you like them tis only a peece
taken out of a new thing of his the whole is very longe & is a
discription of, or rather a paraphrase upon the friendships of
David and Jonathan, tis I think the best I have seen of his and I
like the subject because tis that I would bee perfect In[.]
Adieu   Je suis vostre

Letter 68

[London, Monday] 26 June [1654]

I told you in my last that my Suffolk Journy was layed aside and
that into Kent hastned, I am beginning it to day[1] and I have
Chosen to goe as farr as Graves End by water;[2] though it bee
very stormy weather, if I drowne by the way, this will bee my
Last Letter, and like a will I bequeath all my kindenesse to you in
it, with a charge never to bestow it all, upon another Mistresse
least my Ghost rise againe and haunte you.

I am in such hast that I can say litle else to you now; when
you are come over wee'l think where to meet for at this distance

I can designe nothing only I should bee as litle pleased with the constraint of my B[3] house as You. Pray let mee know whither your Man leav's you and how you stand inclined to him I offer you,[4] indeed I like him Extreamly and hee is commended to mee by People that know him very well and are able to Judge for a most Excelent Servant and faithfull as possible; i'le keep him uningaged till I hear from you   Adieu

My next shall make amends for this short one.

June the 26th

For Mr William Temple
at Sir John Temples house in Damaske Street
Dublin

I received your last of June the 22th since I seal'd up my letter,[5] and I durst not but make an excuse for another short one after you have chid mee soe for those you have received alredy indeed I could not help it nor cannot make a much better wife then I doe a husband[6] if I ever am one; Pardon mon Cher Coeur on m'attend Adieu mon Ame Je vous souhait tout ce que vous desiré

Letter 69

[Knowlton, Kent, Tuesday 4 July 1654]

Because you finde fault with my other letters this is like to bee shorter then they, I did not intende it soe though I can assure you but last night my Brother[1] told mee hee did not send his till ten a clock this morning and now hee cal's for mine at seven, before I am up, & I can only bee allowed time to tell you that I am in Kent and in a house soe strangly Crowded with Company that I am weary as a dog alredy though I have bin heer but three or fower day's; that all theire mirth has not mended my humor,

and that I am heer the same I was in other Places, that I hope
meerly because you bid mee and loose that hope as often as I
consider any thing but yours; would I were easy of beliefe[,]
they say one is soe to all that one desyr's[,] I doe not finde it,
though I am told I was soe Extreamly when I beleeved you
loved mee[.] that I would not finde and you have only Power to
make mee think it[.] but I am call'd upon[.] how faine I would
say more yet tis all but the sayeing with more Circumstance then
I am   Yours

June the 4th[2]

For your Master[3]

Letter 70

[Knowlton, Kent, Monday] 10 July [1654]

I am very sory I spoke too late, for I am confident this was an
Excelent Servant;[1] hee was in the same house where I lay and I
had taken a great ffancy to him upon what was told mee of him
and what I saw; the Poore ffellow was soe pleased that I undertook to inquire out a place for him that though mine was as I
told him uncertain, yet upon the bare hopes ont hee refused two
or three good condition's[2] but I shall sett him now at Liberty;
and not think at all the worse of him for his good Nature; sure
you goe a litle too farr in your condemnation on't; I know it
may bee abused as the best things are most subject to bee, but in
it self tis soe absolutely necessary that where it is wanting nothing
can recompence the misse on't; the most contemptible Person in
the world if hee has that cannot be Justly hated and the most
considerable without it, cannot deserve to bee loved; Would to
god I had all that good Nature you complaine you have too
much of, I could finde wayes Enough to dispose ont amongst

my self and my friend's; but tis well where it is and I should
sooner wish you more on't then lesse.

I wonder with what confidence you can complaine of my
short Letters that are soe guilty your self in the same kinde. I
have not seen a Letter this month, that has been above halfe a
sheet; never trust mee if I write more then you that live in a
desolated Country[3] where you might ffinish a Romance of ten
Tomes before any body interupted you; I that live in a house the
most filled of any since the Arke and where I can assure [you?][4]
one has hardly time for the most necessary occasion's Well there
was never any one thing soe much desired and aprehended[5] at
the same time as your retourne is by mee, it will certainly I think
conclude mee a very happy or a most unfortunate Person. Sometimes mee thinks I would faine know my doome, what Ever it
bee and at others I dread it soe Extreamly that I am confident the
5 Portugalls and the 3 Plotters which were tother day condemned[6] by the high Court of Justice had not half my fears upon
them. I leave you to Judge the constraint I live in what Alaram's
my thought[s] give mee and yet how unconcern'd this company
requires I should bee. They will have me Act my Part in a Play,
the Lost Lady[7] it is, and I am she[,] pray God it bee not an ill
Omen; I shall loose my Ey's and you this Letter if I make it
longer[.]   Farwell   I am   Yours

July the 10th

Letter 71

[Knowlton, Kent, Saturday 15 July 1654]

I see you can chide when you please and with athority; but I
deserve it I confesse and all I can say for my self is, that my fault
proceeded from a very good principle in mee; I am apt to speak
what I think; and to you have soe accoustumed my self to dis-

cover all my heart, that I doe not beleeve twill ever bee in my power to conceal a thought from you; therfore, I am affrayed you must resolve to bee Vexed with all my sencelesse aprehensions as my Brother Pe is with some of his wives,[1] who is, though a very good woman, the most troublesome one in a Coach that ever was, wee dare not let our tongues lye more on one side of our mouths then tother for fear of overturning it.

You are sattisfyed I hope ere this that I scaped drowning; however tis not amisse that my will is made you know now how to dispose of all my wealth whensoever I dye but I am troubled much you should make an ill Journy to soe litle purpose, indeed I writt by the first Post after my arrivall heer, and cannot imagin how you cam to misse of my Letter. Is your f. retourned yet and doe you think of comeing over imediatly[?] how welcome you will bee but alas I cannot talke on't at the rate that you doe[.] I am sencible that such an absence is misfortune Enough, but I dare not promise my self that it will conclude ours, and tis more my beleife that you your selfe speak it rather to incourage mee and to shew your wishes, then your hopes; my humor is soe ill at present that I dare say noe more least you should Chide againe[.] I finde my self fitt for nothing but to converse with a Lady below that is fallen out with all the worlde because her husband and she cannot agree[,] tis the pleasantest thing that can bee to hear us discourse[.] she takes great pain's to diswade mee from ever marryeng and say's I am the veryest foole that ever lived if I doe not take her councell; now wee doe not absolutly agree in that point but I promise her never to marry unlesse I can finde such a husband as I discribe to her and shee beleev's is never to bee found soe that upon the matter wee differ very litle; and whensoever she is accused of maintaining opinions very distructive of society and absolutly prejudiciall to all the young People of both sexes that live in the house, she call's out mee to bee her secconde & by it has lost mee the favour of all our young galants whoe have gott a Custome of Expressing any thing that is noe where but in fiction by the name of Mis O: husband[.] for my life I cannot beat into theire head's a passion that must bee subject to noe decay[,] an Even Perfect Kindnesse that must last perpetualy without the least intermission[.] they Laugh to hear mee say that one unkind word would distroy all the sattisfaction of my life and that I should expect our kindnesse should increase every day if it were posible but never lessen[;] all this is perfect nonsence in theire opinion but I should not doubt the convincing them if I could hope I should ever bee soe happy as to bee

Yours

Letter 72

[Knowlton, Kent, Saturday 22 July 1654]

How long this letter will bee I cannot tell; you shall have all the time that is allowed mee but upon condition that you shall not Examin the sence on't too strickly; for you must know I want sleep extreamly the sun was up an hower before I went to bed to day, & this is not the first time I have don this since I cam hither[.] twill not bee for your advantage that I should stay heer longer for in Earnest I shall bee good for nothing if I doe; wee goe abroad all day and Play all night and say our Prayers when wee have time; well in sober Earnest now I would not live thus a twelve month to gaine all that the K.[1] has lost unlesse it were to give it him againe; tis a mirracle to mee how my B.[2] indures it tis as contreary to his humor as darkenesse is to light and only shew's the Power hee lets his wife have over him[.] will you bee soe good natured[?] hee has certainly as great a kindenesse for her as can bee and to say truth not without reason but of all the People that ever I saw I doe not like his Carriage towards her; hee is perpetualy wrangling and findeing fault and to a Person that did not know him would apeare the worst husband and the most imperious in the world, hee is soe amongst his Children

too though hee loves them passionatly[.] hee has one son and
tis the finest boy that ere you saw and has a notable spirritt
but yet stands in that awe of his Father that one word from
him is as much as twenty whippings.

You must give mee leave to entertaine you thus with Discourses of the Famely for I can tell you nothing Else from hence;
Yet now I remember I have another storry for you. You litle
think I have bin with Lilly,[3] in Earnest I was, the day before I
cam out of Towne and what doe you think I went for, not to
know when you would com home I can assure you, nor for any
other occasion of my owne but with a Cousen[4] of mine that has
long designed to make her self sport with him and did not misse
of her aime; I confesse I alway's thought him an imposture but I
could never have imagin'd him soe simple a one as wee founde
him; in my life I never heard soe rediculous a discou[rse][5] as hee
made us and noe old woman that passes for a witch could have
bin more to seek what to say to reasonable People then hee was;
hee asked us more questions then wee did him and caug[ht][6] at
Every thing wee sayed without discerning that wee abused[7] him
and sayed things purposly to confound him which wee did soe
perfectly that wee made him contradict himselfe the stranglyest
that Ever you heard; Ever since this adventure I have had soe
great a beleife in all things of this nature that I could not forbeare layeing a Pescod with nine Pease in't under the doore Yesterday and was informed by it that my husbands name should
bee Thomas, how doe you like that, but what Thomas I cannot
imagine for all the servants I have gott since I cam hither I know
none of that name.

Heer is a new songe[8] I doe not send it to you but to your
Sister, the tune is not worth the sending soe farr; if shee pleases
to put any to it I am sure it will bee better then it has heer[.]

Adieu

Letter 73

[Knowlton, Kent, Saturday 2 September 1654]

I wonder you did not come before your last letter, 'twas dated the 24th of August, but I received it not till the 1st of September; would to God your Journy were over; Every litle storme of winde fright's mee soe that I passe heer for the greatest Coward that ever was borne though in Earnest I think I am as litle soe as most women Yet I may bee deceived too for now I remember mee you have often tolde mee I was one and sure you know what kinde of heart mine is better then any body else.

I am glad you are pleased with that discription I made you of my humor,[1] for though you had disliked it I am afrayde tis past my power to helpe[.] you need not make Excuses neither for yours noe Other would please mee halfe soe well[.] that Gayete which you say is only Esteem'd, would bee unsuportable to mee and I can as litle indure a tongue that's alway's in motion as I could the Clack of a Mill; of all the Company this Place is stored with there is but two Person's whose conversation is at all Easy to mee one is my Eldest Neece[2] whoe sure was sent into the world to shew tis posible for a woman to bee silent; the Other is a gentleman[3] whose Mistresse Dyed Just when they should have maryed and though tis many year's since, one may read it in his face still[.] his humor was very good I beleeve before that accident for hee will yet say things pleasant enough but tis soe seldome that hee speak's at all and when hee dos tis with soe sober a look that one may see hee is not moved at all himself when hee diverts the Company most. You will not bee Jealous though I say I like him very much, if you were not secure in mee you might bee soe in him[.] hee would Expect his Mistresse should rise again to reproach his inconstancy if hee made court to any thing but her memory; Mee thinks wee three (that is my Neece, and hee, and I,) doe become this house the

worst that can bee; unlesse I should take into the Number my
Brother P himselfe too, for to say truth his for another sort of
Melancholy is not lesse then ours. What can you imagin wee did
this last week when to our Constant Company there was add a
Coll:[4] and his Lady a son of his and two daughters, a mayde of
honour to the Queen of Bohemia[5] and another Coll:[6] or a Major
I know not which besides all the trayne they brought with them
the men the greatest drinkers that ever I saw which did not at all
agree with my Brother whoe would not bee drawne to it to save
a Kingdom if it lay at stake and noe other way to redeem it[.]
but in Earnest there was one more to bee pittyed besides us and
that was Col: Thornhils Wife as pritty a Young Woman as I
have seen. She is Sir John Greenvils sister[7] and has all his good
Nature, with a great deal of beauty and modesty and witt
enough, this innocent Creature is sacrified to the veryest beast
that ever was, the first day she cam hither hee intended it seem's
to have come with her but by the way called in to see an old
acquaintance and bid her goe on hee would overtake her but did
not come till next night After and then soe drunk that hee was
layed imediatly to bed whither she was to ffollow him when she
had supped. I blessed my selfe at her Patience, as you may doe
that I could finde any thing to fill up this paper withall.

Adieu

Letter 74

[Knowlton, Kent, Saturday 9 September 1654]

I did soe promise my selfe a letter on fryday that I am very
angry I had it not though I know you were not come to Towne
when it should have bin writt[.] but did not you tell mee you
should not stay above a day or two[?][1] what is it that has kept
you longer[?] I am pleased though to know that you are out of

the Power of soe uncertaine things as the winde and the sea, which I never fear'd for my selfe but did Extreamly aprehende for you. You will finde a Pacquett of Letters to read and may bee have mett with them alredy[,] if you have you are soe Tyred that tis but reasonable I should spare you in this. To say truth I have not time to make this longer besydes that if I had my pen is soe very good that [it] writes an invisible hand I think I am sure I cannot read it my selfe if your Ey's are better you will finde that I intended to assure you

I am   Yours

Letter 75

[Knowlton, Kent, Saturday 16 September 1654]

I am but newly waked out of an unquiet sleep and I finde it soe late that if I write at all it must bee now, some company that was heer last night kept us up till three a clock and then wee lay three in a bed which was all one to mee as if wee had not gon to bed at all; Since dinner they are all gon and our company with them part of the way and with much adoe I gott to bee Excused that I might recover a little sleep but I am soe moaped yet that sure this letter will bee nonsense; I would faine tell you though that your f is mistaken and you are not if you beleeve that I have all the Kindenesse and Tendernesse for you my heart is capable of; Let mee assure you (what ere your f: thinks) that had you £10000 a year I could love you noe more then I doe and should bee far from showing it soe much least it should look like a desire on your fortune which as to my self I valew as little as any body breathing; I have not lived thus long in the world and in this Age of Changes but certainly I know what an Estate is[.] I have seen my fathers reduced [from] [1] better then £4000 to not £400 a yeare and I thank god I never felt the change in any thing that I thought necessary; I never wanted nor am confident I never shall; but yet I would not bee thought soe inconsiderat a person as not remember that it is Expected from all people that have sence that they should act with reason[,] that to all persons some proportion of fortune is necessarry according to theire severall qualitys[,] and though it is not required that one should tye on's self to just soe much and somthing is left for on's inclination and the difference in the person's to make[,] yet still within such a compasse[,] and such as lay more upon those considerations then they will bear shall infallibly bee condemned by all sober persons. If any accidentes out of my power should bring mee to necesity though never soe great[,] I should not doubt with gods assistance but to bear it as well as any body[,] and I should never bee ashamed on't if hee pleased to send it mee[,] but if by my owne ffolly I had puld it upon my selfe the case would be Extreamly alter'd; if Ever this comes to a treaty I shall declare that in my owne choyse I prefferr you much before any Other person in the world and all that this inclination in mee (in the Judgments of any persons of honnour and discretion) will beare I shall desyre may bee layed upon it to the uttermost of what they can allow and if your f: please to make up the rest I know nothing that is like to hinder mee from being Yours[.] but if your father out of humor shall refuse to treate with such friends as I have² let them bee what they will it must End hear[,] for though I was content for your sake to loose them and all the respect they had for mee yet now I have don that i'le never lett them see that I have soe litle interest in you and yours as not to prevaile that my Brother may bee admitted to treat for mee. Sure when a thing of Course and soe much reason, as that (unlesse I did declare to all the world hee were my Enemy) it must bee Expected whensoever I dispose of my self, hee should bee made noe Stranger to it[,] when that shall bee refused mee I may bee justly reproached that I deceived my self when I Expected to bee at all Valewed in a famely that I am a Stranger to or that I should bee consider'd with any respect because I had a Kindenesse for you that made mee not Valew my owne interest. I doubt much whither all this bee sence or not[,] I finde my head soe heavy but that which I would say is in short this. If I did say it once that my B should have nothing to doe int twas when his Carriage towards mee gave mee such an occasion as I could justi-fie the keeping that distance with him, but now it would Look Extreamly unhandsome in mee and sure I hope your f: would not requir[e] it of mee[.] if hee dos I must conclude hee has noe Valew for mee and sure I never disobliged him to my knoledge and should with all the willingnesse imaginable serve him if it lay in my power[.] good god what an unhappy person am I; but all the world is soe almost Just now they are telling mee of a gentle-man neer us that is the most Wretched Creature made (by the Losse of a wife that hee passionatly Loved) that can bee. If your f: would but in some measure sattisfie my freinds that I might but doe it in any Justifiable manner you should dispose mee as you pleased, carry mee whither you would all places of the world would bee alike to mee where you were & I should not despaire of carryeng my self soe towards him as might deserve a better opinion from him.

I am   Yours

Letter 76

[Knowlton, Kent, Saturday 23 September 1654]

My doubts and fear's were not at all Encreased by that which gives you soe many nor did I aprehende that your f: might not have bin prevailed with to have allowed my Brothers being seen in the Treaty[,] for as to the thing it selfe whither hee apear int or not twill bee the same[.] hee cannot but conclude my B. P. would not doe any thing in it without the Others consent.[1]

I doe not prettende to any share in Your F: kindenesse as

haveing nothing in mee to merrit it but as much a stranger as I am to him I should have taken it very ill if I had desyred it of him and hee had refused it mee. I doe not beleeve my Brother has sayed any thing to his prejudice unlesse it were in his per-swasions to mee,[2] and there it did not not injure him at all[.] if hee takes it ill that my B. appear's soe Very averse to the match, I may doe soe too that hee was the same, and nothing lesse then my kindenesse for you could have made mee take soe patiently as I did his Sayeing to some that knew mee at York[3] that hee was forced to bring you thither and afterwards to send you over least you should have marryed mee. This was not much to my advantage nor hardly Civill I think to any woman yet I never soe much as took the least notice on't nor had not now but for this occasion[.] yet sure it concern's mee to bee at least as nice[4] as hee in pointes of honour. I think tis best for mee to End hear least my anger should make mee loose that respect I would alwayes have for your father and twere not amisse I think that I deverted it all toward's you for being soe idle as to run out of your bed to catch such a Colde[.] if you come hither, you must Expect to bee chidden soe much that you will wish you had stayed till wee cam up when perhap's I might have almost forgott halfe my quarrell to you. At this present I can assure you I am pleased with nobody but your Sister and her I love Extreamly and will call her pritty say what you will. I know she must bee soe though I never saw more of her then what her letters show; Shee shall have two spotts[5] if she please (for I had just such another given mee after you were gon)[6] or any thing Else that is in the power of   Your

Letter 77

After a longe debate with my selfe how to sattisfie you and remove that rock (as you call it) [1] which in your aprehensions is of soe great danger I am at last resolved to let you see that I valew your affection for mee at as high a rate as you your selfe can sett it and that you cannot have more of Tendernesse for mee and my Interest's then I shall ever have for Yours. The particulers how I intende to make this good you shall know when I see you; which since I finde them heer more irresolute in point of time though not as to the Journy it selfe then I hoped they would have bin, notwithstanding your quarrell to mee and the aprehension you would make mee beleeve you had that I doe not care to see you pray come hither and try whither you shall bee welcome or not[.] in sober Earnest now I must speak with you, and to that End if your occasions will g[ive you leave,] [2] as soone as you have rec[eived this, com]e [3] downe to Canterbury, send[ing word whe]n [4] you are there [5] and you shall have further dirrections. You must bee contented not to stay heer above two or three howers I shall tell you my reason when you come & pray informe your self of all that your f: will doe in this occasion that you may tell it mee only therfore let it bee plainly and sincerely what hee intends and all.

   I will not hinder your comming away soe much as the making this letter a litle longer might take away from your time in reading it; tis Enough to tell you   I am   Ever

Yours

Monday
October the 2d [6]

You are like to have an Exelent housewife of mee I am abed still and slept soe soundly nothing but your letter could have waked mee you shall hear from mee as soone as wee have dined farewell can you indure that word, noe out upont, i'le see you anon.

Fye upon't I shall grow too good now, I am taking care to know how your Worship slept to night better I hope then you did the Last. Send mee word how you doe and dont put mee off with a bitt of a Note now, You could write mee a fine Long Letter when I did not deserve it halfe soe well.

Appendices

A Letters Written During the Marriage

Letter A

My Dearest Heart

'Twas kindly don not to forget my scrips. I wayted for it all day and would not have missed it for two such basketts of grapes as cam with it though they were Excelent good ones. I will bee very Carefull of my selfe and my Aunt[1] dos assure mee I cannot misse of a good midwife in the Towne whensoever I shall have occasion for her.[2] Your horses shall bee looked to too as well as William[3] and I and Jane[4] and Mrs Gouldsmith[5] can doe it, for wee understand it much alike mee thinks. I wish my Aunt's buisnesse a happy dispatch,[6] and my dearest home again with his

D. Temple

Letter B

Dearest Heart

Tom[1] will give you an account of his Journy to Moore Parke and I can only tell you that wee are all well hear and that you need not presse Mrs Carter[2] to come downe yet for my Aunt is of

Opinion as well as I that I shall not come soe soon. My Lady
Vachell[3] was hear yesterday and my Cousin Mary Hamond &
both sayed you were an arrant Gadder therfore I would advise
you to make what hast home you can to save your Creditt but
most because you know how welcom you will bee to Your

D. Temple

Letter c

Tis mighty well too that I have satt upon thornes these two
howers for this sweet scrip full of reproaches. Pray what did you
Expect I should have writt, tell mee that I may know how to
please you next time. But now I remember mee you would have
such letters as I used to write before we were marryed, there are
a great many such in your cabinet[1] that I can send you if you
please but none in my head I can assure you. Tis not the great
aboundance of diversion I finde heer though, nor want of any
kindnesse (I think) that hinders mee from being Just what I was
then, but a dullnesse that I can give no accounte of and that I am
not displeased with but for your sake and because it is many
times an occasion for the making good one of my Brothers
prophesy's who used to tell mee often I had more kindnesse for
you then became mee, and that I might assure my selfe if I ever
came to bee your wife you would reproach mee with it, I might
perhaps though bee som thing more dull then ordinary when I
writt last for as I remember I was sleepy too and not soe much
with sitting up late as with riseing Early which I have done ever
since you went Either because I am weary of my bed or that tis
good to make me leave again but know soe little what to doe
with myselfe when I am up that I am fain to send for Jack[2] into
my chamber, see him drest there, and when I am weary of
playing with him goe to worke for him, but alasse, he has a
greate defecte[3] his Coate was made and I had gott him linnen

redy to weare with it but Mrs Carter[4] has sent him noe shoo's and stockings[.] I believe twas Tom's[5] fault that did not carry her Janes[6] letter soone enough. You tell mee nothing of my Aunt[7] nor of my cousin Thorolde.[8] I suppose tis that you have not seen any of them yett. I shall observe your order to morrow and write to you againe on Monday[.] tis like to bee a great faire[9] they say, somthing more then ordinary sure it will bee or else Mr Mayor[10] and his brethren would nere have put themselves to the trouble of comeing all to my Aunt[11] two days agon. Do tell her that they would pull downe our friend Mrs Harrisons[12] hedge to make roome for it[.] they threatend her Garden too and question her right to the ffishing and the hundred Egg's. Mighty hott words past and many more then the buisnesse was worth I thought, but that the gravity of Mr Mayor's Ruffe bore it out well would I could borrow it to send with this letter for tis a litle to the purpose mee thinks as all that hee sayed. See what you get by putting mee upon long letters[,] if you confesse it you are glad with all your heart to finde yourselfe soe near the end on't. Good night to you my dearest. I am, your

D. Temple

Letter D

My Dearest Heart

After all Mr Mayor's[1] preparations 'twas a very poore faire, Not a good horse in't besides Sawyers[2] Teame in which was the Mare hee told you of, and hee brought her downe to the Stable to match her with my Aunt's[3] and they doe very well together hee says but I did not see it for though I sent twenty Messengers to him Sadler[4] would not come near mee all the faire day but sent mee word at night what hee had don which was that on Satterday next heer would come two Mares for you to see. To day I sent for him againe and hee tels mee that the Mares are both Sawyers, both 4 years old, and full as large as my Aunts and the same Couler and both come to about £30[.] one of them hee has bin offered £16 for and hee takes her to be better then my Aunts there was but that one heer but Sawyer tells him the Other is full as good as my Aunts and if you like them you may have them if not thers noe harm done, hee is not fond of selling them.[5] I have seen the Young ffellow[6] hee looks plain and honnest, will undertake he says to Looke to your 4 horses very well and with as much care as any man. Sadler commends him Mightily hee drove his Brother's coach the Gloucester Rode a great while, he asks £12 a year and cannott take under hee sayes, hee had as much at Sadler's Brother and has as good as £16 where he now is.[7] Sadler and hee goes up together to morrow, there you may see him and Sattisfye your selfe but with all this I must tell you too that they say Sadler is generally taken Notice on for a Gift he had of Lyenge and therefor what his Mares will come to I cannot tell. Can you tell me when you intende to come home, would you would, I should take it mighty kindly good deare make haste I am as weary as a dog without his Master,[8] your poore Jack is all the Entertainment I have, hee mem's his little duty and grow's and thrives Every day. When the sun shines his mayde has him abroade to use him to the Aire against his Journy and hee is to goe to Coley[9] upon a solemne invitation. My deare Hearte bee sure I have a scrip by Tuesday's coach and noe reproaches, remember that, indeed I don't deserve them I thinke, for Ime sure I infinitly love my dearest dear hart and I am his   D. Temple

If you can conveniently I should bee glad you payd the Grocers bill.[10]

Letter E

My dearest best Heart

I saw your new man [1] to day and heard him to my cost – Ah, 'tis a sad story my deare but he says your best Mare is good for nothing she has the glanders [2] extremely, and a soare heel, which the Fairier says is a surfett [3] she has had that now breaks out there[.] is not Sawyer bound to take her againe that warranted her sounde to you. Saddler that knewe what she was before [4] I believe for hee will not come neer mee, though I have sent for him twice today. I thought fitt to lett you know it before you come down that you might consider what you had to doe, I am affrayde it will disorder us a little. John found it as soone as ever hee saw her I beleeve the fellow has good skill in horses hee looks very honestly too and like to make a good servant I think. I gave Jack the kiss you sent him and he mems his little duty and gave mee another for you that you shall have as soone as you come home and twenty more from

Your   D.T.

Letter F

My Dearest Heart

I send you here a letter that will amaze you I beleeve as much as it did mee, but tis most Happy that hee [1] is thus discovered before hee has don a worse mischiefe. Rid your hands of him quickly for God sake, since I know I have broken open his boxe but founde nothing there but his owne things, his new sute and most of his linnen, unlesse it bee the Cape of your Cloak which I have sent lest you might want it. Poor Mr Rolles[2] brought this letter through all the rain to day. My dear dear heart make hast home, I doe soe want thee that I cannot imagin how I did to Endure your being soe long away when your buisnesse was in hande. Goodnight my dearest, I am   Your   D.T.

Letter G

My best dear heart

How kindly I take this little scrip you sent mee deed my dear you shall never want one as longe as I have fingers to write, yet never trust me if I know what to tell thee besydes that were all well heer and were at the fall of the great Wall today.[1] I would have cryed over it mee thoughts, it fell soe solemnly and with soe good grace after it had stood out all their Battery's soe long and mett with the same fate that all the great thing's in the worlde doe when they fall, The People shouted at it and were pleased, ran in to trample ont because twas down and tooke a pride in[2] treading where they durst not have sett a foot whilest it was up.[3] Well the man has a huge Bargaine ont there is I am confident five times more free stone int then anybody could have imagin'd but all this is nothing to your Mares & truth is my deare I can give you but a slender accounte of them. I hope they are well (& soe forth) but 'tis soe durty I cannot goe down to the stable and Tom[4] is resolved I shall see him noe more I think for I have not don it since you went. To day indeed hee took his Phisick and soe kept his Chamber but where he bestowed himself all yesterday I know not. Jane[5] is at an End of all her patience with him too, for it seems Robins Master seeing his letters open read them and Robin[6] took it soe ill that they went together by the Ear's aboute it and great disorders it has caused, but those are common things. I thought wee should have had a Combatt between my poor Aunt[7] and her grandsonne to Night they fell out soe Terribly at Cards & doe you thinke that Rude boy should have the confidence to throw up his Cards in a snuffe (after hee had disputed it with her halfe an howre) and say hee would play noe more because when hee has dealt twice shee told him ont and would have the cards to deal her selfe as twas her Turne. Ah my deare if Ever Jack should doe such things, sure I shall make bold to beat him as long as I were able, but poor childe hee looks soe honestly I know hee never will, deed my Hearte 'tis the quietest best little boy that Ever was borne, I'me afray'd hee'l make mee grow fonde of him doe what I can, the only way to keep mee from it is for you to keep at home for then I am lesse with him, now hee is all my Entertainment besydes what I find in thinking of my dearest and wishing him with his   D. Temple

I think it will bee much the best not to bring downe the Coach but to try to borrow my Aunts.[8]

Letter H

My Dearest Heart

Tooby[1] did me great wrong in not delivering the long scrip I sent you[.] I know if you had seen it before you writt yours would have been something longer than it is. But I am thankful however and indeed you send mee very good news, of my Aunt's[2] stay in Towne for the thought of that Journy was not very pleasant to mee. I am glad you have found a footman too, and Tom shall bee sent up as you apoint but how will you doe to retourne your mony I am in some paine for you. Mr Lamport[3] has made up a bill of £15 od money £5 wee had before and £5 now[4] and the linnen with some od things you had, Buttons & Silke, &c. I sent it to our neighbour Mr

Osgood[5] to know if hee could help us, but hee is not provided
at present hee says. I doe not think but that Mr Warde[6] of
Newgate Markett could doe it, he has acquaintance heare for I
have had letters sent mee from him by Town's men, if you
have any from Irlande pray let mee have them to Entertaine
my selfe withall till you come. It seems tis true that my Aunt
Temple[7] comes away, for my cousin Mary Hammond[8] writes
my Aunt word that she and my Lady Waller[9] were at Battersey to see my uncle and where they told her they Expected
her very suddenly. Poore woman I am soe sorry for her tis
certainly the dread of us that frights her away. To morrow
Jack is invited to Coly a-shroving, but my Lady say's shee
beleev's shee is never to see you there, I sayed what I could to
Excuse you, but you are concluded the Arrantist gadder in the
Country, none matter though my deare I love you for all that
soe while hast home againe. Doe you mean to look for some
lodgings and rooms to lay our goods in that must be thought
on, I mem'd to stand out of harm's way when the Great Wall
fell downe. Here com's Creeper[10] that will lett mee say noe
[more?] but that we are both

Yours

If Tom goes remember Mrs Fountains hood.[11]

Letter 1

Hague, 31st October [1670]

My Dearest Heart

I received your letter from Yarmouth,[1] and was very glad you
made so happy a passage. 'Tis a comfortable thing, when one is
on this side, to know that such a thing can be done in spite of
contrary winds. I have a letter from P., who says in character

that you may take it from him that the Duke of Buckingham[2]
has begun a negotiation there, but what success he may have in
England he knows not, that it were to be wished our politicians
at home would consider well that there is no trust to be put in
alliances with ambitious kings, especially such as make it their
fundamental maxim to be base.[3] These are bold words, but they
are his own. Besides this, there is nothing but that the French
king[4] grows very thrifty, that all his buildings, except fortifi-
cations, are ceased, and that his payments are not so regular as
they used to be. The people here are of another mind; they will
not spare their money, but they are resolved – at least the States
of Holland, if the rest will consent – to raise fourteen new
regiments of foot and six troops of horse; that all the companies,
both old and new, shall be of 120 men that used to be 50, and
every troop 80 that used to be 45. Nothing is talked of but the
new levies, and the young men are much pleased. Downter[5]
says they have strong suspicions here you will come back no
more, and that they shall be left in the lurch; that something is
striking up with France and that you are sent away because you
are too well inclined to these countries; and my Cousin Temple,
he says, told him that a nephew of Sir Robert Long's,[6] who is
lately come to Utrecht, told my cousin Temple, three weeks
since, you were not to stay long here, because you were too
great a friend of the people, and that he had it from Mr Williamson,[7] who knew very well what he said. My cousin Temple
says he told it Major Scott[8] as soon as he heard it, and so 'tis like
you knew it before; but here is such a want of something to say
that I catch at everything. I am my best dear's most affectionate　　　D.T.

B William Temple's Letter from Ireland

[Dublin, Thursday] 18 May 1654

This is no artificiall humility, no I am past all that with you, I know well enough that I am as other people are, but at that rate that me things[1] the world goes, I can see nothing in it to putt a value upon besides you, and beleeve mee whatever you have brought mee to and how you have done it I know not but I was never intended for that fond thing which people tearme a lover. I am calld upon for my letter, but I must have leave first to remember you of yours, for Godsake write constantly while I am heere or I am undone past all recovery, I have livd upon them ever since I came but had thrivd much better had they been longer[.] unless you use to give mee better measure I shall not bee in ease to undertake a journey into England. The dispaire I was in upon the not hearing from you last weeke and the beleefe that all my letters were miscarried (by some treachery among my good friends[2] who I am sorry have the name of yours) made mee press my father by all means imaginable to give mee leave to goe presently[3] if I heard not from you this post, but hee would never yeeld to that, because hee said upon your silence hee should suspect all was not likely to bee well between us and hee was sure I should not bee in condition to bee alone, hee rememberd too well the letters I writt, upon our last unhappy differences[4] and would not trust mee from him in such another occasion. But withall hee told mee hee would never give mee occasion of any discontents which hee could remedy, that if you desird my comming over, and I could not bee content without, hee would not hinder mee, though hee very much desird my company a month or two longer, and that it that time twas very likely I might have his.[5] Well now in very good earnest doe you thinke tis time for mee to come or noe, would you bee very glad to see mee there,[6] and could you doe it in less disorder and with less surprisse then you did at Ch:[7] I aske you theese questions very seriously, but yett how willingly would I venture all to bee with you. I know you love mee still, you promised it mee, and thats all the security I can have for all the good I am ever lik to have in this world, tis that which makes all things else seeme nothing to it, so high it setts mee, and so high in deed that should I ever fall twould dash mee all to pieces. Methinks your very charity should make you love mee more now then ever, by seeing mee so much more unhappy then I usd, by beeing so much farther from you, for that is all the measure can bee taken of my good or ill condition. Justice I am sure will oblige you to it, since you have no other means left in the world of rewarding such a passion as mine, which sure is of a much richer value then any thing in the world besides. Should you save my life againe,[8] should you make mee absolute master of your fortune and your person too, yett if you love mee not, I should accept none of all this in any part of payment, but looke upon you as one be-hindhand with mee[9] still. Tis no vanity this, but a true sense of how pure and how refind a nature my passion is, which none can ever know besides my owne heart unles you finde it out by beeing there.

How hard tis too of ending when I am writing to you, but it must bee so, and I must ever bee subject to other peoples occasions, and so never I thinke master of my owne. This is too true both in respect of this fellows hast that is bawling at mee for my letter, and of my fathers delays, they kill mee, but patience, would any body but I bee here, yett you may com-mand mee over at one minutes warning. Had I not heard from you by this last, in earnest I had resolvd to have gone with this[10] and given my F. the slip for all his caution. Hee tells mee still of a little time,[11] but alas who knows not what mis-chances and how great changes have oftend[12] happend in a little time, for Godsake lett mee know of all your motions,[13] when and where I may hope to see you, lett us but escape this cloude, this absence, that has overcast all my contentments and

I am confident theres a cleare skye attends us. My dearest deare adieu. I am

Yours

Pray where is your lodging. Have a care of all the despatch and security that can bee in our intelligence. Remember [me] to my fellow servant,[14] sure by the next I shall write some learned epistle to her, I have been so long about it.

May 18
1654

C Genealogies

The genealogical tables have been compiled with the assistance of Lady Osborn; they are based on Collins (1720 and 1727), Wotton (1727 and 1741) and Burke (1980), and on private family records, and differ in some respects from the details given in Moore Smith (1928). The present Lady Osborn is not only a Hammond by descent, but is also a long-standing expert on genealogy, and I am deeply indebted to her for her assistance, although I must take full responsibility for any errors the tables may contain.

K.P.

Sir John Osborne, Bt (1552—1628) of
Chicksands, Beds.; born in prison, where
his father was confined by Mary I;
Treasurer's Remembrancer of the Exchequer

=

Dorothy Barlee (1562—1638),
d. of Richard Barlee of Elsenham Hall, Essex;
Lady in Waiting to Anne, Queen of Denmark

Peter Osborne (1521—92),
of Tyld Hall, Lachington, Essex;
Keeper of the Privy Purse and Treasurer's
Remembrancer of the Exchequer to Edward VI

=

Anne Blyth (d. 1615),
d. of John Blyth, 1st Regius Professor of
Physick in the University of Cambridge

Catherine Osborne (b.1575)

=

Sir Thomas Cheke of Pyrgo, Essex,
married (ii) Essex Rich., eldest d. of
1st Earl of Warwick

Robin Cheke

Thomas Cheke (1628—88);
Colonel in the Army; Lieut.-Governor
of the Tower of London

=

Letitia, d. of the Hon. Edward Russell;
married (ii) her cousin, Lord Robert Russell

Frances Cheke

=

2nd Earl of Manchester; she was
the third of his five wives

Elizabeth Cheke

=

Richard Franklin of Moor Park,
Herts.

The Osborne
Family Tree

Anne Osborne (b. 1610)
=

Sir Peter Osborne, Kt (1585–1654),
of Chicksands, Beds.; Treasurer's
Remembrancer of the Exchequer;
Lieutenant-Governor of Guernsey
=
Dorothy Danvers (1590–1650), d. of
Sir John Danvers of Dauntsey, Wilts.
(s. of 1st Earl of Danby, K.G.; grandson
of Sir John Danvers, the regicide;
great-grandson of Sir Charles Danvers,
member of the Essex plot)

Sir Thomas Peyton (1613?–84)
of Knowlton, Kent, who married
(ii) Cecilia, widow of Sir Thomas Swan
(iii) Jane, widow of Sir Timothy Thornhill

— Dorothy Peyton (b. 1638)
=
Sir Basil Dixwell (d 1668)
of Bromehouse, Kent

Sir John Osborne, Bt (1611–96)
of Chicksands, Beds.; created first
baronet, 1662 ; Privy Councillor to Charles II
=
Eleanor Danvers (d. 1677), d. of
Sir Charles Danvers of Baynton, Wilts.

— Katherine Peyton
=
Sir Thomas Longueville, Bt
of Winterton
(Waterton ?), Bucks.

Christopher Osborne (b. 1586);
Captain in the Navy;
died unmarried

Henry Osborne (1614–45);
Lieut.–Colonel of Foot;
Killed at the battle of Naseby

— Elizabeth Peyton
=
William Longueville,
of the Inner Temple

Thomas Osborne (1588–1651)
of North Fambridge Manor, Essex

Thomas Osborne (1615–37);
unmarried;
died of smallpox in France

Richard Osborne (1590–1623);
Lieutenant in the Army; page to
Queen Elizabeth of Bohemia, sister
of Charles I; killed at Sedan, France,
in the Bohemian War

Francis Osborne (b. 1617);
died young

Francis Osborne (1593–1658);
Master of Horse to the Earl of Pembroke;
author of Advice to a Son (1656)
=
(i) Anne Ufflet, d. of William Ufflet
(ii) Anna Draper of Nether Watton,
Oxon., sister of William Draper, Colonel
in the Parliamentary Army

Sir Henry Osborne, Kt (1618–75);
Treasurer of Sick and Wounded Soldiers
at Greenwich; diarist; died unmarried

Charles Osborne (1620–43);
Lieut.–Colonel of Foot; unmarried;
killed in the market place at
Hartland, Devon, fighting on the
Royalist side

Elizabeth Osborne (b. 1623)
=
Edward Duncomb of Battlesden, Beds.

— Six died in Ireland

Robert ('Robin') Osborne (1626–53);
died unmarried

Dorothy Osborne (1627–95)
=
Sir William Temple, Bt (1628–99);
diplomat; statesman; author

— John Temple (1664–89);
Secretary for War
=
Marie du Plessis
of Rambouillet, France

Mary Osborne (1620–30)

— Diana Temple (1663–79);
died of smallpox

The Temple Family Tree

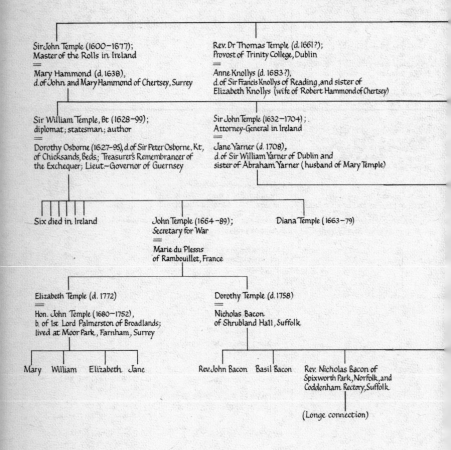

Sir John Temple (1600–1677);
Master of the Rolls in Ireland
=
Mary Hammond (d. 1638),
d. of John and Mary Hammond of Chertsey, Surrey

Rev. Dr Thomas Temple (d. 1661?);
Provost of Trinity College, Dublin
=
Anne Knollys (d. 1683?),
d. of Sir Francis Knollys of Reading, and sister of
Elizabeth Knollys (wife of Robert Hammond of Chertsey)

Sir William Temple, Bt (1628–99);
diplomat; statesman; author
=
Dorothy Osborne (1627–95), d. of Sir Peter Osborne, Kt,
of Chicksands, Beds; Treasurer's Remembrancer of
the Exchequer; Lieut.–Governor of Guernsey

Sir John Temple (1632–1704);
Attorney-General in Ireland
=
Jane Yarner (d. 1708),
d. of Sir William Yarner of Dublin and
sister of Abraham Yarner (husband of Mary Temple)

Six died in Ireland

John Temple (1664–89);
Secretary for War
=
Marie du Plessis
of Rambouillet, France

Diana Temple (1663–79)

Elizabeth Temple (d. 1772)
=
Hon. John Temple (1680–1752),
b. of 1st Lord Palmerston of Broadlands;
lived at Moor Park, Farnham, Surrey

Dorothy Temple (d. 1758)
=
Nicholas Bacon
of Shrubland Hall, Suffolk

Mary   William   Elizabeth   Jane

Rev. John Bacon   Basil Bacon   Rev. Nicholas Bacon of
Spixworth Park, Norfolk, and
Coddenham Rectory, Suffolk

(Longe connection)

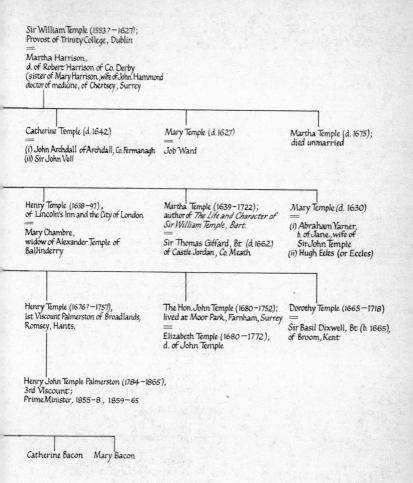

Sir William Temple (1553? – 1627);
Provost of Trinity College, Dublin
=
Martha Harrison,
d. of Robert Harrison of Co. Derby
(sister of Mary Harrison, wife of John Hammond
doctor of medicine, of Chertsey, Surrey

Catherine Temple (d. 1642)
=
(i) John Archdall of Archdall, Co. Fermanagh
(ii) Sir John Vell

Mary Temple (d. 1627)
Job Ward

Martha Temple (d. 1675);
died unmarried

Henry Temple (1638 – 97),
of Lincoln's Inn and the City of London
Mary Chambre,
widow of Alexander Temple of
Ballinderry

Martha Temple (1639 – 1722);
author of *The Life and Character of
Sir William Temple, Bart.*
=
Sir Thomas Giffard, Bt (d. 1662)
of Castle Jordan, Co. Meath

Mary Temple (d. 1630)
=
(i) Abraham Yarner,
b. of Jane, wife of
Sir John Temple
(ii) Hugh Eeles (or Eccles)

Henry Temple (1676? – 1757),
1st Viscount Palmerston of Broadlands,
Romsey, Hants.

The Hon. John Temple (1680 – 1752);
lived at Moor Park, Farnham, Surrey
=
Elizabeth Temple (1680 – 1772),
d. of John Temple

Dorothy Temple (1665 – 1718)
=
Sir Basil Dixwell, Bt (b. 1665),
of Broom, Kent

Henry John Temple Palmerston (1784 – 1865),
3rd Viscount;
Prime Minister, 1855 – 8, 1859 – 65

Catherine Bacon   Mary Bacon

John Hammond (d. 1617); doctor of medicine
of Chertsey, Surrey;
Physician to James 1

==

Mary Harrison (d. 1649 or 1650),
d. of Robert Harrison of Co. Derby and
sister of Martha (wife of Sir William Temple,
Provost of Trinity College, Dublin)

— Robert Hammond (d. 1623)
of Chertsey, Surrey

==

Elizabeth Knollys (d. 1657),
d. of Sir Francis Knollys of Reading and
sister of Ann Knollys (wife of Rev. Dr
Thomas Temple of Trinity College, Dublin)

— Thomas Hammond,
one of the judges at the trial of
Charles 1

— George Hammond

— Henry Hammond (1605–60);
Doctor of Divinity; Fellow of Magdalen
College, Oxford; author of *Practical
Catechism*; invested with the living at
Penshurst, he supervised the education
of William Temple; died unmarried

— Jane Hammond

==

Sir John Dingley (1593–1671)
of Wolverton, Isle of Wight

— Mary Hammond (d. 1638)

==

Sir John Temple (1600–1677);
Master of the Rolls in Ireland

The Hammond
Family Tree

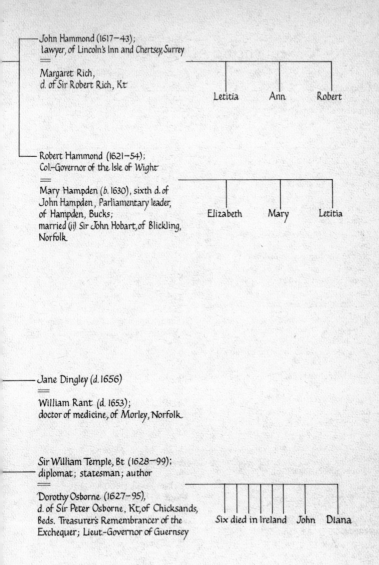

John Hammond (1617–43);
lawyer, of Lincoln's Inn and Chertsey, Surrey
=
Margaret Rich,
d. of Sir Robert Rich, Kt

Letitia   Ann   Robert

Robert Hammond (1621–54);
Col.-Governor of the Isle of Wight
=
Mary Hampden (b. 1630), sixth d. of
John Hampden, Parliamentary leader,
of Hampden, Bucks;
married (ii) Sir John Hobart, of Blickling,
Norfolk

Elizabeth   Mary   Letitia

Jane Dingley (d. 1656)
=
William Rant (d. 1653);
doctor of medicine, of Morley, Norfolk

Sir William Temple, Bt (1628–99);
diplomat; statesman; author
=
Dorothy Osborne (1627–95),
d. of Sir Peter Osborne, Kt, of Chicksands,
Beds. Treasurer's Remembrancer of the
Exchequer; Lieut.-Governor of Guernsey

Six died in Ireland   John   Diana

D Sequencing of the Letters

No.	First line	Manuscript (1891)	Parry (1888)	Gollancz (1903)	Parry (1903, 1914)	Moore Smith (1928)	Folio Society (1968)
1	You may please to lett my Old . . .	2-3	2	2	1	1	1
2	If there were any thing in my . . .	4	3	3	2	2	2
3	There is nothing moves my Charity . . .	1	1	1	3	3	3
4	Since you are soe easy to please . . .	5	5	4	4	4	4
5	Not to confirme you in your beleife . . .	6	4	5	5	5	5
6	I am soe great a lover of my bed . . .	9	7	7	6	6	6
7	You have made mee soe Rich . . .	10	8	8	7	7	7
8	Though I am very weary after my . . .				8	8	8
9	I was soe kinde as to write to you . . .	11-12	9	9	9	9	9
10	Your last letter came like a . . .	13-14	10	10	10	10	10
11	I am soe farre from thinking . . .	15-16	11	11	13	11	11
12	Your fellow servant upon the news . . .				11	12	12
13	I am glad you scaped a beating . . .	19-20	13	13	15	13	13
14	I know not how to Oblige . . .	7-8	6	6	12	14	14
15	There shall bee two Post's . . .	17-18	12	12	14	15	15
16	I did receive both your letters . . .				53	16	16
17	I received your letter to day . . .	24-5	17	17	18	17	17
18	That you may bee sure it was . . .	21	14	14	17	18	18
19	I am sory my last letter frighted . . .	30-31	20	20	21	19	19

No.	First line	Manuscript (1891)	Parry (1888)	Gollancz (1903)	Parry (1903, 1914)	Moore Smith (1928)	Folio Society (1968)
20	I doe not know that any body ...	32-3	21	21	24	20	20
21	I'le tell you noe more of my servants ...	36	23	23	26	21	21
22	You must pardon mee I could not ...	22	15	15	16	22	22
23	If it were the Carryers fault ...	23	16	16	22	23	23
24	I have bin reckoning up how many ...	26-7	18	18	19	24	24
25	If to know I wish you with mee ...	28-9	19	19	20	25	25
26	You are more in my debt then ...	34-5	22	22	25	26	26
27	You amaze mee with your story ...	37-8	24	24	27	27	27
28	In my opinion you do not ...				30	28	28
29	I can give you leave to doubt ...	47-8	29	29	34	29	29
30	The day I should have received ...	41-2	26	26	31	41	41
31	I received your last sooner ...				28	30	30
32	Your Last cam safe, and I shall ...	43-4	27	27	32	31	31
33	I doe not lay it as a fault ...	45-6	28	28	33	32	32
34	Jane was soe unlucky as to come ...	57-8	34	34	41	33	33
35	You cannot imagin how I was ...	49-50	30	30	35	34	34
36	That you may be at more certainty ...	68-9	40	40	45	39	39
37	'Tis most true that I could not ...				23	35	35
38	It was sure a lesse fault in mee ...	51-2	31	31	36	36	36
39	If want of kindenesse were ...	65-6	39	38	37	38	38
40	All my quarrells to you ...	53-4	32	32	38	37	37
41	Pray let not the aprehension ...	55-6	33	33	40	40	40

No.	First line	Manuscript (1891)	Parry (1888)	Gollancz (1903)	Parry (1903, 1914)	Moore Smith (1928)	Folio Society (1968)
42	Nothing that is paper can scape mee . . .	59	35	35			
43	You have furnish'd me now with . . .	39–40	25	25	29	42	42
44	You would have mee say somthing . . .	66–7	38	39	43	43	43
45	Why are you soe sullen . . .	60–61	26	26	29	44	44
46	You say I abuse you . . .	62–3	37	37	42	45	45
47	Had you the bitt of paper . . .				44	46	46
48	Haveing tyr'd my selfe with . . .	70–71	41	41	46	47	47
49	Tis most true what you say . . .	77	45	45	50	49	49
50	I am extreamly sorry that . . .	72–3	42	42	47	48	48
51	I can say litle more then I did . . .	74–5	43	43	46	50	50
52	If you have Ever Loved mee . . .	76	44	44	49	51	51
53	That which I writt by your Boy . . .	78–9	46	46	51	52	52
54	Tis but an howr since you went . . .	82–3	48	48	54	54	54
55	Tis never my humor to doe injury's	80–81	47	47	52	53	53
56	. . . of what she saw till hee was gon . . .	84–5	49	55	55	55	55
57	Whoe would bee kinde to one . . .	86–7	50	50	56	56	56
58	Tis well you have given over . . .	92–3	53	53	59	57	59
59	The lady was in the right . . .	88–9	51	51	57	58	58
60	They say you gave order for . . .	90–91	52	52	58	59	59
61	You bid mee write Every week . . .	94–5	54	54	60	60	60
62	How true it is that a misfortune . . .	96	55	55	61	61	61
63	There was never any body more . . .	97–8	56	56	62	62	62
64	This world is composed of nothing . . .	101–4	58	58	64	64	64

No.	First line	Manuscript (1891)	Parry (1888)	Gollancz (1903)	Parry (1903, 1914)	Moore Smith (1928)	Folio Society (1968)
65	I see you know how to punish . . .	105-6	59	59	65	65	65
66	You have sattisfied mee very much . . .	107-8	60	60	66	66	66
67	I promised in my last to write . . .	109-10	61	61	67	67	67
68	I told you in my last . . .	111-12	62	62	68	68	68
69	Because you finde fault . . .	113-14	63	63	69	69	69
70	I am very sory I spoke too late . . .	117	66	66	70	70	70
71	I see you can chide when you . . .	115	64	64	71	71	71
72	How long this letter will bee . . .	116	65	65	72	72	72
73	I wonder you did not come before . . .	118-19	67	67	73	73	73
74	I did soe promise my selfe a . . .	120	68	68	74	74	74
75	I am but newly waked . . .	121-2	69	69	75	75	75
76	My doubt's and fear's . . .	123	70	70	76	76	76
77	After a long debate . . .	124	71	71	77	77	77
App. B	This is no artificiall humility . . .	99-100	57	57	63	63	63

E The Physick Well at Barnet
(*See* LETTER 6; note 5)

The Physick Well at Barnet was discovered around 1650; the earliest record occurs in *The Perfect Diurnall* of 5 June 1652: 'There is lately found at Barnet 10 miles from London an excellent purging water, it springs from a salt nitre mine, half the quantity works as effectually as that of Epsom Water Mill, it is much approved by several eminent physicians. They that have occasion to make use of it may repair thither and take it free.' This last statement is incorrect: the waters were sold, and the money from the sale was earmarked for poor relief – the Barnet Local History Museum holds a Churchwarden's Book of Accounts which meticulously records the assistance given at that time.

Although Barnet never became a resort to rival either Epsom or Tunbridge Wells, it nevertheless developed a considerable reputation. Pepys visited it at least twice, as the following entries from his Diaries show:

11 July 1664. – Betimes up this morning, and getting ready, we by coach to Holborn, where at nine o'clock they [the rest of the party] set out, and I and my man Will on horseback by my wife to Barnett . . . Here we stayed two hours and then parted . . . Thence I and Will to see the wells, half a mile off, and there I drank three glasses, and walked, and came back and drank two more: and so we rode home, round by Kingsland, Hackney, and Mile End, till we were quite weary; and, not being very well, I betimes to bed.

11 August 1667 – *Lords Day*. Up by 4 a-clock and ready with Mrs Turner to take coach before 5; which we did, and set on our Journey and got to the Wells at Barnett by 7 a-clock, and there found many people a-drinking; but the morning is a very cold morning . . . So after drink[ing] three glasses and the women nothing, we by coach to Barnett.

Popular familiarity with these waters may be judged from an advertisement of 1663, which offers:

At the Angel and Sun, in the Strand, near Strand Bridge, is to be sold every day fresh Epsum-water, Barnet-water, and Tunbridge-water, and Epsum-ale and spruce-water.

A graphic picture of the well, as it was at around the time Dorothy Osborne writes about it, occurs in the Diary of the Hon. Celia Fiennes, who visited it regularly in the years 1701 to 1703.

In 1676, John Owen, a wealthy fishmonger and Alderman of the City of London, left the sum of £1 for the reparation of the well and, by another deed, left instructions that

if any obstructions should take place in the use of the Physick Well or the same should be forsaken and disused so as to produce no profits to the tenants or town aforesaid, in that case the said £1 should be paid to the school master of the said Free School [of Barnet, to which John Owen had left £3 to teach '3 poore boyes of Barnet without charge' and £3 towards the reparation of the Free School] for the instruction of one or more poore boy of the said town of Barnet in like manner as the other three boys.

The strategic position of the well had been a focus for friction since its discovery, to such an extent that one section of a 1729 Act of Parliament laid down that:

Provided nevertheless that nothing in this Act shall extend or defeat, abridge or exclude the inhabitants or parishioners of Chippen Barnet from free access and regress to and from the medicinal springs or wells on the said waste common for the using the medicinal waters which are upon the said great waste and benefit only as of antient time they have been accustomed to use the same.

Although the records are incomplete it would appear that the well was apparently pulled down around 1840 and the land used for farming, with a farmhouse being erected on the site; the records are then silent until 1907, when interest was rekindled, so that in 1912 a new analysis of the water, made by the Rev.

William Trinder, M.D., recorded that one gallon of water contained '96 grams of sulphate of magnesia; 12 grams of muriate of magnesia; 16 grams of carbonate of lime; 7 grams of extractive material'.

Thereafter, and especially during the years 1922 to 1938, the well was restored. The Minutes of the General Purposes Committee of the Barnet Urban District Council are superbly revealing of local political attitudes; for instance, they record a willingness to restore the well once it is discovered that half the cost of the reparation would come out of John Owen's legacy, as shown by the following resolutions:

That a request be made to the Governors of Queen Elizabeth Grammar School to utilise so much of the amount [it was then about £14] as may be necessary in cleaning out the Physick Well under the supervision of the officials of this Authority. (Thursday 29 June 1922)

That application be made to the Governors [of the school] for the money now in their hands from the gift of John Owen for the repair of the Physick Well, to be paid over to this Authority, in order that the Council may take the necessary steps to protect the interests of the town in relation to the Well and in accordance with the terms of the gift in question. (Thursday 2 November 1922)

That, with the exception of the provision of a pump, the Surveyor be authorized to carry out the works ... at an estimated cost of £23, and that upon the completion of the works, application be made to the Governors of Queen Elizabeth's Grammar School for the amount now in their hands [then approximately £12] towards the cost incurred. (Thursday 1 March 1923)

The Minutes also record the conclusions of a new analysis, which showed the waters to be 'slightly ferruginous, fairly highly saline ... [they] might no doubt be regarded as a mineral water' ... 'from a chemical point of view the water showed unusual purity in its low ammonia and freedom from nitrates and nitrites'.

In 1924, the Urban District Council purchased the site and commenced restoration, which revealed an underground chamber with steps leading down to it. The well was finally re-opened in 1938, and the Council Minutes record that it was insured for £450, a considerable sum in those days. On 28 August 1937 the local newspaper, the *Barnet Press*, carried an illustration of the restored well.

In the years after the Second World War the well once again suffered a decline, and although the actual well and cavern are intact to this day, it is now enclosed in a structure of mock-Tudor design, and encircled by one of the housing estates of the local authority; all that records its past are street names: Well-house Lane; Pepys Crescent; Well Approach; Trinder Road.

Aspects of the history of the Barnet Physick Well are related in the following:

S. H. Widdicombe, *A Chat About Barnet and its History* (1912);

B. R. Leftwich, *Annals of the Parish and Township of Chippen Barnet* (1951, manuscript);

Horace William Pettit Stevening, *Old Barnet* (1886);

W. M. Trinder, *The English Olive Tree* (n.d.).

I should like to express my gratitude to Mrs Joanne Corden, Archivist at the Barnet Local History Museum, for her generous and kind assistance – K.P.

F Litigation Between William and Dorothy Temple and Sir Henry Osborne, Kt.

Henry Osborne's Diary for the year 1655 records:

Feb. 1, Thursday. – I received a sub poena by one Sutton from T. and my sister to appear in Chancery.

Feb. 16, Friday. – I received my sisters bill in Chancery by Mr R. Skinner.

Feb. 28, Wednesday. – I putt in my Answer, which Mr Peeke drew up, and Sir O. Bridgeman, and Mr Chute corrected it.

The bill, dated 13 February 1655, reads:

William Temple Esq. son and heir apparent of Sir John Temple Kt Master of the Rolls in Ireland and Dorothy his wife the sole daughter of Sir Peter Osborne late of Chicksands, co. Bedford Kt deceased declare that whereas Sir Peter Osborne did by his Indenture tripartite 21 February 1649 . . . grant unto Sir Thomas Payton Bart, Sir Thomas Hatton of Long Stanton co Cambs Kt and Bart, Samuel Browne, Serjeant at Law Henry Osborne the second son and Robert Osborne the youngest son of Sir Peter Osborne the manor of Chicksand . . . of yearly value of £1000 or thereabouts for 99 years for several uses, among others for the raising and paying unto your Oratrix a sum of £4000 whereof £2000 was directed to be raised with all possible speed and another £1000 within a year and the other £1000 within two years, and that till the said £2000 were raised and paid, the Trustees should pay her £50 a year at Lady Day and Michaelmas. By virtue whereof the said trustees took over the trust and about two years afterwards for the better securing of the payment of £2000, part of your Oratrix's said portion, assigned her for some long term of years a farm called Fawnes Grange of the yearly value of £120 by a deed which the said Henry Osborne took into his custody on pretence that he would procure your Oratrix's brother Robert, then absent, to sign. After in 1653 Sir Peter Osborne died, no part of the said portion of £4000 being paid.*

* Quoted from Moore Smith, op. cit., pp. 185 ff.

In order to understand how this Bill in Chancery came about, and to follow the subsequent proceedings, it is perhaps wise to trace the events as recorded in Henry Osborne's Diary; he notes:

[1652] Feb. 16, Munday. – Sir T. Peyton, Sir T. Hatton, S. Browne and my selfe [four of the five trustees of Sir Peter Osborne's estate] sealed at S. Browne's chamber the Indenture to Holforde for the keeping the writings by S. Browne and the Lease to my sister for £2000 of her portion.

Feb. 27, Friday. – My father sealed the Lease to my sister for £2000 ... he told my sister there was provision made for her, and that when I asked him if he pleased to deliver it to the use of my sister he said yes with all his heart and I pray God saies he blesses it to her.

Apr. 8, Thursday. – I went to Mr Latche *about selling land with my sisters consent* ...

[1654] March 9, Thursday. – *My sister told mee she would marry Temple.*

Mar. 13. – *My sister told mee shee had tied up her han[d]s that shee would marry no body but Temple.*

Oct. 17, Tuesday. – My Lady Peyton and my sister &c., came to London from Knolton Sir Thomas Peyton staying behinde ... my sister came up and stayed supper with mee, and then declared *shee would marry Temple.*

Dec. 13, Wednesday. – Sir J. Temple came to Sir T. Hattons about a Treaty with my sister.

Dec. 22, Friday. – I carried Sir T. Hatton Sir J. Temples draught for settling thinges upon mariage with the corrections of Sir O. Bridgeman, which he seemed to consent to all but the £1500 that was to returne to the family in case her issue failed, as he said, but he, in truth, would only meddle with the businesse of the £1000 and would have nothing to doe with the other £3000 whereupon Sir T. Hatton told him that without he did one we should [not?] doe the other, and that it was not in my sisters power to hinder it. Upon this, he quite flew of and said he would doe nothinge and so parted. The next day my sister told it mee, and wee utterly fell out about it.

Dec. 25, Munday. – Being Christmasse day my sister was married, and went as shee said to Mr Franklins.

Dec. 28, Thursday. – Temple and my sister writ to mee to deliver up the writings [deeds] of her Portion, which I answered by the same bearer.

[1655] Feb. 1, Thursday. – I received a sub poena by one Sutton from T. and my sister to appear in Chancery.

Feb. 16, Friday. – I received my sisters bill in Chancery by Mr R. Skinner.

Feb. 28, Wednesday. – I putt in my Answer, which Mr Peeke drew up, and Sir O. Bridgeman, and Mr Chute corrected it.

Henry Osborne's response to the subpoena is interesting for the insight it provides into marriage settlements. He substantially concedes that the details as set out in the claim by William and Dorothy Temple are correct, but he seeks to explain why the provisions had not been met; his explanation is concentrated upon a relation of his fears about the marriage itself, and the financial settlement appertaining to it. His answer notes that:

It is true that Sir Peter Osborne . . . died when no part of the said portion was paid. After which time, and also before, he this defendant did profess and really had a great affection and kindness for her which made him perceiving there was a possibility of marriage between her and the other complainant and having cause to think that neither William Temple or his father Sir John Temple could settle upon their posterity nor upon her for her jointure an estate answerable to such her portion (although as she informed this defendant the said William Temple had told her that his father would make appear such an estate as should satisfy her friends) for that after several treaties had thereabout and pretences made of a considerable estate, no satisfaction could be given by them that they, or either of them, could settle upon her any jointure or estate upon her children proportionable to what her portion deserved and to the satisfaction of her friends . . . and remembering the strict commands left him [H.O.] by his deceased father and mother to have a special care to her, and out of his own great affaction to her, he did advise her to secure her said portion and to that end to make it over to the trustees of her father's estate. Whereupon she willingly and freely consented to secure her said portion, but chose rather to have it made over to him, Henry Osborne. Yet because he, H.O., did conceive that William Temple and his father might have some prejudice against him . . . he was willing and did so declare to her

... that he would make over all his interest therein to them the trustees.*

The rest of the entries in the Diary pertaining to this matter is a record of the time it took to reach a settlement, and the nature of the agreement:

Mar. 5, Munday. – When I came home Temples man stayed for mee with a note from him and my sister to desire mee to send the Counterpart of the Deede shee made mee, I told the man I had it not here, but I would take order it should be sent some time to-morrow.

Mar. 6, Tuesday night. – Temple sent his man againe, I said I had now brought it home, and was just sending it, so gave it to him, and my Lady Dianas picture to returne it to my sister.

Mar. 7, Wednesday morninge. – I heard by Evans that he had sent up the Table Linnen for my sister and the other Linnen all in one trunke.

Mar. 12, Munday. – I sent my sister the trunke with Linnen, and my Lady Osborne told mee shee was there when my letter came and that my sister seemed extreamely pleased with it, and said that the Letter was very kinde and that it was more then shee expected from mee. Yet that night she writ to mee againe a Letter where she was unsatisfied, and very unkinde.

Mar. 15, Thursday. – She writ againe and two or three Letters went betweene us.

Mar. 16, Friday. – This day T. came to Mr Ward to bid him if any money were returned up for him he should keepe it in his hands, and my man told mee Mr Ward not well understanding what order I gave to R. Compton, mistooke and said I denied I had given him order not to pay any money to my sister, when I denied that I had given him order not to pay any money till our Lady day; for I had ordered him and he had promised to send it up ten dayes before. So I went that night to him and made him understand the businesse right, and he said that if any money came to him for my sister he would send mee worde, and if T. sent to know whether any was returned up for him he would say no. / The 14 of this moneth T. sent his man over the way with a Coachman to beate Owen.

* Quoted from Moore Smith, op. cit., pp. 188 ff.

Mar. 21, Wednesday. – I was with Sir T. Hatton who told mee
Temple and my sister had beene with him, and that he had
offered him a bill, which he refused to take.

Mar. 22, Thursday morninge. – Sir T. Peyton came to mee and
told mee Temple had been with him and given him a bill
against the Trustees desiring up [sic] to send it to S. Browne,
and desire him to draw up an answer, which he told mee he
had done, thereupon I writ this day a letter to S. Browne to
desire him not to doe it. / I writ to R. Compton that he should
returne up the £120 to mee, and not to my sister, of both
these last letters I have Copies.

Mar. 30, Friday. – Owen received of Mr Ward £120 that R.
Compton had returned to mee for my sister. Owen went to
Stacys, &c., to enquire how I might send to my sister, but shee
knew not. / I retained Attorney Prideaux against *my brother*
[Temple].

Apr. 2, Munday. – I retained Mr Chute against *my brother*.

Apr. 3, Tuesday. – I retained Sergeant Maynard against *my
brother*.

Apr. 5, Thursday. – I sent a Letter by Owen to Mrs Grizells to be
sent to my sister to acquaint her I had £120 for her, shee they
say is at Battersey.

Apr. 7, Saterday. – My sister writ mee a Letter by one Cornwall to
pay the £120 to him, I told him on Munday at 3 a clocke in
the afternoone he should receive it.

Apr. 9, Munday. – Cornwall came, but he would not signe the
acquittance because it was mentioned to be payd for interest to
my sister due at our Lady day last, he said he had no order for
it, but would acquaint my sister with it, and come againe to
morrow morninge.

Apr. 10, Tuesday. – Cornewall came and received the £120 and
said it was onely his scruple.

May 10, Thursday. – I came to London.

May 11, Friday. – I was served with a sub poena from Temple.

May 19, Saterday. – I received the bill of Temple against the
Trustees as well as my selfe. I sent it to S. Browne.

May 25, Friday. – The Trustees mett and my brother. Mr Keeling
demanded Land security for my Lady Briars. Sir John Temple
and Mr Rant came, where wee treated concerning my sisters

portion, and my brother and I consented to an agreement between us, and S. Browne was to draw the heads.

May 30, Wednesday. – Temple came from Redding and desired a meeting of the Trustees to conclude concerninge my sisters portion, but I putt of the meeting, for I said I would conclude nothinge unlesse my sister were present, so shee was sent for.

June 1, Friday. – Wee mett at S. Brownes chamber my brother, Sir T. Hatton, my sister, Sir J. Temple, Mr Raworth and my selfe where wee made an agreement, and Raworth tooke the heads of it.

June 9, Saterday. – When I was abroad somebody left a draught for mee of an Agreement about my sisters Portion.

June 18, Munday. – One from Mr Raworth came to know if I had persued the Deede. I told him I had, and that there was not one thinge right putt downe, and so sent it him againe.

June 27, Wednesday. – I went with O. Bridgeman to Kensington with Sir J. Temples booke corrected, and Sir Orl: made notes upon it, and I left it with those notes at my lodgings for Mr Temple.

June 29, Friday. – Wee had a meeting at S. Brownes chamber onely Sir J. Temple, and his sonne and Mr Raworth and my selfe where wee agreed that a booke should be drawn up according to Sir O.B. notes, and then I would goe with it againe to Sir O.B. and if they differed in any matter of law, S. Browne should determine betweene them.

July 20, Friday. – Wee sealed the Writings of agreement betweene mee and my sister and Sir John Temple, &c.

Notes

The Notes have been compiled from many sources, including:

The Dictionary of National Biography (*DNB*)
The Dictionary of Scientific Biography (*DSB*)
Compact Edition of the *Oxford English Dictionary* (*OED*)
The New Columbia Encyclopedia
Dictionary of British History, edited by J. P. Kenyon (New York: Stein & Day, 1983)
English Historical Facts 1603–1688, edited by Chris Cook and John Wroughton (Totowa, New Jersey: Rowman & Littlefield, 1980)

INTRODUCTION

1. *The Life and Character of Sir William Temple, Bart* (London, 1728). This *Life* was prefixed to editions of Temple's *Works* of 1740, 1754, 1757 and 1770. Commentators who assert that it was omitted from the edition of 1731 are in error; the *Life* was incorporated in a new Preface to the second issue of that edition, with additions and revisions.

2. See G. C. Moore Smith, *The Early Essays and Romances of Sir William Temple, Bart* (Oxford: Clarendon Press, 1930), for the complete text of the Giffard *Life*, together with critical apparatus.

3. For a history of these events, see Ferdinand Brock Tupper, *The Chronicle of Castle Cornet* (Guernsey: Stephen Barnett, and London: Simpkin, Marshall, 1851).

4. I am grateful to the Rector of St Giles in the Fields, Holborn, the Rev. Canon Gordon Taylor, M.A., and his verger, Mr Wheatland, for their assistance.

5. Julia G. Longe, *Martha, Lady Giffard* (London: George Allen & Sons, 1911).

6. Two recent books deal with the events of this period: K. H. D. Haley, *An English Diplomat in the Low Countries: Sir William Temple and John de Witt, 1665–1672* (Oxford: Clarendon Press, 1986), and H. H. Rowen, *John de Witt: Statesman of the 'True Freedom'* (Cambridge: C.U.P., 1986), which is a re-working of his monumental *John de Witt, Grand Pensionary of Holland, 1625–1672* (Princeton, N.J.: Princeton U.P., 1978).

7. For this period, see A. C. Elias, *Swift at Moor Park: Problems in Biography and Criticism* (Philadelphia: University of Pennsylvania Press, 1982). This is a superb exercise in scholarly reconstruction; it comprehensively evaluates conventional views of the Swift–Temple relationship, including those of the eighteenth century (Dean Swift, *Essay Upon the Life, Writings and Character of Dr Jonathan Swift*, London, for Bathurst, 1755; Thomas Sheridan, *Life of the Rev. Dr Jonathan Swift*, London, for C. Bathurst, W. Strahan, *et al.*, 1784); of the nineteenth century (Macaulay – see Bibliography; Thackeray, *English Humourists of the Eighteenth Century*, London, Smith, Elder, 1853); and of the twentieth century (Woodbridge – see Bibliography; Irvin Ehrenpreis, *Swift: the Man, his Works, and the Age*, London, Methuen, 1962, Vol. I).

8. Narcissus Luttrell, *A Brief Historical Relation of Affairs of State, from September 1678 to April 1714* (Oxford, 1857), Vol. 1, p. 524. See also *Correspondence of the Family of Hatton, A.D. 1600–1704*, ed. E. M. Thompson, Camden Society, Vol. II, pp. 131–3; Abel Boyer (see Bibliography), pp. 416ff. This account is accepted by biographers, including Woodbridge, and by historians, for example David Ogg, *England in the Reigns of James II and William III* (Oxford: Clarendon Press, 1955).

Richard Talbot, Duke and Earl of Tyrconnell (1630–91), was an Irish Jacobite who escaped from Ireland in the aftermath of Cromwell's 1649 campaigns, but then returned to the household of the Duke of York (later James II) after the Restoration. Although he was arrested for his alleged involvement in the Popish Plot (a fictitious Jesuit plot to assassinate Charles

I), he was created an earl by the new King, and sent to Ireland as commander-in-chief, where he placed many Catholics in key positions. After the 'Glorious Revolution', Tyrconnell sought to hold the island for the fallen James, but he was defeated at the Battle of the Boyne (1690), went to France to seek help, returned in 1691, but died just before the final defeat of the Irish Jacobites.

9. 'William Temple, of Moor Park, in the Surrey countryside, caused this monument, such as it is, to be erected to the memory of himself and those most dear to him: his beloved daughter Diana Temple; his fondly conjoined wife Dorothy Osborne; his very best of sisters Martha Giffard.'

10. T. P. Courtenay, *Memoirs of the Life, Works and Correspondence of Sir William Temple, Bart* (London, 1836), Vol. II, pp. 273–337.

   The Rt Hon. Thomas Peregrine Courtenay (1782–1841) was Member of Parliament for Totnes (1810); Secretary to the India Commission (1812–28); and Vice-President of the Board of Trade (1828–30). In addition to the book on Sir William Temple, he wrote pamphlets, and Commentaries on Shakespeare's history plays.

11. T. B. Macaulay, *Literary Essays. Contributed to The Edinburgh Review* (Oxford: O.U.P., 1913).

   Thomas Babington Macaulay (1800–1859), historian, was educated at Cambridge. He was a regular contributor to the *Edinburgh Review* after publication in it of his essay on Milton (August, 1825). Called to the Bar (1826) and elected to Parliament (1830), Macaulay was a distinguished orator in support of Whig ideology. He was in India from 1834 to 1838, where, as a member of the Supreme Council of the East India Company, he helped to re-formulate both the education system and the legal code. Upon his return to England he concentrated on the writing of history, while simultaneously holding public office (Secretary for War, 1839–41; Paymaster to the Armed Forces, 1846–7; Member of Parliament, 1839–47 and 1852–6). He was created Baron Macaulay of Rothley in 1859. As a historian (some would say *the* historian) of the nineteenth century, he is best remembered for his *History of England from the Accession of James the Second* (5 vols., 1849–61). Macaulay also wrote several short biographical essays on key figures in English history, including Warren Hastings and Samuel Johnson, as well as a work of poetry, *The Lays of Ancient Rome* (1842).

12. Edward Abbott Parry (ed.), *Letters from Dorothy Osborne to Sir William Temple, 1652–54* (London: Griffith, Farren, Okeden & Welsh, 1888).

   Sir Edward Parry (1863–1943) was a barrister in the Middle Temple; a Circuit Court judge in Manchester (1894–1911); chairman of the West Kent Appeal Tribunal (1916) and of the Industrial Unrest Commission, N.W. Area (1917); president of the Pensions Appeal Tribunal (1916); and a judge of the Circuit Court at Lambeth (1911–27). He was knighted in 1927. Parry was a prolific author: apart from books on legal matters (among others, *The Law and the Poor*, 1914; *The Law and the Woman*, 1916; *The Drama of the Law*, 1924), he wrote stories for children and adapted prose works for production as plays on the London commercial stage.

13. Sir Edward Parry, *My Own Way* (London: Cassell & Co., 1932).

14. Raymond Williams, *The Long Revolution* (London: Chatto & Windus, 1961), Pt. 2, Ch. 2: 'The Growth of the Reading Public,' from which I also acknowledge the Arnold extract.

15. Parry (1888).

16. 1906; 1914.

17. Israel Gollancz/Alexander Morning, *The Love Letters of Dorothy Osborne to Sir William Temple* (London: The De La More Press, 1903).

18. E. J. MacGillivray, *Copyright Cases* (London, 1903). I am grateful to my colleague Michael Slade, Head of the Department of Law in the North East London Polytechnic, for his assistance.

19. G. C. Moore Smith (ed.), *The Letters of Dorothy Osborne to William Temple* (Oxford: Clarendon Press, 1928).

20. For Henry Osborne, see letter 10, note 3. Extracts from the Diary were edited by Moore Smith and published in *Notes and Queries*, 12th Series, Vol. VII (16 October 1920, and subsequent weeks).

21. Kingsley Hart (ed.), *Letters of Dorothy Osborne to Sir William Temple 1652–54* (London: The Folio Society, 1968).

22. Genie S. Lerch-Davies, 'Rebellion Against Public Prose: The Letters of Dorothy Osborne to William Temple', in *Texas Studies in English Literature* (20 March 1978), pp. 368–415, reported in *Abstracts of English Studies* (1982).

23. For letters which might not have arrived, see, for example, letter 17, note 2; letter 33, note 1; letter 51, note 5; letter 62, note 1; letter 65, note 3; letter 68, note 4; letter 73, note 1.

24. Selection of a few titles from a vast and ideologically diverse range is contentious; nevertheless ... the most accessible statement of the debate is probably R. C. Richardson's *The Debate About the English Revolution* (London: Methuen, 1977); the most scholarly 'traditional' histories are arguably those by Ivan Roots, *The Great Rebellion, 1642–1660* (London: Batsford, 1966) and Robert Ashton, *The English Civil War: Conservatism and Revolution* (London: Weidenfeld & Nicolson, 1978); while the clearest political study is that by Brian Manning, *The English People and the English Revolution* (London: Heinemann, 1976). But, without doubt, the most profound scholar of the English Revolution in our time is Christopher Hill, whose vast output includes the best biography of one of the main actors (*God's Englishman: Oliver Cromwell and the English Revolution*, Harmondsworth: Penguin, 1972); the most valuable synthesis of the complexities of the event (*Intellectual Origins of the English Revolution*, Oxford: O.U.P., 1965), and the most elegant theoretical speculations (*Some Intellectual Consequences of the English Revolution*, London: Weidenfeld & Nicolson, 1980).

25. Alan Everitt, *The Local Community and the Great Rebellion*, Historical Association pamphlet (1969); see also his study, *Change in the Provinces: The Seventeenth Century* (Leicester: Leicester U.P., 1969). See also J. S. Morrill, *The Revolt of the Provinces: Conservatism and Radicalism in the English Civil War 1630–1650* (London: Longman, 1976). The classic study of the gentry is G. E. Mingay's *The Gentry: The Rise and Fall of a Ruling Class* (London: Longman, 1978).

26. Mark Girouard, *Life in the English Country House: A Social and Architectural History* (New Haven and London: Yale U.P., 1978).

27. See an excellent recent study by Virginia Kenney, *The Country House Ethos in English Literature 1688–1750: themes of personal retreat and national expansion* (Brighton: Harvester Press, 1985). See also the reference in letter 44, note 7.

28. Lawrence Stone and Jeanne C. Fawlter Stone, *An Open Elite? England 1540–1880* (Oxford: O.U.P., 1985).

29. Lord David Cecil, *Two Quiet Lives* (London: Constable & Co., 1947).

30. For the family see, *inter alia*, Ralph A. Houlbrooke, *The English Family 1450–1700* (London: Longman, 1984); A. MacFarlane, *The Origins of English Individualism: The Family, Property and Social Transition* (Oxford: Basil Blackwell, 1978); Lawrence Stone, *The Family, Sex and Marriage in England 1500–1800* (Harmondsworth: Penguin, 1982); L. Charles and L. Duffin (eds.), *Women and Work in Pre-Industrial England* (Beckenham: Croom Helm, 1985); Alice Clark, *Working Life of Women in the Seventeenth Century* (London: Routledge & Kegan Paul, 1982 – a reprint of the 1919 edition); Patricia Crawford (ed.), *Exploring Women's Past* (Carlton, Australia, 1983); Mary Prior (ed.), *Women in English Society 1580–1800* (London: Methuen, 1985).

31. It is perhaps appropriate to note here why I use the abbreviations D.O. and W.T. throughout. The 'normal' usage would have been 'Dorothy' and 'Temple' or 'Dorothy' and 'William', but these forms have, rightly, been criticized. The use of both first names and family names throughout would have led to in-elegancies, so (in the absence of an appropriate non-sexist formulation) the use of initials seems to be a suitable 'English compromise'.

32. Lawrence Stone, *The Family, Sex and Marriage in England 1500–1800* (Harmondsworth: Penguin, 1982), p. 72.

33. *Notes and Queries*, 7th Series, Vol. V, No. 130 (23 June 1888), p. 499.

34. Virginia Woolf, *The Common Reader*, Second Series (London: The Hogarth Press, 1932).

35. In the *New Republic* (24 October 1928); *The Times Literary Supplement* (25 October 1928).

36. *The Diary of Virginia Woolf*, Vol. 3, 1925–1930, edited by Anne Olivier Bell, assisted by Andrew McNellie (New York: Harcourt Brace Jovanovich, 1982), pp. 197–9.

37. G. C. Moore Smith, *The Early Essays and Romances of Sir William Temple, Bart* (Oxford: Clarendon Press, 1930), contains *A True Romance, or The Disastrous Chances of Love and Fortune sett forth in Divers Tragicall Stories which in thees later ages have been but too truely acted upon the stage of Europe*. The title-page lists nine stories, of which those with an asterisk appear to be the only ones which have survived: *The Labyrinth of Fortune*; *The Fate of Jealosie*; ★*The Constant Desperado*; ★*The Force of Custome*; ★*The Generous Lovers*; *The Incestuous Paire*; ★*The Maids Revenge*; ★*The Disloyall Wife*; *The Brave Duellists*.

38. Recent critical studies include H. S. Bennett, *English Books and Readers 1603 to 1660: Being a Study of the History of the Book Trade in the Reign of James I and Charles I* (Cambridge: C.U.P., 1970); Margaret Spufford, *Small Books and Pleasant Histories: Popular Fiction and Its Readership in Seventeenth-Century England* (London: Methuen, 1981); David Cressy, *Literacy and Social Order: Reading and Writing in Tudor and Stuart England* (Cambridge: C.U.P., 1980). Two easily accessible collections of the political prose are Howard Erskine-Hill and Graham Storey (eds.), *Revolutionary Prose of the English Civil War* (Cambridge: C.U.P., 1983) and Andrew Sharp, *Political Ideas of the English Civil War 1641–1649* (London: Longman, 1983). A representative collection of the range of prose of the period is *Seventeenth-Century Prose 1620–1700*, edited by Peter Ure, being Volume 11 of *The Pelican Book of English Prose*, edited by Kenneth Allott.

39. Nicholas Maw, *The Voice of Love: A Song Cycle*, with poems by Peter Porter (London: Boosey & Hawkes, 1968).

40. John McCabe, 'Concertante Variations on a Theme of Nicholas Maw' (Borough Green, Kent: Novello, 1976).

41. This poem, 'Dorothy Osborne in the Country', can be found in Peter Porter's *Collected Poems* (Oxford: O.U.P., 1983); it is also included in *A Porter Folio* (Oxford: O.U.P., 1969).

LETTER 1

1. The 'Old Servant' is W.T. D.O. and her friends use the word 'servant' in the sense of 'professed lover; one who is devoted to the service of a lady' (*OED*).

2. The 'ten poundes' claimed by W.T. apparently refers to a wager he had made with D.O. that she would pay him that amount if she married.

3. W.T. had been travelling on the Continent (see letter 2, note 1).

4. The date of this letter is corroborated by the endorsement 'Decemb: 24, 1652', by W.T., on the reverse.

5. That this is probably the first letter in the sequence might be deduced not only from her invitation to him to continue to write ('to Confirme it to mee by another'), but also by the instructions on the reverse: those concerned with delivery are intended for the carrier; those relating to collection are for Mrs Painter.

LETTER 2

1. There is some uncertainty about when, and why, W.T. left England. *DNB* suggests that in the period between 1648 (when he left Cambridge, without taking his degree) and 1652 (when the sequence of letters commences), he travelled to Paris, Brussels and Madrid in order to study French and Spanish. What is clear from the letters is that the separation was much longer than D.O. had initially anticipated – which might help to explain her annoyance when she found out that, on his return to England, W.T. had gone to York to see his father, and had passed through Bedford without making the short detour from there to Chicksands to visit her. (See also the reference in letter 76.)

2. The date is corroborated by Henry Osborne's Diary, 1653:

> Mar. 15, Munday. – My sister went to London *about Sir T. Osborn* [see note 3, below] and lay at Sir T. Peyton's [see letter 24, note 5]. The same day came hither Mr Edwards [not identified] *about Sir T. Isham* [see letter 3, note 6]. / Mar. 30, Wednesday. – I received a letter *from my Lady Osborn about my sister.* / April 1, Thursday. – I came to London *about my sister and Sir Thomas Osborn.* / April 8, Thursday. – This evening *my lady Osborn broke of the match* [intended to be made between Sir Thomas Osborn and D.O. But compare this version with the comment which D.O. makes in letter 43, where she writes that, according to rumour, what persuaded Sir Thomas to his eventual choice of a wife was that the lady concerned was the daughter of an earl].

3. Thomas Osborne (1631–1712), Earl of Danby, Marquess of Carmarthen and Duke of Leeds. Under the patronage of George Villiers, 2nd Duke of Buckingham (1628–87), Osborne was appointed Treasurer of the Navy (1668), a Privy Councillor (1672) and Lord Treasurer (1673–8). A staunch royalist and fervent Anglican, he was opposed to any alliance with France. He helped to end England's involvement in the Dutch War (1674), and assisted in the negotiations concerning the marriage between William and Mary (1677). However, while telling parliament that he was raising money for war with France, he was at the same time negotiating – albeit reluctantly, according to some commentators – with that country for an alliance with Charles II (1677). Impeached for treasonable communications with an enemy (1678), he was put in prison (1679–84). Upon his release, his protestantism ensured his support for those who opposed James II (1633–1701; King of England, Scotland and Ireland, 1685–8), and he became a signatory to the petition for William and Mary to accede to the throne. Although he was suspected of having Jacobite sympathies he continued to be influential under the new monarchs, so that in 1690 he became President of the Council. However, he was impeached once more in 1695 – this time in connection with alleged bribes involving the East India Company – and resigned; although he was exonerated and restored to royal favour, he did not thereafter hold office. He was created Marquess of Carmarthen (1689) and Duke of Leeds (1694). He married (1654) Lady Bridget Lindsay (d. 1704), second daughter of Montague Bertie, Lord Lindsay; there were three

sons and five daughters of the marriage. The standard biography is by A. Browning, *Thomas Osborne, Earl of Danby*, 3 vols. (Glasgow, 1944–51); for his political management, see J. R. Jones, *Court and Country* (1978), and for his financial administration see C. D. Chandaman, *The English Public Revenue 1660–1688* (Oxford, 1975).

4. Probably the family solicitor.

5. Sir William Briers (1569–1653) of Upbury, Pulloxhill, Beds. (only a few miles from Chicksands), with whom the Osborne family had a complicated personal as well as financial relationship. Entries in Henry Osborne's Diary, 1652–6, note:

July 25, Sunday. – I went with my sister and my Lady Grey [see letter 14, note 5] and Mrs Pooley to dinner to Sir William Briers. / July 29, Thursday. – R. Compton came to mee from Mr Barbor who informed my father would be sequestrated againe for not producing his discharge to the Committee at Bedforde upon a pretended order we had to doe so. / Oct. 19, Tuesday. – I went to Sir W. Briars but he could not tell whither the bargaine he was upon would goe forward till a fortnight or 3 weekes, if it did not he would helpe me to £1300. / 1653, Mar. 28, Monday. – R. Compton told me Wheeler had brought him worde that now Sir W. Briars was content that my father should have £1300 upon our personall security till the other of Hawnes was free. / June 7, Tuesday. – I went to the buriall of Sir William Briars. / July 16, Saturday. – Wee dined with my Lady Grey at my Lady Briars. / Dec. 30, Friday. – Mr Yelverton [see letter 45, note 17] and my Lady Briars, &c. dined at Chicksands. / Dec. 31, Saterday. – Wee all dined at my Lady Briars. / 1654, Apr. 17, Munday. – My Lady Briars and my sister and I came away from Easton [Maudit], Mr Yelverton and his sister and my Lady Ruthin came with us to Bedforde where my Lady Briars coach mett them, and my sister went that night to my Lady Briars. / Apr. 20, Thursday. – My sister went to St Albons in my Lady Briars coach, and from thence in a hackney to London. / June 6, Tuesday. – I wente to my Lady Briars in her new Chariott my sister made stay there that night and the next day came to Chicksands. / 1655, May 25, Friday. – The Trustees mett and my brothers, Mr Keeling demanded Land security for my Lady Briars. / 1656, May 22, Thursday. – I payed my Lady Briars £1000. / 1657, June 5, Friday. – I payed my Lady Briars at Mr Rees her bond of £1300.

6. There is some uncertainty about the date of Lady Osborne's death. The date given by D.O. (1651, rather than 1650, as given

on the memorial – see below) is almost certainly correct. Henry Osborne's Diary records the death and burial of his father (as announced by D.O. in letter 62) as 11 March and 13 March. The memorial in Campton Church reads:

In Honour and Duty to the Memory / of / Sir Peter Osborn of Chicksand Kt. / Sonne of Sir Iohn Osborn / He was Treasurers Remembrancer of the Exchr / And for the space of 28 Years Governour of / Islands / and Castle of Guarnsey / for / King Iames and King Charles / He was buryed here / The 13th Day of March 1653 / Being / Almost 69 Yeares Old / And here lies Dorothy Danvers wife of Sir Peter / Osborn. She was the 6th and Youngest daughter of / Sir Iohn Danvers of Dantsey in the Covnty of Wilts. / Knight / And of Elizabeth Nevill his wife / the 4th and Youngest Daughter and coheire of Iohn / Nevill Lord Latimer and of Lady Lucy Somerset / his wife second daughter of Henry Somerset / Earl of Worcester / and / The said Dorothy was Sister to Henry Danvers / Earle of Danby, Privie Covncellr to King Charles / and Knight of the Order of the Garter / She / was buryed here the 1st Day / of October 1650 / Being 60 Yeares Old.

7. The Law Terms were:

Hilary:	23 January (or, if a Sunday, 24 January) to 12 February.
Easter:	The Wednesday fortnight after Easter Day to the Monday after Ascension. (1653: 27 April to 23 May; 1654: 12 April to 8 May).
Trinity:	The Friday after Trinity Sunday to the following Wednesday fortnight (1653: 10 June to 29 June; 1654: 26 May to 14 June).
Michaelmas:	23 October (or, if a Sunday, 24 October) to 28 November.

LETTER 3

1. Goring House was the town house of George Goring, Earl of Norwich (1608–17). Goring was a royalist commander during the Civil War, having previously served with the Dutch army. In 1641, while stationed at Portsmouth, he was one of the participants in the 'first army plot', which had as its objective the attempt to force parliament to obey Charles I. Goring later

betrayed his fellow conspirators because (it was alleged) he was annoyed at not being appointed leader of the plotters. He apparently continued to play a double role until 1645, when he was forced to flee the country. He died on the Continent in 1657 (Moore Smith gives the date of his death as 1662, and *DNB* gives it as 1663). The house D.O. writes about stood on the site of the former Mulberry Garden – almost exactly where Buckingham Palace now stands. Moore Smith notes that in the Works Accounts of the Treasury Records for 1646–7 there is a payment for refurbishing the house for the use of the French Ambassador Extraordinary, and from this letter we might infer that D.O. had visited there to attend a social function; the house was apparently used for that purpose by the parliamentary government as well. In 1665 it belonged to Henry Bennett, 1st Earl of Arlington (1618–85), Secretary of State under Charles II, and a member of the Cabal (Clifford, Arlington, Buckingham, Ashley and Lauderdale). It was destroyed by fire in 1674.

2. It has not been possible to identify D.O.'s suitor.

3. The two previous editors differ about the identity of the aunt. Parry (1914) identifies her as the wife of Sir John Danvers (1588?–1655), the regicide. Sir John and D.O.'s mother were brother and sister, and the aunt would have been Sir John's third wife, Grace, daughter of Thomas Hughes of Kimerton. Sir John had previously been married to (i) Magdalen, the widow of Richard Herbert of Montgomery Castle. She was the mother of the poet Lord Herbert of Cherbury and was twice her husband's age at the time of their marriage; (ii) Elizabeth Dauntsey (1604–36), with which marriage Sir John acquired the lavish mansion of West Lavington, Wiltshire. The Danvers town house in London was reputed to be sumptuous and elegant; it stood near Chelsea Old Church and next to the house in which Sir Thomas More had lived.

Moore Smith identifies the aunt as Katherine, Lady Gargrave, who was the only surviving sister of Dorothy's mother. She married Sir Richard Gargrave, of Nostell and Kinsley (or Kingley) Park, Yorkshire; his claim to fame was the rapidity with which he managed to squander his estate (which, it is said, was so immense that he could ride on his own land all the way from Wakefield to Doncaster). A consequence of this profligacy was that Lady Gargrave was often in dispute over property matters with her relatives, or with the parliamentary government: Sir John Danvers, for instance, sought to have a legacy in her favour annulled on the grounds that, had he not been a regicide, the legacy would have been his. In 1649, Lady Gargrave was allowed to compound (the payment of a fine by royalists to avoid prosecution or confiscation of properties) for her estates.

I lean towards Moore Smith's identification because it seems to me that (i) it would have been totally out of character for Lady Danvers to wish to intervene to the extent of summoning D.O. to London to recommend a husband; (ii) we know from Henry Osborne's Diary (see note 8, below) about the visit to London by Lady Gargrave, and her central role in all the marriage transactions.

4. It has not been possible to identify this suitor.

5. Stepmother.

6. Sir Justinian Isham (1610–74) of Lamport, Northants., was admitted Fellow Commoner of Christ's College, Cambridge, in 1627. A supporter of Charles I, to whom he lent money, Isham was imprisoned during the Civil War and had to compound for his estates at Shangton, Leicestershire, but was elected Member of Parliament for Northamptonshire after the Restoration. Isham's first wife was Jane, daughter of Sir John Garrard, Bart, of Lamer, Hertfordshire. Having successfully survived the birth of four daughters (Jane; twins, Elizabeth and Judith; Susanna), Lady Isham died on 3 March 1639, after giving birth to a son, who survived her by only a few days.

Sir Justinian was about forty-two at the time of his proposal to D.O., who was then about twenty-five. His second wife was Vere, daughter of Thomas, Lord Leigh of Stoneleigh, Warwickshire (who was the second son of Sir Thomas Leigh, member of the Merchant Adventurers' Company, and Lord Mayor of London in 1558). See also *The Diary of Thomas Isham of Lamport (1658–81)*, kept by Him in Latin from 1671 to 1673 at his Father's command, translated by Norman Senn; Introduction by Sir Gyles Isham, Bart (Farnborough, Hants., Gregg International Publishers, 1971), especially Introduction; Appendix D.

Henry Osborne's Diary shows us vividly the intensity of passions and actions of some of the participants in the proposed marriages to Sir Justinian and to Sir Thomas Osborne (see note 8, below). With regard to Sir Justinian, the Diary records (1652):

Mar 9 [8?]. – Being Monday Mr *Vaughan* [not identified] sent to Mrs *Goldsmith* [wife of the vicar of Campton] about *Isham for a plaine answer* [from which we might deduce that the negotiations had been in progress for some time].

Mar. 15, Munday. – The same day came hither Mr Edmonds [not identified] *about Sir Isham.*

April 20, Tuesday. – I went to see *Mr Edmonds.*

May 5, Wednesday. – I went up to London *about Sir I. Isham.*

May 14, Friday. – In the morning my sister came to Towne to meet me . . .

May 17, Munday. – Sir I. Isham came to Towne and came to my sister . . .

June 18, Friday. – I writ that evening to Mr Seth Ward [one of the founder members of the Royal Society] . . . about *Sir I. Isham.*

June 23, Wednesday. – Tuesday *Mrs Goldsmith writ to Mr Vaughan of the epistle from Mr Gibson* [the vicar of the church at Hawnes, who appears to have been instructed to write on behalf of the Osborne family].

Sunday the 4th of July I went to *Sir I. Isham who* [upon?] *the* [reception?] *of Mr Gibsons letter said he had entertained of a new treaty* [was seeking to marry someone else; later letters will make numerous references to the progress of Sir Justinian's search for a new wife].

7. Lord Coleraine was Hugh Hare (1606?–67), scholar, traveller, landscape gardener and noted royalist; he is said to have lost in excess of £40,000 in his support of Charles I, who in 1625 rewarded him with an Irish peerage. Coleraine married Lucy, second daughter of his stepfather, Henry Montagu, 1st Earl of Manchester, in 1632, and lived in the village of Totteridge, north of London.

8. Henry Osborne's Diary shows a similar intensity around the proposals relating to Sir Thomas Osborne (see letter 2, note 2):

Feb. 6, Friday. – I received a letter from my Lady Osborn in answer to mine concerning her £100 when she mentioned the [fitenesse?] *of her sons marriage.*

Feb. 15, Munday. – This day I went to my L. Osborn who was newly come to Towne.

Mar. 15, Munday. – My sister went to London *about Sir T. Osborn* . . .

Mar. 30, Wednesday. – I received a letter from *my Lady Osborn about my sister*.

Apr. 1, Thursday. – I came to London *about my sister and Sir Thomas Osborn*.

Apr. 8, Thursday. – . . . this evening *my Lady Osborn broke off the match*.

May 14, Friday. – In the morninge my sister came to Towne to mee at Sanders house.

May 19, Wednesday. – My Aunt Gargrave and my C. Thoreld [see letter 10, note 2] came to Towne and lay in Queene street.

May 21, Friday. – My sister and my L. Osborn mett at my Aunt Gargraves. My L. Osborn *told her story*.

May 24, Munday. – My L. Osborn went into Norfolke. My sister told my Aunt Gargrave *her story*. The same day my Aunt Gargrave afterwards told it mee.

June 5, Saterday. – I mett Sir T. Osborn after his returne out of Norfolke who said he would come to speake with mee next morninge.

June 7, – Sir T. Osborn came to mee *and gave mee an account of what hee had said to his mother*.

June 8, Tuesday. – My sister came to mee from Chicksands.

June 10, Thursday. – My sister went backe againe for Chicksands.

June 18, Friday. – I went to my C. Thorelds, and heard my L. Osborn and Charles were gone to Cornebury. Yesterday I writ to my A. Gargrave the story of *Sir T.O. and my Lady* [Osborn].

July 28, Wednesday. – *I vowed a vow to God to say a prayer everie day for my sister and when shee is married to give God thanks that day everie day as long as I lived*.

9. The break-up of the attempt to marry her to Sir Thomas Osborne.

10. Henry Osborne's Diary records (1652):

Aug. 16, Munday. – My sister went to London to go to Ebsham [Epsom] to drink the waters.

Sept. 4, Saterday. – My sister with Mr Goldsmith and his wife came home from Ebsham water.

Epsom in Surrey was a famous spa town in the seventeenth and eighteenth centuries. Epsom salts, a water-soluble, bitter-tasting compound, used medically as a purgative and industrially in leather tanning, and as a filter in cotton goods and paper, was prepared from the waters as early as 1618. Aubrey visited the town in 1654 and 1655, and Sir William Temple's essay, *Of Health and Long Life*, is appropriate reading.

11. This 'servant' was almost certainly Dr (afterwards Sir) Charles Scarborough (1616–94), the physician and mathematician, who was a former student of Seth Ward and one of the founder members of the Royal Society, and who was educated at St Paul's School and Caius College, Cambridge. He was elected a Fellow of his College in 1640, but was ejected during the Civil War, whereupon he transferred to Merton College, Oxford, where Ward himself had been, and there worked with William Harvey (1578–1657), the distinguished physician who is considered to have laid the foundations of modern Western medicine. Admitted a Fellow of the Royal College of Physicians in 1650, Scarborough had a distinguished list of patients, including Charles II, James II, Queen Mary, and Prince George of Denmark. He was elected Member of Parliament for Camelford in Cornwall (1685–87). He is buried at Cranford, Middlesex, where there is a monument to him which (according to *DNB*) was erected by his widow, although *DSB* does not give her name.

From Henry Osborne's Diary, we learn that Scarborough was a member of the party which came to Chicksands from Epsom on 4 September. The Diary shows considerable ingenuity and effort on Henry's part to marry his sister either to Dr Scarborough or to his friend, Edmund Wyld (another of the founder members of the Royal Society, and later a patron of John Aubrey):

Feb. 2, Munday. – This day or the day following I went to Dr Scarborough about *Wilde*. [The next day he received Lady Osborn's letter about her son, and the negotiations with him and with Sir Justinian Isham then intervened; but it appears that Dorothy's visit to Epsom made her brother start again.]

Aug. 23, Munday. – Mr Gibson went to see *Doctor Scarborough* but founde him gone to Battlesden.

Sept. 4, Saterday. – My sister with Mr Goldsmith and his wife came home from Ebsham waters. Dr Scarborough came downe with them.

Sept. 5, Sunday. – Dr Scarborough came over to Chicksands *he spoke of Wild and said I should heare from him.*

Oct. 11, Monday. – Mr Gibson *went to* [London?] *to Doctor Scarborough.*

Oct. 23, Saterday. – I sent a note to *Doctor Scarborough.*

Oct. 30, Saterday. – *Doctor Scarborough came to mee in Westminster hall he said I should heare from him this night or to morrow morning.*

Nov. 2, Tuesday. – I receved a letter from my sister where shee was not of opinion that *Mr Gibson should come aboute Doctor*

Scarborough. I writ her worde that I had *heard nothing from him.*

Nov. 21, Sunday. – I mett by Sommersett house *Doctor Scarborough, wee had hot talke he desired to meete on Tuesday night at the Diuell taverne.*

Nov. 23, Tuesday. – Yesterday night I met *Doctor Scarborough* according to appointment at the Diuell Taverne.

Dec. 2, Thursday. – *Doctor Scarborough* came to mee and wee appointed to *dine at his house on Sunday with Wilde.*

Dec. 5, Sunday. – *I dined with Wilde.*

Jan. 29, Saterday. – I went to *Doctor Sc*: and spoke of *Wilde.*

LETTER 4

1. A humorous allusion to the effect that if she had married Sir Justinian Isham she would have attempted to arrange a marriage between W.T. and one of the four grown-up step-daughters she would have acquired by her own marriage.

2. Henry Pierrepont, Lord Dorchester (1607?–80), succeeded his father as Earl of Kingston-on-Hull (1643), and was created Marquess of Dorchester, Dorset (1645). He was educated at Emmanuel College, Cambridge, and represented Nottinghamshire in the 1628–9 parliaments as Viscount Newark. His first wife was Cecilia, daughter of Paul, Viscount Bayning; by this marriage there were two daughters – Anne (who married John Manners, Lord Ross, from whom she was divorced by Act of Parliament in 1666) and Grace (who died unmarried in 1703). Lord Dorchester's second wife was Catherine, third daughter of James Stanley, 7th Earl of Derby (beheaded in 1651). She was born around 1633, so that she was a very young bride: about nineteen to his forty-six. In letter 64, D.O. mentions Lord Dorchester as a probable participant in a plot against Cromwell, but the record is unclear: while there is evidence that Dorchester was fined heavily for sitting in the Oxford parliament, *DNB* also notes that in 1658 *Mercurius Politicus*, the journal of the Protectorate, praises him for giving the nobility of England a 'noble example how to improve their time at the highest rate for the advancement of their honour and the benefit of mankind'. It is known that after the end of the war Lord Dorchester resumed his medical and legal studies, and that he was elected a Fellow of the Royal College of Physicians (to which he left a valuable

library) as well as being admitted to Gray's Inn. *DNB* also notes that according to his biographer, Dr Charles Goodall (1878), Dorchester met his end by taking his own medicines, but again the record is unclear – in any event, he was about seventy-two years old.

3. Moore Smith notes that this is a reference to Acts 26:24: 'And as he thus spoke for himself, Festus said with a loud voice, Paul thou art beside thyself; much learning doth make thee mad.'

4. Henry Osborne's Diary records (1652):

> Apr. 9 – We removed my sister from my brother Peyton's [see letter 24, note 5] because my Lady and Doll [not identified] had the smallpox./Apr. 12, Munday. – I went to see Sir Tho: Osborn sicke. My sister and I came out of Towne and lay at Hatfeilde [Hatfield, Herts.].

5. Lady Diana Rich was one of her closest friends. She was the youngest daughter of Henry Rich, who was created Earl of Holland by James I (see note 6, below), and Isabel, daughter of Sir Walter Cope. Lady Diana had four sisters, whose names will recur in these letters: Frances, who married William, Lord Paget; Isabella, who married Sir James Thynne; Susanna, who married James, Earl of Suffolk; and Mary, who married John, Earl of Breadalbane. Lady Diana never married despite many attempts (as the letters will show) by D.O. to seek a suitable husband for her.

6. Henry Rich (1590–1649), 1st Earl of Holland, was the second son of Robert, Lord Rich, 1st Earl of Warwick, and Penelope Devereux (1562–1607), the 'Stella' of Sir Philip Sidney's *Astrophel and Stella* (1591). He was educated at Emmanuel College, Cambridge, was Member of Parliament for Leicester (1610; 1614), and was created Baron Kensington in 1623, taking this title for his baronetcy because his father-in-law, Sir Walter Cope, lived there. Rich, who became Chancellor of the University of Cambridge, was one of the lords-proprietors of Newfoundland, thus making part of his fortune out of marriage and part out of colonization, though his preferred method was through monopolies and Crown grants. In 1631 he was made Chief Justice in Eyre, south of the Trent, and thereby became implicated in the administration of one of the most unpopular acts of the reign, that of the revival of obsolete forest laws. Rich was executed in

1649 for being party to the attempt to rescue Charles I from the Isle of Wight. Defeated at the Battle of Kingston-on-Thames (7 July 1648), he was kept in the Tower until after the execution of Charles I; he was then tried, sentenced and beheaded before the gate at Westminster Hall, together with the Duke of Hamilton and Lord Capel. Parry (1914) quotes the Earl of Leicester's observation that there were '30 voyces for him and 31 against him; so his life was lost by the small part of one man's breath'.

Holland House, where he lived, was originally called Cope Castle, and was built around 1606 by Holland's father-in-law, Sir Walter Cope, who was Chancellor of the Exchequer to James I. Under Sir Walter's will his widow inherited the house on condition that she did not re-marry; when she did, it passed to her daughter, and thus to Lord Holland. After his execution, the house was confiscated by parliament (Cromwell is said to have walked in the gardens there with Ireton in order to seek to prevent eavesdroppers from overhearing what he had to shout to his deaf son-in-law), but it was returned to Lady Holland after the Commonwealth, and she had plays performed there privately in defiance of the laws of the time. The house became the social centre for Whigs in the late eighteenth and early nineteenth centuries, was severely damaged by bombs in the Second World War and left derelict until 1952, when the London County Council bought the property and managed to preserve and restore parts of it to public use.

7. For the dates of the Law Terms, see letter 2, note 7. Henry Osborne's Diary gives her visit to London as 12–22 February.

8. Henry Osborne's Diary corroborates this observation. It shows that he is away on business (mainly to do with various legal matters) as follows (1652): 3–17 July; 30 July – 7 August; 25–27 August; 13 September – 10 October; 5 October; 19 October; 22 October – 26 November; 29 November – 8 December; 27 January – 5 February.

9. Theatrical performances, including masques, took place at various times throughout the Commonwealth period, not only (though mainly) in private houses and the Inns of Court, but even in some of the large inns, which were never totally closed during the period.

LETTER 5

1. Lady Temple died in November 1638; she is buried at Penshurst Rectory.

2. A posy (poesy) ring is one which incorporates a short motto, or a line of (usually highly stylized) verse.

3. William Lilly (1602–81), the astrologer and author of *Christian Astrology* (1647), was the son of a yeoman farmer. He was born at Diseworth, Leicestershire, and educated at Ashby-de-la-Zouch Grammar School under John Brinsley. Arriving in London, Lilly obtained employment as a domestic servant in the house of one Gilbert White (who made his fortune out of property development and rental, but who could neither read nor write, and who thus found his servant helpful with the preparation of accounts). Lilly later married his former master's widow, Grace (née Whitehaire, White's second wife), and thereafter took up astrology, becoming a pupil of the 'mechanick preacher', Rhys 'Arise' Evans (about whom there is an excellent article in Christopher Hill, *Change and Continuity in Seventeenth-Century England*, 1974). The new career of astrologer was apparently so successful that Lilly could retire to the country (at Hersham, Surrey), but he returned to London in 1641, and soon numbered the rich and famous as his clients. In 1644 he began to publish his famous almanac, *Merlinus Anglicus Junior* (*The English Merlin Revived*), which became an annual publication, until his death. Lilly is reputed to have taken part in the attempt to secure the release of Charles I from Hampton Court, but he was also the favourite astrologer of parliament, on behalf of which he went to France as a spy, and which rewarded him with a pension. The government also used his services to encourage soldiers, with his predictions of victory. See also Bernard Capp, *Astrology and the Popular Press: English Almanacs 1500–1800* (London, 1979).

4. Sir Justinian Isham (see letter 3, note 6).

5. One possible reading of her comments may be that, in her view, Sir Thomas could not always be trusted to tell the truth – which might therefore indicate a reason for her critical attitude towards

him; though, according to Lady Giffard's *Life* of her brother (1728), there was a very close friendship between W.T. and Sir Thomas. Certainly, in the years 1674 to 1679, when negotiations to end the Dutch War and to effect the marriage between William and Mary were at their height, W.T. was one of Sir Thomas's most committed supporters.

6. This is a reference to the story of Amasis, king of Egypt, and Polycrates, tyrant of Samos, in which the former broke off a pact of friendship with the latter in order that, when Polycrates finally met with his destined calamity, Amasis would be freed from the need to feel compassion, since Polycrates would no longer be his friend. Parry suggests that D.O. might have read the story in a French translation – he mentions those by Pierre Saliat (1580) and P. de Ryer (1646). Moore Smith notes that there was also a translation into English by B. R., in 1585. The most accessible present-day source is Herodotus, *The Histories* (Penguin, 1954, rev. ed. 1972), pp. 220–21.

7. W.T. was a keen tennis-player and played the game regularly until late middle age, when he was forced to give it up because of gout. (See his essay, *Of Health and Long Life*.)

8. Lady Diana Rich (see letter, 4, note 5). There is some play here between D.O. and W. T. about 'sore eyes'. While the observation in letter 4 clearly refers to a physical ailment, the response by W.T. is equally clearly intended to draw attention to Lady Diana's beauty, which had the effect of giving 'sore eyes' to her admirers. D.O. writes about her loveliness in letter 7.

9. For the carriers, see Introduction, p. 20.

LETTER 6

1. Moore Smith speculates that W.T. must have complained, in an earlier letter, about the annoyance caused by church bells (which is another minor – but not negligible – insight into the 'normality' of some aspects of life, even in these days of Puritan hegemony; indeed, especially noticeable if it is to be presumed

that W.T. was not then living near Covent Garden, since he had to get up at four o'clock to deliver his letter to Mrs Painter).

2. For the Law Terms, see letter 2, note 7.

3. Philip Sidney (1619–98) was the eldest son of Robert Sidney (1596–1677), 2nd Earl of Leicester (see letter 44, note 6); he was created Lord Lisle in 1627, and succeeded his father to the earldom in 1677. After accompanying his father on embassies to Denmark (1632) and France (1636), he represented Yarmouth, Isle of Wight, in the Short Parliament (1640) and in the Long Parliament (1640–60). In 1642 he commanded a regiment of horse in Ireland; this troop plundered Monaghan so comprehensively that the parliamentary forces wanted him as their commander-in-chief. Sidney was appointed Lord-Lieutenant of Ireland in April 1646 (though he was unable to take office until February 1647), but after his landing in Munster was unsuccessful the appointment was not renewed. Like his brother, Algernon (see letter 7, note 3), Philip was appointed one of the judges at the trial of Charles I, but he declined to serve. A member of the first, second, fourth and fifth Councils of State of the Commonwealth, Sidney was selected in December 1652 to be Ambassador to Sweden; but his instructions were not ready until March 1653, and he had not set out when Cromwell ejected the Long Parliament. He then resigned his ambassadorship, and Bulstrode White-locke (see letter 39, note 10) went in his stead. A prominent Puritan and a great favourite with Cromwell, he seems to have exercised very little political influence despite his influential position – which might explain why he was not a victim of Restoration retribution. In 1645 Lisle married Catherine Cecil (d. 1652), daughter of William, 2nd Earl of Salisbury.

4. For his journey to Yorkshire to visit his father, see letter 2, note 1; letter 76, note 3.

5. Two other resorts, apart from Epsom (see letter 3, note 10), were fashionable at that time: Tunbridge Wells and Barnet. The Tunbridge Wells waters were reputed to have been discovered by Lord North (1606), but the fashion for going there appreciated considerably and rapidly after Henrietta Maria, Queen Consort of Charles I, visited there on medical advice in 1630, following

the birth of the future Charles II. The history of the Physick Well at Barnet is less well known, and for that reason elements of its history are given as Appendix E.

6. Lady Sunderland was Dorothy Sidney (1617–84), eldest daughter of Robert Sidney, 2nd Earl of Leicester (see letter 44, note 6). She was therefore sister to Algernon Sidney (see letter 7, note 3) and Lord Lisle (see note 3, above), and reputedly the 'Sacharissa' of the poet Edmund Waller (1606–87) (see letter 41, note 15); others who admired her included the Lords Russell, Devonshire, and Lovelace. W.T. had her portrait – she was one of Van Dyck's favourite subjects – hung in his closet (see letter 46, note 7). In 1639 she married Lord Spencer of Wormleighton (1620–43), later Earl of Sunderland, who was killed at the Battle of Newbury. Four children were born of this marriage: Dorothy and Robert, afterwards 2nd Earl of Sunderland, were born in Paris; Penelope and Henry (who was born two weeks after the death of his father, and who died at the age of five) were born at Penshurst. Lady Sunderland spent the first few years of her widowhood at Penshurst, but then returned to 'Allthrope' (Althorp, near Brington, Northants.) in 1650. She married Robert Smith, or Smythe, of Sutton-at-Hone and Boundes, Kent, in 1652, from which marriage there was one child, Robert (1653). Lady Sunderland died soon after the execution of her brother Algernon.

7. Thomas Howard, Earl of Arundel (1566–1646), was probably the first great English collector and patron of the arts. Educated at Trinity College, Cambridge, he married (1605) Alathea, third daughter of Gilbert Talbot, Earl of Shrewsbury, and a god-daughter of Queen Elizabeth. Always closely connected with the Court, Howard was made a Privy Councillor in 1616 and Earl Marshal in 1621. He was imprisoned for his hostility to Buckingham (1626–7), and was later a general in the army against the Irish (1639), and president at the trial of Strafford in 1641. He was close to many of the intrigues of his time, especially to the colonizing activities of Raleigh and others. Both Rubens and Van Dyck painted portraits for Howard of himself and of his wife; he brought Hollar from Prague and employed him to make drawings, and was the patron of Inigo Jones, who accompanied

him on his visits to Rome, where Howard acquired statues which (together with other sculptures, including the Parian Chronicle) were given to the University of Oxford in 1667 and which became known as the Arundel Marbles. Most of these are now in the Ashmolean Museum. Howard's library was given to the Royal Society, and the manuscripts known as the Arundel Collection were transferred to the British Museum in 1831.

8. Apparently Mr Smith married Lady Sunderland because another woman whom he wished to marry, Lady Isabella Blount, had rejected him in favour of Nicholas, 3rd Earl of Banbury. Lady Isabella died in 1655, and is buried in St Martin-in-the-Fields. She and her sister, Lady Anne Blount (see letters 48 and 49), were daughters of the 1st Earl of Newport, who was the illegitimate son of Charles Blount, Duke of Devonshire, and Penelope Devereux, Lady Rich, Philip Sidney's 'Sacharissa' (see note 6, above).

9. D.O. admonishes W.T., in several of her letters, about his moods. Lady Giffard, in her biography of her brother, writes:

> He was an exact Observer of Truth, thinking none that had fail'd once ought ever to be trusted again; of nice points of Honour; of great Humanity and Good-nature; taking pleasure in making others easy and happy; his Passions naturally warm and quick, but temper'd by Reason and Thought; his Humour gay, but very unequal from cruel Fits of Spleen and Melancholy, being Subject to great Damps from sudden Changes of Weather, but chiefly from the Crosses and surprising Turns of his Business, and Disappointments he met with so often in his Endeavours to contribute to the Honour and Service of his Country, when he thought himself two or three times so near Compassing, that he could not think with Patience of what had hinder'd it, or of those that he thought had been the occasion of his Disappointments.

LETTER 7

1. D.O. here offers a commentary on the seals which she had asked W.T. to send her (letter 5). Some of the letters (for example, letters 15, 20, 34, 51, 52, 53 and 61) still show traces of the seals – though these may not all be the ones he sent her. The short notes

written during her London visit (see note 5, below) have especially well-preserved examples of, respectively, a female figure sitting astride a dolphin; a helmeted male figure; and a female figure (goddess of fruitfulness?) against a background of what appear to be ears of wheat.

2. Philip II (1165–1223), King of France from 1180 to 1223, consolidated and extended royal power at the expense of feudal barons. He took part in the Third Crusade, was involved in several wars, and his victory at Bouvines (1214) established France as the pre-eminent European power of those times. Philip was also responsible for several administrative reforms; he commenced the construction of Notre Dame and built the first Louvre; and he paved the main streets and walled the city of Paris. His first wife was Isabella, daughter of Baudouin V of Hainault (later King Baudouin VIII of Flanders). After her death, Philip married Isamboin, daughter of Waldemar I of Denmark, but he later repudiated her in favour of Agnès de Méranie, daughter of Berthold V, Count of Meran (Tyrol). It is not clear where D.O. got her story.

3. Algernon Sidney (1622–83) was the second son of Robert Sidney, 2nd Earl of Leicester (see letter 44, note 6), and of Dorothy Percy, daughter of Henry Percy, 9th Earl of Northumberland; younger brother of Philip Sidney, 3rd Earl of Leicester (see letter 6, note 3); and brother of Dorothy Spencer, Countess of Sunderland (see letter 6, note 6). Algernon Sidney served under his brother's command in Ireland (1642); fought on the parliamentary side, and was wounded at Marston Moor (1645); was governor of Colchester (1645); Member of Parliament for Cardiff (1646), and Lieutenant-Governor of Horse in Ireland (1647). Nominated as a commissioner for the trial of Charles I, Sidney opposed as invalid both the constitution and proceedings of the High Court (as well as the subsequent 'engagement' which ratified these proceedings). Although he became a member of the Council of State (1653), he disengaged from the Protectorate after the dissolution of the Rump, only to be appointed once again to the Council in 1659. As one of the four commissioners who mediated between Sweden and Denmark (1659–60), Sidney refused to give pledges about his behaviour on his return to Charles II, and remained abroad:

he was in Rome from 1661 to 1663, where an attempt (inspired, it is suggested, by the new King) was made on his life; in Holland in 1665; and in France in 1666, where he negotiated with Louis XIV to seek to raise a revolt, but without success. In 1667 he returned to England, where he successfully defended himself to the King against a charge of nonconformist plotting. He was influential, especially with Whig leaders, so that when the Rye House Plot (a conspiracy to assassinate the King and his brother James, Duke of York, as they travelled from Newmarket to London past Rye House in Hertfordshire, which was aborted, but nevertheless betrayed to the King – see letter 58, note 17) was uncovered, Algernon Sidney was one of those sent to the Tower. He was tried before Jeffreys on three overt charges of treason and, despite an able defence and almost certain innocence, was executed on Tower Hill, and buried at Penshurst. With him were executed Lord William Russell (1639–83), who was subsequently vindicated by the reversal of the bill of attainder against him. Algernon Sidney's chief writings include *The Apology of A. Sydney in the Day of his Death*, and the not negligible *Discourses Concerning Government* (published in 1698), an answer to Filmer's *Patriarcha* (published posthumously in 1680).

4. The 'Arundel Howard' to whom D.O. refers was the son of Thomas Howard, Earl of Arundel (see letter 6, note 7). Parry observes that D.O. is correct in her reference to him as 'Arundel Howard' in order to distinguish him from the family of the Earl of Berkshire.

5. The dates of her visit to London are given in Henry Osborne's Diary (1653):

Feb. 11, Friday. – I went up to London.
Feb. 12, Saterday. – My sister came up to London with my Lady Diana Rich and lay at My Aunt Gargraves by Charing Cross and I lay at Palins.
Feb. 22, Tuesday. – Wee came to Chicksands in a coach of Jack Peters at 35 shillings and 6 horses.

6. Moore Smith is of the opinion that these two notes were written to W.T. during her visit to London; he dates them as both having been written on 14 February. The first, in which she informs him of her address and asks him to visit her, strengthens the case

for the view that the aunt who had summoned her to London was Lady Gargrave and not Lady Danvers (see letter 3, note 3). The second note appears to be her response to his complaint that she had not seen him on the Saturday or the Sunday. Since D.O. again mentions the cold to which she had made reference in her letter, it seems appropriate to include the note here. (See also letter 46, note 12.)

7. Past tense of 'rose'. See also letter 9, where she writes: 'I . . . risse a thursday'; letter 59; letter 64, note 2.

LETTER 8

1. Parry (1914) suggests that the shortness of this letter indicates that D.O. must have written it immediately after her return to Chicksands, and sent it to London with the coachman Jack Peters (see letter 7, note 5). This suggestion of Parry's seems to be substantiated by the opening line of the next letter, 'I was soe kinde as to write to you by the Coachman . . .'.

2. Address on the reverse of the letter.

LETTER 9

1. Rose.

2. An indication that W.T., too, was discomposed by the parting.

3. A reference to the proposed embassy by Lord Lisle to Sweden (see letter 6, note 3).

4. Moore Smith notes: 'A proposal had been made for a marriage between W.T. and a rich young lady. Sir John T. had left it to W.T. to decide whether to accept it.'

5. Colonel Robert Hammond (1621–54) was the son of Robert Hammond and Elizabeth, daughter of Sir Francis Knollys of Reading Abbey, and a cousin of W.T.: both were grandsons of Dr John Hammond, physician to James I. Hammond was Governor of the Isle of Wight during the period when Charles

I was imprisoned in Carisbrooke Castle; D.O. and W.T. first met there in 1648 – when Hammond condoned her brother's offence of writing the slogan 'And Hamon [Hammond] was hanged on the gallows they had prepared for Mordechai', for which D.O. took the blame in order to prevent her brother from being punished. Hammond became a member of the Irish Council in 1654, for which services parliament initially gave him an annuity of £500, later changed to a pension of £400, but which eventually became a grant of land valued at some £600 per annum. Hammond married Mary, sixth daughter of John Hampden (1594–1643), the parliamentary leader who opposed Charles I, was imprisoned for refusing to pay ship-money, helped to impeach Strafford, and died from wounds received at Chalgrove Field. At the time this letter was written, Hammond – who had just been chosen as High Steward and Burgess in Parliament for Reading – was probably living in Reading, perhaps at the house of his wife's stepmother, Lady Vachell of Coley Park. After their marriage, William and Dorothy Temple lived for some years in Reading, perhaps with Colonel Hammond's mother at Reading Abbey.

6. Martha, Lady Giffard (1639–1722), sister of W.T., married Sir Thomas Giffard of Castle Jordan, Co. Meath in Ireland on 21 April 1662. After his death two weeks later, Lady Giffard devoted herself to caring for her brother and his wife, and went to live with them. She wrote a *Life* of her brother, was engaged in disputes with Swift over the W.T. literary remains, and was the employer of Esther Johnson, Swift's 'Stella'. (See also Julia G. Longe, *Martha Lady Giffard*, 1911.)

7. Marguerite de Valois (1553–1615), Queen of France and Navarre, was the daughter of King Henry II of France and Catherine de Medici. Her marriage in 1572 to Henry, Protestant King of Navarre (later Henry IV of France), which was intended to make the peace between Catholics and Protestants, became instead the prelude to, and pretext for, the massacre of Protestants on St Bartholomew's Day, beginning in Paris on 24 August 1572. The marriage was one of mutual toleration. Marguerite took part in the intrigues of her brother Francis, Duke of Alençon and Anjou; in 1583, her brother, Henry III, had to

exile her from Paris because of her promiscuous behaviour, notably with Bussy d'Ambois, one of her brother's attendants. (Bussy d'Ambois is the hero of George Chapman's play of that name (1607), and of the novel *La Dame de Montsoreau* (1846), by Dumas.) Estranged therefore from her husband as well as her brother, Marguerite took up arms against them and seized Agen, but was captured in 1586 and imprisoned in the castle at Usson – although she soon managed to make herself mistress of the place rather than its prisoner. She refused at first to comply with her husband's demand that their marriage be annulled in order that he could be free to marry his mistress, Gabrielle d'Estrées, but finally agreed to the annulment in 1599, after the latter's death. In her retirement at Usson (1587–1605) she maintained a small court, in which literary men were prominent. She spent the last ten years of her life in Paris, and her autobiography, *Mémoires de la Reyne Marguerite*, the story of her life to 1582, was published in Paris in 1628 and received the commendation of the French Academy for its prose style.

8. The *Mémoires* contain the story of Mlle de Tournon and the Marquis de Varanbon, which bears a marked resemblance to that of the doomed affair between Hamlet and Ophelia. Although an English translation of the *Mémoires* was published in 1641, it is clear from the letter that D.O. had read the story in the original. Moore Smith speculates that W.T. might have brought a copy with him on his return from the Netherlands.

9. *Cléopâtre*, by Gautier de Costes, sieur de la Calprenède (1609?– 33), the French novelist and dramatist, appeared in 10 volumes in France; 12 volumes in Holland (1646–8). Again, it is evident that D.O. had read it in the original.

10. Moore Smith speculates that W.T. had intended a visit to Chicksands, apparently to bid farewell to D.O. before embarking with Lord Lisle on the embassy to Sweden, but that the visit did not take place.

11. Sir Justinian Isham (see letter 3, note 6).

12. Her companion, Jane Wright, whom he called his 'fellow servant'. Parry suggests that Jane Wright and Mrs Goldsmith,

wife of the Rector of Campton, were sisters, and Moore Smith suggests further that these two women were the daughters of Thomas Wright, Sir Peter Osborne's bailiff and at one time his agent in Jersey, and that the daughters had been taken into the Osborne household.

13. Parry suggests that the 'Old Knight' was probably Sir Richard Cook, a Bedfordshire gentleman who was knighted at Ampthill on 21 July 1621. Moore Smith suggests that it is a further reference to Sir William Briers (see letter 2, note 5), but that cannot be so if the dating of this letter as February 1653 is correct: we know from Henry Osborne's Diary that he had attended the funeral of Sir William in June, so he would still be alive at this time.

LETTER 10

1. For the two carriers, see Introduction, p. 20.

2. The 'widdow' was Mrs Elizabeth Thorold, daughter of Mary, Lady Carr of Sleaford, and granddaughter of Lady Gargrave (see letter 3, note 3); she was the very young widow of William Thorold, son of William Thorold of Marston, Lincs. She married, secondly (after 1669), Sir William Trollope of Casewick House, Uffington, but died in childbirth in 1671, leaving one daughter, Elizabeth. Henry Osborne's Diary again corroborates dating:

   1653, Mar. 2, Wednesday. – My cousin Thorold came to Chicksands. / Mar. 4, Friday. – Shee went away, and I went with her the first night to Stilton.

3. Henry Osborne (1619–75), royalist and colonel in the army, and compiler of the unpublished Diary used in these notes. He was the strongest opponent of the marriage between D.O. and W.T., and lived at Chicksands from 1649 (when the estate was freed from sequestration) until 1654 (the date of his father's death). Henry Osborne was one of the royalists who accompanied the five peers who went to fetch Charles II back to

England. The King apparently promised him the governorship of the island of Guernsey, but although this appointment was made it was almost immediately cancelled, and when it again fell vacant (1662) his application was turned down. In 1669, he is described as treasurer to the Commission for the Sick and Wounded, as well as Commissioner for the Navy; he was knighted in January 1673. Moore Smith notes that Henry Osborne's translations of the sixth and tenth books of Juvenal's *Satires*, together with a preface advocating 'free translation', constituted part of the papers preserved by the Longe family (see Introduction, page 18).

4. One of several remedies fashionable at that time.

5. A further reference to the lady who had been proposed as a wife for W.T. (see letter 9, note 4). It has not been possible to establish her identity.

6. John Osborne (1616–98), elder brother to D.O. He succeeded to the baronetcy of Chicksands upon the death of his father in 1653, and was created baronet in his own right in 1662. At the time of this letter he was living in Gloucestershire, having married his second cousin, Eleanor, daughter of Charles Danvers of Baynton: she was the sister of Jane Danvers, who married (i) George Herbert, the poet, and (ii) Sir Robert Coke of Highnam, Gloucestershire (see letter 37, note 8). John Osborne was one of the Gentlemen of the Privy Chamber to Charles II.

7. Henry Molle (1597–1658), of Eton and King's College, Cambridge, where he was elected to a Fellowship in 1620. He was Bursar from 1627 to 1629, and Vice-Provost and University Public Orator in 1639, but was expelled from his offices for refusing the take up the Engagement (a controversial Cromwellian oath of allegiance). He then went as fellow-commoner to Trinity College until 1654, when he was reinstated by Cromwell. He is buried in King's College chapel. (See Moore Smith, Appendix VII, especially for a biography of Henry Molle's father, John Molle (or Mole), who was imprisoned by the Inquisition in Rome for thirty years for being in possession of Protestant literature. See also *Notes and Queries*, 12th Series, Vol. VII (13 November 1920) for the family connections be-

tween the Osbornes, Molle, and the Chekes; Tom Cheke, the Countess of Manchester, and Mrs Franklin (see letters 27 and 30).)

8. This refers to the story of Gyges, a shepherd of the King of Lydia, as told in Plato, *Republic*, II.359, 360. The story is that, as a consequence of a storm and an earthquake, a deep chasm opened in the place where Gyges was feeding his flock. The shepherd entered this chasm and found a hollow bronze horse which contained the dead body of a larger-than-life human being, from whose finger he took a golden ring; by turning the bezel of the ring he was able to make himself invisible. With this power Gyges contrived to get himself selected to be one of the messengers sent to the King's court, where he seduced the Queen and plotted with her to kill her husband, and so obtain the crown.

9. *The Pleasant Comedy of Old Fortunatas*, by Thomas Dekker (1752?–1632), first produced in 1599. A sultan presents Fortunatas with a cap which enables the wearer to be transported to any destination simply by wearing it.

10. Harry Danvers, son of Sir John Danvers (1588?–1655), a regicide, by his second wife Elizabeth, daughter of Ambrose Dauntsey of West Lavington. Harry Danvers died of smallpox on 19 November 1654, and was buried in West Lavington church on what would have been his twenty-first birthday; the dates are corroborated by an entry in Henry Osborne's Diary for 29 November 1654.

LETTER 11

1. A further reference to the infusion of steel (see letter 10, note 4), but with the added interest of a description of how it was administered.

2. Jane Wright (see letter 9, note 12).

3. A child's game which became a fashionable adult pastime during the reign of James I. More precisely, 'battledore and shuttle-

cock', in which a shuttlecock is hit with a battledore (paddle); the precursor of the modern game of badminton.

4. Almanzor was originally identified by Parry as the story of Almanzor (later to be be the hero of Dryden's *Conquest of Granada*, 1670, 1671), which was based on *Almansor the Learned and Victorious King that Conquered Spaine, His Life and Death*, published by Robert Ashley (1627), which was a translation of a Spanish romance by a fictional Arabian author, Ali Abencufian. Moore Smith reminds us that, in his essay *Of Heroick Virtue*, W.T. appears to treat Almanzor as a real figure in history (so too, apparently, does Colonel Prideaux in *Notes and Queries*, 9th Series, Vol. XII, No. 292 (1903), pp. 81–2). But, as Courtenay (II. 264) reminds us, it was Gibbon (*Miscellaneous Works*, V. 554) who showed that W.T. had been deceived. See also Moore Smith, Appendix VIII, 'Almanzor or Amaran'.

5. There is some uncertainty about the identity of the person whom D.O. calls 'your Aunte my lady R.'. Lady Temple appears to have had only one sister, Jane, who married Sir John Dingley of Wolverton, Isle of Wight. It was their daughter Jane who married Dr William Rant of Morley, Norfolk (see letter 43, note 9), but if this is the person to whom D.O. refers here, it is not clear why she should call her 'your aunt' rather than 'your cousin'. Sir John Temple's sisters – Catherine, who married (i) John Archdall, and (ii) Sir John Vell; Mary, who married Job Ward; and Martha, who died unmarried – do not fit this description.

6. Her interrogators were her brothers Henry and John. Moore Smith notes that 'interrogatories' is a legal term, denoting questions put to a witness who is under oath, and cites several instances in Shakespeare, including Gratiano's speech in *The Merchant of Venice*, V.i.300ff., and the speech of the King in *King John*, III.i.147ff.

7. The gentleman who had to be carried upstairs in a basket may have been her elder brother, John (see letter 10, note 6), who had come to Chicksands to recover from the ague, to which illness she refers in letter 13. Henry Osborne's Diary has the following entry (1653): 'Mar. 10, Thursday. – My brother John came to Chicksands, where he had his ague.'

8. Word omitted.

9. Henry Cromwell (1628–74), second son of Oliver Cromwell, was born in Huntingdon, in the same year as D.O. A captain in the parliamentary army under Harrison (1647) and a colonel in Ireland under his father, Henry Cromwell represented that island in the Barebones Parliament (1653), in which year he also married Elizabeth, daughter of Sir Francis Russell of Chippenham, Cambridgeshire; she died in 1687. In 1654 he was sent to Ireland to suppress Anabaptists, and was promoted to the rank of major-general and to membership of the Irish Council, becoming Lord-Lieutenant of Ireland (1657). But he wearied of transplanting the Irish and replacing them with English settlers, saying that it brought disquiet to body and mind (which gives a very different picture of him from that of Mrs Hutchinson, who described him as a 'debauched ungodly Cavalier'). Henry Cromwell retired to Cambridgeshire at the Restoration. Moore Smith speculates that D.O. might have met him during the years 1645 to 1649, when, it is thought, Sir Peter Osborne and his family lived in London after their return from France. The sentence '. . . H.C. will bee as acceptable to mee as any body else' has been variously interpreted. Courtenay maintains that he was the suitor to whom she was most inclined, after W.T.; Moore Smith disagrees: for him the sentence means that 'if not T., then any man, even H.C.'. This seems to me a perverse reading. It is plain that, while she thinks highly of Henry Cromwell (see, for instance, letters 18, 22, 25) and that she would probably have married him if driven to it by her parents, the cumulative impression given by the letters is of a mind set upon marrying W.T. (see letter 12, note 2) and clear about the kind of qualities she would wish in a husband.

10. Betray.

LETTER 12

1. Henry Osborne's Diary records: 'Mar. 18, Friday. – R. Squire carried Jane [Wright] to London to goe for Guarnsey.' It must

be presumed that this unusually short letter was written in order
that Jane should take it with her to London to deliver to W.T.
Squire was Henry Osborne's groom (see also opening paragraph,
letter 13).

2. This is an unequivocal offer on the part of D.O. to marry W.T.,
should he wish to accept her offer.

LETTER 13

1. The words 'hee could not but' are written twice.

2. If W.T. were to agree to marry his Mrs Cl.

3. For Cleopatra, see letter 9, note 9; letter 10.

4. D.O. here means the New Exchange, built in 1608–9 on the
south side of the Strand on part of the gardens of Durham Place,
which had been leased to Robert Cecil, 1st Earl of Salisbury
(1563–1612). It was inaugurated by James I (who named it
'Britain's Burse') and his Queen, Anne of Denmark, and was
erected partly on the plan of the Royal Exchange in the City of
London (built around 1566–71), which was itself modelled on
the Antwerp Exchange. The New Exchange had vaults below,
with an open and paved arcade above, and above that again
were walkways with shops occupied by perfumiers, publishers,
milliners, etc. It was here that Pepys bought gloves for his wife,
Mrs Pierce and Mrs Knibb. The New Exchange became very
fashionable after the Restoration, when it took over much of the
business previously conducted by the Royal Exchange; but its
popularity declined after the death of the Queen, and it was
dismantled in 1737, when shops were built on the site.

5. Parry (1888) could not find any record of 'The Flower Pott',
above the Exchange, although he lists several others, including
one in Leadenhall Street and another in St James's Market. He
also gives a fascinating account of the origins of the shop sign: it
is said to have derived from the earlier representations of the
salutation of the Angel Gabriel to the Virgin Mary, in which
lilies were either placed in his hand, or set in a vase as accessories.

Then, as popery declined, the angel disappeared and the lily-pot became a vase of flowers; subsequently the Virgin was omitted, and there remained only the vase of flowers. Moore Smith traced an advertisement in the *Tatler* for a perfumier who sold orange-flower water, claiming that it had various reviving qualities.

6. Salisbury House was erected in 1602 by Robert Cecil, 1st Earl of Salisbury, who had built the New Exchange as well as Hatfield House, Hertfordshire (1607).

   This Salisbury House should not be confused with another of that name, later called Dorset House, which was built on land belonging to the Bishops of Salisbury from as early as the twelfth century, and which was in the parish of St Bride's in Fleet Street.

LETTER 14

1. Lady Diana Rich (see letter 4, note 5). We know from letter 10 that D.O. had hoped that Lady Diana might marry Harry Danvers, so the suitor mentioned here must have been someone else.

2. Not identified; probably now not identifiable.

3. Lady Jane Seymour (1637–79) was the youngest daughter of William, 1st Marquess and 2nd Earl of Hertford, created Duke of Somerset (1660), and of Frances Devereux, daughter of Robert, 2nd Earl of Essex. In 1661 she married Charles (Parry calls him Richard) Boyle, Lord Clifford, of Lanesborough, Yorkshire, who was also known as Viscount Dungarvan, and who was the eldest son of Richard, 1st Earl of Burlington and 2nd Earl of Cork. Lady Jane is buried in Westminster Abbey.

4. Lady Anne Percy (1633–54) was the daughter of Algernon, 10th Earl of Northumberland, and a niece of Lady Carlisle (see letter 44, note 3). She married Philip, Lord Stanhope (1633–1713), who in 1656 succeeded his grandfather as the 2nd Earl of Chesterfield. After her death (probably in childbed; she is buried at Petworth House, Sussex, together with her infant son), Stanhope went to Rome, but returned to England in 1656, when (it is asserted)

Oliver Cromwell offered him command of the army as well as the hand of his daughter in marriage, but the proposal (as well as a later one: of marriage to one of the daughters of Fairfax) was withdrawn because Stanhope had by then developed a notorious reputation for drunkenness, as well as for his affairs with Barbara Villiers (afterwards Duchess of Cleveland) and Elizabeth Howard (afterwards Mrs John Dryden). In 1658 Stanhope was committed to the Tower for dangerously wounding an opponent in a duel, and in 1659 he was once again imprisoned – this time for reputedly being implicated in a rising against Cromwell. In 1660 he killed an opponent in a duel and fled to France, but returned to England after obtaining a pardon from Charles II. In that year he married, secondly, Lady Elizabeth Butler, eldest daughter of James Butler, 12th Earl and 1st Duke of Ormonde. Lady Elizabeth herself had to be packed off from London to Derbyshire in order to insulate her from the attentions of, among others, the Duke of York and her cousin, James Hamilton. (This second Lady Chesterfield was the confidante of Martha, Lady Giffard; some of her letters are included in Julia Longe, *Martha, Lady Giffard*, 1911.) Stanhope married for a third time (1665) Lady Elizabeth Dormer, elder daughter of Charles, 2nd Earl of Carnarvon. Like Lord Holland (see letter 4, note 6), Stanhope was appointed a Chief Justice in Eyre of the royal forests south of the Trent.

5. Lady Grey de Ruthin was the daughter of Charles Longueville, Baron Ruthin, and a peeress in her own right. She was still single at the time of this letter, but she later married Sir Harry Yelverton (see letters 25, 45, 56 and 57).

6. Both previous editors identify Lady Anne Wentworth as the daughter of Thomas Wentworth, Earl of Strafford (executed in 1641), both give her as marrying Edward Watson, Lord Rockingham, whose more famous descendant was the patron of Edmund Burke.

7. Lady Diana Rich (see letter 4, note 5).

LETTER 15

1. 'Nan' is Nan Stacy, who appears to have been trusted by both parties. Moore Smith speculates that she might have come from the village of Campton, and that she had been employed by D.O.; there is also quite clearly a close link between Nan Stacy and Jane Wright, but it is not obvious that it is one rather of family relationship than common interest.

2. See letter 5, note 7. Parry reminds us that tennis continued to be played during this period, despite strong Puritan disapproval; he cites, for instance, the petition by John Tilson, 'gentleman, and others' (17 October 1654), seeking 'to prohibit Charles Gibbons, a tennis court keeper, from erecting another tennis court to the disturbance of his neighbours and ill example of others in this time of Reformation' (*CSP Dom.*, 1654).

3. On reverse of letter.

LETTER 16

1. This appears to be a reference to a letter which D.O. had written, at the request of W.T., to a third party; but the circumstances are unclear.

LETTER 17

1. Henry Osborne's Diary has the following entries (1653):

   Apr. 10, Easterday, Sunday. – My father fell ill in the chapell which was the beginning of his sicknesse.
   April 12, Tuesday. – He fell ill againe of a fitt, and I sent for Dr Spencer.
   Apr. 24, Sunday. – Placatt [not identified, but it might be the 'Poore moaped fellow' who gave D.O. some of his ale; see note 5, below] came to tend my father at night.

2. It is not possible to establish the circumstances which nearly led to the dismissal of the servant. Moore Smith speculates that an earlier letter, containing details concerning the circumstances of

Sir Peter Osborne's illness, might be missing, and he may be correct: it is certainly odd that there is no letter from D.O. to W.T. which goes into detail about the dramatic events described in her brother's Diary, and the writing about the servant would depend upon prior knowledge, based on correspondence.

3. Henry Osborne's Diary of 20 April records that: 'The Army dissolved the Parliament', which action aborted the projected embassy to Sweden (see letter 6, note 3); when the embassy eventually set out, it was led by Bulstrode Whitelocke (see letter 39, note 10).

4. D.O. turns the paper through ninety degrees to write in the margin (see Introduction).

5. D.O., having had her share of the ale, returns to complete the letter.

6. Lady Newcastle (1623–73) was Margaret Lucas, second wife of William Cavendish (1592–1676), Duke of Newcastle, royalist, patron of the arts, and dramatist. Her publications, which showed a keen interest in (for instance) chemistry, natural philosophy, and the political ideas of Thomas Hobbes, included: *Poems and Fancies* (1653); *Philosophicall Fancies* (1653); *Nature's Pictures* (1655); *Philosophical Letters* (1664); *Observations upon Experimental Philosophy* (1666); a biography of her husband (1667) and an edition of her plays (1668). Although Pepys wrote of her as being 'mad, conceited and ridiculous', Charles Lamb refers to her as being 'chaste and virtuous, but again somewhat fantastical and original-brained'. Critics suggest that Lady Newcastle met her husband when they were both in exile: she, having accompanied Queen Henrietta Maria, to whom she was one of the maids of honour; he, following flight after defeat at the Battle of Marston Moor (1644). As a wealthy royalist Cavendish had not only lent Charles I a vast sum of money, but had also sought to raise an army in the campaigns in the North. The couple returned to England with Charles II, but retired to his estate to become patrons of the arts and supporters of dramatists and poets (Shirley, Dryden, Shadwell). Ben Jonson wrote two masques for the entertainment of Charles II at Newcastle's Welbeck estate.

There is an excellent assessment by Virginia Woolf in *The Times Literary Supplement* of 2 February 1911. See also Sarah Mendelson, *The Mental World of Stuart Women: Three Social Biographies*, Brighton, Harvester Press, 1987.

LETTER 18

1. Robert and Willian Spencer, sons of Lord Spencer of Wormleighton and Penelope Wriottesley, who was the daughter of Henry Wriottesley, 3rd Earl of Southampton (to whom Shakespeare dedicated *Venus and Adonis* and *The Rape of Lucrece*). Their brother, the Earl of Sunderland, was killed at Newbury, and his widow thereafter married Mr Smith (letter 6, note 6).

2. This refers to the dissolution of parliament (see letter 17, note 3). As D.O. mentions Algernon Sidney (letter 7, note 3) in connection with this event, it is perhaps appropriate, following both Parry and Moore Smith, to quote from the diary of Algernon Sidney's father, Lord Leicester, which records:

> The Parliament, sitting as usual, and being in debate upon the Bill with the amendments, which it was thought would have been passed that day, the Lord General Cromwell came into the House, clad in plain black clothes, with gray worsted stockings, and sate down as he used to do in an ordinary place. After a while he rose up, putt off his hat, and spake; at the first and for a good while, he spake to the commendation of the Parlement for theyr paines and care of the publick good; but afterwards he changed his style, told them of theyr injustice, delays of justice, self-interest and other faults; then he sayd, Perhaps you think this is not Parlementary language, I confesse it is not, neither are you to expect any such from me, then he putt on his hat, went out of his place, and walked up and down the stage or floore in the middest of the House, with his hat on his head, and chid them soundly, looking sometimes, and pointing particularly upon some persons, as Sir R. [B.] Whitlock, one of the Commissioners for the Greate Seale, Sir Henry Vane, to whom he gave very sharpe language, though he named them not but by his gestures it was well known that he meant them. After that he sayd to Corronell Harrison (who was a Member of the House) 'Call them in', then Harrison went out, and presently brought in Lieutenant Collnel Wortley (who commanded the Generall's own regiment of foote,) with five or six files of musqueteers, about 20 or 30, with their musquets, then the Generall, pointing to the Speaker in his chayre, said

to Harrison, 'Fetch him downe'; Harrison went to the Speaker, and spoke to him to come down, but the Speaker sate still, and sayd nothing. 'Take him down' sayd the Generall; then Harrison went and pulled the Speaker by the gowne, and he came downe. It happened that day, that Algernon Sydney sate next to the Speaker on the right hand; the Generall sayd to Harrison, 'Put him out', Harrison spake to Sydney to go out, but he sayd he would not not go out, and sate still. The Generall sayd again, 'Put him out', then Harrison and Wortley putt theyr hands upon Sydney's shoulders, as if they would force him to go out, then he rose and went towards the doore. Then the Generall went to the table where the mace lay, which used to be carryed before the Speaker, and sayd, 'Take away these baubles', so the soldier's tooke away the mace, and all the House went out, and at the going out, they sayd, the Generall sayd to young Sir Henry Vane, calling him by his name, that he might have prevented this extraordinary course, but he was a Juggler, and had not so much as common honesty. All being gon out, the doore of the House was locked, and the key with the mace was carryed away, as I heard, by Corronell Otley. (*Sydney Papers*, ed. R. W. Blencowe (1825), p. 139.)

3. Lord Lisle (see letter 6, note 3).

4. Henry Cromwell (see letter 11, note 9).

5. 'the G' refers to Oliver Cromwell (1599–1658), Lord Protector. No note can do justice to this complex man, and students might best approach him through his biographers, who include: Sir Charles Frith (1900); Maurice Ashley (1957); Christopher Hill (1970); Antonia Fraser (1973); C. V. Wedgwood (1973).

6. John Pym (1584–1643), parliamentary politician; the eldest son of Alexander Pym of Brymore, near Bridgwater, Somerset, he was educated at Pembroke College, Oxford, and became Member of Parliament for Calne (1614; 1621; 1624) and for Tavistock (1625; 1626; 1628). Pym was opposed equally to Arminianism in the Anglican Church and to Catholicism, and was one of the earliest opponents of Charles I. He was one of the chief organizers of the impeachment of George Villiers, 1st Duke of Buckingham (1626), as well as of the Petition of Right (1628); he was also one of the key supporters of the colonization of the East Indies by the Providence Island Company (1629–40), and the unquestioned leader of the House of Commons in the years immediately preceding the Civil War. It was his long speech in the Short Parliament (1640), in which he listed popular griev-

ances, which led to the dissolution of that parliament. In the subsequent Long Parliament, Pym was one of the initiators of the prosecution of Thomas Wentworth, Earl of Strafford, and of Archbishop Laud. Pym also urged the abolition of episcopacy; helped to draft the Grand Remonstrance (1641), and is perhaps best known for being one of the Five Members – the others being John Hampden, Hollis, Hesibridge, and Strode – whom Charles I tried to remove by arrest by the military (1642). He should also be remembered for being the first to introduce excise duties, which had hitherto been unknown in England. His last major contribution was an alliance with the Scots, based on English acceptance of the Solemn League and Covenant (1643). Pym was buried in Westminster Abbey, but the body was removed after the Restoration. Pym was in many ways an unlikely political leader: he was associated with neither Court nor country; he was scrupulously honest, pursuing his dominant joint interests of religion and state finance. There is, as yet, no good biography of Pym; the most accessible book is probably that by J. H. Hexter, *The Reign of King Pym* (Cambridge, Mass., 1941), but the best short statement probably continues to be the entry in *DNB*.

LETTER 19

1. W.T. may have expressed concern over her state of mind. See the end of letter 18.

2. Moore Smith suggests that she is here referring to his Diary, concerning which she had written: 'I shall expect your Diary next week' (letter 18).

3. See letter 10, note 7. Henry Osborne's diary records: 'Apr. 14, Thursday. – My Cousen Molle came in the coach from Cambridge sicke of quartan fever.'

4. We can only infer that he must have offered to release her from their unofficial engagement, which, we must assume, had been agreed when they met on their visit to London (see letter 7), which in turn culminated in her offer to him of marriage (see letter 12, note 2).

5. See letter 6, note 3.

6. Sir John Temple was appointed (21 November 1653) a commissioner to advise on the entitlement of the Irish to estates in Ireland after the end of the Civil War; he went there in September 1653, and remained until the summer of 1654.

7. Address on reverse of letter.

LETTER 20

1. See letter 19 for her reference to 'an Ague that with two fitts has made mee soe very weak'; also letter 21, and those following.

2. For Sir Peter's illness, see letter 17, note 1; for her brother's, see letter 11, note 7, and the final paragraph of letter 13.

3. Bedlam – the Bethlem Royal Hospital, the oldest institution for the confinement of the mentally ill in England, and one of the oldest in Europe – was founded in 1247 by Sheriff Simon Fitz Mary as the Priory of St Mary Bethlehem outside Bishopsgate. A hospital for the treatment of general illness was added in 1329, and the treatment of 'distracted patients' – generally by being kept chained to the wall by the ankle or the leg, and by whipping and drenching with water when violent – began around 1377. The Priory and hospital came under the protection of the Mayor and Corporation of the City of London in 1346, and when the Priory was dissolved in 1547 the City bought the site from the Crown and re-established the hospital as an asylum, which in 1557 was placed under the administration of Bridewell. Bedlam was moved in 1675 to a new building at Moorfields, designed by Robert Hooke; at the entrance it had statues of 'Madness' and 'Melancholy', said to have been modelled on inmates. In the seventeenth century visitors were allowed to look at the inmates, and Bedlam became one of the regular sights of London until about 1770, when the practice was discontinued. In 1815 a new Bedlam was inaugurated at Lambeth, and, at the request of the government, the category of 'criminal lunatics' was added; these continued to be sent there until 1854, when they went to Broadmoor. The present Bethlehem Royal Hospital is at Beckenham, Kent, and the central block of

the Lambeth hospital (the wings being demolished) is now the Imperial War Museum.

4. Lady Diana Rich (see letter 4, note 5).

5. Henry Osborne's Diary records (1653): 'May 2 [3?], Tuesday. – I went up to London to the Terme.' (See letter 2, note 6, for dates of the Law Terms.)

6. Sir Thomas Osborne, afterwards Lord Danby (see letter 2, note 3).

7. A willow garland, the gift for forsaken lovers. Shakespeare, in *3 Henry VI*, III.iii.227–8 has:

> Tell him in hope he'll prove a widower shortly,
> I'll wear the willow garland for his sake.

8. Parry (1914) identified him as Levinus (called Richard in the 1888 edition) Bennet, Sheriff of Cambridgeshire. He was the son of Thomas Bennet, an alderman of the City of London, who had bought an estate near Cambridge called Babram or Babraham, which had once belonged to Sir Horatio Palavicino (or Palavicini). We can assume that Bennet was a royalist; he was created a baronet in 1660. His name is not mentioned in Henry Osborne's Diary, but as he appears in letter 21 as 'Mr B.' in connection with Henry Molle (where the Cambridge don is described as his 'agent'), we might assume further that he came to Chicksands at the invitation of the scholar; he might even be one of the visitors mentioned in letter 19, who proffered 'expert advice' on the treatment of ague.

Palavicino, who was the Pope's Collector of Taxes in England, apparently abjured popery after the accession of Queen Elizabeth to the throne, and built his estate at Babraham, some six miles south-west of Cambridge, around 1576 out of (it is alleged) monies which he should have remitted to Rome. He died in 1587, and Moore Smith gives his epitaph, which is revealing:

> Here lies Horatio Palavazene
> Who robb'd the Pope to lend the Queen.
> He was a theefe! A theefe? Thou lyest,
> For whie? He robb'd but Antichrist.

> *Him death with besom swept from Babram*
> *Into the bosom of old Abram,*
> *But then came Heracles with his club*
> *And struck him down to Belzebub.*

(See also Lawrence Stone, *An Elizabethan: Sir Horatio Palavicino*, Oxford, 1956.)

9. *OED* gives this as a reference to 'the calcareous structure in the stomach of a lobster', fancifully supposed to resemble a seated female figure; it records the first attribution to Swift, *The Battle of the Books* (1704), where the Dean, describing the encounter between Virgil and Dryden, writes: 'The helmet was nine times too large for the head, which appeared situate far in the hinder part, even like the lady in a lobster.' Parry (1888) gives an even earlier example, one that is roughly contemporaneous with this letter, from Robert Herrick's 'The Fairy Temple, or, Oberon's Chapel', from *Hesperides* (1648):

> The Saint, to which most he prayes
> And offers *Incense* Nights and dayes,
> The *Lady* of the *Lobster* is.

Parry also notes that the expression was still known to fishmongers at the time of his first edition, and further cites a written use in a letter from Charles Lamb to Bernard Barton, 5 December 1828.

10. Written by Madeleine de Scudéry (1607?–1701), a French novelist, who was prominent at the salon of Catherine de Vivonne, Marquise de Rambouillet, but who later set up her own and made it one of the pre-eminent places of its kind in Paris. Her two chief literary works, *Artamène; ou, Le Grand Cyrus* (1645–53) and *Clélie* (1654–60), are lengthy pseudo-historical novels, which were extremely popular in France as well as in England. The title pages of the novels give only the name of Madame de Scudéry's brother, Georges (1601–67), but it appears that he was only a minor collaborator; he wrote plays, and is perhaps best known for his attacks on Corneille's *Le Cid*. As was the case with *Cléopâtre* (letter 9, note 9), D.O. would have read this in the original, though both novels were translated into English by one 'F.C. Gent'.

11. Address on the reverse, together with the remnants of a seal showing a female figure against a trellis-work background.

LETTER 21

1. Yet another example of the ability of W.T. to establish the identity of her 'servants'.

2. *OED* gives this sentence, and the one in letter 54, as the first examples of the use of 'romance' as 'having the character or attribute associated with Romance, chivalrous, romantic'. She also uses the word in letter 57.

3. The 'county force' or 'Posse Comitatus': 'the body of men above the age of fifteen in a county (exclusive of peers, clergymen, and infirm persons), whom the sheriff may summon or "raise" to repress a riot or for other purposes; also, a body of men actually so raised and commanded by the sheriff' – *OED*.

4. Reveries.

5. This is one of the salutary examples which demonstrate the unwisdom of seeking to construct a rigid pattern for the writing and despatch of the letters.

6. D.O. here means 'household': the members of the family collectively; an organized group, which would include servants and attendants living in the same house.

7. Lady Gargrave (see letter 3, note 3).

8. Henry Osborne's Diary records (1653):

   May 2 [3?], Tuesday. – I went up to London to the Terme.
   May 16. – My brother John came up.
   June 3, Friday. – I came to Chicksands in a coach with my neisse D. Peyton.

   We should also note, from information later in this letter, that Molle had returned to Cambridge, and that John was still at Chicksands, waiting to travel to London, which journey is confirmed in Henry's Diary.

9. Harry Danvers (see letter 10, note 10). D.O. apparently continues to hope that he will marry Lady Diana Rich.

10. A neat deflation of the views of Sir Justinian Isham, in particular, but perhaps also a more general comment upon prevailing male attitudes.

LETTER 22

1. An indication of one possible reason why so few of his letters to her have survived: while he could preserve hers in a special cabinet, in the relative safety of his lodgings in or near London, she had to be constantly on her guard against family interference, especially on the part of her brother Henry.

2. Parry identified him as the Anabaptist preacher, the Rev. William Erbury (1604–54), who was born in or near Roath Dagfield, Glamorgan. Erbury studied at Brasenose College, Oxford, and was afterwards the incumbent of St Mary's, Cardiff. He was apparently regularly at odds with the Church hierarchy; after being declared a schismatic by the Bishop of Llandaff (Laud) in 1634, he was forced to resign (1638), whereupon he began his preaching against episcopacy (1640) and ecclesiastical ceremony, and became chaplain of Major Skipton's troop in the parliamentary army, where he is reported to have preached antinomian doctrines. In 1645 he went to London, where he began to preach the doctrine of universal redemption. In that same year, at Bury St Edmunds, he affirmed that Adam's curse could only be imputed to Adam, and denied the divinity of Christ. Although he went to live in Ely, Erbury retained his links with the army; when he was forced to leave Ely (and, later, Oxford) because of his Socinian views, he returned to London, where he preached at Christ Church, Newgate Street, until he was summoned to defend his unorthodoxies before a Committee for Plundered Ministries (1652), which Committee refused to accept his profession of faith and which reputedly had him put in prison. After his release, he disputed with John Webster in a church in Lombard Street, a confrontation which became so serious that it ended in riot. After his death in 1654, his widow became a

Quakeress; she was imprisoned in 1656 for paying divine honours to James Nayler – she alleged that Nayler was the Son of God, and that he had raised her from the dead. (See also Christopher Hill, *The Experience of Defeat: Milton and Some Contemporaries*, London, 1984.)

3. Moore Smith speculates that W.T. may have taken her to the same church on Sunday 20 February, but this is doubtful: the second note incorporated in letter 7 is quite clear – Saturday had been spent in the company of Lady Diana, while a cold kept her indoors on Sunday. It is possible that they might have gone together to listen to Erbury on another day, but it is difficult to see when that might have taken place during the visit. Their excursion may have been at an earlier time, for instance in the period of their meeting at Goring House (see letter 3).

4. One of the surviving sons (Oliver, b. 1626; John, b. 1632; Nathaniel, b. 1636) of Sir Samuel Luke (d. 1670), who was a neighbour of the Osbornes, being Lord of the Manor at Hawnes (Haynes), near Chicksands. Sir Samuel was a well-known colonel in the parliamentary army; he commanded a troop of horse at Edgehill (23 October 1643), and, after assisting in the recovery of Newport Pagnell from the royalist forces, became governor of the town, and was later Scoutmaster-General of the counties of Bedford and Surrey. He was a member of both the Short and Long Parliaments, and in 1643 parliament expressed thanks to him for his services. However, with the promulgation of the 'Self-Denying Ordinance' of 26 June 1645 (a proposal by Cromwell's supporters that no Member of Parliament should hold an army commission; it was a response to the defeats of 1644, and an attempt to remove incompetent officers), Luke was relieved of his command, and stripped of his parliamentary duties as a consequence of 'Pride's Purge'. Although *DNB* casts doubt on the story, it is usually asserted that Luke was the model for the butt Hudibras in the mock-heroic epic of that name by Samuel Butler (1612–80).

5. The name of the shopkeeper from whom she ordered the orange-flower water (see letter 13, note 5).

6. Levinus Bennet (see letter 20, note 8).

7. For her 'fighting Servant', see letter 3.

8. 'The Lord of Lorne and the False Steward' was a broadsheet ballad of the sixteenth century; it was entered, with two other ballads, to Master Walley, on 6 October 1580. The text is readily available in *The Oxford Book of Ballads*, ed. James Kinsley (1969), pp. 285ff.

9. Henry Osborne's Diary records (1653): 'July 28, Wednesday. – *I vowed a vow to God to say a prayer everie day for my sister and when shee was married to give God thanks that day everie yeere so long as I lived.*'

LETTER 23

1. Parry's research is once again exemplary. He informs us that the story of which she makes mention is that of the trial of George Brydges, 6th Lord Chandos, a royalist who fought at Naseby and later in the West Country and who had to pay a large sum of money to parliament at the end of the war. He died suddenly of smallpox in 1654/5. He had been twice married: first, to Susan, a daughter of the Earl of Manchester, by whom he had three daughters; secondly, to Jane, daughter of John Savage, Earl Rivers, by whom he had another three daughters.

   The event to which she refers was the trial of Lord Chandos for killing a Mr Henry Compton at Putney on 13 May 1653. Although this trial is not reported in the State Trials, Parry discovered its details in the Journals of the Earl of Leicester, who noted that: 'Towards the end of Easter term, the Lord Chandos, for killing in a duel Mr Compton the year before' (that is to say, in March: the new year began on 25 March) 'and the Lord Arundel of Wardour, one of his seconds, were brought to the trial for their lives at the Upper Bench in Westminster Hall, when it was found manslaughter only, as by a Jury at Kingston-on-Thames it had been formerly. The Lords might have had the privilege of peerage . . . but they declined it by the advice of Mr Maynard and the rest of their Counsel, least by that means the matter might have been brought about again, and therefore they went upon the former verdict of manslaughter, and so were acquitted; yet to be burned in the hand, which was done to them both a day or two after, but very favourably.' The Earl of Leicester went on to observe that the trial was important for the following reasons: Lord Chandos and Lord Arundel, despite being royalists, had consented to be tried by the parliamentary authorities; they had waived the privilege of peerage; and they were burnt in the hand – the first peers to whom this was done. These observations prompted Parry to reflect that 'the democratic Earl of Leicester expresses at the event some satisfaction, and seems to derive from the whole circumstances of the trial comfortable assurance of the power and stability of government'.

In the 1914 edition, Parry tells us the reason for the duel, as given in Collins' *Peerage*: 'The Lord Chandos had a difference with Colonel Henry Compton ... about a lady he had recommended to the Colonel, whose person and fortune were below few matches in the kingdom, which unhappily ended in a duel.'

2. Lady Carey was Mary, illegitimate daughter of Emmanuel Scrope, Earl of Sunderland. She married Henry Carey, Lord Leppington, who became the Earl of Monmouth (1639); he died in 1649, and their son (whose death D.O. mentions, and who was buried in Westminster Abbey a few days before this letter was written) died in 1653. In 1654, Lady Carey married Charles Paulett, Lord St John, later Duke of Bolton. We read in the next letter that Compton, killed in the duel, had left his estate to Lady Carey. (See also letter 37, note 2; letter 41, note 12.)

3. Thomas Osborne, afterwards Earl of Danby (see letter 2, note 3).

4. W.T. must have asked her to stop ending her letters with phrases like 'your humble servant' or 'your faithful friend and servant', and inspection of the letters which follow will reveal that she stopped using those forms until letter 51, when she again adopted the formal style as an indication of what she intended to be the end of their love affair.

5. Sir William Briers (see letter 2, note 5).

6. Portion and jointure: *OED* defines 'portion' as 'The part or share of an estate given or passing by law to an heir, or to be distributed to him in the settlement of an estate.' This masculine formulation

has its female equivalent in 'dowry' or 'marriage portion'; it is also defined, more generally and ideologically, as 'That which is allowed to a person by providence, lot, destiny, fate.' *OED* defines 'jointure' as 'The holding of property to the joint use of a husband and wife for life in tail, as a provision for the latter, in the event of her widowhood.' See also Introduction, section iv: 'Family, Gender, and Feminism'.

7. Sir Peter Lely (1618–80), a Dutch painter who settled in England, was originally known as Pieter van de Faes. After studying in Haarlem, he came to England in 1643, and succeeded his compatriot, the Flemish Sir Anthony van Dyck (1599–1641), as Court painter (1661); he painted many of the great figures of the Court of Charles I, the Protectorate, and the Restoration. Lely did eventually paint his portrait of Lady Diana Rich for D.O. at Lord Pagett's house (see letter 45), and he also completed portraits of both D.O. and W.T.

8. It is noteworthy that D.O. was unswerving in her defence of her brother against outside criticism, despite his behaviour towards her. This is particularly striking in the letters towards the end of the sequence, where there is opposition by Sir John Temple to Henry Osborne taking part in the marriage settlement negotiations (see letter 75, note 2; letter 76, note 1).

LETTER 24

1. Lord Lisle (see letter 6, note 3).

2. Henry Molle (see letter 10, note 7).

3. Levinus Bennet (see letter 20, note 8).

4. Moore Smith speculates that D.O. might here be unconsciously echoing Virgil: '*O fortunatas nimium sua si bona norint Agricolas*' (*Georgics*, II. 458). which R. C. Trevelyan translates as 'O husbandmen too fortunate, could they come to know their own felicity' (C.U.P., 1944, p. 73). While Moore Smith is probably correct in his additional observation that some of her spellings (he cites 'apear'; 'exelently'; 'aprobation') 'suggest that the Latin

forms were not familiar to her', that would not be surprising in view of the ways in which education was biased in favour of males. But there is possibly another explanation, which is that her evocation of the tranquil English pastoral scene does not require a learned tradition; it was obvious to her, capable of being observed and reiterated – despite the world being turned upside down, and despite the fact that this world of tranquil rurality was itself the consequence of uninterrupted human intervention and construction.

5. We know from Henry Osborne's Diary that he had brought his niece, Dorothy Peyton, to Chicksands on Friday, 3 June (see letter 21, note 8). Dorothy Peyton was the eldest daughter of Sir Thomas Peyton of Knowlton, Kent. Sir Thomas, who was the second baronet, was born about 1613, and died in 1684. He was a prominent Kentish royalist, who had to compound for his estates (1645), and who became one of the leaders of the Kentish rising which was put down by Fairfax (1648). A member of the Short as well as the Long Parliament, Peyton spent seven years in prison for his royalist sympathies, but was granted the duty on sea-coal after the Restoration.

   His first wife was Elizabeth (not Anne, as stated in Parry), eldest sister of D.O., whom he married in 1636, in St Bride's Church, London; she died in 1642. Peyton married, secondly, Cecilia, the widow of Sir Walter Swan, Lord Mayor of London; she died in 1661. His third marriage was to Jane, widow of Sir Timothy Thornhill.

6. Walker was the man who set the seals (see letter 7, note 1).

7. Lady Leppington (see letter 23, note 2; letter 37, note 2; letter 41, note 12).

8. Obscured by the binding.

LETTER 25

1. See letter 24.

2. Opened in 1632.

3. See letter 14, note 5. Parry (1914) suggests that Lady Grey de Ruthin might at this time have been living at Meppershall, which is near Chicksands, where she had family connections.

4. It has not been possible to identify this person.

5. See letter 3, note 10.

6. See letter 19, note 6.

7. See letter 11, note 9.

8. Charles Fleetwood (1618?–92) was the second husband of Oliver Cromwell's daughter, Bridget. A famous general in the parliamentary army, he had fought with Cromwell in several battles in England and in Scotland. Fleetwood became a member of the Council of State (1651) and succeeded his new wife's first husband, Henry Ireton (1611–51), as commander-in-chief in Ireland (1652–55), where he continued his predecessor's policy of settling English soldiers on lands confiscated from Irish owners. In 1659 he led the coup that forced Richard Cromwell (1626–1712, third son and successor to Oliver Cromwell as Lord Protector) to dissolve parliament. At the Restoration, Fleetwood was barred from holding further office. Moore Smith notes that Fleetwood's mother was a member of the Luke family, of Woodend, close to Chicksands, and he speculates that she might have been related to Sir Samuel Luke (letter 22, note 4). In Letter 41, D.O. reports that her dogs had arrived, and acknowledges the assistance of Henry Cromwell.

9. Mastiff, 'any of a breed of large, powerful, smooth-coated dog with hanging lips and drooping ears, formerly used for hunting and as watchdogs' (*OED*).

10. Perfect.

11. It would appear from this comment that W.T. was not living in London and, furthermore, that even D.O. was not aware of his precise address. (See also letter 6, note 1.)

12. See letter 18, note 1.

13. There is some doubt as to which Lady Lexington she refers. Robert Sutton of Aram (Averham?) (1594–1668) was created

Baron Lexington of Aram in 1645. He was married three times: (i) to Elizabeth, daughter of Sir George Manners of Haddon Hall, and sister of John, 8th Duke of Rutland; (ii) to Anne, daughter of Sir Guy Palmes of Lindley, who was the widow of Sir Thomas Browne, Bt, of Walcott, Notts., who left two co-heiresses; (iii) to Mary, daughter of Sir Anthony St Leger, Warden of the King's Mint. Parry suggests that the Lady Lexington to whom D.O. refers was the third wife, but Moore Smith disputes that, claiming that since the third marriage took place in 1661, we have to do here with the second wife. I suspect that Moore Smith is correct because Parry noted that he could not find a daughter of Lady Lexington who had married a Spencer, but if we assume that the daughter mentioned in D.O.'s letter was a Browne, that would explain all.

14. See letters 3, 5, 6, 9 and 22.

LETTER 26

1. Shakespeare, *Richard III*, V.iii.

2. 'To make a leg' involved the male scraping one foot on the ground while bowing to the female, who would curtsey in response. It was this act which made D.O. and her brother the 'most Complementall Couple' – abounding in acts of formal politeness.

3. See letter 25, note 5.

4. See letter 7, note 1, and letter 24, note 6.

5. According to Parry, Mr Ralph Freeman of Aspenden Hall, Hertfordshire, who died in 1714, aged about eighty-eight, and was therefore about thirty-seven at the time of this letter. He may be the same Mr Freeman whom D.O. (then Lady Temple) mentions as her friend in letters which are reprinted in Julia Longe's book.

6. Humphry Fysshe, Esq., of Ickwell Green, about six miles from Campton, was Sheriff of Bedfordshire in 1644. Parry tells us that he came from Southill, near Campton.

7. The dates for the Law Terms are given in letter 2, note 7.

8. Robert (Robin) Osborne (see letter 29, note 8).

LETTER 27

1. Sir Thomas Cheke of Pyrgo (Purgo?), near Havering atte Bower, Essex, was a second cousin of Sir John Osborne. However, when Sir Thomas Cheke married Sir John Osborne's sister Catherine, he became not only an uncle to Sir Peter Osborne, but also a great-uncle to Sir Peter's children, including D.O. After the death of Catherine, Sir Thomas married, secondly, Essex Rich, daughter of the Earl of Warwick; this marriage produced seven children, including the Tom Cheke mentioned in this letter, as well as Frances (not Essex, as given by Moore Smith), Countess of Manchester, and Elizabeth (later, Mrs Franklin: see note 4, below). It is these seven children to whom the Osbornes refer as 'cousins'. Henry Molle (see letter 10, note 7) was a first cousin to the Cheke family, because his mother Elizabeth was a sister of Sir Thomas Cheke. Parry points to a longstanding relationship between the two families, noting that a Sir John Cheke, who was Professor of Greek in the University of Cambridge, had taught Roger Ascham (1515–68), tutor to Queen Elizabeth and Edward VI; Ascham is perhaps best remembered for *The Schoolmaster* (1570).

The Tom Cheke mentioned here was born in Romford in 1628; he married a famous beauty, Letitia, daughter of the Hon. Edward Russell – she survived him, and married, secondly, her cousin Lord Robert Russell. Tom Cheke, who was a colonel in the army, and Lieutenant of the Tower of London in the reigns of Charles II and James II, died in 1688, and was buried in the chapel at Pyrgo Park.

2. Kimbolton, near St Neots, Huntingdonshire, was the seat of the Earl of Manchester (see note 3, below). The original medieval mansion was remodelled in the reign of William and Mary, and further rebuilt by Vanbrugh after a fire (1707). Robert Adam added an outer gatehouse and gateway to the north side, *c.* 1776.

3. Edward Montagu (1602–71), 2nd Earl of Manchester, was educated at Sidney Sussex College, Cambridge, and was Member of Parliament for Huntingdon (1623; 1625). He became Lord Kimbolton (1626) and Earl of Manchester (1642), and was also known as Viscount Mandeville; he was the leader of the Puritans in the House of Lords, and was the only peer who sided with the Five Members (see letter 18, note 6). Montagu raised a regiment to fight at Edgehill, reconquered Lincolnshire, and was commander at the battle of Marston Moor, at which time (Parry reminds us) Cromwell was one of his officers. However, at the second battle of Newbury, Cromwell accused him of palpable negligence, and he resigned his command (1645). Montagu opposed the trial of Charles I, as well as the establishment of the Commonwealth, and retired from public life until after the Restoration, when he became one of the Commissioners of the Great Seal, was restored to his lord-lieutenantcy of Huntingdonshire and Northamptonshire and elected to the chancellorship of the University of Cambridge. Montagu, who was created a Knight of the Garter (1661), was married five times: (i) to Susanna, daughter of John Hill of Honiley, Warwickshire, and his wife Dorothy Beaumont; (ii) in 1626, to Anne, daughter of Robert Rich, 2nd Earl of Warwick, from which marriage there were three children (Robert, his successor; Frances, who married Henry Sanderson, later Bishop of Lincoln; Anne, who married Robert Rich, 3rd Earl of Holland and 5th Earl of Warwick); (iii) to Essex, daughter of Sir Thomas Cheke, from which marriage there were six sons and two daughters; (iv) in 1659, to Ellinor, daughter of Sir Richard Wortley, of Wortley, Yorkshire – it was her fourth marriage; (v) in 1657, to Margaret, daughter of Francis Russell, 4th Earl of Bedford – she was the widow of James Hay, 2nd Earl of Carlisle.

4. Moor Park, Herts. Sir Richard Franklin, Kt, married Elizabeth, daughter of Sir Thomas Cheke (see note 1, above), who bought the park and mansion from the Earl of Monmouth (1652) and the manor from Sir Charles Harbord (1655). The gardens were laid out to a design by Lucy Harrington, Countess of Bedford. Temple, in his essay on gardens, described them as 'the perfectest figure of a garden I ever saw, either at home or abroad'. It is

here that Sir William and Lady Temple spent their honeymoon, and it is after this Moor Park (now a famous golf club) that Temple, in 1680, re-named the house near Farnham where they lived. The latter is now a finishing school.

5. Cooper and Hoskins were celebrated English miniaturists. Not much is known about John Hoskins, except that he painted Charles I and his Queen Henrietta Maria, and that he is buried in St Paul's, Covent Garden. Samuel Cooper (1609–72) was his nephew and pupil. He was born in London and is perhaps best known for his portrait of Oliver Cromwell, although he also painted some of the other key figures of his time, including Lilburne, Ireton, Hampden, Hobbes, and James II (when he was Duke of York). He lived in France for several years, and his widow was awarded a pension by the French government; he was promised one by the English, but this never materialized.

LETTER 28

1. This is a continuation of the sentiments expressed at the end of letter 27. Parry speculates that D.O. might have been thinking of the lines in Ovid, *Metamorphoses*, VIII, in the 1626 translation by George Sandys; these lines are given in letter 54, note 14.

2. See letter 26, where D.O. gives her reasons why W.T. should not go to visit her at Chicksands.

3. Sir Justinian Isham (see letters 3, 5, 6, 9, 22 and 25).

4. Although Sir John Temple had recommended a potentially suitable wife to his son (see letter 9, note 4; letter 10, note 5), he appears not to have applied pressure on W.T. to comply with parental recommendation.

5. Moore Smith notes the similarity of this expression to the one in *Macbeth*, V.v.24ff.:

> *Out, out, brief candle!*
> *Life's but a walking shadow, a poor player*
> *That struts and frets his hour upon the stage*
> *And then is heard no more.*

6. A continuation of the matter raised in letter 27.

LETTER 29

1. See letter 28, note 2.

2. Moore Smith speculates that W.T. might have been in St Malo in 1648, after his visit to the Isle of Wight; that he and D.O. had met again in London, but that she had forgotten him. (See also letter 44.)

3. Moore Smith draws attention to the line in *The Merchant of Venice*, I.i.80: 'With mirth and laughter let old wrinkles come . . .'

4. Jane Wright (see letter 9, note 12; see also letter 12, note 1 for details of her departure for Guernsey, via London).

5. In letter 34 we are informed that Jane Wright has returned, which suggests that she was in Guernsey (or, at least, away from Chicksands) for some five months.

6. The man who set the seals (see letter 7, note 1).

7. Henry Osborne's Diary does not give a precise date for John Osborne's arrival at Chicksands; it does, however, record that Henry postponed his return to Chicksands to 4 July, because John had arrived in London on 1 July. The Diary confirms that Henry sent his man, Owen, to Greenwich on 25 July, and that John went to London with him. We next hear of John on 1 September, when the Diary records that he has gone to Gloucestershire, having heard of the death of their younger brother, Robin (see note 8, below). It seems a reasonable assumption, therefore, that John was at Chicksands sometime between 24 July and 1 September.

8. We know from letter 26 that she had expected that her brothers would arrive together, but this hope of a family reunion was dashed because, as Henry Osborne's Diary records (1653):

Sept. 1, Thursday. – My brother John went from Chicksands into Gloucestershire with my lady Cooke's man upon the death of my brother [Lady Cooke, *née* Danvers, John Osborne's sister-in-law, had been the wife of George Herbert, the poet]. This day came a Letter from P. Froude of my brother Robin's death with one inclosed from Mr Dowdeswell who writes he died upon friday night about 12 a clocke being the 26 day of August [Colonel Philip Frowd had fought on the royalist side in the Civil War; he received a knighthood after the Restoration, and was made governor of the Post Office. Mr Dowdeswell is not known].

9. Dorothy Peyton had arrived on Friday, 3 June (see letter 21, note 8; letter 24, note 5).

10. Lady Gargrave (see letter 3, note 3).

11. Mrs Thorold (see letter 10, note 2).

12. It has not been possible to trace this motto.

LETTER 30

1. Lady Briers of Upbury, Pulloxhill, Beds. (see letter 2, note 5). Henry Osborne's Diary notes (1653): 'July 16, Saturday. – Wee dined at my L. grey de Ruthin at my Lady Briars.' This is one of several letters where dating is uncertain: Parry dates the letter as 31 July, whereas Moore Smith places it in the first week in October, because it appears to him to relate clearly to those which follow, and because Saturday is the day upon which letters would normally be expected. Moore Smith's case might be contested, for (at least) the following reasons: (a) it is unlikely that D.O. would have gone to what was apparently a very convivial dinner so soon after the death of her brother, who had died at the end of August; (b) the letter does not say that D.O. had received the letter from W. T. on the Saturday – it records that she had received the invitation on that day (Thursday), for the Saturday; (c) the letter continues the references to Walker and the business of the seals, as well as the arguments with her brother about marriage, especially with regard to Tom Cheke and Mrs Franklin, which were raised in letter 29, and are to be continued. I would therefore wish to suggest a date after mid July but before the end of August.

2. Disappointed.

3. Cousin Franklin is Elizabeth, wife of Richard Franklin of Moor Park, Herts. She was the sister of Tom Cheke and the youngest

daughter of Sir Thomas Cheke, by his second wife, Essex (see letter 27, notes 1 and 4).

4. Sir Thomas Cheke's daughters were Essex, who married Edward Montagu, 2nd Earl of Manchester (see letter 27, note 3); Frances, who married Sir Lancelot Lake; Anne, who married Lord Rich, afterwards 3rd Earl of Warwick; and Isabella, who married a Mr Gerrard.

5. It is evident that he must have met Elizabeth Franklin in London. It is understandable that D.O. should interrogate him in this letter if we recall that it was Tom Cheke who had apparently spread the rumour of their engagement (see letter 27). What is also important to note is that the friendship between the two parties developed to such an extent that the newly married William and Dorothy Temple spent their honeymoon at Moor Park.

6. Walker, who set the seals (see letter 7, note 1).

7. Fleur de lys: the heraldic lily, well known because it was a prominent constituent of the royal arms of France before the revolution of 1789.

8. For once, neither of her brothers will be at Chicksands.

LETTER 31

1. Nan Stacy (see letter 15, note 1). The information she offers could have been sent by letter, or she could have visited Chicksands or Campton.

2. See letter 29, note 7.

3. Lady Diana Rich (see letter 4, note 5).

4. The carrier involved in gathering in the harvest would be Harrold.

5. The Rev. Edward Gibson (1618?–90) was vicar of Hawnes, or Haynes. Moore Smith suggests that he was at this time unmarried and living at Chicksands, which seems to be a reasonable suggestion if we are to account for the numerous references to him in

Henry Osborne's Diary. He seems to have married some time
after the date of these letters, because Moore Smith notes that
the Hawnes parish register records the baptism of a daughter
on 10 November 1658, and a son on 14 August 1661, to
'Edward Gibson and Margaret his wife'. Gibson was born in
Rutland and, after attending Uppingham School, was admitted
sizar (a student paying reduced fees in return of performing certain menial tasks) to Sidney Sussex College, Cambridge. He
graduated B.A. (1637), M.A. (1640), and was elected to a fellowship, but was ejected in 1644 by the Earl of Manchester (see
letter 27, note 3), himself a former student of the college and
later Chancellor of the University. We can judge D.O.'s high
regard for Mr Gibson from letter 60, where she writes: 'I can
gett Mr Gibson if you will to bring you a letter, tis a Civill
well natur'd man as can bee, of Excellent Principles, and an
Exact honesty. I durst make him my Conffessor though hee is
not Obliged by his orders to conceal any thing that is told
him.' We also know from Henry Osborne's Diary that Mr
Gibson was used as an intermediary in the negotiations with Dr
Scarborough (see letter 3, note 11).

6. The story of the 'litle Marquise' was reconstructed by Courtenay, Parry, and Moore Smith. She was Elizabeth de Mayenne
(1633–53), who married (1652) Pierre de Caumont, the 'Buffle
headed' Marquis de Cugnac, a Huguenot refugee from a very
distinguished French family. The 'litle Marquise', who died in
childbed, and to whom there is a monument in the south wall
of the chancel of Chelsea Church, was the daughter of the distinguished physician Sir Theodore de Mayenne (1573–1655),
who was born near Geneva, studied at Montpellier, practised
in Paris, and settled in London (1611), becoming physician to
Charles I and Henrietta Maria (1625). After the execution of
Charles I, Sir Theodore retired to Chelsea, but this letter would
seem to indicate that he must have gone to live there earlier
than the date usually assigned. The letter also indicates that
D.O. knew the doctor and his family before she first went to
France, which offers some corroboration for the view that she
and her mother might have stayed with Sir John Danvers and
his family (letter 3, note 3), not only in the period prior

to joining Sir Peter in St Malo, but also after their return.

7. This letter also confirms that the 'litle Marquise' had previously been betrothed to Henry, Lord Hastings, the eldest son of Ferdinando, 6th Earl of Huntingdon. Henry died on 24 July 1649, aged nineteen, of smallpox, on the eve of his marriage – which death became the occasion for the publication of some 100 elegies under the title *Lachrymae Musarum*, collected by R.(ichard) B.(rome) (1650). Among the contributors to this collection of elegies were John Dryden (1631–1700) and Robert Herrick (1591–1674), whose contribution, 'The New Charon', was set to music by Henry Lawes (1596–1662). (See R. J. Kaufman, *Brome, Caroline Playwright*, 1964.)

LETTER 32

1. See the opening paragraph of letter 31, where D.O. asks W.T. to designate a new address.

2. She uses the word in the *OED* sense of 'freedom or licence, of speech and manners'.

3. D.O. wrote: 'Doe you doubt it would I say, – hee were not happy int else', which makes perfect sense. Moore Smith emends it to: 'Do you doubt I would? I say, hee were not happy int else', which seems to me perverse; not only does the editor's emendation fail to help the sense, but it also results in a tortured style.

4. The meaning is not clear. Moore Smith interprets it as D.O. informing W.T. that her elder brother could not be so unkind as to make her intended marriage the cause for an estrangement between brother and sister, particularly since (as the next sentence shows) she had not quarrelled with him for not taking her into his confidence about his own marriage.

5. See letter 3, note 10.

6. The injunction not to complain almost certainly came from W.T., who invariably counselled a stoic response in the face of adversity.

7. 'To meet beforehand, or anticipate' (*OED*).

8. Althorp, near Brington, Northants, the home of the Spencer family since 1508. Queen Anne, wife of James VI of Scotland, stayed there on her way to join her husband in London when he became James I of England (1603), for which event Ben Jonson wrote the masque 'Entertainment of the Queen and Prince at Althorp'. The mansion is of medieval origin, but was altered in 1573, 1660, 1733 and 1787. Robert Spencer (1640–1702), 2nd Earl of Sunderland, installed paintings by Dutch and Italian masters in the Picture Gallery, which is over a hundred feet long. Note also that it was to Althorp that Lady Sunderland took her new husband, Mr Smith (see letter 6). Evelyn describes a visit there in 1675.

9. D.O. means that marriage to Sir Justinian would have entailed going to live at his estate at Lamport, Northamptonshire, which was some six miles from Althorp, thus making her a near neighbour of the Spencer family.

10. There is no evidence (at least, not in these letters) that Sir Justinian ever courted Lady Diana Rich. What is interesting is that the estimation she makes here of Sir Justinian is consistent with previous ones.

LETTER 33

1. There is a considerable difference between the two editors about the date of this letter. Parry shows no interruption in the sequence, while Moore Smith suggests that a letter must have been lost here, because 'nothing in letter 32 could bear this interpretation'.

2. See letter 19, note 6.

3. Word omitted.

4. See letter 3, note 10.

5. Henry Osborne's Diary records (1653): 'July 11, Munday. – Wee went to see Mr Hilsden and his wife who were newly come into

the country.' Moore Smith, using *The Visitation of Bedfordshire* (1634), says that this must have been the Hillesden family, formerly of Elstow, later of Ampthill – both places within a few miles of Chicksands. Elstow is, of course, famous for its association with John Bunyan, who was born near there, at Harrowden, in 1628, and who had returned there, in the year that D.O. is writing these letters, from service in the parliamentary armies (1644–7) to be a lay preacher to the Bedford Baptist congregation. It is interesting to note that while D.O. would go to hear Erbury (see letter 22, note 2), she does not mention Bunyan.

6. See letter 29, note 6.

7. Her observations highlight not simply the changes in language usage which are taking place, but also the sharpness of the mind registering these changes. *OED* defines the word 'wellness' as 'the state of being well or in good health', with 1654 as the date of first usage and with this letter as the second example, based on Parry (1903); but *OED* is incorrect in giving the date as *c.* 1655.

8. This is a Christian version of a familiar fable. According to that fable, the Emperor Decius (*c.* 250 A.D.) commanded the inhabitants of Ephesus to worship a statue which he had erected in their city. When seven youths fled the city and hid themselves in the caves of Mount Celion rather than worship the statue, the Emperor had the cave entrances sealed. While there is some difference about the length of the time the youths were incarcerated, most versions agree that they re-awakened in the mid fifth century, whereupon they were taken to Theodosius II, Roman Emperor of the East; that event restored that king's faith in Christianity, and the youths returned to their cave to sleep until the Day of Judgment. The story is generally said to have been popularized by the historian-saint Gregory of Tours (538–94); and 27 July is designated as the feast day of the Seven Sleepers. The most famous reference in English is probably in John Donne's 'The Good Morrow' (*Songs and Sonnets*, 1635–69).

> I Wonder by my troth, what thou, and I
> Did, till we lov'd? were we not wean'd till then?
> But suck'd on countrey pleasures, childishly?

Or snorted we in the seaven sleepers den?
T'was so; but this, all pleasures fancies bee.
If ever any beauty I did see,
Which I desir'd, and got, t'was but a dreame of thee.

LETTER 34

1. Jane Wright (see letter 9, note 12).

2. Nan Stacy (see letter 15, note 1).

3. See letter 24, note 5.

4. The word 'them' was written, then deleted, but clearly deleted in error.

5. Sir Thomas Osborne, Earl of Danby (see letter 2, note 3).

6. Here there is a hole in the paper.

7. Jane Wright.

8. We know from letter 31 that Harrold would not be used again until after the ending of the harvest period. Judging by these instructions (on the reverse), we can see that the harvest period is over.

LETTER 35

1. Sir John Temple (1632–1704), younger brother of W.T., who was Solicitor-General in Ireland (1660), Member of Parliament for Carlow, and Speaker of the Irish parliament (1661). He was forced to flee to England during the campaign by Tyrconnell (see Introducton, note 8) when his name was included in a list of persons proscribed by the Irish parliament and his estates to the value of £1,700 per annum were sequestrated. After the Restoration, Temple was appointed Attorney-General (1690); he continued in that office until his retirement to his estate at East Sheen in 1695. He married Jane, daughter of Sir Abraham Yarner of Dublin, in 1663; there were several children, of whom the

eldest son, Henry (1676–1757), became the 1st Viscount Palmerston and is therefore the Temple link to the 3rd Viscount, Henry John Temple Palmerston (1784–1865), Prime Minister (1855–8; 1859–65).

2. Lady Anne Wentworth (see letter 14, note 6).

3. A small newspaper, in common use from about the 1640s to the turn of the century; it replaced the pamphlets or broadsheets of the first two decades of the century, and the double-columned half-sheet, or small folio coranto, of the third decade; it was usually of quarto size, and consisted of between eight and twenty-four pages, according to the supply of news, which was given as factually as possible.

4. Lord Lisle (see letter 6, note 3).

5. This is a reference to a statute passed on 24 August by the Barebones Parliament (named after Praisegod Barebones, one of its members; it was an assembly of some 140 'godly men', chosen by Cromwell, which sat between 4 July and 12 December 1653, but which foundered because of the gulf between the competing religious ideologies of its members, which proved unbridgeable). This statute laid down that in future only marriages conducted by a justice of the peace would be lawful. Since most justices, especially in the country, were rich landowners, this statute was both a secularization and a gentrification of the marriage service: it required that the names of those who intended to marry should be displayed, together with certain other details, upon the door of the 'common meeting-house' (which was, in effect, often the parish church, re named) and that the marriage could not take place until three weeks after these details had been verified through an examination of the couple and other witnesses. The Barebones Parliament also laid down a new form of words for the marriage vows:

I, A B, do hereby in the presence of God take thee, C D, to be my wedded wife, and do also in the presence of God, and before these witnesses, promise to be unto thee a loving and lawful husband.

In the woman's response, 'lawful' was replaced by 'faithfull and obedient'. The vows, as given in the Book of Common Prayer, at that time read:

I, N, take thee, N, to be my wedded wife, to have and to hold, from this day forward, for better or worse, for richer for poorer, in sickness and in health, to love and to cherish, till death us do part, according to God's holy ordinance, and thereto I plight thee my troth.

In the woman's response, 'and to obey' was added after 'cherish' and 'plight' was replaced by 'give'.

6. Mrs Cl: (see letter 9, note 4; letter 10, note 5).

LETTER 36

1. It must be assumed that this letter, sent with Harrold, was lost.

2. This change was almost certainly forced upon them by her fear that Jones the saddler knew her name, and might report the letter to her brother (see letter 39, note 8).

3. These remarks prefigure the dark mood which will permeate the letters soon to be written.

4. Robin Osborne (see letter 29, note 8; letter 38, note 5).

5. See letter 26, note 5.

6. Dorothy Peyton (see letter 24, note 5).

LETTER 37

1. Sir William Uvedale (1586–1652), who lived at Wickham, Hants., was knighted in 1610 and was a Member of Parliament (1612–13). His first wife was Anne, daughter of Sir Edmund Carey; his second wife, whom he married in 1642, was Victoria, daughter of Henry Carey, 1st Viscount Falkland, and sister of Lucius Carey, Lord Falkland, who was killed at Newbury. Sir William had a son by his first marriage, and this son is described as 'deceased' in his father's will of 1651; yet, as this letter shows, not only was he alive, but father and son were rivals for the

same woman. It also shows that the son had died at the age of twenty-eight shortly before the father (aged fifty-six) had married his second wife (aged twenty-two). It is probably this first son, William, who was buried in Westminster Abbey (30 November 1614). By the second marriage there was a further son, also named William, and two daughters. After Sir William's death in 1652 the widow married (14 April 1653) Bartholomew Price, Esq., of 'Lithlington and of Wickham, Hants.', and Moore Smith points out that this bears out the observation that her husband lived in the house with her.

2. Moore Smith discovered that John Frescheville (or Frecheville), born in 1607, had a warrant dated 25 March 1645 for his elevation to the peerage, with the title of Lord Frecheville of Staveley Musard and Fiztralph, but that, because the warrant did not pass the Great Seal, Frecheville had to wait until the Restoration for a new warrant to be issued (16 March 1665). This warrant provided that, in the absence of male heirs, inheritance should devolve upon John Frecheville's eldest surviving daughter, Elizabeth, and her male heirs; or, failing that, upon the youngest daughter, Frances, and her male heirs. John Frecheville and his first wife (who died in 1629) had no children. His second wife was Sarah, daughter of, and heiress to, Sir John Hampton. She died in 1665, having given birth to three daughters: Christian, born 13 December 1633, who married Charles Paulett, Lord St John, on 28 February 1652 and who died in childbirth on 22 July 1653; Elizabeth; and Frances. Lord St John married, secondly (12 February 1655), Mary Carey, Lady Leppington (see letter 23, note 2).

3. Moore Smith suggests that the two Misses Bishop were the daughters of Edward Bishop of Parham, Sussex. He was the second baronet, and he married Mary, fourth daughter of Nicholas, Earl of Thanet, in 1626.

4. The only information about Mr Hemingham concerns his matrimonial affairs: in letter 45, D.O. mentions him as being interested in Lady Grey de Ruthin, and as a possible husband for D.O. herself; in letter 64 we are told that a Miss Gerard had rejected his proposal.

5. The comparison with Sir Justinian Isham gives an excellent insight into the consistency of D.O.'s arguments (see also letter 32, note 10).

6. Lady Diana Rich (see letter 4, note 5).

7. See Appendix E.

8. Sir Robert Coke (1586–1653) was the eldest son of the eminent jurist, Sir Edward Coke (1552–1634). Sir Robert married Theophila, eldest sister of the 8th Lord Berkeley; she was celebrated in poetry and prose not only for her physical grace and beauty, but also for her intellect. She died in April 1643, and her husband in July of that year, a month or so before the date of this letter.

9. Her brothers.

10. See letter 1, note 2.

LETTER 38

1. See letter 35.

2. Sir John Temple is still in Ireland; Martha Temple is still in London, living near enough to W.T. to enable him to visit her.

3. Sir Thomas Peyton (see letter 24, note 5). Henry Osborne's Diary records (1653):

   > Oct. 25, Thursday [Tuesday?]. – Sir Th. Peyton and my Lady Cooke [née Danvers, John Osborne's sister-in-law, previously the wife of the poet George Herbert] came to Chicksands.
   > Oct. 28, Friday. – They went to St Albons toward London and carried mee and my sister with them . . .

4. For the Law Terms, see letter 2, note 7.

5. D.O. is in mourning for the death of her brother (see letter 29, note 8).

6. See letter 25 for Sir Peter Temple's departure for Ireland.

7. George Monck (Monk), 1st Duke of Albemarle (1608–70). He took part (1625) in the disastrous expedition to Cadiz, and

thereafter fought against the Spanish in the Netherlands. After service in the Bishops' Wars (two brief campaigns, in 1639 and 1640, by the Scots against Charles I to overturn that monarch's attempts to strengthen episcopacy by imposing the Book of Common Prayer), Monck was given a command in Ireland and was there when the Civil War broke out (1642). He returned to England to fight on the royalist side, was captured at Nantwich (1644) and kept in prison until 1646. He then managed to gain the confidence of the parliamentary government to such an extent that he was appointed to assist with the subjugation of the Irish, and, later, the Scots – he accompanied Cromwell to Scotland in 1651 and was left in command when Cromwell returned to England: a fine example of the subsuming of political difference at home in order to pursue national interest abroad. In 1652, Monck became a general of the fleet in the first of the Dutch wars, but he returned to Scotland in 1654 to resume command there, and held that position until 1660. When Richard Cromwell's Protectorate collapsed in 1659, Monck supported the Rump against the army under General George Lambert, but thereafter he sought to reconcile the (largely republican) army to the growing civil demands for the Restoration; when the strongly royalist Convention parliament was elected in 1660, Monck openly espoused the cause of Charles II. Indeed, it appears that it was on Monck's advice that the new king issued the Declaration of Breda (4 April 1660), which made the concessions that laid the foundations for the Restoration. These included a free and general pardon (with some exceptions) for regicides; confirmation of all sales of royalist lands made during the Civil War; swift payment of arrears owed to the army; and some measure of religious liberty. All clauses were to be subject to ratification by parliament.

Monck was the recipient of many honours. He was created 1st Duke of Albemarle; he shared command of the fleet in the second Dutch War with the Prince Regent (1666), and was in charge of London at the time of the Great Plague (1665) as well as the Great Fire (1666).

This letter refers to Monck's secret marriage to Anne Clarges, which some historians date as having taken place as early as

1649, but which became public knowledge only in 1653. Moore Smith quotes the tendentious Clarendon as describing her as a woman 'of the lowest extraction, without either wit or beauty', and Pepys observed that 'she became the laughing-stock of the Court, and gave general disgust'. Monck was probably living at Greenwich Palace at this time, and D.O.'s observation must mean that Anne Clarges, Duchess of Albemarle, would be as much at home in that residence as Cromwell's wife was in Whitehall.

8. Nicholas Monck, Vicar of Kilkhampton, Cornwall. Moore Smith notes that he was rector of Langtree, near Torrington, Devon (1640–52), which is close to where the Monck brothers were born, and where in 1646 Fairfax defeated Hopton and his Cornish army, thereby establishing the power of the parliamentary government in the West Country. After the Restoration, Nicholas Monck became Provost of Eton and Bishop of Hereford.

9. Charles Osborne, fifth son of Sir Peter Osborne, was born in 1620; he was killed at Hartland, Devon, probably in February 1646. Henry Osborne's Diary records the event (1646):

My brother Charles was killed at Hartland in Devonshire and buried at Hartland, But Mr Carey of Clovelly neere Hartland said he would remove his body to Clovelly where he was then quartered at Mr Carey's house, to whom he had been much obliged.

10. Instead of with Mrs Painter, in Covent Garden.

11. See letter 20, note 10.

12. Obscured by the binding.

LETTER 39

1. See opening sentences of letter 38.

2. Characters in *Le Grand Cyrus* (see letter 20, note 10).

3. Stephen Marshall (1594?–1655), Presbyterian divine, was born at Godmanchester, the son of a glover. After studies at Emmanuel College, Cambridge (M.A., 1622), Marshall married a rich

widow (1629), by whom he had one son (who was drowned at Hamburg), and six daughters. Marshall was vicar at Finchingfield in Essex at £200 per annum, but in 1636 was reported for 'want of conformity'. In 1642 he was appointed to St Margaret's, Westminster, as one of the seven preachers who preached daily, in rotation, and in that year he also became chaplain to the regiment of the 2nd Earl of Essex. Because of his consistent advocacy of liturgical reform and support for the abolition of episcopacy, Marshall was selected in 1643 as one of the delegates to discuss reform with Scots divines. In 1645 he waited on Archbishop Laud before his execution; in 1647 he was chaplain to Charles I on the Isle of Wight, and in 1651, having completed a 'Shorter Catechism', he was town preacher at Ipswich. A controversial preacher, Marshall gave addresses to the parliamentary armies, and was the orator at the funeral of Pym (see letter 18, note 6). He was buried in Westminster Abbey, but after the Restoration his body was exhumed and cast into the pit 'at the back door of the prebendary's lodgings' at St Margaret's, Westminster. He is today perhaps best remembered as one of the contributors to the Smectymnuus debate: Bishop Hall had written *An Humble Remonstrance to the High Court of Parliament* in defence of episcopacy; five Presbyterian divines thereupon composed a reply, under a pseudonym made up of their initials (Stephen Marshall, Edmund Calamy, Thomas Young, Matthew Newcomen, William Spurstow); Hall responded with his *Defence of the Humble Remonstrance*, which provoked Milton's famous *Animadversions upon the Remonstrant's Defence Against Smectymnuus*. This in turn led to *A Modest Confutation*, probably written by Hall's son, to which Milton responded with his *An Apology Against a Pamphlet called A Modest Confutation of the Animadversions of the Remonstrant against Smectymnuus*.

4. Disappointed.

5. Moore Smith suggests that D.O. perhaps remembers 'The Church Porch', by George Herbert (1593–1633), who was the first husband of Lady Cooke, née Danvers, and sister-in-law to John Osborne (see letter 38, note 3). The relevant stanzas (77, 73) are:

> Judge not the preacher; for he is thy judge:
> If thou mislike him, thou conceiv'st him not.
> God calleth preaching folly. Do not grudge
> To pick out treasures from an earthen pot.
>   The worst speak something good: if all want sense,
>   God takes a text, and preacheth patience.
>
> He that gets patience, and the blessing which
> Preachers conclude with, hath not lost his pains.
> He that by being at church escapes the ditch,
> Which he might fall in by companions, gains.
>   He that loves Gods abode, and to combine
>   With saints on earth, shall one day with them shine.

6. The Barebones (Nominated) Parliament (see letter 35, note 5) was at that time considering whether or not to oppose the levying of tithes; there was great opposition to the payment of clergy from the purportedly voluntary offerings by congregations.

7. See letter 40, where D.O. writes, 'there is noe such thing as perfect happynesse in this world'.

8. Letters are now left with Jones instead of with Mrs Painter (see letter 36, note 2).

9. The quince marmalade referred to in letter 43.

10. Bulstrode Whitelocke (1605–75), graduate of St John's College, Oxford, was called to the Bar (Middle Temple) in 1626. He was Member of Parliament for Stafford (1626) and for Marlow (1640). A distinguished parliamentarian and diplomat, his career was long and varied. He was chairman of the committee which managed the impeachment of Strafford one of the Commissioners of the Great Seal, with Lord Lisle (see letter 6, note 3) and Richard Keble, in 1648, 1649, and 1654–5 (when he was deposed by Cromwell), only to be reinstated in 1659; one of the committee appointed to draw up the indictment and proposals for managing the trial of Charles I, though later he refused to serve; Ambassador to Sweden (1653–4); Member of Parliament for Oxford, and one of the Commissioners of the Treasury (1654); a member of the delegation appointed to urge Cromwell to accept the Crown (1655); a member, and, later, president of the new Council of State after the fall of the administration of

Richard Cromwell and a member of the Committee of Safety which succeeded that Council; and a member of the committee appointed to draft a new constitution. Whitelocke received a royal pardon after the Restoration, and lived in retirement, producing two texts which are of considerable documentary value as source material for the period: *Memorials of English Affairs*, published in 1682, and *Journal* of the Swedish Embassy, published in 1772. (See Ruth Spalding, *The Improbable Puritan: a Life of Bulstrode Whitelocke 1605-75,* London, Faber and Faber, 1975.)

11. The Barebones Parliament abolished the Court of Chancery in August 1653.

12. Joseph Keble (1632–1710) was the son of Richard Keble, Fellow of All Souls and (with Lord Lisle and Bulstrode Whitelocke) one of the Commissioners of the Great Seal. Joseph Keble qualified as a barrister and was admitted to Gray's Inn, but never practised; he became, instead, a law reporter and the author of 'Reports in the Court of the Queen's Bench' (1685), but his reports were so confused that judges ruled that his writing should not be used in their courts.

13. The reference to 'my Lord my father' is unclear; there is no evident link – or reason for a link – between Sir Peter Osborne and Joseph Keble. D.O. may have intended to write 'my Lord his father' in order to indicate that the son owed his preferment as a reporter to the position of his father.

LETTER 40

1. See letter 9, opening paragraph.

2. *Le Grand Cyrus*, Book III, Part I (see letter 20, note 10).

3. The title page gives the name of Georges de Scudéry and not that of his sister Madeleine, who was the actual author. D.O.'s error is therefore unintentional, but understandable, and the subterfuge points once again to the obliteration of the female contribution to authorship.

4. Lady Ormonde was Elizabeth, daughter of the Earl of Desmond. In 1629 she married James Butler (1618–88), 12th Earl and 1st Duke of Ormonde, who became one of the most influential

royalists in Ireland during the Civil War (he was Lord-Lieutenant on three separate occasions). The letter draws attention to a time when the family were in severe financial difficulties – *DNB* informs us that, in August 1652, Lady Ormonde had to travel from Caen to England to plead with Cromwell to honour his pledge to reserve for her that portion of the estates which had been hers by inheritance, and that it was only after great delay that she obtained £500 and a grant of £2,000 per annum out of her Irish lands in Galway.

5. Sir Francis Annesley, Lord Valentia (d. 1660), was born in Newport Pagnell, Bucks. He was married twice: (i) to Dorothy, daughter of Sir John Phillips, Bt; (ii) to Jane, daughter of Sir John Stanhope. At the time of this letter, Lord Valentia was Secretary of State in Dublin.

6. Moore Smith glosses this as 'I should have chosen single life with some amenities', and reminds us of the old saying that an old maid would lead apes in hell, which is a reference to the prediction about the ultimate fate of spinsters, although the meaning is in some dispute: one view is that such a task is fitting punishment for women who avoid fulfilling their role as bearers of children; another is that it is a fitting punishment for those women who entice men for whom they do not really care.

7. Shakespeare: 'The ancient saying is no heresy: / Hanging and wiving goes by destiny' (*The Merchant of Venice*, II.ix.82–3).

8. Sir Justinian Isham is, at last, successful; in 1653 he married Vere, daughter of Lord Leigh of Stoneleigh, Warwickshire, and of Ursula Hoddesdon, who came from Leighton Buzzard, Bedfordshire – which might explain why D.O. writes of the new Lady Isham as 'my Country Woman'.

9. The sign of disappointed love (see letter 20, note 7).

10. Moore Smith suggests that these might have been visits of condolence on the death of her brother Robin.

LETTER 41

1. See letter 24, note 5.

2. Word omitted.

3. Word obscured by one of the very few blots in the text.

4. Word omitted.

5. Henry Molle (see letter 10, note 7).

6. Sir Justinian Isham (see letter 3, note 6).

7. 'A stand containing ink, pens and other writing materials and accessories; an inkstand; also an inkpot' (*OED*).

8. 'as' in text.

9. *Polexandre* (1653), a huge folio (of over 350 pages) romance, by Martin le Roy de Gomberville, set in Mexico, translated into English by W. Browne as *The History of Polexander* (1647). *Ibrahim, ou i'illustre Bassa* (1641) by Georges de Scudéry (see letter 20, note 10), was translated into English by H. Cogan as *Ibrahim, or the Illustrious Bassa* (1652).

10. *La Prazimène* and *Suite de la Prazimène* (1643), by Le Maire, was translated by Roger Boyle (see note 13, below).

11. Obscured by the binding.

12. Henry Carey, Lord Leppington, 2nd Earl of Monmouth (1596–1661), educated at Exeter College, Oxford, was the father-in-law of Lady Leppington (see letter 23, note 2). By his wife Martha, eldest daughter of Sir Lionel Cranfield (later Earl of Middlesex), he had two sons and eight daughters; the eldest son was killed at Marston Moor, and the younger died of smallpox, leaving one son and heir, who died in 1653. Henry Carey was a well-known translator; his works included *An Historicall Relation of the United Provinces; A History of the Wars in Flanders;* and *A History of Venice.*

13. Roger Boyle (1621–79), 1st Earl of Orrery, Irish politician and writer, created Baron Broghill in 1627, was the son of Richard Boyle (1566–1643), 1st Earl of Cork, and brother of the scientist Robert Boyle (1627–91). He was educated at Trinity College, Dublin, and thereafter fought in the 1641 campaigns against the Irish. Although Boyle was a royalist, he served with the parliamentary armies after 1647 because of his support for Cromwell's Irish policy – indeed when Boyle was involved in a

plot to restore Charles II, Cromwell intervened personally to persuade him to serve the Commonwealth, for which he was given large tracts of land in Ireland and made Lord President of the Council in Scotland. However, when the Restoration of Charles II became inevitable, Boyle went to Ireland to secure allegiance for the new monarch. He was made Earl of Orrery (1660) and a Lord Justice; served in the parliament of 1661, and as Lord President of Munster until 1668. Boyle was a friend and patron of writers, but he also wrote several rhymed verse tragedies, including *Henry the Fifth* (1668); *Mustapha* (1668); *The Black Prince* (1669); a military treatise; and the romance, *Parthenissa* (1654–76; see letter 59, note 7). (See also K.M. Lynch, *Roger Boyle, First Earl of Orrery,* Tennessee U.P., 1975.)

Boyle's grandson, Charles (1676–1731), 4th Earl of Orrery (he succeeded to his brother's title in 1703), was one of the supporters of W.T. in the controversy with Richard Bentley (1662–1742), the critic and philologist, who had exposed *The Epistles of Phalaris* as a fraud. But, since Charles Boyle was the editor of these epistles, his support for W.T. in what later became known as the controversy over ancient and modern learning must be considered as not totally objective. Boyle had one other claim to fame: he was a patron of the inventor George Graham, who designed a forerunner of the planetarium, to which he gave the name 'orrery'.

14. William Fiennes (1582–1662), 1st Viscount Saye and Sele, was a Puritan member of the House of Lords. Although he was, for a short time, a supporter of the Earl of Buckingham, Fiennes was also (because of his religious convictions as well as his commercial interests as one of the main participants in the attempt to establish the New England colonies in the 1630s) a determined opponent of Charles I. He nevertheless sought to act as intermediary between the king and parliament, on behalf of that faction which sought not to remove the king, but to vest his powers in parliament. When that attempt failed, Fiennes apparently retired to the island of Lundy during the period of the Protectorate, but returned from his voluntary exile after the Restoration, to become Lord Chancellor of the Household and Lord Privy Seal.

15. Edmund Waller (1606–87), poet; a student at King's College, Cambridge (he may have left before taking his degree), Waller

was admitted to Lincoln's Inn in 1622. He married (i) Anne Banks (1631; she died in 1634); Mary Bracey (1644; she died in 1677). Waller was a wealthy landowner – he inherited extensive estates in Beaconsfield, Bucks. – who was elected to parliament for Amersham at the age of sixteen (1622); for Ilchester (1624); for Chipping Wycombe (1626); for Amersham again (1628–9); and for St Ives in the Long Parliament, where he defended episcopacy, conducted the impeachment of Sir Francis Crawley (1641), and opposed the raising of troops by parliament. Appointed to the commission negotiating with Charles I at Oxford, Waller conceived what became known as the 'Waller Plot' to seek to secure the City of London on behalf of the king (1643). For this he was expelled from parliament and imprisoned in the Tower (1643–4), then banished (though two of his accomplices were hanged). After seven years he returned, on the revocation of his banishment order, and became a supporter of Cromwell, about whom he wrote the impressive valediction, 'Upon the Late Storm and Death of His Highness'. In 1661, he was elected Member of Parliament for Hastings, and remained that town's representative until his death. Waller's earlier poems were addressed to 'Sacharissa' (Dorothy Sidney; see letter 44, note 6), who refused to marry him; and it is for those poems, and for lyrics like 'Go, lovely Rose', or 'On a Girdle', that he is now probably best remembered, though his verse was very popular in his own time. The first edition of his *Poems* ran into three editions in their year of publication (1645), and five more before the end of the century; they were followed by his less interesting *Divine Poems* (1685), and *The Second Part of Mr Waller's Poems* (1690, with a further four editions by 1722). Waller had an important influence on Pope and Dryden, and he is generally credited (with Denham) as the first poet to make extensive use of the heroic couplet. (See A. W. Allison, *Towards an Augustan Poetic: Waller's 'Reform' of English Poetry*, 1962; W. L. Cherniak, *The Poetry of Limitation: A Study of Waller*, 1968.)

16. See letter 42, note 1.

17. Obscured by the binding.

18. See letter 25.

19. See letter 33.

LETTER 42

1. This letter is written on the reverse of the letter from Sir Thomas Peyton, to which D.O. refers in letter 41. Although Parry (1888) had this as a separate letter (number 35), he incorporated it with letter 41 in 1914, and this was followed by Moore Smith. This seems to me to be perverse: not only is it palpably a separate letter, but that this was D.O.'s intention is made clear by the writer's comments in letter 41: 'I will send you'; 'as litle Roome as I have left'. In letter 42, she says 'I would tell you how many Letters I have dispatch'd since I Ended yours', and, most tellingly, 'I had forgott, *in my Other*' (my emphasis). She clearly intended this as a separate letter – even if only to chide W.T. later on, as elsewhere, about his failure to reciprocate.

Sir Thomas Peyton's letter reads:

Good Sister – I am very sorried to heare of the losse of our good Brother [Robin Osborne: see letter 29, note 8] whose short time gives us a sad example of our fraile condition. But I will say the lesse, knowing whom I write to; whose religion & wisdome is a present stay & support in all wordly accidents.

Tis long since wee resolved to have given you a visit, & have releived you of my Daughter. But I have had the following of a most laborious affaire, which hath cost mee the travelling, though in our owne Country still [Kent], fifty miles a weeke; & have bin lesse at home then elsewhere ever since I came from London [Henry Osborne's Diary shows Sir Thomas Peyton to be in London from 16 February to 9 April]: which hath cost mee the more in regard I have bin detayned from the desires I had of being with you before this time. Such entertainment however must all those have that have to doe with such a purse-strong and willfull person as Sir Edw. Hales [of Woodchurch, Kent; created baronet 1611, died 1654, and buried at Tunstall, near Sittingbourne]. The next weeke being Michaelmas weeke wee shall end all, & I be at liberty I hope to consider my owne contentments. In the meane time I knowe nott what excuses to make for the trouble I have putt you to already, of which I growe to bee ashamed; should much more bee soe, if I did not knowe you to bee as Good as you are Faire: in both which regards I have a great Honour to be esteemed

My good Sister
Your faithfull Brother & Servant
Thomas Peyton

2. Neither these verses nor those by Lord Byron (see note 3, below) have survived.

3. John, Lord Byron (d. 1652), 1st Baron, Member of Parliament for Nottingham (1624–5). He fought in the Dutch Wars, and against the Scots (1640); was Lord-Lieutenant of the Tower (December 1641–February 1642); joined Charles I at York, then held Oxford for the royalist forces; he won at Powick Bridge (22 September), and fought at Edgehill, Newbury and Ormskirk. He was created Baron Byron of Rochdale in October 1643. After surrendering at Carisbrooke Castle, Byron went to Paris; in 1648 he was sent to seize Anglesey, an attempt which failed, and he was finally forced to live out his life in exile after parliament had him prosecuted for his part in trying to pursue the king's fortunes in Ireland. Byron married (i) Cecilia, daughter of the Earl of Delaware, who was then the widow of Sir Francis Bindloss, Kt; (ii) Eleanor, daughter of Robert Needham, Viscount Kilmorey, who was then the widow of Peter Warburton of Cheshire; she was, according to Pepys, 'the king's seventeenth mistress abroad' (26 April 1676).

4. As a nightcap, or as a sleeping draught; hence 'aproved' in the medical sense of *probatum est* (it is proved), placed upon prescriptions.

LETTER 43

1. See letter 42 for the dispute about riches and passions.

2. Sir Thomas Osborne, Earl of Danby (see letter 2, note 3).

3. Mrs Franklin (see letter 27, notes 1 and 4).

4. Not 'malicious', but in the sense of 'inclined to tease'.

5. See letter 29, note 2.

6. A reiteration of sentiments expressed in letter 27.

7. I suggest that we should deduce from this that W.T. had sent his father's letter to D.O. for her to read.

8. 'e' obscured by binding.

9. Jane Rant, née Dingley, was first cousin to W.T.; her father

was Sir John Dingley of Wolverton, Isle of Wight, and her mother was Jane Hammond of Chertsey. (Dr John Hammond of Chertsey was maternal grandfather to W.T.) Jane Dingley married, at the age of nineteen, the distinguished physician William Rant of Morley, Norfolk, when he was thirty years of age. A monument at Thorpe Market gives the date of Dr Rant's death as 15 September 1653, but that date is disputed. See, e.g., the contributions by Colonel W. F. Prideaux and Walter Rye, of St Leonard's Priory, in (respectively) *Notes and Queries*, 9th Series, Vol. XII, No. 292, 1 August 1903, pp. 81–2; No. 299, 19 September 1903, pp. 230–31.

10. William, 5th Lord Paget (1609–78), married Lady Frances Holland, eldest sister of Lady Diana Rich (see letter 4, note 5). Paget had his estate sequestrated because he raised a regiment in support of Charles I at Edgehill; he later had to compound for it in order to have the order lifted (1644); at the Restoration, he and his wife petitioned unsuccessfully for grants of sinecures to compensate for their losses.

11. Lady Isabella Rich had married Sir James Thynne; in the next letter we find that it is not a very happy marriage.

12. See letter 20, note 3.

13. See also letter 41, where she observes that 'these great Schollers are not the best writer's, (of Letters I mean, of books perhaps they are)'.

14. The present sent by Jane Wright, mentioned in letter 39.

15. Parry cites the *Autobiography of Mary, Countess of Warwick*, ed. T. C. Croker (1848). The Countess was born on 8 November 1625; she was the daughter of the Earl of Cork, and sister of Lord Broghill (see letter 41, note 13), and the episode concerning Mistress Harrison and the Queen is explained as follows. Her brother Francis, after his marriage to a Mrs Elizabeth Killgrew,

was in love with a maid of honour to the Queen, one Mrs Hareson [daughter of Sir Richard Harrison of Hurst, Berkshire] that had been a chamber-fellow to my sister-in-law while she lived at Court, and that brought the acquaintance between him and my sister. He continued to be much with us for about five or six weeks, till my brother

Broghill then grew also to be passionately in love with the same Mrs Hareson. My brother then having a quarrel with Mr Thomas Howard, second son of the Earl of Berkshire, about Mrs Hareson (with whom he was also in love), Mr Rich [second son of Robert, Earl of Warwick] brought my brother a challenge from Mr Howard, and was second to him against my brother when they fought, which they did without any great hurt of any side, being parted. This action made Mr Rich judge it not civil to come to our home, and so for some time forbore doing it; but at last my brother's match with Mrs Hareson being un-handsomely (on her side) broken off, when they were so near being married as the wedding clothes were to be made, and she after married Mr Thomas Howard (to my father's great satisfaction), who always was averse to it, though, to comply with my brother's passion, he consented to it.

Parry fixes the date of the duel as 1640, based upon a reference in a letter to the Earl of Cork. Rich married Mary Boyle in July 1641, and succeeded his brother as Earl of Warwick in 1658; Mr Howard became 3rd Earl of Berkshire in 1679.

16. It has not been possible to trace the origin of this saying.

17. Edward Nevill of Keymer, Sussex.

18. The word 'Eternaly' is placed in such a manner that it can be read as applying to either the words 'last' or 'I am Yours', which flank it.

LETTER 44

1. The letter from Sir Thomas Peyton (see letter 42, note 1).

2. Mrs Rant (see letter 43, note 9).

3. Lucy, Countess of Carlisle (1599–1660), was a daughter of Henry Percy, 9th Earl of Northumberland, and Dorothy, formerly the widow of Sir Thomas Perrot; a sister of Dorothy, Countess of Leicester, she was thus an aunt to both Lady Sunderland (see letter 6, note 6) and Algernon Sidney (letter 7, note 3). She married James Hay, Earl of Carlisle (then Lord Hay of Sawley), in 1617, despite the opposition of her father, who stated that, as a Percy, he 'could not endure that his daughter should dance any Scotch jigs'; he kept her for some time with him in the

Tower, where he was at the time a prisoner, but could not prevent the marriage. Hay is said to have been instrumental in procuring his father-in-law's release in order to gain approval for the marriage, but the release did not take place until 1621. Lady Carlisle was very popular at the court of Charles I – she is reputed to have taught Queen Henrietta Maria how to paint; she was also a great friend of Strafford, but after his execution she allied herself with the leaders of the opposition, especially Pym (see letter 18, note 6). Clarendon claims that this was because of the influence of the Earl of Holland (see letter 4, note 6) and is reputed to have warned of the intended arrest of the Five Members. During the latter years of the war, she was close to those aristocrats and presbyterians who wanted to remove Charles I but retain the monarchy, and for these intrigues she spent some two years in the Tower. She was known for her beauty and wit, and was celebrated by poets (Cartwright, *A Panegyric to the Most Noble Lady, Countess of Carlisle*; Carey addresses her under the name of Lucinda, and Herrick names her in *Hesperides*; *DNB* notes that she is the subject of a 'by no means platonic dialogue between Carew and Suckling'. The death of her husband in 1636 led to Davenant and Waller writing consolatory poems to her).

4. Lady Isabella Rich (see letter 43, note 11). Parry reminds us that she had an affaire with the Duke of Ormonde (see letter 40, note 4), by whom she had a son; here, however, D.O. is writing about an apparently quite different matter.

5. There is disagreement between Parry and Moore Smith about the identity of Lord Pembroke. Parry suggests that he was the Lord Pembroke who, according to Clarendon, 'pretended to no other qualification ". . . than to understanding horses and dogs very well, and to be believed honest and generous", whose stables vied with palaces, and whose falconry was furnished at vast expense, but whose private life was characterized by gross ignorance and vice, and whose public character was marked by ingratitude and instability.' Parry adds that the life of his second wife was embittered by this man for nearly twenty years, and that she was finally compelled to separate from him, living alone until his death in 1650. He was born Philip Herbert (1584), and

was the younger son of the 2nd Earl; a great favourite of James I, he received a grant of Trinidad, Tobago, Barbados and Fonseca (though this last was disputed by James Hay, Earl of Carlisle: see note 3, above), and in 1628 was a member of the Councils of both the East India Company and the Virginia Company. In 1641, he voted against Strafford; in 1642 he was a member of the Committee of Safety, and parliamentary Governor of the Isle of Wight. As vice-chancellor of the University of Oxford (where he was a student at New College for some three months) in the years 1641–50, he supervised the visitation of colleges in order to seek out and eject royalists. Pembroke married (i) Lady Susan Vere, third daughter of Edward, 17th Earl of Oxford, in 1604; she died in 1628, having given birth to seven sons and three daughters; and (ii) Anne, daughter of George Clifford, Earl of Cumberland, and widow of the Earl of Dorset. Parry's reference to 'vice' and to the embitterment of his wife's life relates to the fact that a daughter of the Earl of Berkshire had lived with Pembroke as his mistress for several years, until she, too, eventually ran away from him.

Moore Smith suggests that D.O. was referring to the son, Philip Herbert (1619–69), who had succeeded his father in the earldoms of both Pembroke and Montgomery; like his father, he was on the side of parliament – he was Member of Parliament for Glamorgan in the Long Parliament, and (for a short period in 1652) President of the Council. He made his peace with Charles II after the Restoration, and continued his father's exploitation of the colonies. He married (i) Penelope, daughter of and heiress to Sir Robert Naunton (she was the widow of Paul, Viscount Bayning); and (ii) Catherine, daughter of Sir William Villiers, Bart, of Brooksby, Leicester.

I tend here to side with Parry: in letter 45, D.O. writes of a husband that 'hee must not be soe much a Country Gentleman as to understand Nothing but hawks and dog's and bee fonder of Either then of his wife', from which it appears that she had the father, not the son, in mind.

6. Robert Sidney (1595–1677), 2nd Earl of Leicester. He studied at Christ Church, Oxford, was admitted to Gray's Inn in 1618,

served in the Netherlands from 1614 to 1616, and was Member of Parliament for Wilton (1614); Kent (1621), and Monmouthshire (1624 and 1625). A distinguished diplomat, he went on embassies to Christian V of Denmark, to the Duke of Holstein, and to France (1636–41); he was appointed Lord-Lieutenant of Ireland in succession to Strafford, but he never assumed office because of the outbreak of the Irish rebellion. He was in Oxford with Charles I (1643–4) but was not trusted by the royalists because of his reputed moderation and irresolution, and he finally retired to Penshurst (see note 7, below). In 1616 he married Dorothy, daughter of Henry Percy, 9th Earl of Northumberland; she died in 1659, having given birth to six sons and seven daughters. Of the former, four lived to maturity: Philip, who became 3rd Earl of Leicester; Algernon (see letter 7, note 3); Robert, who was a soldier and who died unmarried – according to scandal, he was the father of the Duke of Monmouth; and Henry, afterwards Earl of Romney. Of the daughters, Dorothy was the inspiration for Edmund Waller's 'Sacharissa' (see letter 41, note 15).

7. Penshurst, the castellated mansion five miles west of Tonbridge, Kent, renowned for the sixty-foot-high roof of chestnut beams in the Great Hall. It was begun in 1339, and the building was added to at later periods in its history. One of its early owners was Humphrey of Gloucester (1391–1447), youngest son of Henry IV and Mary de Bohun, who was a patron of scholars and whose gift of books formed the nucleus of the Bodleian Library. Later, the estate was given by the young Edward VI to Sir William Sidney, grandfather of Robert and Philip Sidney, who were born and spent part of their youth there. Sir Philip Sidney inherited the estate when he was Governor of Flushing in the Netherlands; after his death from wounds received at the Battle of Zutphen (1586), the estate passed to his brother Robert (created Lord Sidney, 1603; Viscount Lisle, 1605; Earl of Leicester, 1618), the father of the Lord Lisle who was appointed Ambassador to Sweden (see letter 6, note 3). Sir Robert and his daughter Mary (who married Sir Robert Wroth at Penshurst in 1604) were friends of Ben Jonson (1572–1637), who celebrated the place in his famous poem, 'To Penshurst'. For a magnificent

new study, see Don E. Wayne, *Penshurst: the Semiotics of Place and the Poetry of History* (London: Methuen, 1984).

8. Digest.

9. Households.

10. Stout sticks or staves laid loosely across the bedstocks of old wooden beds to support the bedding.

11. To drum; from tabour, a small drum used in conjunction with a pipe or trumpet.

12. Martha Temple, Lady Giffard (see letter 9, note 6).

13. A further reference to quince marmalade (see letters 39 and 43).

14. Dorothy Peyton (see letter 24, note 5).

LETTER 45

1. In letter 44, D.O. had commented upon the apparently altered state of mind of W.T.

2. Moore Smith comments: 'Dorothy evidently means some particular lady, but who she is and why she is thus styled, is not clear.' But I suspect that D.O. here (and below, note 16; also in letter 6) means no more than the *OED* definition: 'Applied as a term of affection, to a female friend', and that she might therefore be referring to Nan Stacy. See, for instance, letter 58, where Nan Stacy seems to be the 'vile wench' who sees all their letters.

3. D.O. had written 'has is'.

4. See letter 43.

5. D.O. had written 'his standing', i.e. his class at school or university, or at the Inns of Court, but had deleted this and replaced it with 'his forme'.

6. D.O. probably means here one of the general staff of officers in regular attendance and service, especially in a royal household.

7. To wear what is fashionable, even at the risk of discomfort.

8. There is no record of Henry Molle's comments, but W.T. (in his essay *Upon the Gardens of Epicurus*, 1685) writes that 'the perfectest figure of a garden I ever saw, either at home or abroad, was that of Moor Park in Hertfordshire'.

9. It is to be assumed that Sir John Temple has at last landed in Ireland.

10. Lady Carlisle (see letter 44, note 3).

11. Sir Peter Lely (see letter 23, note 7).

12. Lord Paget (see letter 43, note 10).

13. Mr Hemingham (see letter 37, note 4).

14. See letter 20, note 7.

15. Lady Grey de Ruthin (see letter 14, note 5).

16. She was perhaps living at Meppershall, near Chicksands (see letter 25). Moore Smith reminds us that Queen Mary II, in her letters to her friend Frances Apsley (*Letters of Two Queens*, ed. B. Bathurst, 1925), speaks constantly of Frances as her 'husband' and of herself as 'wife' to Frances.

17. Sir Henry Yelverton (1653–70) was the son of Sir Christopher Yelverton, 1st Baron of Easton Maudit; he succeeded his father in 1654, having married Lady Grey de Ruthin in April 1653, when he was about twenty years old. They had one daughter, who married Lord Hatton. Sir Henry Yelverton was educated at St Paul's School, London, and Wadham College, Oxford, where his tutor was Cromwell's brother-in-law, the mathematician Dr Wilkins (1614–72).

18. Frances, daughter of Edward Nevill of Keymer, Sussex; she was the widow of Charles Longueville, who succeeded to the barony of Grey de Ruthin in 1639; he died in 1643, and his widow in 1668.

19. Mr Hemingham.

20. By marrying a woman without a substantial settlement or inheritance.

21. John's wife was Eleanor, youngest daughter of Charles Danvers of Baynton (see letter 10, note 6).

LETTER 46

1. Henry Osborne's Diary records (1653):

   Oct. 25 [27?], Thursday. – Sir Th. Peyton and my Lady came to Chicksands. / Oct. 28, Friday. – They went to St Albons towards London and carried mee and my sister with them, who lay at Mr Cales a plommer at the catt a mountaine in Fleete streete.

2. See letter 31, note 5.

3. It has not been possible to identify the 'two dumbe Gentlemen'.

4. See letter 20, note 10. The story mentioned here is in Book I of Tome 5.

5. Lady Carlisle (see letter 44, note 3).

6. See letter 45.

7. It would appear that W.T. had a portrait in his lodgings of Lady Sunderland, the former Dorothy Sidney, whom he knew from their youth when he was at Penshurst Rectory. (See letter 6, note 6.)

8. In letter 47, we find that the portrait is about to be returned to Chicksands.

9. Sir Justinian Isham (see letter 3, note 6).

10. Obscured by the binding.

11. Obscured by the binding.

12. The manuscript in the British Library contains ten short notes (the last of which is included in error: it is not by D.O.) on pieces of paper of various sizes. Parry, who is largely responsible for the order of the letters in the manuscript, suggests that these were written near the time of the betrothal, but internal evidence would seem to indicate otherwise: two have been assigned to the first London visit (see letter 7, note 6), five are assigned to the visit she is now making, and only two to the betrothal – though even these last two could have been assigned here.

13. John Osborne (see letter 10, note 6).

14. Cousin Franklin (see letter 30, note 3).

15. Roehampton, near Sheen, was the home of Christian, Duchess of Devonshire.

16. Tear in the manuscript.

17. Tear in the manuscript.

18. Tear in the manuscript.

19. 'I slept hardly any more than you did and my dreams were no less troubled, besides a set of fiddlers came to play under my window and they tormented me to such an extent that I doubt if I should be able to stand them ever again. And yet I am not in a very bad temper and as soon as I am dressed I'll go and see what I can do to satisfy you – afterwards, I'll come and give you an account of our business, and whatever may happen you shall never ever doubt that I love you more than anything on earth.'

LETTER 47

1. Henry Osborne's Diary for Friday, 25 November, contains the information that: 'This day my sister went to St Albons where our Coach met her.' It must be assumed that D.O. sent the note to which she refers here (and which is lost) with the coachman who had brought her from London.

2. At Chicksands.

3. Her elder brother, John. It is assumed that John had brought his wife with him: the entry in Henry Osborne's Diary for 25 November also records: 'it was determined that my brother and his wife should come to Chicksands the day before *he and I agreed*' (about D.O. and W.T. – see note 5, below).

4. Moore Smith gives this as 'a quantity of flesh', but she probably means it more precisely in the *OED* sense: 'A thick fold of flesh on the body as evidence of a well-fed condition.' *OED* also

reminds us that 'Collop Monday', when bacon (collops) and eggs are beaten, is the day that precedes Shrove Tuesday.

5. A further indication of the strain imposed upon both of them by the difficulties of their London reunion after the long separation. Recall that in letter 46, she had written that 'I never resolvd to give you an Etternell ffarwell but I resolved at the same time to part with all the comfort of my life'. Henry Osborne's Diary records how the pressure was constantly being applied: 'Nov. 28, Munday. – *Sir T. Peyton and I [tell?] S. Br. Wh.* [not identified] *of my sister. I went to Chicksands to speak with her.* / Nov. 29, – *My sister resolved not to marry Temple.*'

6. See letter 46, note 8.

7. Moore Smith speculates that the reference here is to the cloisters in Westminster Abbey, and wonders if W.T. was then living near Westminster. My feeling is that D.O. is here not referring to a particular place, but that she is admonishing him not to live in the cloistered and withdrawn seclusion to which he was prone when depressed.

LETTER 48

1. See letter 47, note 5. Apart from the difficulties encountered during the visit to London, we need to bear in mind that her younger brother had recently died; her niece had gone back to Kent; Jane was ill; and she was aware that her father was dying. Marriage, in the weeks preceding the Christmas festivities, seemed an impossibility.

2. To release her from their unofficial engagement (see letter 19, note 4; letter 50, note 5).

3. 'I have seen all the works that are done under the sun; and, behold, all is vanity and vexation of spirit. / Then I looked in all the works that my hands had wrought, and on the labour that I had laboured to do: and, behold, all was vanity and vexation of spirit, and there was no profit under the sun. / Therefore I hated life; because the work that is wrought under

the sun is grievous unto me: for all is vanity and vexation of spirit' (Ecclesiastes i.14; ii.11, 17).

4. It has not been possible to trace the origin of this observation.

5. We shall see from letter 50 that her brother Henry and his groom were to go to London on the day after the letter from W.T. should (in theory) have arrived. Henry went to London on Friday, 9 December, which leads to the conclusion that the first part of this letter was written on Thursday the 8th, and the postscript on Saturday the 10th, the day on which the groom returned.

6. Nan Stacy (see letter 15, note 1).

7. Lady Anne Blunt (or Blount) was the daughter of Mountjoy Blount, Earl of Newport (1597?–1666), who was the illegitimate son of Charles Mountjoy, Earl of Devonshire, and Penelope Devereux, Lady Rich, Sir Philip Sidney's 'Stella' (see letter 4, note 6). Lady Anne Blount was therefore the younger sister of Isabella, Lady Banbury (see letter 6, note 8). According to *SPDom.*, Vol. lxix, no. 71 (1654), Lady Anne Blount had, on 18 April in a petition to Oliver Cromwell, denied that she had contracted to marry one William Blunt (no relation) because (according to her petition) she did not have her father's permission to marry. But, since Blunt was insisting that he would marry her whether she wished or no, her petition was that a discreet commission should be set up to investigate, because these false accusations would prejudice her integrity. Cromwell ordered that the commission be set up, that it should summon Blunt to give evidence before it, and that it should come to judgment.

Four months earlier (8 December 1653) the Council had referred a petition of the Earl of Newport to two commissioners, about (apparently) the same matter. This letter would appear to indicate that Lady Anne Blount did eventually marry William Blunt, but there is no evidence that that happened, or that he was ever charged with either seduction or abduction. The saga does not end there: on 27 February 1655, the Protector in Council issued a warrant 'To apprehend Thomas Porter and bring him before Council for taking Lady Anne Blount out of the house of her father, the Earl of Newport'. This Thomas Porter was the son of the distinguished diplomat and patron of poets, Endymion Porter. The accused was about nineteen at the time of his arrest and imprisonment; the 'contract' was declared null and void at the Middlesex Quarter Sessions. There appears, however, to have been a happy ending: Lady Anne Blount and Thomas Porter eventually married; they had one son, George.

8. William Wentworth (born 1626) was the son of Thomas Wentworth, Earl of Strafford. A new peerage was created for the son, who, after the reversal of the attainder against his father, had his rights restored (1662). He was invested Knight of the Garter (1661) and elected Fellow of the Royal Society (1668). He married (i) Anne, daughter of James Stanley, 7th Earl of Derby (she died in 1685); (ii) Henrietta, daughter of Charles de la Roye de Rochefoucauld, Count of Roye and Rouci. There were no children from either marriage.

9. *Le Grand Cyrus* (see letter 20, note 10).

10. For Lady Diana Rich (see also letters 20 and 26).

LETTER 49

1. A reference to Henry Cromwell (see letter 11, note 9). The remark is particularly apposite – and a corroboration of the sequencing of the letters – since Cromwell had been made Lord Protector on 15 December 1653. Henry Osborne's Diary does not record the event, but it does have: 'Dec. 12 – My cause was to be heard but the Parliament was dissolved this morninge, and the Committee that was to heare it.'

2. Despite the dark mood of these three letters, we know from Henry Osborne's Diary that D.O. dutifully took part in the Christmas preparations and festivities. The relevant entries are:

Dec. 24, Saturday. – I came home to Chicksands.
Dec. 27, Tuesday. – Mr Yelverton [see letter 45, note 17] came to Campton.
Dec. 28, Wednesday. – My sister and I dined there.

Dec. 29, Thursday. – Wee all dined at my Lady Oxfords, but my Ly Grey de Ruthin that was sicke.

Dec. 30, Friday. – Mr Yelverton and my Lady Briers, &c. dined at Chicksands.

Dec. 31, Saturday. – Wee all dined at my Lady Briars.

LETTER 50

1. See letter 48, note 5.

2. See letter 48, postscript.

3. See letter 48, note 7.

4. See letter 30, note 3.

5. If W.T. were to release her from her offer to marry him (see letter 48, note 2).

6. One cannot help reading this as her comments on the events of the time. But recall also the general context (given in, for instance, the Norwegian captain's response to Hamlet, about why they will fight for an apparently useless piece of land, of no significance: their war is neither against the main part of Poland, nor against its frontiers, but 'We go to gain a little patch of ground / That hath in it no profit but the name' – IV.iv.18–19).

7. At Chicksands, particularly in view of the need to nurse her father.

8. Stain on the manuscript.

9. Stain on the manuscript.

10. Jones the saddler (see letters 38 and 39). Moore Smith suggests that the saddler's shop might have been next door to the town house of the Earl of Suffolk, near Charing Cross, which later became Northumberland House.

LETTER 51

1. To fear.

2. Moore Smith notes that 'the description is clearly that of a pathological condition of mind', which seems to me to betray a confidence of diagnosis that is perhaps not only excessive, but also misguided.

3. See letters 46, 48, 49, and 50, where D.O. denies charges of falseness and inconstancy.

4. For the first time since letter 14 she signs 'D. Osborne' as well as 'humble Servant' and we must interpret these emendations, after his request to her not to do so (see letter 23), as deliberate on her part, to signal her change and strength of feeling.

5. This may refer to the letter reported lost in letter 48, or to the letter I suspect as lost, from letter 50.

6. Of her engagement to W.T.

LETTER 52

1. D.O. says in letter 53 that she had written to him in 'much hast and distraction'. Moore Smith is probably correct in his surmise that W.T. had been so disturbed by the contents of letter 51 that he had sent an immediate response. This short note from her would then be a quick response, before the more measured one of letter 53. The one surviving letter from W.T. to D.O., given as Appendix B, indicates his state of mind at that time.

2. Tear in the manuscript.

3. See letter 51, note 3.

4. Address on reverse.

LETTER 53

1. See letter 52, opening sentence.

2. Letter 52.

3. Not identified.

4. Address on reverse.

LETTER 54

1. See letter 55, note 5, for Henry Osborne's revelation that when he returned from London he found W.T. at Chicksands.

2. To preserve the peace.

3. Ireland.

4. The day of W.T.'s visit.

5. See letter 21, note 2.

6. Not identified.

7. 'A case of small instruments; an etui' (*OED*).

8. A reference to the popular belief that the gift of a knife or a pair of scissors is unlucky, that it will 'cut love' between giver and recipient.

9. D.O. is now prepared to acknowledge their engagement in public. But see also letter 57 – she will do so discreetly.

10. There is no record of a ring of this description in the family records. One assumption might be that it was buried with her.

11. This may be a reference to the continuing saga of the affaires of Lady Anne Blount. See letter 48, note 7.

12. Lady Grey de Ruthin (see letter 14, note 5). For her marriage to Sir Harry Yelverton, see letter 45, note 17.

13. Herm, one of the Channel Islands. Parry (1913) suggests that D.O. and W.T. might have visited the island (which is only

two miles from Guernsey) during their first meeting, in 1648. Parry also notes that in 1889 Miss Henrietta Tupper, daughter of the historian of Guernsey (Ferdinand Brock Tupper, *The Chronicle of Castle Cornet*. Guernsey: Stephen Barnett; London: Simpkin, Marshall, 1851), wrote to him to say that a document believed by her father to be in the handwriting of Sir Peter Osborne, and written about 1630, refers to the 'isle of Arme'.

14. According to Greek mythology, the Phrygian husband and wife, Philemon and Baucis, were the only humans who were willing to offer hospitality to Zeus and Hermes when these gods visited the earth in human form. As a reward, they were not only saved from the flood which Zeus created to punish humankind, but were also made priest and priestess to the gods. They died together and were turned into trees whose branches intertwined. Parry (1914) notes that D.O. could have read the story in the translation of Ovid's *Metamorphoses* by G. Sandys (1626). He quotes the following extract from Book VIII:

> Jove, in a humane shape: with Mercury;
> (His heeles unwing'd) that way their steps apply.
> Who guest-rites at a thousand houses crave;
> A thousand shut their doores: One onely gave,
> A small thatch't Cottage: where, a pious wife
> Old Baucis, and Philemon, led their life
> Both equall-ag'd. In this, their youth they spent,
> In this, grew old: rich onely in content.
> Who poverty, by bearing it, declin'd,
> And made it easie with a cheerfull mind.
> None Master, nor none Servant, could you call:
> They who command, obay: for two were all.

It is interesting to compare the sentiments expressed in the final couplet with the views she expresses in letter 28 about the 'Law's of freindship'.

Moore Smith notes that after the publication of his edition, a Mr S. J. Cranford of University College, Southampton, wrote to say that he had bought in a local bookshop a copy of Ovid's *Metamorphosis Englished . . . by G. S.*, 1632, with the signature 'D. Osborne' at the top of the title page, and 'From the Author' at the foot of the page in a different hand. Sandys died in 1644, when D.O. was seventeen.

15. In the process of starting a new sheet of paper, D.O. omits 'ten' in 'contented': one sheet ends in 'con' and the next starts with 'ted'.

LETTER 55

1. D.O. here comes to recognize that W.T. will continue to wish to marry her, despite her entreaties to him to stop. This letter thus marks the moment of her acceptance of what will happen, and with that a new tone can be discerned in the writing.

2. Chicksands.

3. We know from letters 47 and 48 that, although the visit to London had been difficult, the parting had been marked by mutual affection and regard, and that it was the journey back and the arrival at Chicksands which had precipitated the mood of despair.

4. Wife of Robert Rich, 2nd Lord Holland, who had succeeded his father (see letter 4, note 6) after the latter's execution in 1649, and who became 5th Earl of Warwick (1673). Parry (1913) identifies the 'Young Lady Holland' as the second wife, Anne Montagu, who was the daughter of the Earl of Manchester (see letter 27, note 3) but, on the basis of dating, Moore Smith's identification of the first wife, Elizabeth, daughter of Arthur Ingram, must be preferred.

5. Henry Osborne's Diary records (1654): 'Jan. 13, Friday morninge. – I came to Chicksands before dinner. *I found Mr Temple here and my sister broke with him, God be praised.*'

6. Cromwell had been created Lord Protector on 15 December 1653.

7. Moore Smith comments: 'One wonders why he [W.T.] had not found employment before now.' This seems to me to be a perverse reading – D.O. does not here mean 'employment' in the sense of a job, but is surely suggesting that W.T. must seek

some diversions against the 'thousand inconveniencys' to be faced in the immediate future.

8. *Le Grand Cyrus* (see letter 20, note 10).

LETTER 56

1. This appears to be the continuation of a letter of which the earlier part is lost. Moore Smith suggests that this sentence might have had as a beginning: 'She did not tell mee any thing . . .', and what appears to be under discussion are poems which have been presented to Lady Grey de Ruthin by a new admirer of D.O. Although this 'servant' is not named, Moore Smith identifies him from the available data; he writes:

> In letter 57 we hear that Temple called him 'a whelp' and had told a story of his prevailing over his tutor by importunity. In letter 59 it is clearly the same man who appears as 'my Servant James'. In Letter 60 he is 'James B.'. In Letter 63 she says 'J.B. cryes out on mee for refusing him and choosing his Chamber ffellow . . . hee knew you before I did'.
>
> Noting that 'James B.' was a Bedfordshire man who had been at college with Temple, I was able to identify him. In the Easter term of 1644 W. Temple and James Beverley were matriculated together as fellow-commoners of Emmanuel. Meanwhile the heraldic visitation shows that Sir James Beverley of Begurney, Beds., and of Cainho Park, Clophill, Beds., had an eldest son who was five years old in 1634. Clophill lies between Chicksands and Wrest, where Dorothy met her admirer, and where perhaps Lady Grey [de Ruthin] was then living . . . It is he, no doubt, who accompanied Henry Osborne from White-chapel to Chelmsford for the assizes on 26th March 1655, and came home with him in a hackney-coach on the 28th . . . H.O. mentions him again: '1656 – Oct. 30. I went to see Mr Beverley.'

James Beverley was knighted on 11 July 1660.

2. Lady Grey de Ruthin, called 'Lady Grey' at other times.

3. To tease.

4. 'Difficult to satisfy; careful as to the standard of excellence' (*OED*).

5. See letter 27. There is no trace of the whereabouts of this miniature.

6. Pester; persecute.

7. Serious.

8. See the opening lines of letter 41.

9. See letter 45, note 17, on Lady Grey de Ruthin's marriage to Mr Yelverton.

10. Silliness; foolishness.

LETTER 57

1. 'Always the same.' See also the ending of letter 9.

2. See letter 56, note 1.

3. Encouragement; credence.

4. Francis Osborn (1593–1658), D.O.'s uncle, mentions the story in his *Advice to a Son*: '. . . the voluptuous death of that Taylor reported to have whined away himself for the love of Queen Elizabeth'. Parry (1888) quotes from Agnes Strickland, *Life of Queen Elizabeth* (1864): 'Mention is made by Stowe [John Stow (1525?–1605) was one of the most reliable chroniclers of his time] of a foolish little tailor of the City of London who about the time (1588) suffered his imagination to be so much inflamed by dwelling on the perfections of his liege lady, that he whined himself to death for love of her.' Parry also attributes a poem by one of the Court wits, Lord Charles Cavendish, as corroboration: 'I would not willingly / Be pointed at in every company / As was the little tailor that to death / Was hot in love with Queen Elizabeth.'

5. Christina (1626–89) succeeded her father Gustavus II as Queen of Sweden (1632) – though she ruled under a regency headed by the famous Chancellor Oxenstierna from 1632 to 1644. She is reputed to have disliked the idea of marriage so vehemently that she designated her cousin Charles (later Charles X) as her successor; she abdicated in 1654. It is said that she left Sweden disguised as a man. She was received into the Catholic Church

in 1655 and retired to Rome, from where she returned in 1660 to seek to reclaim the throne upon the death of Charles X, but failed to do so. After a further attempt in 1667, she was denied entry into Stockholm because of her Catholicism, whereupon she returned to Rome, where she died, and was buried in St Peter's.

The 'King of Scott's' is the future Charles II, who had been crowned at Scone on 1 January 1651 and who was at times called by this title; Parry gives a contemporary reference – Richard Falconer's sworn affidavit against Lord Craven (in the former's trial for perjury) given in Thomas Howell (ed. William Cobbett, *State Trials*, Vol. V, 325 (1809–26). He also quotes from the 'Nicholas Papers', Camden Society, N S No. 40 (1886), an extract from a letter of November 1652 to Edward Hyde: 'It is most certain that the Queen of Sweden is of late much inclined to the rebels of England against the King, which some say is because she, having declared a successor, despairs of having the King as a husband', which may not have been true, since Moore Smith quotes from *Mémoires . . . tirez des Despeches de M. Chanut Ambassadeur pour le Roy en Suède*, ii. 194 (1675):

1651, Avril. La Reine ne manquoit pas de volonté d'assister ce Roy, mais les choses n'y estoient pas encore disposées, il falait que quelque succès extraordinaire en ouvrit le chemin, avant qu'il y eust seureté pour les autres Couronnes de se mesler de ses affaires. Cependant il passoit sous main des armes, & des munitions de Suède en Ecosse, & l'on ne pouvoit juger si c'estoit par l'ordre de la Reine: on disoit qu'il faloit qu'il y eut intelligence entre ce Prince et elle, car avant qu'il passast en Ecosse il fit sonder cette Princesse par le Chevalier Balandin, qui fit deux voyages exprès en Suède, pour voir si elle souffriroit qu'il luy fist parler de mariage, & pour donner entrée à ce discours il luy envoya son portrait, mais elle luy fit si bien connoistre qu'elle estoit fort esloignée d'entendre à de semblables propositions, qu'on ne luy donna pas la peine de s'expliquer plus ouvertement d'un refus.

[April 1651. The Queen was not lacking in the will to assist this King, but circumstances were not yet propitious; some extraordinary success was required to open the way, before it could become safe for other kingdoms to interfere in his business. Yet he had had weapons and munitions transported from Sweden to Scotland and it was impossible to tell whether this was upon the Queen's orders: it was rumoured that there must have been some connivance between this Prince and the Queen for, before travelling into Scotland, he had had this Lady sounded by Chevalier Balandin, who travelled twice to Sweden for this very purpose, to find out if she would hear talk of marriage, and by way of introduction to this kind of discourse he had had his portrait sent to her, but she had made him understand so clearly that she was very far from listening to such proposals that she was spared having to make her refusal plain.]

Moore Smith also notes that, according to Christina's biographer (F. W. Bain, *Christina*, 1890), she responded in her own hand to Balandin, the envoy sent on behalf of Charles II, 'regretting her inability to provide any remedy for the incurable evils of the age, and hoping that time which cures all things might put an end to his evil fortune and furnish her with opportunities to assist him without detriment to her own interets and obligations'.

6. See letter 56, note 1.

7. Wrest, in Bedfordshire, was the estate of Anthony Grey, Earl of Kent; he inherited it as well as the title in 1639 from his cousin Henry, Lord Grey de Ruthin. At the time this letter was written the title was held by the grandson, Anthony, then aged about nine, who lived there with his widowed mother. Moore Smith notes that at that date the barony of Grey de Ruthin (but not the earldom of Kent) had passed to the late Earl's nephew by marriage, Charles Longueville, and at his death in 1643 to his sister, who was D.O.'s friend. Wrest House and Wrest Park are about six miles from Chicksands, opposite the village of Silsoe. The house is now the headquarters of the National Centre for Agricultural Engineering.

8. See letter 56, note 1.

9. Fear.

10. Lady Grey de Ruthin (see letter 14, note 5). The letter appears to indicate that she is now living at Wrest, though she may also have lived at nearby Meppershall.

11. To make a sufficiently generous financial settlement in order to enable them to marry. D.O. did not wish to make an im-

provident marriage, and W.T. was reluctant to pressure his father. We shall see later, from Henry Osborne's Diary, that the financial negotiations which preceded the marriage created some difficulties.

12. See letter 21, note 2.

13. The end of the sheet of paper.

14. When Sir Peter Osborne returned to England from St Malo in 1649.

15. See letter 5, note 2, for 'posy rings'.

16. Nan Stacy (see letter 15, note 1).

17. Moore Smith notes: 'Dorothy is surely recalling the doctor's words in the sleepwalking scene in *Macbeth*: "What a sigh is there! The heart is sorely charged"'(V.i.55).

18. To Ireland to seek to persuade his father to agree to the marriage, and to negotiate a financial settlement.

LETTER 58

1. See Letter 57, opening sentence.

2. 'It is not possible to prevent people being the subjects of discussion.'

3. See letter 17, note 6.

4. See letter 55, note 5. Henry Osborne had returned to Chicksands on Friday 13 January, to find W.T. there.

5. See letter 6, note 3; Lord Lisle was considered to be an atheist.

6. See letter 26, note 2.

7. See letter 31, note 5.

8. For which ailment she went to Epsom for treatment (see letter 3, note 10).

9. Until D.O. and W.T. are married.

10. Nan Stacy. In letter 57, D.O. had asked W.T. to allow Nan Stacy to cut a lock of his hair to send to her at Chicksands.

11. The Franklin family at Moor Park.

12. Robin Cheke (see letter 27, note 1).

13. 'I am astonished . . .'

14. The estate of the Earl of Manchester (see letter 27, note 2).

15. See letter 57, note 11.

16. D.O. means it in the religious sense: 'of persons, their actions, or occupations: dead to sin or the world; having the appetites and passions in subjection; ascetic' (*OED*).

17. This charge against W.T. was first made by Bishop Burnet. Gilbert Burnet (1643–1715), after studying abroad (1665–9), returned to Scotland to become vicar of Saltoun, and Professor of Divinity in the University of Glasgow (1669). In 1673 Burnet went to London, where he was lecturer at St Clement's until his defence of his friend Lord William Russell made it unsafe for him to remain in England after the Rye House plot (see letter 7, note 3). Burnet's anti-Catholic fulminations were so extraordinary that he was barred from the Court of James II; but he became a trusted adviser to William and Mary, and was made Bishop of Salisbury. His most celebrated works are the highly selective but informative *History of My Own Times* (1723–4) and the three-volume *History of the Reformation in England* (1679–1714). Burnet accused W.T. of being an Epicurean, both in principle and in practice, but Courtenay rebuts the accusation that W.T. was irreligious. It is evident, though, from the writings that, while W.T. was neither an atheist nor irreligious, his views in this regard were not orthodox.

18. Parry identifies two Bagshawes. Edward Bagshawe the elder, of Brasenose College, Oxford, and of the Middle Temple, had been in the earlier part of the century an exceptionally stern Puritan. His orations to show, *inter alia*, that bishops may not meddle in civil affairs, and that a parliament may be held without the attendance by the bishops, were apparently banned by Laud. Bagshawe was in the King's Bench Prison from 1644 to 1646

for joining Charles I at Oxford; he died in 1662. His son, Edward (1629–71), and Sir Henry Yelverton (see letter 45, note 17), who married Lady Grey de Ruthin, clashed on the question of the Church of England; the younger Bagshawe published (1671) an 'Antidote Against Mr Baxter's Treatise on Love and Marriage'. Moore Smith writes that he sees 'no grounds for identifying this Bagshaw' with either of the two identified by Parry, and certainly the lists of their publications would appear to support that view; yet D.O. would not have made a mistaken identification, and it is now too late to settle the matter.

19. Parry identifies her as Mrs Hannah Trupnel, who is referred to in 1654 in an old newsbook as 'having lately acted her part in a trance so many days at Whitehall'. Parry relates that she appears to have been full of mystical anti-Puritan prophecies, and that she indicted Cromwell for being a 'rogue and a vagabond'. She apparently abandoned preaching after she had been convicted and bound over to keep the peace. It could, however, have been any one of many women who preached at that time, of which perhaps the most famous was Mrs Attaway. (See Christopher Hill, *The World Turned Upside-Down*, 1975, Ch. 6: 'A Nation of Prophets'; Ch. 8: 'Sin and Hell'; Ch. 15: 'Base Impudent Kisses'.)

LETTER 59

1. We do not know the identity of the person who described W.T. as a 'pritty gentleman', but the portraits clearly corroborate her observation.

2. Anne, daughter of John, Baron Boteler, of Bramfield, Herts.; wife of Mountjoy Blount, 1st Earl of Newport. *DNB* records that, in March 1652, she was granted permission to leave England on condition that she would not perform acts prejudicial to the State while she was abroad. She was the mother of Lady Isabella Blount, who married Nicholas, 3rd Earl of Banbury, rather than Mr Robert Smith (see letter 6, note 8) and of Lady Anne Blount (see letter 48, note 7). In 1637 she was induced by her sister (who had married Endymion Porter) to follow the

fashion and declare herself a Catholic. Her husband, angered by this turn of events, asked Laud to punish those who had sought to influence his wife, and the archbishop's endeavours to do so led him into conflict with the queen. *DNB* suggests that it is possible that the Earl of Newport's temporary adherence to the leaders of the parliamentary opposition was the consequence of his irritation produced by his wife's conversion.

3. Moore Smith suggests that D.O. might here have in mind the Italian proverb, 'Se non è vero, è ben trovato' ('if not true, it is cleverly fabricated').

4. Robert Rich, 3rd Earl of Warwick, succeeded his father (who had demanded Sir Peter Osborne's surrender at Castle Cornet) in 1658; his first wife was Anne, daughter of William Cavendish, Earl of Devonshire, and of Christian, the daughter of Lord Bruce of Kinloss. Their son Robert married Frances Cromwell in 1657, but he died in February 1658, so that the title passed to the earl's brother, Charles Rich. The earl married, secondly, Anne, the daughter of Sir Thomas Cheke (see letter 27, note 1) and sister of Tom and Robin Cheke, of the Countess of Manchester, and of Mrs Franklin. Parry observes that the Warwick family was 'not a desirable family to marry into. The sons were idiots and the women seem to have conducted themselves with scant propriety' (1914, p. 206), which observation might be said to be sustained by interpreting D.O.'s remarks here as evidence that, at Lady Devonshire's behest, the earl had interfered in a proposed second marriage between his son and one of the daughters of Lady Newport. We also learn later (letter 64) that the earl himself is contemplating a third marriage, to Lady Betty Howard.

5. See note 4, above.

6. A particularly pertinent example of D.O.'s awareness of current ideological disputes, and her reactions to them.

7. *Parthenissa*, in three parts, is perhaps the most pretentious example of an English romance derived from the French pattern developed by writers like La Calprenède (letter 9, note 9) and Madame de Scudéry (letter 20, note 10); it was the work of

Roger Boyle, 1st Earl of Orrery (letter 41, note 13). Parry notes that the first part of the romance was dedicated to Lady Northumberland, and was advertised in *Mercurius Politicus* on 19 January 1654.

8. Henry Osborne was in London from 6 February to 25 February.

9. 'Surprising'. Moore Smith draws attention to D.O.'s fondness for introducing a French word, or the use of an English word in a French sense, of which the following are examples: 'resve' (letter 31); 'devoyr' (letter 33); 'sans raillerie' (letter 48); 'faiseurs de Romance' and 'Jealoux' in this letter.

10. Part One of *Parthenissa* tells the story of the Siege of Pettely by the Carthaginians under Himilco (a colleague of Hannibal) who also sacked Acragas (present-day Agrigento) in 406 B.C. It is said that in this siege some two thousand women, led by Amazora, left the city voluntarily in order that provisions for the men who were defending the city would last longer; the defenders were, however, all slain. D.O. objects to that part of the story, in Book Four, where a letter from Amazora is discovered in which she confesses her love for the enemy leader, Perolla.

11. *L'Illustre Bassa*, a novel by Madame de Scudéry (letter 20, note 10). Moore Smith identifies the passage to which D.O. refers as from the Preface:

> Vous y verrez Lecteur (sie je ne me trompe) la bien-seance des choses et des conditions, assez exactement observée: et je n'ay rien mis en mon livre, que les Dames ne puissent lire sans baisser les yeux & sans rougir. Que si vous ne voyez pas mon Heros, persecuté d'amour par les femmes, ce n'est pas qu'il ne fust aimable, et qu'il ne pust estre aimé: mais c'est pour ne choquer point la bien-seance, en la personne des Dames, et la vraisemblance en celle des hommes, qui rarement font les cruels, & qui n'y ont pas bonne grace. Enfin, soit que les choses doivent estre ainsi, soit que j'ayre jugé de mon Heros par ma foiblesse; je n'ay point voulu mettre sa fidellité à cette dangereuse épreuve.
> ['You will see in it, Reader (if I am not mistaken), the propriety of things and conditions rather accurately observed: and I have put nothing in my book that Ladies could not read without lowering their eyes and blushing. So that if you do not see my Hero

persecuted with the love of women, it is not because he was not lovable or that he could not be loved, but it is in order not to offend against propriety in the person of ladies and with verisimilitude in that of men, who seldom behave in a cruel manner and who do not come out to their advantage whenever they do so. Finally, whether because that is how things should be or because I have judged my Hero in the light of my own foibles, I did not wish to put his loyalty to such a perilous test.']

12. *OED* gives the date for the first use of 'ambition'd' in this way as 1670, but credits D.O. with the first example of this particular use of 'concern'.

13. See letter 20, note 10.

14. Martha Giffard (see letter 9, note 6), who was to accompany W.T. to Ireland (see letters 54, 56 and 61).

15. The cabinet in which the letters were kept (see letter 58). There is a photograph of the cabinet in Julia Longe, *Martha, Lady Giffard* (1911).

16. James Beverley (see letter 56, note 1).

17. Bailiff.

18. Wife of the Rector of Campton.

19. Jane Wright (see letter 9, note 12). Jane Wright and Mrs Goldsmith may have been sisters.

20. At once.

21. Rose. A similar usage occurs in letter 64. D.O. also uses 'risse' (letter 9).

22. Sir John Temple evidently did not subscribe to the view that D.O.'s actions were wholly motivated by her love for his son.

23. *OED* cites Lady Mary Worth, *Uriana* (1621): 'What is pleasinger then varietie, or sweeter then flatterie.'

24. The lock of hair mentioned in letters 57 and 58.

25. The ring mentioned in letter 54.

LETTER 60

1. D.O. from now on writes on paper of a much increased size, and it would appear from her comment that W.T. was somehow responsible for this change; see Introduction, p.19.

2. Jeremy Taylor (1613–67), bishop, theologian, devotional writer; he was distinguished as a preacher and as author of some of the most celebrated religious works of his time. After completing his studies at Cambridge and taking holy orders, Taylor was nominated (1635) by Laud to a fellowship at All Souls, Oxford. He became chaplain to Laud and rector of Uppingham, Rutland (1638), but as a chaplain-in-ordinary to Charles I, he left his parish to join the king at the outbreak of war (1642). After the defeat of the royalist forces at Cardigan Castle, Taylor was briefly imprisoned, but in 1645 he became principal of a school in Carmarthenshire and served as private chaplain to the 2nd Earl of Carbery, at whose home, Golden Grove, he wrote some of his best works. *The Liberty of Prophesying* (1647) was a noteworthy call for toleration, and his *Great Exemplar . . . the Life of Jesus Christ* (1649) was followed by his key devotional works: *Holy Living* (1650), *Holy Dying* (1651), *The Golden Grove* (1655) and *The Worthy Communicant* (1660), and his learned treatise *Ductor Dubitantium; or, The Rule of Conscience* (1660) was dedicated to Charles II. After the Restoration, Taylor was made Bishop of Down and Connor, in Ireland, and appointed vice-chancellor of Trinity College, Dublin. At Dromore, which was added to his see, Taylor built (1661) the church in which he is buried; his tenure as bishop, from 1660 to 1667, was a period of turbulent dispute with Presbyterian ministers, who refused to acknowledge episcopal jurisdiction. Parry notes that D.O. may have had in mind here a passage from *Holy Living*:

> There is a very great peace and immunity from sin in resigning our wills up to the command of others; for provided that our duty to God be secured, their commands are warrants to us in all else; and the case of conscience is determined, if the command be evident and pressing; and it is certain, the action that is but indifferent, and without reward, if done onely upon our own choice, is an act

of duty and religion, and rewardable by the grace and favour of God, if done in obedience to the command of our Superiors.

3. 'Contentment is the best paint.' I am indebted to Robert Pring-Mill of St Catherine's College, Oxford, for establishing that, while there appears to be no precise match, the nearest would be: '*El afeite que más hermosea es la dávida buena*' (lit. 'The cosmetic which most beautifies is the good present' – i.e. 'A good gift does more than anything else to enhance a woman's beauty'). Pring-Mill notes, additionally, that he expects the proverb to start with '*El afeite que más hermosea . . .*' and continue with something like '*es el contento*' – or else to run, '*El contento es el mejor afeite*', or words to that effect. 'Paint', he adds, is undoubtedly being used in the sense of '*afeite*', i.e. something applied as a facial cosmetic. The version he quotes is No. 1361 in Luis Martínez Klein, *Refranero general ideológico español* (Real Academia Española, Madrid, 1953).

4. See letter 58, where D.O. refers to herself and her brother as 'two hermitts conversing in a Cell they Equaly inhabitt'.

5. To Ireland.

6. Approaching from Dunstable, Little Brickhill is about two miles, and Great Brickhill about four miles, from present-day Bletchley. W.T. would have travelled this way on the London–Chester road, to reach the coast to embark for Ireland.

7. See letter 31, note 5.

8. See letter 6, note 6.

9. It has not been possible to identify 'Mrs Camilla'.

10. This may be either a trunk in which china objects were stored, or a piece of china in the shape of a trunk.

11. Fernão Mendes Pinto (1509?–83), a Portuguese traveller in Asia and Africa for over twenty years; he often endured great hardship – including a period of enslavement. The account of his travels, *Peregrinação* (1614), was translated into several languages and D.O. may have read it in French: *Les voyages . . . de F.M.P. . . . traduicts . . . par B. Figuier* (Paris, 1628, 1645). Parry

makes the interesting observation that the change in reading material might indicate that D.O. had tired of romances.

12. Moore Smith notes that one of the Proverbs in Camden's *Remains* is: 'A traveler may lye with authority.'

13. Sister, not of Lady Grey de Ruthin, but of her mother the dowager baroness. Henry Osborne's Diary notes (1652):

> June 29, Tuesday. – I and my sister went to my Lady Grey and Mrs Pooley to the burial of Mrs Rolf [not identified].
> July 25, Sunday. – I went with my sister and my Lady Grey and Mrs Pooley to dinner with Sir William Briars.

14. The Old Spring Gardens were situated at the north-west edge of St James's Park; they are shown in Morden and Lea's 1682 map as being roughly where the Admiralty now stands. It is not clear when the gardens were opened to the public, but they were certainly in use from about 1634. They apparently derive their name from a fountain which was activated by spectators tripping a hidden mechanical device. The gardens became a bowling green, which was closed *c.* 1635 because of riots which had purportedly taken place there, though, if Evelyn is to be believed, they were reopened as New Spring Gardens in June 1649, when he took some ladies there for entertainments. Cromwell closed the gardens in May 1654, soon after the nightly visits there by D.O. (see letter 65). After the Restoration, the gardens were built over and the entertainments were transferred to Vauxhall. Parry quotes a contemporary witness, one Lady Alicia Halkett, who noted in 1644: 'so scrupulous was I of giving any occasion to speake of me as I know they did of others, that though I loved well to see plays, and to walk in the Spring Gardens sometimes (before it grew something scandalous by the abuses of some), yet I cannot remember three times that ever I went with any man besides my brother'. Parry also reminds us, most appositely, that 'it is a little astounding to read, as one does in this and the last letter [as well as letter 65, and the references to masques in letter 4], of race meetings, and Dorothy habited in a mask, disporting herself at Spring Garden or in the Park. It opens one's eyes to the exaggerated gloom that has been thrown over England during the Puritan reign by those

historians who have derived their information solely from state papers and proclamations.' It might perhaps be observed that despite the fact that modern historians have sought to redress the record, popular wisdom about the 'Puritan reign' appears to have remained largely intact and unaltered.

15. This was originally the Roman feast of Lupercalia, which was christianized in memory of the martyrdom of St Valentine in A.D. 270; his name, in medieval times, became associated with the union of lovers under conditions of difficulty.

16. Jane Wright (see letter 9, note 12).

17. Humphry Fysshe (see letter 26, note 6).

18. James Beverley (see letter 56, note 1).

19. Here and in other instances in this part of the letter, the word is partly obscured by the binding.

20. The usage is unclear. *OED* offers only two definitions: (i) the father of one's husband or mother; (ii) the misused 'stepfather'. Since neither of these definitions could apply here, one wonders if D.O. might have meant 'grandfather'. See also her use of 'Mother in Law' (letter 3, note 5).

LETTER 61

1. How the letter will reach W.T. in Ireland.

2. Nan Stacy (see letter 15, note 1).

3. Jane Wright (see letter 9, note 12). It appears from this letter that she had returned to London from Guernsey (letter 12, note 1), and that she is now looking for employment.

4. W.T. acted as escort for his sister during the voyage (see letter 59, note 14).

5. Familiar with; used to.

6. James Beverley (see letter 56, note 1).

7. Unidentified; the initials also occur in letters 53 and 54.

8. A church near the south side of old St Paul's, destroyed in the Great Fire.

9. See letter 26, note 5.

10. 'so particular about identifying'.

11. Sir Thomas Peyton (see letter 24, note 5).

12. Sir John Tufton (1623–85), son of Sir Humphrey Tufton, 1st baronet, of 'Le Mote', Maidstone. He succeeded his father in 1659, and married (i) Margaret, third daughter and co-heiress of Thomas, 2nd Baron Wotton; (ii) Mary, daughter and co-heiress of Sir James Altham of Monks Hall, Essex.

13. Word omitted.

14. James Beverley (see note 6, above).

15. Moore Smith observes: 'The present passage is especially puzzling, as it does not appear that Temple had sent Dorothy a letter from some lady whom they called his wife, but that Dorothy is giving an account of a supposed letter which Temple had not seen.' We know that D.O. wrote to W.T. on the back of a letter from her uncle; that she wrapped a book in a letter from her brother; that W.T. sent her a letter from his father, and would later send one from his brother. If the 'wife' is, as I believe, Nan Stacy (see letter 45, note 2), and if letters are being sent to Ireland via her (see note 21, below), then there is no reason to assume that the letter mentioned here is not from Nan Stacy to W.T.; otherwise, if it is an account of a letter which W.T. had not seen, how did D.O. acquire it?

16. See letter 58, note 16.

17. Not identified.

18. Mrs Jane Rant (see letter 43, note 9).

19. Not identified.

20. Colonel W. F. Prideaux (*Notes and Queries*, 9th Series, Vol. XII, No. 292, 1 August 1903, pp. 81–2) identifies him as Edmund Smith, a medical doctor, who died of pleurisy in Shoe Lane on 16 February 1654. Dr Smith had apparently bought his house

from Dr Rant (see letter 43, note 9), who in turn had bought it from Lord Paget (see letter 43, note 10).

21. Address on the reverse, with the comment 'All else is but a circle' above the remnants of three seal-marks. It seems that letters to W.T. at this time were transmitted via Nan Stacy; later they will have a Dublin address, once D.O. realizes that she can, with safety, send her letters to W.T. at his father's house.

LETTER 62

1. This letter, and most of the letters which follow, are dated. Note that (i) the dating follows the custom of beginning the New Year on 25 March, the day of the Feast of the Annunciation of the Blessed Virgin (Lady Day); (ii) if we follow Parry's dating, then one letter (25 February) is missing; if we follow Moore Smith, then two letters (4 March; 11 March) are missing. See Introduction, p. 20.

2. Shakespeare: 'When sorrows come, they come not single spies, / But in battalions (*Hamlet*, IV. v.79–80).

3. Henry Osborne's Diary records (1654):

   Feb. 25, Saterday. – I came home to Chicksands.
   Mar. 9, Thursday. – *My sister told mee shee would marry Temple.*
   Mar. 11 – Being Saterday my father died just at eleven a clocke of night being within two moneths 69 yeares old.
   Mar. 13. – *My sister told mee shee had tied up her han[d]s that shee could marry no body but Temple.* This night Mr Goldsmith buried my father at Campton.

4. Moore Smith is doubtless correct when he writes that 'we must interpret this literally, that Dorothy defrayed from her own income the cost of her board and lodging at Chicksands'.

5. Henry Osborne's Diary records that his elder brother had arrived on 22 March (he dates it 24 March) from Gloucester, and that he returned there on Monday, 3 April.

6. Fears.

7. Having told her brother that she intended to marry W.T., and

also to combat the 'malicious' rumours being spread by her brother, D.O. gives W.T. permission to acknowledge the engagement publicly.

8. Anticipate.

9. Inform of; relate.

10. 'this letter'.

11. To discuss with her where she will live following the death of her father, since she would have to leave Chicksands when the estate passed to her elder brother.

12. See letter 61, note 4.

LETTER 63

1. We know from letters 60 and 61 that the journey had been delayed by adverse weather. We assume that W.T. had started his letter at Chester, had completed it on the voyage, and had then sent it from Dublin.

2. James Beverley (see letter 56, note 1).

3. Henry Osborne's Diary gives the following:

Apr. 10, Munday. – I went with my sister to Bedforde where Mr Yelverton [see letter 45, note 17] mett her to carry her to Easton [Easton Maudit, for his marriage to Lady Grey de Ruthin].

Apr. 12, Wednesday. – I went to Easton.

Apr. 13, Thursday. – My Lady Ruthin was married.

Apr. 17, Munday. – My Lady [Diana Rich?] and my sister and I came away from Easton, Mr Yelverton and his sister and my Lady Ruthin came with us to Bedforde where my Lady Briars coach mett them, and my sister went that night to my Lady Briars.

Apr. 20, Thursday. – My sister went to St Albons in my Lady Briars coach, and from thence in a hackney [hired carriage] to London.

Apr. 21, Friday. – I came to London leaving Evans to keepe the house and garden at Chicksands.

Apr. 25, Tuesday. – My A. Gargrave *spoke to my sister of Temple*.

Apr. 27, Thursday. – My A. Gargrave went out of Towne towards Cornebury.

4. Lady Gargrave (see letter 3, note 3).

5. Sir Thomas Peyton (see letter 24, note 5).

6. William Seymour (1588–1660), 1st Marquess and 2nd Earl of Hertford, was the great-grandson of Edward Seymour, Duke of Somerset (1506?–52), Protector of England after the death of Henry VIII (1547–49), and grandson of Lady Catherine Grey, through whom he had a claim to the throne. Seymour made a secret marriage to Arabella Stuart, cousin of James I, for which he was put in the Tower, but he escaped and fled abroad; he returned to England after the death of Arabella (1616) and was made Privy Councillor as well as Marquess of Hertford (1640). He fought on the royalist side during the Civil War; after the Restoration he was made Duke of Somerset. Seymour married, secondly, Frances Devereux, daughter of Robert, 2nd Earl of Essex (1567–1601; executed for treason, despite being Elizabeth's favourite courtier), and sister of Robert Devereux, 3rd Earl of Essex (1591–1646), general of the parliamentary armies. Frances Devereux was the mother of the young Lord Beauchamp, whose death at the age of twenty-eight D.O. deplores.

7. Baptist Noel (1612–82) was 2nd Baron Noel and 3rd Viscount Campden; he was fined very heavily (originally £19,558, reduced to £11,078. 17s.) for raising a corps of foot and a regiment of horse for Charles I (1643), but appointed Lord-Lieutenant of Rutland after the Restoration. He married four times, the fourth wife being Lady Elizabeth Bertie, a daughter of the Earl of Lindsay, whose sister had married Sir Thomas Osborne, Earl of Danby (see letter 2, note 3). There seems to be no account of a duel with Mr Stafford.

8. The writing is much larger and more spaced out than usual.

9. The first letter which is openly addressed to W.T. at his father's address.

LETTER 64

1. See letter 63, note 3.

2. Rose (see letter 59, note 21).

3. The letter from W.T. (see Appendix B). Did this survive because

it was the first letter that D. O. could openly acknowledge and because their engagement was known by then?

4. Steadfastness; courage.

5. Greenland; from the Danish Grønland.

6. Serious.

7. Unlike W.T.'s last visit to Chicksands. See letter 55, note 5, and his letter (Appendix B) which asks: 'Well now in very good earnest doe you thinke tis time for mee to come or noe, would you bee very glad to see mee there, and could you doe it in less disorder and with less surprisse then you did at Ch[icksands].'

8. A reference to one of several attempts to assassinate Cromwell (around 21 May 1654); a large number of arrests were made, and those convicted included John Gerard, beheaded at Tower Hill; Peter Vowell, a schoolmaster, hanged; Somerset Fox, reprieved. Henry Osborne's Diary has no entries for May (he was, in any event, not in London then), but he does record the events preceding the trials as follows: 'June 9, Friday. – I came to London from Chicksands, and the night before there was the great search for cavalliers about killing my Ld. Protector.' There is also no record of the sentences because the Diary records Henry Osborne's departure for 'Knolton' (Knowlton, Kent) via Gravesend on 26 June.

9. See letter 4, note 2.

10. See letter 13, note 6. According to Parry, D. O. was apparently lodging opposite Salisbury House, where Lady Danvers used to stay when she came up from Chelsea.

11. Parry identifies Lady Sandis (Sandys) as Mary, wife of William, Lord Sandys de Vyne of Mottisfont Priory (or Mottisfont Abbey), near Romsey, Hampshire; she was the youngest daughter of William Cecil, 2nd Earl of Salisbury.

12. Colonel W. F. Prideaux states in *Notes and Queries*, 9th Series, 16 May 1903, p. 386, that 'he must surely be the celebrated Col. Panton, the biggest gambler of the day, and a man that no husband of that time would have chosen as the companion of

his wife'. Colonel Panton was the possessor of land in the Haymarket in Piccadilly, and it is from him that Panton Street derives its name. He died in 1681. His daughter married Henry, Lord Arundel of Wardour, after whom Wardour and Arundel Streets are named.

13. Parry suggests that this may have been Sir John Morton, of Milbourne St Andrew, Nottinghamshire.

14. Charles Stanley, grandson of the 6th and nephew of the 7th Earl of Derby (1607–51), who was married to Jane, daughter of Lord Widdrington. Lord Widdrington died in the Battle of Wigan (1651), under the command of the 7th Earl of Derby, who was himself executed after being captured at the Battle of Worcester (1651).

15. Sir Henry Lyttelton, 2nd baronet, of Hagley Park, married Philadelphia Carey, daughter and co-heiress of Robert Carey, 2nd Earl of Monmouth (see letter 41, note 12).

16. See letter 59, note 4.

17. Parry identifies her as the wife of William, fourth son of the 1st Earl of Berkshire.

18. Not identified.

19. See letter 37, note 4.

20. In letter 65, we learn that Elizabeth Gerard, daughter of the 3rd Lord Gerard, married William Spencer (see letter 18, note 1).

21. See letter 23, note 2. D.O. recounts in letter 37 that Lord St John's previous wife had died in childbirth.

22. Indicating.

23. As a consequence of the discovery of the plot to assassinate Cromwell (see note 8, above) a proclamation was issued on 23 May directing the constables of London, Southwark and Westminster to draw up a list of all lodgers within their bounds, and to forbid such lodgers leaving their lodgings unless they had leave to do so.

24. There is no record of D.O. going to Suffolk; she went to Kent, to the estate of Sir Thomas Peyton (see letter 24, note 5).

LETTER 65

1. We know from W.T.'s letter (see Appendix B) that Jane is with D.O.

2. A public house where letters for Ireland could be left?

3. See letter 18, note 1; letter 64, note 20.

4. See letter 60, note 14.

5. Moore Smith explains the shortness of this letter by suggesting that D.O. had returned briefly to Bedfordshire; the entry in Henry Osborne's Diary reads: 'June 6, Tuesday: – I wente downe to my Lady Briars in her new Chariott my sister made stay there that night and the next day came to Chicksands.' The Diary does not make any further reference to D.O.'s movements until 26 June, when brother and sister set out for Knowlton via Gravesend.

LETTER 66

1. Dublin.

2. See letter 64, note 24.

3. See letter 27, note 5.

4. Jane Wright (see letter 9, note 12).

5. See letter 65.

LETTER 67

1. Henry Osborne's Diary records (1654): 'June 15, Thursday. – My Lady Ruthin went out of Towne my A. Gargrave who came to Towne about my C. Thorolds [see letter 10, note 2] businesse went out of towne againe. This day my sister removed from my Lady Ruthins lodging in Queenstreete, to my C. Thorolds lodging in Drury lane.'

2. Henry Osborne's Diary records (1654): 'June 14, Wednesday. –

My A. Gargrave and my Cousin Thorold my sister and I dined at the Swan in Fish streete, *my sister and I had the greate falling out and were friends againe.*'

3. Remedy.

4. Elizabeth Murray (d. 1697) was the daughter of William Murray, Gentleman of the Bedchamber to Charles I and created 1st Earl of Dysart in 1643, and his wife, Catherine Bruce of Clackmannan. Elizabeth Murray married Sir Lionel Tollemache (Talmach), 3rd baronet, of Helmingham, Suffolk, in 1647, and they had three sons and two daughters. After the death of her husband in 1668, she renewed an earlier relationship with John Maitland, Earl of Lauderdale, although his wife was then still alive, and it is to this event that D.O. refers. Elizabeth Murray succeeded her father as Countess of Dysart in her own right (the earldom had been conferred with remainder to heirs male and female, and the earl had no sons), and when the Countess of Lauderdale died (1672) she added that title as well because of her marriage to the earl. Some commentators also note that it is claimed she was one of Cromwell's mistresses, but evidence is slight. Bishop Burnet (see letter 58, note 17) wrote of her: 'Cherub I doubt's too low a name for thee / For thou alone a whole rank seems to be: / The onelie individual of thy kynd / No mate can fitlie suit so great a mind.' After noting, elsewhere, that: 'She was a woman of great beauty, but of far greater parts. She had a wonderful quickness of apprehension, and an amazing vivacity in conversation. She had studied not only divinity and history, but mathematics and philosophy', Burnet also observed: 'She was violent in everything she set about, – a violent friend but a much more violent enemy. She had a restless ambition, lived at vast expense, and was ravenously covetous; and would have stuck at nothing by which she might compass her ends', which opinion might be said to be vindicated by her insistence that Lauderdale should settle the whole of his estate on her. When the earl's brother succeeded to the title, she brought a series of lawsuits against him, which nearly bankrupted him. It has been suggested that the character of the widow Blackalee in William Wycherley's *The Plain Dealer* (1674) was modelled on Elizabeth Murray.

5. Colonel Robert Hammond (see letter 9, note 5).

6. Edmund Ludlow (1617?–92). After graduating from Trinity College, Oxford (1636), and fighting at the Battle of Edgehill (1642), he became Member of Parliament for Wiltshire (1646), one of the instigators of Pride's Purge (1648), and one of the judges of Charles I and a signatory of his death warrant. Later he was a member of the Council of State, a prominent military commander and commissioner for civil government in Ireland (1650–55). However, after the proclamation of Cromwell as Lord Protector, Ludlow refused to acknowledge his authority or to give security for his peaceable behaviour; he was allowed to retire to his Essex estate in 1656, but when the Long Parliament was recalled, he was made a member of the Committee of Safety, a member of the Council of State, and commander of the army in Ireland. Ludlow was impeached by the Restoration parliament, and surrendered to the proclamation requiring all judges of Charles I to do so. Allowed his liberty after providing sureties, Ludlow escaped to Switzerland, but returned to England in 1689 in the hope of obtaining some preferment at the Court of William III, but when the new monarch published a proclamation for his arrest, he escaped once again and died abroad. Ludlow's *Memoirs* (published 1698–9) provide a valuable insight into republican factional opposition to Cromwell – one of the features which led to the overthrow of that administration in 1659.

7. Parry identifies her as Ursula, daughter of Walter Giffard of Chillington, Staffordshire, who married Sir Thomas Vavasor (or Vavasour), 2nd baronet, of Haselwood, Yorkshire; they had a son (born in 1653), and a daughter who died at birth. Parry tells us, further, that they were a Roman Catholic family, and that the husband claimed descent from those who held the ancient office of King's Vavasour ('a feudal tenant ranking immediately below a baron' – *OED*). Moore Smith also suggests that it could have been Olive, the wife of Sir William Vavasour, of Copmanthorpe, Yorkshire, whose daughter Frances was born on 26 October 1654 (although he inverts the names of the men to read Thomas Giffard, Viscount Fauconberg, and Sir Walter Vavasour).

8. See letter 64, note 8.

9. See D.O.'s earlier strictures against civil marriages, in letter 35.

10. We will find in the letters which follow that Sir John Temple acted on behalf of his son, and Sir John Peyton (assisted by Henry Osborne, after some initial opposition to him) acted for D.O. in the marriage negotiations.

11. Probably at the dinner where brother and sister had 'the greate falling out and were friends againe' (see note 2, above).

12. The proposed journey to Suffolk (see letter 64).

13. Abraham Cowley (1618–67), one of the 'Metaphysical Poets'. At the outbreak of the Civil War he was, like others, ejected from Cambridge, but found Oxford a congenial refuge. The scriptural epic *Davideis* (1656), to which reference is made here, must have been started at about this time. In 1646 Cowley went to France to become a cypher clerk to Queen Henrietta Maria and returned to England in 1655 to act as a royalist spy, but he was arrested, and interrogated by Cromwell. Released, he sought to ingratiate himself with the Protectorate by writing a conciliatory paragraph in the 1656 preface to his poetry – for which his royalist friends never forgave him, and despite which the parliamentarians never trusted him. His poems 'Brutus' and 'Destiny' were interpreted as political allegories justifying the rebellion against Charles I, and the execution of the king.

Parry is almost certainly correct in identifying the verse from 'David and Jonathan', Book II, as the following lines:

> What art thou, love, thou great mysterious thing?
> From what hid stock does thy strange nature spring?
> 'Tis thou that mob'st the world through ev'ry part,
> And hold'st the vast frame close that nothing start
> From the due place and office first ordained,
> By thee were all things made and are sustained.
> Sometimes we see thee fully and can say
> From hence thou took'st thy rise and went'st that way,
> But oft'ner the short beams of reason's eye
> See only there thou art, not how, nor why.

Moore Smith quotes some other lines, which we cannot help but compare with those of the final couplet quoted from Ovid, *Metamorphoses*, where the story is told of Philemon and Baucis (see letter 54, note 14). Cowley writes:

They mingled fates, and both in each did share,
They both were servants, they both princes were.
If any joy to one of them was sent,
It was most his, to whom it least was meant,
And Fortune's malice betwixt both was crost,
For, striking one, it wounded th'other most.

LETTER 68

1. Henry Osborne's Diary records (1654):

   June 26, Munday. – My sister and I went to Gravesend towards our way to Knolton.
   June 27, Tuesday. – My brother Peyton mett us at Sittingbourne, and his coach mett us at Canterbury and that night wee came to Knolton.

2. Moore Smith points out that: 'People going into Kent would often go by water as far as Gravesend, in a tilt boat [a boat with an awning against the weather]'.

3. Sir Thomas Peyton (see letter 24, note 5).

4. In another lost letter.

5. This is a small piece of paper ($5\frac{1}{2}'' \times 5''$) given as folio 112 in the manuscript; it was clearly written to send with letter 68.

6. As 'husbandman' (of her time).

LETTER 69

1. We know from Henry Osborne's Diary (letter 68, note 1) that they arrived at Knowlton on Tuesday, 27 June. The Diary also records that he left Knowlton on the morning of Thursday, 13 July.

2. This is clearly a mistake; it should read 'July the 4th'.

3. This letter is again addressed 'For your Master', so we must presume that Nan Stacy is back in London and acting as inter-mediary, though why the letter should not have been sent directly to Dublin is not clear.

LETTER 70

1. See letter 68. It would appear that D.O. failed to engage the servant because a letter had either gone astray or perhaps arrived too late.

2. Moore Smith glosses this as 'situations held by servants', and notes that *OED* does not recognize that use, which is correct; but D.O. might have meant it in the equally appropriate sense of 'agreement by settlement of terms; covenant; contract; treaty', which is an *OED* definition. Moore Smith does, however, point out that W.T., in his early romance *The Force of Custome*, writes: 'Vamorin . . . meets with a good condition in a Cardinal's house who taken with the excellence of his voice entertained him in his service.'

3. Kent.

4. Word omitted.

5. Feared.

6. For the '3 Plotters', see letter 64, note 8. The '5 Portugalls' were Dom Pantaleon Sa (aged nineteen) and four of his men. Parry traced the story to *Mercurius Politicus*, November 1653. It appeared that one evening, when Dom Pantaleon (who was the brother of the then Portuguese ambassador) was visiting the New Exchange (see letter 13, note 4), he claimed that a Colonel Gerard had insulted him, and that this had provoked a scuffle in which Colonel Gerard and one of Pantaleon's aides were injured. According to the evidence, Pantaleon returned to the Exchange on the following evening, accompanied by some fifty armed men, one of whom shot dead a Mr Greenway, who had gone to the Exchange with his sister and his fiancée to buy gifts for their wedding which was to take place two days later. For this Pantaleon and four of his associates were tried by a special commission, and sentenced to death. Pantaleon was beheaded on 10 July at Tower Hill, along with John Gerard who had been separately convicted of attempting to assassinate Cromwell.

7. *The Lost Lady*, a tragicomedy by Sir William Berkeley (1606–77), appointed colonial Governor of Virginia (1641). Berkeley was an uncompromising royalist; he made war on the Indians as well as on the Dutch, refused to recognize the Commonwealth, and sought to make Virginia a safe haven for supporters of Charles I. When a Puritan force was sent out in 1652 to depose him, he retired to his plantation until 1660, when he was re-appointed Governor, but this second term was marked by economic difficulties brought about by the fall in tobacco prices as well as by accusations of favouritism towards friends, which led to 'Bacon's Rebellion' – a popular revolt of 1676, led by Nathaniel Bacon, which ousted the Governor, but which then collapsed after the sudden death of the rebellion's leader. Reinstated for a third time, Berkeley proceeded to hang many of the conspirators, in defiance of the express wish of a royal commission which had arrived with pardons for all except Bacon. Berkeley finally retired to England, where he died in disgrace.

LETTER 71

1. Sir Thomas Peyton (see letter 24, note 5). D.O. means 'some of his wife's fears'.

LETTER 72

1. Charles II. I think that D.O. is making reference here to the Anglo-French negotiations of 1654, which forced Charles to leave France for Germany (and later the 'Spanish' Netherlands). It is noteworthy that D.O. writes of Charles, not to be restored to the throne until 1660, as 'the K.'.

2. Her brother-in-law, Sir Thomas Peyton, not her brother.

3. William Lilly, the astrologer (see letter 5, note 3).

4. Mrs Elizabeth Thorold (see letter 10, note 2).

5. Obscured by the binding.

6. Obscured by the binding.

7. Mocked.

8. Unfortunately this song was not preserved.

LETTER 73

1. In another missing letter?

2. Dorothy Peyton (see letter 24, note 5).

3. Not identified.

4. Henry Osborne's Diary reads (1654): 'Aug. 18, Friday. – I came to Knolton. While I was at Knolton [until 11 September] came Coll: Thornhill and his wife and Ascott'. See also notes 6 and 7, below.

5. Elizabeth, Queen of Bohemia (1596–1662), was the daughter of James I. She married Frederick, King of Bohemia (1596–1632), Elector Palatine as Frederick V (1610–20) after the Protestant Diet of Bohemia had deposed the Roman Catholic King Ferdinand (Holy Roman Emperor Ferdinand II). Influenced by his minister Christian of Anhalt, Frederick accepted but did not receive the aid he had expected from his father-in-law and from the Protestant Union (an alliance of German Protestant and city leaders, 1608–21), so that his armies were eventually defeated at the White Mountain in 1620. He was forced to leave Bohemia, and the derisive title of 'The Winter King' derives from his short reign. These battles of Frederick mark the opening campaigns of the Thirty Years War (1618–48). From Frederick and Elizabeth are descended, through their daughter Sophia (who was the mother of George I), the Hanoverian succession in England. After the death of her husband, Elizabeth returned to England, where she maintained a Court despite severe financial hardship, and where she encouraged writers; she numbered among her close friends the poets Francis Quarles (1592–1644) and Sir Henry Wotton (1568–1639). Indeed, the latter's fame rests, in large part,

upon his tribute to Elizabeth in his poem, 'You meaner beauties of the night'.

6. Perhaps the 'Ascott' mentioned in Henry Osborne's Diary (note 4, above).

7. G. Thorn Drury, writing in *Notes and Queries*, 9th Series, Vol. XI, no. 284, 6 June 1903, p. 445, writes that there is, in Wye Church, a memorial to Lady Joanna Thornhill (1635–1708). Lady Thornhill's father, Sir Bevill Grenville, died at the Battle of Lansdowne, near Bath, on 5 July 1653, while leading a Cornish battalion against the parliamentary forces under Waller. Her brother John was born at Kilkhampton, Cornwall; he fought at the second Battle of Newbury, where he was severely wounded, after which he retired to Jersey. He was made Earl of Bath after the Restoration. Lady Thornhill's husband, Richard, had to compound for his estates for the (then) vast amount of £1,054.17s.; he was apparently also fined (and paid) £3,000 by parliament.

LETTER 74

1. In London, before proceeding to Knowlton.

LETTER 75

1. Word omitted.

2. Sir John Temple is clearly not keen to agree that Henry Osborne should be one of the negotiators on behalf of D.O. See letter 67, note 10.

LETTER 76

1. D.O. holds the view that Sir John Temple should realize that Sir Thomas Peyton would not agree any details in the marriage contract without the participation of Henry Osborne, even if the latter was not officially one of the negotiators.

2. This assertion of the family bond and the defence of her brother's rights are significant, despite what she may have said about him previously.

3. When W.T. went to see his father (who was then at York) before his trip to the Netherlands, D.O. mildly castigated him for not having attempted to make a detour from Bedford in order to visit her (see letter 2, note 1).

4. Particular; scrupulous.

5. 'A variety of domestic pigeon, having white plumage with a spot of another colour above the beak' (*OED*).

6. To Ireland.

LETTER 77

1. Not identified; perhaps in another missing letter?

2. Page torn.

3. Page torn.

4. Page torn.

5. It has not been possible to establish whether or not W.T. went to visit D.O. at Knolton during this period, but Henry Osborne's diary records:

   Oct. 17, Tuesday. – My Lady Peyton and my sister, &., came from [?] to London from Knolton Sr Thomas Peyton staying behinde. I kept my chamber that day and they stopt at my lodging at Mr Palins, and my sister came up and stayed supper with mee, and then declared that *shee would marry Temple*. They lay at Honnybuns in

Drury Lane, and the small pox being there they removed to Mrs Broadstreetes in Queenestreete.

6. It is to this period that we should assign the two short notes which follow (numbered 125 and 126 in the manuscript).

Appendix A   Letters Written during the Marriage

LETTER A

1. Identified by Moore Smith as Mrs Elizabeth Hammond, widow of Robert Hammond, Temple's maternal uncle, and by Julia Longe as Lady Danvers. However, if we accept the earlier dating of these letters (see Introduction, p. 8), then Julia Longe's identification cannot be right.

2. She is expecting a child. If it is the first, then the letter must have been written before or about October 1655.

3. Their general handyman.

4. Jane Wright (see letter 9, note 12).

5. Mrs Goldsmith, wife of the vicar of Campton and possibly a sister of Jane Wright.

6. Temple must have gone to London to deal with matters on behalf of Mrs Hammond.

LETTER B

1. Tom is the man who looked after the horses.

2. Mrs Carter is possibly the midwife who was engaged to assist with the confinement.

3. Moore Smith identifies her as Letitia, widow of John Hampden, and stepmother to Mary Hammond (Hampden's sixth daughter). She was probably living at Coley Park, Reading (which Charles

I had made his headquarters before the Battle of Newbury in 1644). Mary Hammond's husband, Colonel Robert Hammond, had lived in Reading until 1654, when he went to Ireland. He died soon after his arrival there. Mary Hammond later married Sir John Hobart.

LETTER C

1. The cabinet in which W.T. kept her letters.

2. Jack, born 18 December 1655; he died in Ireland.

3. Moore Smith has 'defeate' but, although that would agree with similar usage (see letters 30 and 39), Julia Longe's transcription as 'defecte' is probably more likely.

4. See letter B, note 2.

5. See letter B, note 1.

6. Jane Wright (see letter 9, note 12).

7. Lady Gargrave (see letter 3, note 3).

8. Mrs Thorold (see letter 10, note 2).

9. Moore Smith notes that this fair took place on St Matthew's Day, 21 September.

10. Mr Mayor is the Mayor of Reading; neither Sheen nor Chertsey had a mayor at that time.

11. Mrs Robert Hammond (see letter 9, note 5).

12. Not identified.

LETTER D

1. See letter C, note 10.

2. Sawyer, the horse-owner.

3. Mrs Robert Hammond (see letter 9, note 5).

4. The horse-dealer.

5. 'not keen to sell them'.

6. The 'Young ffellow' might be John, who appears in the letters which follow.

7. An excellent basis for comparison of annual payments for what was a common form of employment with not only the price of a horse, but also the size of dowries.

8. 'without his Master' is omitted from the Moore Smith edition.

9. Coley Park, Reading; see letter B, note 3.

10. This postscript was omitted in Julia Longe's transcription.

LETTER E

1. The 'new man' is most likely to be one and the same as the 'Young ffellow' of letter D, note 6, and the one who is called 'John' later on in this letter.

2. 'A contagious disease in horses, the chief symptoms of which are swellings beneath the jaw and discharge of mucous matter from the nostrils' (*OED*).

3. 'An eruptive disease in horses and other animals, arising from immoderate feeds and other causes' (*OED*).

4. 'before' is omitted in Moore Smith's edition.

LETTER F

1. It is clear that Sawyer and Sadler had not only cheated them in the transaction with the horses, but that they had also sought to recommend an employee whom they knew to be dishonest. The sense of outrage of the opening lines of this letter is understandable, given the glowing testimonials of the earlier letter – for once, D.O. is taken in.

2. Moore Smith has 'Mr Bolles', but 'Mr Rolles', Julia Longe's transcription, seems more likely to be correct, although neither has been identified.

LETTER G

1. Presumably this was a wall at Reading Abbey.

2. 'a pride in' omitted from Julia Longe's transcription.

3. If this passage is to be read as one of those in which she comments on political affairs, then it might be applied to one of the Cromwells; if so, it must call into question Moore Smith's dating of February 1656 or February 1657; it must also be near Shrovetide (letter H is written just before that festival). If 1656, it would mean that Jack was two months old when he went a-shroving; if 1657, he would have been about fourteen months. It could not apply to Oliver Cromwell because his death in September 1658 would not coincide with the Shrovetide period (and also because none of her earlier letters speak of him with such sharpness), but to date this letter a year later (1659) would not only make Jack that much older and more capable of going a-shroving, but it would also give a date nearly coinciding with the fall of the regime of Richard Cromwell. Although his administration formally continued until May 1659, it effectively fell on 22 April 1659, when the army forced him to dismiss parliament.

4. See letter B, note 1.

5. Jane Wright (see letter 9, note 12). Either she is living with the Temples, or she is a frequent visitor.

6. 'Robins Master' can only be Tom, which makes Robin the stable-boy.

7. The aunt is Mrs Hammond (see letter A, note 1) and the grandson is Robert, the only son of John Hammond of Chertsey; he was then about sixteen or seventeen.

8. Omitted in Julia Longe's transcription.

LETTER H

1. Julia Longe transcribes this name as 'Forby', but Moore Smith, transcribing it as 'Tooby', identifies him as the father and predecessor of 'Toby Hamond the coachman' who was buried in St Mary's, Reading, on 6 August 1702, and who had children baptized there between 1685 and 1692.

2. Lady Gargrave (see letter 3, note 3).

3. Julia Longe has 'Lawfort', but no identification has been possible.

4. These references to bills indicate that in the early days of their marriage the Temples had some financial difficulties.

5. Not identified.

6. Not identified.

7. Aunt Temple is either an unmarried sister of Sir John Temple, or the wife of his brother.

8. See letter B, note 3.

9. Julia Longe has 'Lady Walker', but Moore Smith identifies her as the wife of the parliamentary general, Sir William Waller.

10. The affectionate name by which they knew their son, Jack.

11. The postscript is not in Julia Longe's transcription; Mrs Fountain has not been identified.

LETTER I

1. This letter is taken from Courtenay's biography, Vol. 1, pp. 345ff. It is clear from the letter that W.T. had returned to England and had written from Yarmouth (presumably his port of entry) on arrival there. The events referred to must be those surrounding the king's change of mind about adhering to the Triple Alliance, for which W.T. was largely responsible; on his return to England, W.T. was asked to denounce the Alliance and to break off rela-

tions with De Witt, the Netherlands statesman. In 1670, the Treaty of Dover, with 'secret' clauses, was signed with the French, and W.T. was recalled from his post as Ambassador in The Hague. From that time he lived largely in retirement, devoting himself to gardening and to writing.

2. George Villiers, 2nd Duke of Buckingham (1628–87). He was brought up with the children of Charles I, served in the Civil War, fled to France (1648), but returned briefly to fight at Worcester (1651). He went back into exile until 1657. He became a member of the Privy Council in 1662, helped to bring about the fall of Clarendon, and became a member of the Cabal. He was not, however, privy to the secret Treaty of Dover (see note 1, above), but became the focus of parliamentary dissatisfaction, and was dismissed in 1674. Buckingham was a playwright as well as a statesman; his best-known work is probably *The Rehearsal* (1671).

3. A reference to Charles II.

4. Louis XIV.

5. Thomas Downton, one of the secretaries to W.T. in the period from 1665 to 1672.

6. Sir Robert Long was Chancellor of the Exchequer from 1660 to 1667.

7. Sir Joseph Williamson was Under-Secretary of State (1665), Ambassador to Cologne, and Secretary of State (1674–8); he was also President of the Royal Society.

8. Not identified.

Appendix B:
William Temple's Letter from Ireland

1. Methinks.

2. Henry Osborne.

3. Immediately.

4. See letter 51.

5. Permission to leave Ireland.

6. In London.

7. Chicksands.

8. This might be a reference to the events surrounding their first meeting on the Isle of Wight, where D.O. took responsibility for the graffito perpetrated by her brother.

9. 'in debt to me'.

10. 'With this letter'.

11. 'My father still wants more time'.

12. Often.

13. Intentions.

14. Jane Wright (see letter 9, note 12).

Index

1. Dorothy Osborne and William Temple are referred to as D.O. and W.T.
2. All references are to page numbers; figures in italics refer to the Notes Section.
3. Reference is made to the Notes
   (a) where it helps to identify an ambiguous reference in the text (e.g the reference to Levinus Bennet on page 79 is indexed as 79n8);
   (b) where significant information is given in a note about a subject not mentioned in the corresponding text (e.g. Alliance, Triple, *383–4n1*);
   (c) to draw attention to a detailed biographical note (e.g. Beverley, James, *349n1*).

FOR THE BEST IN PAPERBACKS, LOOK FOR THE

In every corner of the world, on every subject under the sun, Penguin represents quality and variety – the very best in publishing today.

For complete information about books available from Penguin – including Pelicans, Puffins, Peregrines and Penguin Classics – and how to order them, write to us at the appropriate address below. Please note that for copyright reasons the selection of books varies from country to country.

In the United Kingdom: For a complete list of books available from Penguin in the U.K., please write to *Dept E.P., Penguin Books Ltd, Harmondsworth, Middlesex, UB7 0DA*

In the United States: For a complete list of books available from Penguin in the U.S., please write to *Dept BA, Penguin, 299 Murray Hill Parkway, East Rutherford, New Jersey 07073*

In Canada: For a complete list of books available from Penguin in Canada, please write to *Penguin Books Canada Ltd, 2801 John Street, Markham, Ontario L3R 1B4*

In Australia: For a complete list of books available from Penguin in Australia, please write to the *Marketing Department, Penguin Books Australia Ltd, P.O. Box 257, Ringwood, Victoria 3134*

In New Zealand: For a complete list of books available from Penguin in New Zealand, please write to the *Marketing Department, Penguin Books (NZ) Ltd, Private Bag, Takapuna, Auckland 9*

In India: For a complete list of books available from Penguin, please write to *Penguin Overseas Ltd, 706 Eros Apartments, 56 Nehru Place, New Delhi, 110019*

In Holland: For a complete list of books available from Penguin in Holland, please write to *Penguin Books Nederland B.V., Postbus 195, NL–1380AD Weesp, Netherlands*

In Germany: For a complete list of books available from Penguin, please write to *Penguin Books Ltd, Friedrichstrasse 10 – 12, D–6000 Frankfurt Main 1, Federal Republic of Germany*

In Spain: For a complete list of books available from Penguin in Spain, please write to *Longman Penguin España, Calle San Nicolas 15, E–28013 Madrid, Spain*

PENGUIN CLASSICS

THE LIBRARY OF EVERY CIVILIZED PERSON

John Aubrey	**Brief Lives**
Francis Bacon	**The Essays**
James Boswell	**The Life of Johnson**
Sir Thomas Browne	**The Major Works**
John Bunyan	**The Pilgrim's Progress**
Edmund Burke	**Reflections on the Revolution in France**
Thomas de Quincey	**Confessions of an English Opium Eater**
	Recollections of the Lakes and the Lake Poets
Daniel Defoe	**A Journal of the Plague Year**
	Moll Flanders
	Robinson Crusoe
	Roxana
	A Tour Through the Whole Island of Great Britain
Henry Fielding	**Jonathan Wild**
	Joseph Andrews
	The History of Tom Jones
Oliver Goldsmith	**The Vicar of Wakefield**
William Hazlitt	**Selected Writings**
Thomas Hobbes	**Leviathan**
Samuel Johnson/ James Boswell	**A Journey to the Western Islands of Scotland/The Journal of a Tour to the Hebrides**
Charles Lamb	**Selected Prose**
Samuel Richardson	**Clarissa**
	Pamela
Adam Smith	**The Wealth of Nations**
Tobias Smollet	**Humphry Clinker**
Richard Steele and Joseph Addison	Selections from the **Tatler** and the **Spectator**
Laurence Sterne	**The Life and Opinions of Tristram Shandy, Gentleman**
	A Sentimental Journey Through France and Italy
Jonathan Swift	**Gulliver's Travels**
Dorothy and William Wordsworth	**Home at Grasmere**

THE LIBRARY OF EVERY CIVILIZED PERSON

PENGUIN CLASSICS

THE LIBRARY OF EVERY CIVILIZED PERSON

FOR THE BEST IN PAPERBACKS, LOOK FOR THE

THE PENGUIN LIVES AND LETTERS SERIES

A series of diaries and letters, journals and memoirs